Thief of Hearts

As I slipped out of the rift, I made a grab, my hand closing around her arm before she even realized I was there. I spun her around, snatching the hood from her head in the same movement.

And then I forgot to breathe.

In my shock, I released her, staggering back with a choked cry, stumbling over my own feet and ass-planting in the fallen leaves. For a long moment, I could only stare up at the woman before me, unable to accept what my eyes were seeing.

"You," I finally managed to croak, tears of disbelief blurring my vision. "It's *you.*"

The Transplanted Tales series by Kate SeRine

Ever AFTER

A TRANSPLANTED TALES NOVEL

KATE SERINE

KENSINGTON
PUBLISHING CORP.

www.kensingtonbooks.com

For D.J.S., who's been there with me from the beginning.

Acknowledgments

As always, I owe a tremendous debt of gratitude to my amazing team at Kensington whose hard work is sincerely appreciated. So, thank you to Alicia, Alex, Michelle, Rebecca, Gary, and Jane. And a huge thank you to Nic, my dear friend and tireless agent, for her friendship and guidance and unfailing faith. You all are the best! And it is my pleasure to work with every single one of you.

Also, many thanks to the family, friends, and fans who encouraged me to tell Gideon's story. I fell in love with the stoic fairytale bodyguard the moment I wrote his character in *The Better to See You,* and fell in love all over again when I wrote him in *Along Came a Spider.* But it was the fan response to his few short scenes that convinced me he deserved a story of his own. And what a delight it has been getting to know Gideon and helping him find his own Happily Ever After! I hope you all enjoy reading his tale as much as I enjoyed writing it.

Prologue

"*Marry me.*"

She rose from the bed we shared and wandered a few steps away, the moonlight casting a pale glow upon her fair skin. "Why would you ruin what we have by asking me that?"

I rose up on my elbow, frowning. "How'm I ruinin' it? I want you to be mine forever. Do y'not want the same, lass?"

Her sigh seemed oddly tinged with sorrow. "Of course, I do. It's just . . ." When she turned her head to cast a glance back at me, I swear I saw a flash of light in her eyes, but it faded so quickly, I realized it must've been a trick of my mind. "My father promised my mother forever, love," she explained. "And then he died. Don't make me any such promises. Just promise me *now.* That's all I require."

My chest tightened at the pain in her eyes. "I'll promise whatever y'ask." I extended my hand to her. Without a word, she drifted back to me, slipping under the blanket and letting me wrap her in my arms.

"Tell me you love me," she murmured, her cheek resting on my chest.

I smoothed the satiny length of her dark hair. "I love you with all my heart, you know that. I'll say it as often as y'like."

She lifted her head and placed a slim hand upon my cheek. "Tell me you trust me."

My frown deepened, wondering where this uncharacteristically serious conversation was leading, a sense of foreboding beginning to descend upon me like a shroud. "With my life. Why d'ye ask—"

She pressed her fingertips to my lips, stilling my words. "Tell me that no matter what happens, you know how much I love you."

I shook my head, not liking this line of conversation. "Lass—"

"Tell me," she pleaded, her eyes filling with unshed tears. "Please. I need to know that."

I grasped her nape and pulled her closer, pressing a kiss to each eyelid. "I've no doubts."

Her relief was visible as a smile curved her lips. Then she leaned in and brushed a tender kiss to my mouth, the sweetness of it searing the moment into my memory ever after.

Would that I could've frozen our lives at that point, stopped the inevitable churning of time and held her in my arms forever. But when I woke the next morning, she was gone.

Fearing the worst, I went after her, sending out a spell to track her steps. The path of shimmering silver light took hold in an instant. I latched on to her signature and shifted through time and space, the world about me distorting and folding until I popped out where I had willed myself—and directly into her path.

She slammed into my chest with an audible grunt and staggered backward. I grabbed for her, catching her arm to keep her from falling, and knocking a burlap-wrapped bundle from her arms.

"Oi!" she screeched, snatching the bundle up from the ground and sending a frantic glance over her shoulder toward the cacophony of baying dogs and crashing underbrush as her pursuers gained ground. "What the bloody hell are you doing here?"

"I was concerned y'might be in trouble," I snapped, grabbing her hand and pulling her along. "*Obviously*, I was right. What've y'done this time?"

"Just taking back what's mine," she panted, clutching the bundle tighter as we jumped a stream swollen from the recent rains.

"What happened to stealin' from the rich to give to the poor?" I ground out through clenched teeth as I knocked branches out of my way, grateful when we emerged from the thicket.

She didn't answer, instead sending another glance over her shoulder, her dark eyes going wide. At the same instant, I felt danger—death—coming for her. Without hesitation, I shifted, putting myself directly behind her. Searing pain lanced through my back as the arrows pierced my skin and lodged into my muscle, taking me down to my knees with a strangled groan.

She raced back to me on a choked cry, dropping to her knees and wedging her shoulder under my arm. "Ah, God," she moaned, her voice tight with emotion. "What've I done?"

I wrapped my arms around her, wincing through the agony. "Will y'let me shift you?"

"What?" she gasped, straining as she tried to lift me to my feet.

" 'Tis the only way," I groaned. "Please—just say you'll allow it."

"Yes, I suppose, but—"

In my weakened state, I couldn't control the shift, not knowing where the hell I was taking us—or when. When I could no longer hold it, we burst from the temporal passage I'd created and onto a precipice near a raging waterfall only about a mile from where we'd been. The cool spray of the falls was a relief on my skin, but our reprieve was short-lived. The ground beneath us suddenly crumbled under our weight, and I felt her slip from my grasp.

I made a grab for her, by some miracle catching her wrist, pain from the arrows in my back bringing me to my knees and then flat on my stomach. Crying out in agony, I strained to haul her up, but even the slight weight of her pulled me forward, nearly dragging me off the cliff.

She cried out as we slipped farther, her legs flailing as she twisted in the air and tried to find a foothold. The water churned far below, the roar of the rapids rivaling that of the blood pounding in my head.

"Gimme yer other hand, lass," I ordered, blinking away the tears of anguish that mixed with the water drenching us. Blood from my wounds dripped from my shoulder onto her cheek. "Please, I can't hold you."

She shook her head, her lips trembling. "Let me go or we both fall."

"Never," I ground out, straining to maintain my grasp as I felt her slipping. My voice was choked with tears that had nothing to do with pain this time, "Just let me shift you again, lass."

"They'll never stop searching," she cried over the roar of the water. "Not for this." The ground beneath me began to yield to my weight, and she cast a frightened glance at the churning waters below.

"Drop the treasure and gimme yer other hand, damn it!" I growled, digging into the ground with my knees in desperation, pain making my vision swim as I strained to pull her up. I heard the baying of dogs growing louder. "Quickly, lass! They draw nigh."

Her eyes met and held mine for a heavy moment, filled with heartbreaking sorrow. "I'm so sorry."

And then she let go.

A ragged scream tore from my throat as I grasped for her, encountering only empty air. I tried to shift, but my strength was gone, focus impossible. All I could do was watch in horror as she fell, the mist swallowing her. Feeling as though my heart had been ripped from my chest, I made to follow her, but powerful hands took hold of me, dragging me back from the edge of the cliff.

I struggled, trying to break free, to shift away, but their combined strength was more than I could combat after the amount of blood I'd lost, and soon they had shackled me in enchanted chains, sapping what little magic I could muster. One of the soldiers shoved me forward. Unable to catch myself—and not caring—I slammed into the ground, the impact knocking the breath from my lungs. Numb, disbelieving, I lay there, too stunned to move, mud filling my mouth and nose, choking me. But I didn't give a damn, my will to live as drained as my magic.

The guards dragged me behind them, heedless of my wounds. "On your knees, brigand," one of them ordered gruffly when they finally stopped. When I merely lay mute in the muck, he and his companions pulled me up until I was kneeling.

"Is this the man?" a deep, imperious voice demanded.

"Aye, sire."

The man must've motioned to the guard because a rough hand grasped my hair and jerked my head up, forcing me to meet the calm gaze of none other than the King of Fairies. I knew his face well—all of us did. He was so feared by his subjects that we didn't even dare to speak his name.

"Where is my treasure?" the king asked, his tone even as he stood peering down his nose at me, his great height nearly equal to my own.

I blinked at him through my mud-caked strands of red curls, no doubt appearing as monstrous and contemptible as the aristocracy of Make Believe believed my kind to be. "Gone."

The king's blue eyes sparked briefly. "And the thief? Where is the one they call Robin Hood?"

Sorrow squeezed my throat in its merciless grasp, making it difficult for me to utter the word. "Dead."

An emotion I couldn't decipher passed across the king's face, so fleeting, I doubt anyone else noticed. "You are certain?"

I pushed past the grief that strangled me. "Aye."

There was a long pause and then the king crouched down before me, his gaze level with mine. "I am sorry for that. More than you know." He heaved a sigh, his shoulders hunching ever so slightly.

I let my senses drift, attempting to read him, but the shackles kept me from seeing him clearly. Even so, what I *could* see surprised me. His heart was filled with sorrow that nearly rivaled my own.

He must've noticed as my eyes changed from blue to silver for his own narrowed. "You are an Unseelie," he marveled. "And an empath at that."

I squared my shoulders. "I don't deny it."

He studied me for a moment longer, then motioned to his guards as he rose from his crouch. "Remove your arrows from this man's back. Allow him to heal."

I lifted my brows, baffled by his show of mercy, but my astonishment was soon replaced by the agony of the arrows' removal. It took six of the guards and a sedation spell from the king himself to keep me still while the arrowheads were dug out. Fortunately, with the magic arrows now gone, the healing process was fast and the haze of pain cleared within moments as my flesh knit back together.

"Why restore my health afore y'murder me as you've done the rest of my people?" I panted, glaring up at the man who peered at me with such cool curiosity.

The king's brows came together as if I'd offended him with my question. "I did not destroy your people," he countered. "The Unseelie waged war against *us,* pillaging our villages, murdering our children in their beds. I merely acted to protect my own."

"We waged war for *equality,*" I growled. "We'd no longer be yer subjects, bowing and scraping and kissing Seelie arses just for a chance at yer sloppy seconds."

The king studied me for a moment. "You were a warrior once, were you not?" he finally asked. When I merely glared in response, he continued, "If someone attacked the people you loved, would you not act with every ounce of strength you possessed? You cannot tell me that you would not have done the same in my place."

"I'd fight to the death against any who threatened those in my care," I spat. "And had yer men faced me in fair combat today insteada shootin' me in the back like cowards, I woulda fought to the last breath to protect the woman I love."

The king inclined his head. "I have no doubt of it." Before I realized what was happening, he took hold of one of the shackles around my wrists. Immediately, the chains fell away, leaving only intricate designs encircling my wrists, burned into my skin. They were the symbols of the king's house, his brand, infused with the same shade of blue as his magic. "I bind you to me in service. You will protect me, my family, until such time as I see fit to release you."

I gaped at him. Death would've been preferable to serving my enemy in such a way.

"What is your name?" he inquired, more solicitous than I would've expected.

"Little John," I spat, using the name that had been mine for three years, the name *she* had given me.

The king scoffed, grinning at me with a twinkle of genuine humor in his eyes. "I doubt that very much. That is the name of a thief, a common outlaw. You are no such thing. Tell me your *true* name." When I remained silent, he prompted, "Come now, give me the name of a man who will be my most trusted warrior, my noble protector. I command it."

I lifted my chin higher, fighting against the power of his command but unable to refuse it. "My name," I snarled, "is Gideon Montrose. And one day, sire, you'll be sorry to know it."

Chapter 1

"Who the hell are you working for, Georgie?"

The guy's feet dangled at least a foot above the ground, kicking and twisting to get out of my hold. His eyes were wide with fear, and he clawed the hell out of my hands, which were on either side of his head, threatening to squeeze until his skull popped like an overripe melon.

"I dunno!" he squeaked. "Nobody ever told me. I just move the shit!"

I squeezed a little harder, just enough to make a point. "Sure about that?"

The Tale whimpered a little, and then I'll be damned if the little fucker didn't piss himself.

Disgusted by his cowardice, I held him away from me like a diseased rat. "My patience grows thin."

"I swear to God, man!" he sobbed. "That's the truth!"

I released him, letting him fall into his puddle of piss. "The king will discover who's stealing his transports," I assured him. "And when he does, his vengeance will be visited upon the perpetrators, horrors beyond what they could possibly imagine. No Tale involved will be immune from his wrath—or mine."

I swear I could hear the bastard's gulp as he stared up at me with wide-eyed terror.

"I would suggest you find another line of work," I advised. "You don't want to be associated with the thief when he's caught."

The guy nodded, crab-walking backward until he'd scooted far enough away to be out of my reach. Then he scrambled to his feet and bolted. If we'd been in Make Believe, he probably would've left little tread marks of burning fire from his hasty retreat.

"Go ahead and run, Georgie Porgie," I muttered. "It's the only thing you're good at, you little shit."

I sighed and lifted my face to the sky, checking the progress of the moon to gauge the hour. The night was half over, and I was no closer to getting any answers than I'd been several hours earlier.

Another shipment of the king's fairy dust had gone missing—an occurrence that was becoming far too common. The highly addictive substance was carefully controlled by Tale law in the Here and Now, and the Seelie family were the only ones authorized to manufacture and distribute.

Of course, that didn't mean they were the only ones doing it—a Tale crime lord named Tim "The Sandman" Halloran had made a hefty profit on the illegal trade of fairy dust, or Vitamin D as it was called on the street. Well, he'd made a hefty profit until he struck a deal with the wrong people, choosing to trust the human Agency instead of his own kind for the sake of the almighty dollar. That mistake had cost him his life.

The Agency was a secret branch of the Ordinaries' government charged with controlling any of the paranormal beings that had inhabited the Here and Now long before we came over. In the Ordinaries' urban legends they were often called the Men in Black, but they were far more ruthless and conniving than the Ordinaries ever imagined. They had a hard-on for studying the Tales and figuring out how we'd come to this world and what made us tick. And, as we'd discovered all too well three years before, they were determined to use us to further their own agendas.

Fortunately, we Tales had at least put a stop to the Agency's interference with the fairy dust trade three years ago, and we'd been working hard as hell to maintain the tentative peace between them and the

Fairy Tale Management Authority ever since. But, considering that long-standing history of animosity and distrust, when the dust started going missing again in recent months, my king was quick to blame the Ordinaries.

And I couldn't say I disagreed.

I didn't trust them. I didn't trust this peace. I knew what it was like to hammer out a truce only to have it violated with more brutal and horrific consequences than what had preceded the treaty in the first place. I had lost everyone I cared about to such a violation. I refused to lose my new family—forced upon me though it was this time—to such maneuvering.

I was on the verge of setting off for another targeted area of downtown Chicago when I felt a familiar tingling sensation around my wrists where I still bore the king's brand. I lifted my arm and peered at the marks, the intricate design blazing with the distinctive blue of the king's magic. Whatever he needed, it was urgent.

I took a deep breath and slipped into the temporal rift, arriving in the king's study seconds later. He sat behind his desk, his fingers steepled over his stomach, his brows drawn together in a troubled frown.

"Sire," I greeted with a slight bow.

He glanced up at me with a startled expression as if he'd forgotten he'd summoned me. "Ah, Gideon. Prompt as always." He gestured vaguely toward the ornately carved chair across from him. "Please, have a seat."

I eyed him askance, curious at his behavior. In the hundreds of years I'd served the king, I'd grown accustomed to his every mannerism, could read his mood without even utilizing my ability. And, yet, this was new. He seemed . . . confused.

Cautiously, I accepted his offer and sat down but didn't relax for an instant. "My king," I began guardedly, "you summoned me?"

The smile he gave me was wooden, forced, completely lacking in the warmth and humor I'd come to know. "Indeed."

I made a quick assessment, sifting through a jumble of his emotions to find the root of the matter. "You have received troubling news," I surmised, "and would like me to investigate its validity."

He nodded, clearly distracted by his own thoughts. Finally, he heaved a sigh and rose, coming around to sit on the corner of the desk. "Gideon, you are like the son I never had."

"You *have* a son, sire," I reminded him. When his brows lifted as if I'd provided new information, I added, "Puck? He's mayor of The Refuge. We visited in the spring for the birth of a son delivered of his wife Aurelia."

He sighed. "Oh, yes, yes. Puck, of *course*. But *you* are the son I'd *wished* for, m'boy. Loyal, true, noble. And, if I'm not mistaken, we've become friends—family—over these many long years, have we not?"

"You are not mistaken."

The king grinned. "I wager that even if I removed the spell binding you to this family, you would continue to serve us."

I raised my wrists. "A hypothesis I am keen to test whenever you are, sire."

He chuckled and rose from his perch, returning to his seat behind the desk. "Perhaps another time."

The man was a walking contradiction. Ruthless, powerful, vengeful, he was one of the few Tales worthy of his reputation. But he was pleasant, warm, charming, to those he deemed worthy of his affection. And one would be hard-pressed to find a more generous and loving father to his numerous offspring.

He had always treated me with kindness and respect in spite of my inferior status in his household, insisting that all who served him as his subjects do the same. And when I stood trial for my clandestine relationship with his daughter Lavender some three hundred years after coming into his home, an offense punishable by death among our kind, he came to my defense, refusing to allow my execution. None on the Council dared to question his decision. And nigh on two hundred years later, the members of the Council still dropped their gazes when I came into a room.

Now, after five hundred years together, we'd come to an understanding. I'd become his friend and only confidant. And it'd been at least a century or more since I'd last contemplated slitting his throat while he slept to free myself from his spell.

"Sire," I prompted after a period of prolonged silence on his part, "would you prefer I return at another time? You are clearly preoccupied."

He tilted his head at a contemplative angle. "Preoccupied? Yes, yes. That I am. I have received most troubling news, Gideon—a lead on our thief that I had not anticipated."

My brows shot up. "Indeed?"

"Are you familiar with a Tale named Locksley?" he asked, his tone cautious as he watched me closely.

"No," I replied, curious at his strange behavior. "I can't say that I know the person."

He seemed visibly relieved by this. "I received a report from Al Addin at the Fairytale Management Authority today, providing me a list of all known thieves who'd come over and when. It seems Locksley's arrival in the Here and Now corresponds rather well with the theft of our transports."

"You are abandoning the notion that the Ordinaries are behind the thefts, then?" I asked.

"Not at all. It's entirely possible that the Agency and this person are in league. I want you to bring me this thief. I want answers."

I gave him a curt nod and made to stand, but he held up a hand, staying me. "My king?"

"This thief . . ." he began, searching for words that seemed to elude him. "Well, I think it best if this operation be conducted quickly and quietly. Since arriving in the Here and Now, Locksley has caused quite a lot of trouble, making waves with the Ordinaries that we'd all prefer not to ripple out any further. And from what I understand, Locksley's quite a slippery one, evading all attempts at capture. Al has his own agenda for bringing this one in for questioning, as you can imagine, and has asked that we cooperate with his investigation. But you will bring this mischief maker to *me,* Gideon."

"As you wish, sire."

This time when I stood to go, he didn't stop me. Nevertheless, I paused, studying him in his preoccupation. It was rare that I saw him this pensive. The king was a man who acted decisively, his disposition suited for action more than quiet contemplation. The only other times I'd seen him in such a state was when one of his children had caused him concern—or he'd learned that his escapades had resulted in yet another wee bairn.

The man outwardly doted on his wife, seemed to love her with such blind devotion it was beyond my understanding—especially considering her disagreeable temper and determination to be unpleasant to everyone in her presence. But Queen Mab had not shared her husband's bed for as long as I had been in his house and she encouraged him to seek his pleasure elsewhere. Which he did with a great deal of success—and a shocking amount of potency.

"Sire?" I began, feeling out his willingness to confide. "Is there another child whose mother needs to be provided for? If so, I can visit her immediately and determine her intentions for the child's upbringing and education."

The king's solemn gaze met and held mine before he finally shook his head. "No, no. Nothing of that sort at the moment, my friend. Just concentrate on finding this Locksley as soon as possible. According to Al's report, the last sighting was at the Metropolitan Museum of Art in New York City. Several medieval relics on loan from the British Museum were stolen. There was no fault in the Ordinaries' security system or in their staff. The thief seemed to slip in and out without a trace. The only way it even came to our attention was because a Tale on staff there happened to pick up on a magical signature that was left behind."

I let my senses take him in, immediately picking up on his ire and irritation regarding this evasive thief. There were only a few thieves I'd ever come across—Tale or otherwise—who could slip in and out of a place completely undetected, regardless of the amount of security. And I was one of them. Another was the woman I'd watched fall to her death so many centuries before. The irony of the thief's name didn't escape me, and I doubt it did the king either.

Locksley.

In the Here and Now, the tales told of Robin Hood often ascribed the name Locksley to the lovable rogue of legend. I smothered a wistful smile. How surprised the Ordinaries would've been to discover that the Robin Hood stories they'd learned at their mother's knee were completely and utterly wrong. No one knew that better than I.

But this thief wasn't the same person. Couldn't be. No matter how much I wanted to believe she could still be alive, I had made my peace with her death centuries ago, had finally accepted that she was lost to me forever.

Still, every now and again, that hope resurged—a woman in a crowd whose nose had that same pert upturn at the end. A laugh that had the same joyful abandon. A whisper on the wind that could've been her sigh. But there was no mistaking *this* thief for the one who'd stolen my heart so long ago. For one crucial fact about the evidence crushed those hopes.

"*This* thief has magic," I mused aloud. When I saw the king's inquisitive expression, I offered him a grin to cover the direction of my thoughts and added, "That will make the hunt even more entertaining."

The king chuckled. "Sometimes I think you enjoy this a little too much, Gideon. I believe you miss the days when you were little more than a thief yourself."

He had no idea.

"Perhaps you are correct, sire."

Without thinking, I reached up to place a hand over the silver pendant I wore around my neck and kept hidden beneath my shirt. A series of interconnected, never-ending knots, it was a symbol of my love and devotion that I'd never had the chance to share with the woman whose impudent smile and ready laugh still haunted me all these centuries later.

I made my bow to the king and felt that familiar constriction in the center of my chest that assailed me every time I thought of my lost love. If this Locksley person was even *half* the thief my darling lass had been, then I certainly had my work cut out for me.

Chapter 2

I slipped from the king's study and wandered the halls of the mansion, checking to make sure all was well. There was no reason for concern, I knew. The king's magic was among the most powerful I'd ever seen. Only his daughter Lavender's was more extraordinary. The protection spells around the house were unrivaled.

Yet I still checked every night, making sure those in my charge slept safely. There was only once that I'd failed to detect an intruder—but that had been an attack upon the king's psyche using a glamour to persuade him he was awake and interacting with everyone around him when, in truth, he slept, hovering near death. But that vulnerability had been addressed since then and fortified to ward off illusions more powerful than what even the great Merlin could've conjured.

I grunted at the thought of the famous wizard, unable to keep from grinning. It'd been far too long since I'd visited my old friend. But it appeared that would soon be remedied. I could think of no better person to advise me on the treasures that might tempt a thief who was partial to museum antiquities than a man who had studied all of them in his never-ending search for knowledge.

"You there."

I halted immediately, the sound of Queen Mab's voice jarring me from my stroll down memory lane. Never one to enjoy the queen's company, I set my jaw, squared my shoulders, and turned to face her, counting myself lucky that *I* was the empath.

She stood there before me, haughty and dignified, her lids partially closed over golden eyes, not bothering to mask her disdain for a lowly servant. But she had more reasons than the crime of my birth to dislike me.

I had been under the king's command for only a few months when the queen had invited me to her bed. And I'd declined. Suffice it to say, my lady did not receive my polite refusal well. But her response then paled in comparison to her reaction when we came over to the Here and Now and my secret affair with her daughter was revealed. None had called for my execution more vociferously than Mab. And all these long years later, she still looked at me like she'd love to see my head at her feet.

Never one to do things by halves, Mab was dressed in a pale green evening gown in spite of the late hour, her thick blonde hair piled upon her head in intricate twists, threaded with pearls and jewels. She was a vision of loveliness, one of the most striking women I'd ever seen. It wasn't difficult to see why the king had been so taken with her. What puzzled me was his continued infatuation.

She'd apparently been out all evening, with whom was not for me to know or judge—although I'd noticed such engagements had become more and more frequent. But one thing I'd learned very early on was not to interfere in the affairs of the household. What the royal family did behind closed doors was not my business. I'd attempted to interfere once in the early days of my servitude and warn the king of Mab's conniving before I'd fully understood the peculiar nature of their relationship, and had paid dearly for it. And would continue to do so if the look on Mab's face was any indication.

"My queen," I greeted, keeping my tone even and offering a respectful bow even though respect was the furthest thing from my mind. "How may I serve you?"

"You may inform my husband that I will be expecting him at breakfast in the morning," she said, her tone clipped. "He has failed to join me every day for the past week and I tire of his absence. It's most inconvenient. All I have for company are two of his bastard daughters who are visiting. *Again.* Truly, my nerves are taxed beyond measure."

I was acquainted with Mab's nerves of old and knew well the consequences of their being "taxed." I had my suspicions that the person who'd coined the phrase "drama queen" must've had my lady in mind. From what I could determine, the only reason she wanted the king around was to have someone to fawn over her and provide the attention she constantly craved, but I inclined my head, forcing a compliant smile. "I will relay your message at once. Shall I ask the king's daughters to dine elsewhere? I am certain Lily and Ivy will be happy to oblige."

Having heard the women grumbling about their stepmother in the garden just the day before, vociferously lamenting their poor luck in being stuck with her every meal without the benefit of their father's humor and affection, I had a feeling they would welcome the directive.

But Mab sniffed dismissively. "Just relay the message to my husband."

With that, she swept the length of her dress behind her, sending up a cloud of golden fairy dust. Mab's dust was among the most potent available—and the most addictive, even to other fairies. Most of the time, fairy dust just gave other fairies a mild high or offered a calming effect. I sometimes wondered if it was Mab's dust and not her charming personality that had snared the king and held him captive in so many ways.

I held my arm up to my nose, making sure not to inhale any of the dust she'd shed, and turned to relay the message I'd been given, but drew up short when I caught sight of one of the objects of our discussion, tiptoeing down the hall, carrying her shoes so as not to give away her late return.

"Good evening, Ivy."

She started and spun around with a giggle, then held her finger to her lips. She jogged over to me, a little uncertain on her feet, and swayed when she giggled again. "Don't tell Daddy I got home so late," she said in a loud whisper. "He'd be so *pissed!*"

That he would, especially if he saw her completely shit-faced and glowing from whatever sexcapades she'd been involved in that evening. But who was I to judge? "As you wish."

"And for God's sake, don't tell Lily!" She rolled her eyes. "I'd have to listen to yet another lecture about responsibility and self-respect and whatever wild hair she'd gotten up her ass lately." She flapped her fingers like a puppet mouth, "Blah, blah, blah. She *totally* needs to get laid." She tilted her head to one side, sizing me up and down none too subtly. "Think you're up for the job, Gid?"

My brows shot up. It wasn't the first time I'd been propositioned by one of the king's offspring, and it'd been centuries since I'd taken one up on it. What *was* a new experience was one of them asking on behalf of another sister. "A tempting offer," I replied politely. "Lily certainly is a beautiful woman and enchanting in her own way, even if you disapprove of her rather studious nature."

"*Studious?*" Ivy said with a laugh. "She spends all her time holed up in her room hunched over books of magic. That's not studious, Gid, that's *boring*. She needs to get some nookie and get a life."

I inclined my head. "Well, perhaps it's better left to your sister to decide with whom she should spend her time. I doubt she would find my company engaging."

Ivy shrugged. "Suit yourself." She wiggled her fingers at me. "Ta-ta, Gid. Remember—not a word to Daddy!"

I sighed, shaking my head. God help me if I should ever have any daughters. I'd end up locking them in their rooms until they were at least two hundred and twenty.

As soon as Ivy had disappeared down the hallway, I turned my attention to the shadows. "Perhaps you should retire as well, sir."

The man who'd been attempting to cloak himself in darkness stepped forward, his self-satisfied swagger pissing me off more than I cared to admit. He ran a hand over his perfectly coifed dark hair. "Good evening, Gideon," he drawled. "You're up late."

I lifted an eyebrow, keeping my voice even as I said, "As are you, Reginald."

He chuckled. "Yes, well, what can I say? There's too much pleasure to be had in the darkness."

"She's the king's daughter," I reminded him, an edge of warning in my voice.

"Ivy, you mean?" he asked as if he didn't know who I meant. He chuckled. "Yes, well, you'd know a thing or two about the allure of the king's daughters, wouldn't you?"

I was tempted to knock the condescending smirk off his face, but I merely offered him a tight smile. "I understand there's a meeting tomorrow to discuss the security issues plaguing the king's fairy dust transports," I said, pointedly changing the subject. "I hope you take my recommendations seriously."

Reginald gave a curt nod, his eyes betraying the lie even before he said, "But of course. Your suggestions will be valued as always, Gideon. But, as I'm the queen's attaché, you realize I must obey *her* wishes above all others. And, well . . . how do I put this? Her Majesty doesn't care to take advice from her husband's Unseelie *slave*."

I gave him my *fuck you* smile—the one that left the recipient wondering just what was behind it. "Of course."

Based on the look on Reginald's face, it had the desired effect. His swagger wavered a bit as he said, "Well, I'm sure you have somewhere to be, boots to polish, asses to kiss. . . ."

I inclined my head politely, not showing the least irritation at his barbed comment. "As do you. Good night, Reginald."

After finishing my security check, I delivered Mab's message to the king by slipping a note under his bedroom door, not wanting to interrupt the very audible visit from his latest conquest, then left the mansion and went to my own quarters in the carriage house nearby. But instead of slipping through a rift, I strolled across the lawn, breathing in the crisp autumn air, letting it fill my lungs as my thoughts drifted back to the thief I'd been ordered to find, wondering what the next target could be.

The moonlit night was still, no wind to rustle the leaves or whistle through the rapidly thinning branches of the arbors that surrounded the grounds. Which was why the sudden rustling snapped me out of my reverie in an instant.

I scanned the darkness for a sign of the intruder, my eyes narrowed as I watched for even the slightest movement. After a few moments' pause, I continued toward the house, feigning nonchalance but all the while keeping watch.

Just as I reached the door, leaves crackled behind me. My senses snapped to attention, the hair at my neck prickling in warning. Although I couldn't see anyone there in the darkness, I sensed a presence lurking just beyond my sight.

"Who's there?" I demanded, my voice calm. "Reveal yourself and I won't harm you."

I waited, but no response came.

Then, sudden movement, a scattering of underbrush as something bolted like a frightened deer.

I shifted in the direction of the sound, anticipating the direction it would take, and came out just at the tree line. A shadow darted out from behind a particularly large oak tree, racing for the cover of the woods where the moonlight did not penetrate. I hurried after, determined to find out who had made it past the protection spell around the perimeter of the property.

I crashed through the undergrowth, periodically shifting in short bursts to try to intercept the intruder, but each time he seemed to anticipate my moves, darting just out of the way in time to avoid my grasp. As we raced through the woods, I couldn't help grinning, memories of many woodland chases filling my head.

How many times had I been the one pursued? How often had Robin and I made the same sort of desperate dash, panting through our laughter when we'd managed once again to avoid capture?

I chuckled, picturing the twinkle of mischief in her eyes, the elation in her smile as she'd throw herself into my arms, eager for my kiss. With my thoughts so pleasantly distracted, I didn't see the figure swinging down from the tree branch until his feet slammed into my chest, knocking me flat on my back. For a moment, I lay there, stunned more by my lack of foreknowledge than by the blow itself. "What the hell?" I muttered, frowning as my assailant did a backflip off the branch and landed with surprising grace.

The figure was slight of frame, smaller than I'd expected. He paused briefly, casting a glance at me from beneath his hood, then pivoted and bolted again. I scrambled to my feet but there was no sign of him. I conjured a quick sprinkle of fairy dust and blew it from my palm, instantly finding the footprints I sought, but they went only a few yards before vanishing abruptly.

I scanned the branches of the trees above me, scouring the darkness for my acrobatic foe, but whoever he was, he was gone now.

I made one last search of the area, then summoned the king's captain of the guard, a man whose severe countenance and muscular form made him an intimidating presence at the king's estate.

"We've had a visitor," I informed the burly fairy. "Place your men around the perimeter of the grounds to stand watch. No one comes in or leaves without my knowledge."

The captain gave me a curt nod. "It'll be done, Gideon. Shall I wake His Majesty?"

I shook my head. The intruder had meant no harm, that was for certain. If he had, he never could've crossed our barriers. Whatever had brought him here was not the desire to hurt anyone on the premises. So then why *had* he come? What was he after? "No, that will not be necessary. But send for me at once if you encounter anyone."

Knowing I could count on the guards to keep watch or risk my wrath, I headed back to my quarters, mulling over the events of the last few moments. I kept coming back to the same troubling observation.

There was something familiar in the way the intruder had moved.

A faint niggling of recognition tugged at my consciousness, but I shoved it away, unwilling to let my misplaced hopes make such a connection. Still, when I entered my home, I went straight to my study, bypassing the many thousands of volumes I'd read over the years to educate myself to a level worthy to represent my king whenever called upon.

In Make Believe, reading was reserved only for those in the upper echelons of our society—the Lits and Fairytales mostly, and perhaps the few Rhymes who could sneak in education on the sly or who were fortunate enough to straddle the boundaries. Those like me who hailed from folklore were largely left to their own devices, schooling reserved only for the few recognized by the educated Ordinaries who lent them credence.

But my king bucked against such restrictions, insisting that all in his household be able to read and write. One of the first duties he'd commanded of me was to learn to write my name. Then came reading and writing and taking command of the spoken word. I'd never imagined what comfort and pleasure such skills could bring, what pride I would take in obtaining them.

And when we came to the Here and Now, those opportunities only increased, opening whole new worlds to me. My shelves contained books on every subject imaginable from history to science to literature to philosophy to warfare. For all the king's faults—not the least of which was my forced servitude—I would be forever grateful to him for helping me see that I was a man of skill beyond what was found on the battlefield.

But tonight there was only one book I needed.

I pulled from the shelf a tome bound in soft leather, a treasure I'd secured in the Here and Now nearly one hundred years before. The comforting aroma of aged books wafted to me, bringing a faint smile to my lips as I thumbed through the fragile pages. My grin grew as I began to read the story of how Robin Hood had met Little John, how they'd fought with staves, and how Little John had bested the infamous thief, earning respect and a place as one of the Merry Men.

It was a quaint tale, and at least partially true for once.

I stretched out on the sofa in my study and placed the closed book on my chest, closing my eyes to better envision the scenes as they played out in my head. . . .

"No one crosses without paying a toll."

I peered from under the hood of my cloak at the slight figure before me. Dressed in too-large breeches and tunic, with a cowl shadowing a smooth face, the obstacle in my path was far from intimidating. "Out of my way, boy," I chuckled. "You'd be wise not to detain me. Wait 'til yer old enough to grow whiskers afore incurring my wrath."

When I made a step forward, the youth snatched from his back a stave, twisting it with a flourish that was no doubt meant to instill fear. "I've bested men far larger than you, pilgrim."

I somehow doubted that very much. But more amused than annoyed, I shook my head and strode forward, closing the gap between us and hoisting the lad up by the scruff of his tunic before he'd even seen me move. "Away y'go."

I received a hard crack across the shins with his stave for my troubles.

With a shrug, I dropped the lad on his bum right there in the center of the bridge. "G'day to you, lad," I called over my shoulder.
"Mayhap you'll yet get yer fortune from a weary traveler this day."

I was unprepared for the sharp thwack of the lad's stave across
my shoulders. My patience now gone, I whirled around, grabbing the
stave and twisting hard, flipping the lad in midair. He landed with a
startled grunt.

The boy slowly rolled onto one hip, rubbing his bruised posterior.
"Bloody hell."

I extended a hand to help him rise and was surprised to see wide
dark eyes with long dark lashes staring up at me from one of the
loveliest faces I'd ever seen. It seemed the lad was actually a lass,
and a fair one at that. "I'll be—"

Before I could finish the thought, the little shit grabbed my hand,
using my surprise against me, somehow managing to flip me head
over heels. The air shot out of my lungs as I hit the ground.

"Get up, coward," the lovely little brigand taunted. "Fight me
fairly or risk your honor."

I slowly rose to my feet, studying my companion with new eyes.
"I've no wish to fight you—fairly or otherwise. Shouldn't you be home
practicin' yer needlepoint insteada robbin' men on the highway?"

With a growl of outrage, the thief launched herself at me, apparently hell-bent on proving that needlepoint and other feminine pursuits
could be damned. Her attack was swift, graceful, and admittedly adept,
but I had the advantage of my fairy's prescience, and now that I had
the measure of her, easily avoided her strikes. And yet she refused to
let up, her attack becoming more violent with my growing amusement.

As much as I admired her tenacity and skill, she was delaying my
journey. Needing to be on my way, I waited for her to come charging
at me with a mighty roar and calmly stepped out of her way. She had
misjudged me and her attempt to slide to a halt failed. Her feet slid
on the wet wood and sent her careening off the side of the bridge and
into the water below.

"Damnation," I muttered. The jaded and hardened warrior in me
was tempted to leave the troublesome lass to her own devices, but

some vestige of nobility made me toss aside my bundle and cloak and leap into the water after her.

A moment later, I had her in my arms and was dragging her onto the riverbank. She sputtered and coughed, choking as she expelled the water that had filled her lungs. I lifted her arms over her head, making it easier for her to breathe before dropping down beside her.

"Daft lass," I grumbled, pulling my tunic over my head and attempting to wring it out. "We're both fair dreepin' now. What the hell were y'thinkin'?"

She laughed then, a merry sound that unexpectedly warmed the center of me. "I was thinking that there was no way a man could resist a damsel in distress."

With a twinkle in her eye, she raised my purse of coins before my eyes, having divested me of it at some point during my rescue of her. I snatched it back, unable to smother a grin as I leaned back on my elbows. "You risked yer life for a few pieces o' silver?"

She gave me a saucy grin and a toss of her head. "Of course not! I was never in danger. I swim like a fish."

I laughed, shaking my head. " 'Twas all an act then, was it?"

She nodded and snatched off her cowl, letting her dark hair spill out onto her shoulders to frame her heart-shaped face. A few wet tendrils clung to her cheeks, giving her an impish appearance. "You realized I was a woman," she explained, flouncing back onto the grass beside me. "What was I to do? I saw very quickly I couldn't best you in combat. I had to use other weapons at my disposal."

I leaned in conspiratorially. "And you fig'red bein' a man and all, I couldn't resist ye?"

She batted long dark lashes at me. "It worked, didn't it?"

I peered down at her, utterly captivated by soft pink lips that begged to be kissed. "Why're you here in these woods, a slip of a girl like you? 'Tis a dangerous place, this."

"I rob from the rich and give the spoils to the poor, making sure those who have do their part for those who have not—whether willing or no," she explained. "I've made quite a name for myself."

I chucked her gently under her defiant little chin. "And what name fair fits ye?"

She bounded to her feet and bowed with an exaggerated flourish. "Those who dare to speak of me, sir, call me Robin Hood." Her eyes lit up with anticipation as she asked eagerly, "Have you heard of me?"

I had indeed heard of such a person, but it wasn't the legend that so enchanted me at that moment. "That's what they call all the petty thieves. What's yer true name?"

Her mouth curved up in one corner and she gave me a playful wink. "Ah, but we don't use our real names here in Sherwood Forest, friend. Too dangerous, that."

"Then what d'yer men call you?" I tried, sitting up to drape my arms over my knees.

She sent a sidelong glance my way. "What men do you mean, sir?"

I gestured casually toward the wood where I sensed at least a dozen individuals hiding among the trees, some with their bows at the ready to defend their leader should I make one false move.

A slow smile curled her lips and her eyes flashed with amusement. "Clever boy." She waved to her band of thieves, motioning for them to come out in the open. The ragtag bunch slowly emerged, sizing me up as I got to my feet. I easily towered over even the tallest of them. "And what shall I call you, my gallant hero?"

I opened my mouth to tell her, but she held up a finger in warning. "No real names," I recalled, inclining my head. "Very well, then. I suppose you can call me . . . John."

She pursed her lips. "John, what? We've got three among us already. John Good, John Swift, John Fletcher . . ." She eyed me up and down. "Perhaps we should call you John Little, eh?"

"Little?" I repeated with a chuckle, lifting an eyebrow, enjoying this brand of sparring far better than the staves. "I guarantee ye, lass, there's naught little about me."

Her mouth hitched up at one corner in an amused smirk. "I'll be the judge of that." She then turned and addressed the others. "Well, men, what say you? Shall we add another John to the lot?"

There was a little murmur among them, which apparently was enough to assure her that I was welcome. Her coquettish grin growing, Robin strolled toward me, her hands on her hips. "Well, lads," she said, lifting that impudent and lovely face to mine, "it looks as though we now have ourselves a Little John."

* * *

When I awoke the next morning, the book still lay upon my chest where it had been when I'd fallen asleep. Grinning from a night filled with dreams of my little love, I rose to return the book to its coveted spot upon my shelf. But before I set it aside, I took one last glance at the verse on the page.

> *And so ever after, as long as he liv'd*
> *Although he be proper and tall,*
> *Yet, nevertheless, the truth to express,*
> *Still Little John they did him call.*

Then I closed the book and pressed a kiss to the cover, my pleasure from the night's remembrances bittersweet. My fingers lingered for just a moment on the spine before I tore myself away to prepare for the day.

I'd been given a duty to perform. And I would do so. And when I discovered whoever this thief was that threatened my king and his family—*my* family—he would be sorry he'd ever crossed my path.

Chapter 3

I stepped through a rift into a shadowy corner of the Met's medieval exhibit, determined to do a little reconnaissance before meeting with the Tale contact the king had mentioned. It wasn't that I didn't trust a fellow Tale to be truthful about what evidence had already been gathered, but, well, I *didn't*. There was only a handful of Tales I trusted completely, and they had *earned* that privilege. Unfortunately, they were also forbidden to know about my current errand on the king's behalf.

I emerged from the shadows and attempted to blend in, having exchanged my typical uniform of suit and tie for more casual attire, but as I took in the other tourists, I began to wonder if my jeans, combat boots, and biker jacket had been the best choice. Instead of coming off as a cultured tourist, I probably looked more like a reject from *Sons of Anarchy*. The sunglasses I wore to hide my eyes from Ordinaries didn't help that image, but that was far better than having to explain how they changed color when I was reading the emotions and desires of others.

I slowly strolled through the exhibit, taking in the various medieval helms, breastplates, and other implements of war, too many memories of my own battles haunting me, the faces of the foes who'd fallen at the end of my sword as vivid today as the day we'd met upon the field. Would that I could forget them.

Suddenly, I felt a heaviness at the base of my neck, a prickling of my skin, jolting me out of my guilt-infused brooding. A Tale was nearby. And that Tale was watching me, studying my every move. I let my gaze drift around the room and peered through the glass display cases, searching for my observer, but saw only Ordinaries. The weight of that gaze was maddening. It tugged at my consciousness, pulling me toward it, but when I drifted in the direction it called me, it would change again, keeping out of sight. Had I not been in a room filled with Ordinaries, I could've shifted to intercept the Tale.

But then, as suddenly as the weight had fallen upon me, it lifted. I made one last casual pass in search of my observer, but when it proved fruitless, I turned my attention back to the reason I'd come.

After several minutes of wandering the gallery with no sign of residual magic, I finally came to a glass case that contained a variety of finely crafted relics ranging from gauntlets and sword hilts to bridles and bits. But there were three pedestals within the case that stood empty, small signs indicating that the items had been removed temporarily.

That was one way to put it. . . .

In addition to the signs, each pedestal contained a faint trace of magical residue that resembled a sprinkle of fairy dust. Visible only to other Tales, the residue was a dead giveaway that one of our kind had been there, had somehow appropriated the items within the case without breaking the glass or triggering any alarms.

"Quite a remarkable collection, isn't it?"

I turned at the sound of the voice to see a woman with fair hair standing beside me, smiling softly as she gazed on the relics inside the case. "It has taken years to acquire the collection," she continued, her voice smooth and cultured and decidedly of Make Believe. "The Ordinaries had dispersed them quite far afield, selling them off to private collectors. I'm not entirely sure how they came to the Here and Now to begin with, but I was glad to have something of my husband returned to me."

"You're my contact," I deduced, wondering if she'd been the Tale studying me as I strolled the gallery. "You were the one who informed the FMA of the theft."

She turned her head and offered me that quiet smile, her pale blue eyes kind but filled with a distant sorrow. "Yes." She extended her hand in greeting. "Guinevere Pendragon."

I glanced down at the offered hand of the fabled Queen of Camelot. It was slim, elegant. I shook her hand briefly; concerned I might break her fingers if I held on for too long. "Gideon Montrose. I'm here on behalf of the fairy king."

Her delicate brows lifted. "Oh? You're not from the FMA?"

I shook my head. She looked at me as if she expected me to say more. She was disappointed.

"Ah, well," she said at last. "Perhaps we should chat in my office?"

I motioned for her to lead the way and followed her through the halls until we reached a complex of offices. The one we entered was clearly temporary. The desk was almost completely empty except for a laptop and telephone and there was nothing on the shelves or hanging on the walls. The only hint that anyone worked there was a pale pink leather handbag that perfectly matched the shade of the skirt, jacket, and pumps Guinevere wore.

"I must say, I'm surprised the king has taken an interest in this case," Guinevere said, her tone surprisingly haughty as she took a seat behind the desk and motioned for me to take the chair across from her. She lifted her chin as if offended by the mere thought of my king's involvement. "I fail to see how Arthur's missing relics would be any of *his* concern."

I offered her a carefully practiced smile that revealed nothing. "The king's affairs are his own. Perhaps you could tell me when you noticed the items were missing."

"Five days ago," she replied, one meticulously manicured fingertip lightly tapping the edge of the desk. "They sent someone out to take a look . . . some *Rhyme,* if you can believe it. She was quite the sweet-looking little thing with all of those ringlets, but really! A theft of relics connected to one of *the* most celebrated and admired Tales of all time, and that's the best they could assign to the case?"

I ground my back teeth, biting back the furious retort that immediately rose to my lips. Trish Muffet was worth ten of the woman before me, that was for damned sure. But still needing the information my king required, I was forced to settle with, "I can only assume you mean Trish Muffet. I assure you, she's exceedingly capable and one of the best women I know. Indeed, she and her husband are friends to me."

Guinevere had the grace to don a slightly embarrassed smile. "My apologies. I meant only that I had expected more of an investigative team than what was sent. But if you say Ms. Muffet is the best, then I will believe you."

"Perhaps you should tell me what was taken," I suggested, glad to shift the topic but nonetheless making a mental note to visit with Trish as soon as I returned to Chicago to see what she'd discovered.

Her brows came together in a frown that appeared more put out than troubled. "A goblet, a broken dagger, and a penannular brooch. Odd items to take, really, if you consider the significance of the other items left behind. Those taken were by no means the most valuable— although they would most certainly fetch a handsome price. But, then, really—how can one attach a price tag to items so precious?"

I narrowed my eyes behind my shades. There was something about her words that hinted at sarcasm, but the inflection was slight, vague, as if she perhaps was not even aware of the way her expression belied her words.

"Perhaps the thief did not take them for their monetary value," I suggested. "Is there anything significant about these items?"

"Of course!" she snapped in a surprising lapse of poise. "They're *all* significant. They're significant to *me*." Here she paused to take a slow, measured breath, before explaining, "As I'm sure you know, the exhibit is on loan from the British Museum. What you might not know is that I loaned it to the British Museum with the understanding that if the collection was to travel, I was to travel with it in order to handle the relics personally. These items are all I have of Arthur. They are quite precious to me."

I studied her closely, feeling out her emotions. She was being truthful about what the items meant to her, but I sensed something more to it than just sentimental value. "It's a wonder you'd loan them out in the first place if they are so dear to you."

Her smile this time was guarded. "I am a single woman of modest means, Mr. Montrose. I do not have the fortune that I had in Camelot, nor the knights to guard what's mine. The museum offered to insure the items against harm, so I believed their employees would be able to care for the relics better than I could. Obviously, I was mistaken."

Guinevere Pendragon was a puzzle in which the pieces didn't quite fit. From what I could *see* she wanted for nothing. But I didn't need my ability to tell me that. Her designer suit and expensive accessories contradicted assertions of poverty. Why she was pretending to be helpless and penniless was a mystery.

"I've heard rumors that your husband was a friend to my king," I said. "You could've come to him for protection. I'm certain he would've extended you a kindness for the sake of Arthur's memory."

"They were, indeed, friends," she agreed, her eyes taking on a coldness that was at odds with her smile. "But I believe it was your *king* who did Arthur a favor, once upon a time—quite a great one, if I am not mistaken. So, you see, Arthur actually was beholden to *him*."

She observed me intently as if she was waiting for my reaction to some great secret. I kept my expression impassive, betraying nothing. My knowledge of the king's relationship to Arthur Pendragon was mere hearsay, murmurings among the guards and other staff. I seldom listened to idle gossip, but this time I'd paid attention because it had involved my old friend Merlin. If there was any truth to the rumor, then it was my king who'd sent Merlin to the Pendragon family, to serve Uther and then his son. Beyond that, I was unaware of any favors paid to Arthur directly.

"Even so," I said, "I'm certain the king would've been happy to assist you. As you say, you are a woman with limited resources."

She cocked her head to one side, peering at me through lowered lashes, and now plying me with a very different sort of smile. "A *single* woman," she reminded me. "Let's not forget that part."

I inclined my head in acknowledgement. "Of course."

"And what about you, Mr. Montrose?" she asked, her voice going a little breathless. "Has someone ever managed to snare your heart?"

"Yes," I replied, not bothering to elaborate or explain that such an event had occurred long ago.

Her eyes seemed to spark with irritation. "Well, I wish you happy," she said, her voice a bit strained in spite of the sweet tone.

I inclined my head, acknowledging her kind words, however false we both knew them to be. "Thank you for meeting with me," I told her, getting to my feet. "I think I have everything I came for."

I offered her a slight bow in farewell, but before I could leave, Guinevere rose and came around to the front of the desk. She leaned against the edge, bracing herself with her arms in such a way that accentuated her breasts, squeezing them together beneath the thin material of her blouse and lifting them up to be admired.

"Are you sure about that?" she purred. "It's still early. Why not join me for breakfast?" She arched a brow at me. "Or dinner."

I didn't even bother sensing her out to get at her ulterior motives for the invitation. There was no mistaking what she wanted. The story the Ordinaries told of Guinevere's marriage to Arthur, her affair with Lancelot, and all of the variations thereof, paled in comparison to the truth as known to the Tales. Guinevere had been one of the most sought after women in Make Believe. And I suppose she *was* beautiful in the classical fairytale sense. She was fair, angelic, her features in perfect harmony, creating a true vision of loveliness. She was what every man *should* desire.

But while I could see how some would be tempted by her and no doubt I would've found her a most willing partner in my bed, I found her beauty decidedly lacking in character. To me, she was neither enchanting nor captivating. There was nothing fascinating about her features, nothing remarkable or unique, and certainly nothing to entice me to follow her lead. Still, I would have to have been a eunuch not to appreciate what she was offering—and even then, it wouldn't have been totally out of the question. But my reaction was a purely physical one, and not one I was inclined to indulge at the moment.

I longed only for a pair of mischievous dark eyes and an impish smile that held a promise of adventure and danger and the sweetest love a man could hope for. And Guinevere possessed none of those. "Perhaps another time."

From the offended glint that came into her eyes, it was clear Guinevere was not the sort of woman who was used to having her advances ignored, even in the Here and Now. "You may not find my schedule so accommodating again."

I offered a polite incline of my head. "A risk I must accept. Good day."

I didn't wait to gauge her reaction before I strode from her office and back through the museum to the gallery of medieval antiquities. Now that I knew their history, I made another pass at the case from which Arthur's items had vanished. I frowned at the empty pedestals, curious why the thief hadn't also taken the more valuable pieces. If he'd made it this far without detection, why stop with a few baubles?

As I puzzled over the crime, I felt that familiar sensation of being watched again. My head snapped up, my eyes searching all the faces in the crowd. No Tales in sight. Not one.

Then I caught sight of a woman in a red dress, black tights, and biker boots heading for the gallery exit, her face hidden by the gray hood of the hoodie she wore beneath her denim jacket. And in that quick glimpse, I saw it—just a hint of a Tale signature, the faint aura that surrounded each of us, identifying us to one another. Hers was pale, faltering, but it was there.

I cursed the number of Ordinaries present in the blasted museum, preventing me from shifting to intercept my observer as I quickened my pace to catch up to her. Looked like I was going to have to do it the old-fashioned way.

Based on the circuitous route she took, passing through the various galleries, winding her way through fountains and statuary without pausing to admire a single one, it was clear she knew she was being followed. But I kept my distance, always just a few yards behind, waiting for the opportunity to intercept her and find out who the hell she was and why she'd been watching me.

When we eventually came to the Great Hall, she cast a quick glance over her shoulder then bolted toward the exit, surprising me with her sudden burst of speed. I took off after her, losing sight of her for a few seconds until I saw her racing down the stone steps toward the cabs lined up out front.

For a moment, I thought she would dart inside one, but she abruptly changed direction, running down Fifth Avenue toward Seventy-ninth Street. Shifting now was definitely out of the question, but though her legs carried her swiftly, I was quickly gaining ground. I was within a few yards of her when she broke away, turning off into Central Park. Although the paths were lined with trees, their coverage wasn't nearly dense enough for her to lose me. She cast a quick glance over her shoulder, giving me a glimpse of her face, but it was too brief for me to make out more than wide dark eyes.

As we reached a stretch of denser woods, she left the path, seeking the safety of the foliage, but I was too close now and too tired of this bullshit to let the chase go on much longer. As soon as I was convinced that we were beyond the curious eyes of those in the park, I shifted.

As I slipped out of the rift, I made a grab, my hand closing around her arm before she even realized I was there. I spun her around, snatching the hood from her head in the same movement.

And then I forgot to breathe.

In my shock, I released her, staggering back with a choked cry, stumbling over my own feet and ass-planting in the fallen leaves. For a long moment, I could only stare up at the woman before me, unable to accept what my eyes were seeing.

"*You,*" I finally managed to croak, tears of disbelief blurring my vision. "It's *you.*"

Chapter 4

She took a few hurried steps, ready to bolt again, but then halted midstride, indecision making her falter. With a resigned exhale, she turned back to me and swallowed hard, her brows furrowed. Her chest was heaving and a sob hovered in her voice when she whispered, "Hello, love."

I pulled off my shades and pressed the heel of my hand to my eyes, clearing away the stinging blur. "Who are you?" I demanded, although my voice was cracked, ragged with both sorrow and tentative joy. "Why do you torment me with this humorless jest?"

She offered me a sad smile. "Tormenting you was never my intention."

She slowly came toward me then knelt beside me. My breath shot from my lungs when she took my face in her hands, her touch cool on my skin. My own hands trembled as I brought them up to cover hers. I closed my eyes, committing to memory the tenderness of her fingertips, knowing that at any moment this illusion would vanish, leaving me heartbroken once more.

"This isn't real," I rasped, squeezing my eyes tighter, shaking my head, not willing to indulge this cruel fantasy. "I saw you fall . . . I watched you die."

"Aye, you did," she murmured, her thumbs smoothing away the

tears that had made their way to my cheeks. "And for that I'm sorry. I'm *so* sorry. . . ." And then she kissed me, an all too brief brush of her lips against mine. And I no longer gave a damn if she was real or imagined.

My arms went around her, dragging her into my embrace. I buried my face in her hair, inhaling deeply, the sweet scent of honey-suckle—of *her* scent—filling my lungs. I shuddered with the strength of my warring emotions—sorrow, anger, elation, heartache, fear—torn between sobbing with joy at having her in my arms again and fury at her for having let me believe she was dead.

I abruptly took hold of her upper arms and held her away from me, studying her intently, looking for some evidence that the wide dark eyes, pert nose, and defiant chin in that lovely heart-shaped face I'd adored were false, that this was some witch or siren sent to trick me, lure me to some horrifying fate with my own longings.

My hands moved from her arms to her shoulders, over the silki-ness of her hair, reassuring myself that the woman before me was flesh and blood. Then I took her face in my hands, disbelief making my chest heave with ragged breaths.

"You're alive," I murmured, peering into her beloved face again, knowing I could gaze upon her for eons and still never get enough. "You're truly alive. How is it possible? How is it you're here?"

But instead of explaining her miraculous appearance, she studied me silently, her eyes filling with tears as her fingers came up to ca-ress my cheek, the line of my jaw, my lips. "Oh, my love," she breathed, her voice breaking. "I've missed you so."

Then she kissed me again. This time the kiss lingered, drawing out this precious moment that was long overdue. Her lips were as warm and alluring as I'd remembered all these years, parting in the same sweet invitation, drawing me toward a divine bliss where I could lose myself for hours. As the kiss deepened, she straddled my lap, pressing her body closer to mine, her fingers spearing my hair, holding on to me as desperately as I held on to her. And what started as a tender kiss soon became one of longing, of frenzied urgency.

My God, it was like we'd never been apart. That heated kiss melted away the years in an instant. I clutched her jacket in my fists, desperate to keep her from pulling away, but it was unnecessary. At that moment, my little love was in my arms again, her lips and tongue meeting mine with equal hunger, her hands roaming my neck, my shoulders, holding my face to hers.

I could've gone on kissing her over and over again until the sun dipped down below the horizon, making up for the centuries of kisses I'd missed. My lips clung to hers, but it was not enough. Eager to explore every inch of her skin, I tore my mouth away from hers and kissed her cheeks, each eyelid, her forehead, her jaw in the little spot beside her ear that had always made her laugh. And laugh she did, but it was tainted by tears as her arms went around my neck.

She whimpered softly as my hands slid beneath the hem of her dress and up her thighs to grasp her hips. I captured her lips again, and for a moment she melted into me, accepting my kiss. But then she abruptly broke away.

"Oh, God," she said on a choked moan. "I can't do this. I never should've let you know I was here."

She made to move away, but my hold tightened. "What?" I cried, my hurt and anger taking over now that the return of my joy was on the verge of being snatched away. "Why're you running away again?"

"John, I—"

"That's not my name," I snapped, bitterness creeping in. "My name is Gideon Montrose. It always has been. I haven't used the name *you* gave me since that day at the falls." I studied her closely, my stomach sinking as I watched guilt and regret wash over her. "But I guess you already know that."

She averted her eyes, her shoulders sagging. "I can't take back what I've done," she admitted. "But please know that I never wanted to hurt you. I've stayed away, I've tried to leave you in peace, to protect you from exactly this kind of hurt." She heaved a harsh sigh and brought her eyes back up to meet my gaze. "But I just . . . I had to see you before I go."

I laughed bitterly and gently set her away from me, then got to my feet, pacing in tight designs as I brooded on the situation, not sure how I should feel, what I should say. I wanted nothing more than to sweep her away from there, take her back to my bed and make love to her, lose myself in her arms again, regain that peace and happiness we'd once shared. But it had been five hundred years . . . five hundred years of sorrow and remorse that would not abate. And she'd been alive. Alive the entire fucking time, letting me mourn her without respite.

"Before you go," I repeated on a chuckle, the sound harsh and unforgiving. And as heartbreak turned to fury, my voice shook when I roared, "Before you *go*? I don't even know where *the fuck* you've *been*!"

She closed her eyes on a sigh. "I don't know either. Something happened that day in the falls. I don't know where I went or how long I was gone. I *did* come looking for you in Make Believe when I finally became aware again. I had to find you, tell you I was still alive, but by then you were with someone else. You seemed happy."

I blinked at her in disbelief. "That was Lavender Seelie. And we *were* happy—as much as we could be hiding our relationship. But that was three hundred years after you fell."

"I don't understand it any more than you do," she said. "Nor do I understand how I ended up in the Here and Now, as I hear it's called. I was just *here* one day. If it wasn't for Merlin—"

"Merlin?" I growled. "*He* knew you were here?"

She nodded. "Yes, he looked after me when I arrived."

That arrogant son of a bitch and I were going to have one serious chat when I saw him next. And I had a feeling it might end with my hands around his neck.

"He told me you were here, but I . . . I couldn't bring myself to see you. I didn't want to interfere with your new life."

I shook my head, not understanding. "My new life?"

"With the fairy godmother . . . Lavender."

I pulled my hand down my face, vaguely noting that it was getting to be a habit. "Lavender left me," I told her. "I was nearly executed when I stood up for her after the initial relocation and our relationship was discovered. To protect me, she gave me up. That was two hundred years ago, and for a couple of years now she's been happily married to one of the best men I've ever known. I'm to be godfather to their first child."

"I know that *now*!" she retorted. "And when I found out, I again debated seeking you out, just to see if . . . if we could at least try to be friends again, see if there was any hope after all the time we'd lost. But then things became . . . complicated."

"Of course they did," I muttered. "That was always the way of it with you. And, God knows, when it gets too complicated, you cut and run. That was always your problem—no thought of what tomorrow holds, only what you can have today."

"Once upon a time that was enough," she reminded me. "You used to be willing to accept that all we had was *today*."

"Well, I'm not the same person I was then," I shot back. "You made damned sure of that when you disappeared."

She let her head fall back on her shoulders with an exasperated sigh. "This is why I didn't want you to see me. I had a feeling it would be like this."

"Oh, because you know me so well, you mean?" I snarked. "Well, apparently, I never knew *you* at all! Who *are* you anyway? Tell me the truth. No more lies, no more games. Tell me who the fuck you really are *right now*."

I heard her quiet sigh as she debated what to tell me.

"Not sure what to say? Weighing how much you can trust me? *Me?*" I raged, thumping my chest with my fist. "After all I thought we were to each other, now you hesitate to confide in me? After lying to *me* all these years, pretending to be dead and letting me suffer, now you show up out of nowhere and have the *audacity* to sit there and consider whether or not I finally deserve the truth?"

She swiped at the tears on her cheeks, her eyes filling with more to follow. I felt a jolt of remorse for my harsh words, but I shoved it away, my heartbreak taking on an even greater intensity than when I'd believed her to be dead.

And still she was silent.

"Here," I said. "I'll get you started. Answer me this, if you think you can manage a single word of truth. What's yer name?"

She'd been kneeling but now sat back on her heels, resigning herself to my anger.

"And I mean yer *true* name." I informed her, my voice growing louder, the Unseelie accent that had faded after so many years in the Here and Now slipping back in.

She turned her eyes up to me. "My name is Arabella. *Bella* to those who know me."

Clearly, I was not among them. . . .

"Arabella *what?*" I demanded.

She shook her head. "I have no last name, not really."

"Are you calling yourself Locksley?" I pressed. "Are you the infamous thief I've heard tell of?"

"Yes," she admitted. "As Locksley has already been in use here for some time, I thought it would be an appropriate alias for Robin Hood."

"And are y'the one stealin' the king's fairy dust transports?"

I could see the guilt in her expression even before she nodded. "Yes. But, Gideon, it's complicated—"

The horrifying truth nailed me like a two-by-four to the back of the head, bringing me to my knees, my shoulders sagging in despair. I'd expected her to deny it, not confirm the fear that had been building in my gut during our exchange. I took hold of her arms again, my brows coming together in a frown so fierce it made her draw back. "Arabella, I've been commanded to bring you to my king to answer for yer crimes."

She clutched the front of my shirt, giving me a nervous smile. "Just let me go. He doesn't need to know anything about this. About me. Please. You don't understand—"

"No," I interrupted, setting her away from me and dropping back on my ass. "*You* don't understand, lass." I ran my hands through my hair, completely freeing it from the low ponytail I wore, letting my head hang down between my shoulders for a moment as the magnitude of the situation sank in. Then I held up my wrists, revealing the king's bonds upon me. The symbols of his house were glowing blue with the power of his spell and the strength of his command. Arabella's eyes widened when she saw what they were, understanding the implications even before I explained, "I *cannot* disobey. It's not possible, no matter how hard I fight it. I can put it off for a while, resist for a few days maybe, but if he calls me in . . ."

She scrambled over to me. "I can't let you take me to him, Joh— *Gideon*. There's far more going on than you realize. I wasn't stealing the fairy dust for profit."

"Then why're you stealin' it?" I gave her a pitying look. "Are y'addicted? Are y'a junkie?"

She hesitated briefly as if weighing her answer. "No."

I lifted a single brow in challenge. "Sure about that?"

"Yeah, okay, I *need* it, but I'm not *addicted*. There's a difference." She huffed. "I should've known you wouldn't understand. You've never *needed* anything or anyone." When I stared at her in stony silence, she pushed to her feet, groaning in frustration. "This was a mistake."

"Well, I guess that's the theme of our relationship," I mumbled. "And I made the biggest mistake of all, believin' y'ever cared for me."

The sting of her open palm connecting with my cheek caught me off guard.

"Say what you want about the mistakes I've made," she raged, her cheeks growing red with indignation. "There's certainly no shortage of them. But don't you *ever* question how much I loved you! By doing so you insult us both."

I stared at her, literally struck mute.

When I didn't speak, she swallowed a sob and turned away. "I have to go," she called over her shoulder. "I've already stayed too long." Her hurried steps carried her a few yards before I blew out a harsh sigh and let fly a stream of juicy curses, knowing I was a glutton for punishment even as I went after her.

"Arabella! Wait!" I grabbed her arm, bringing her to a stop but releasing her when the wounded look in her eyes cut me to the core. I put my hands on my hips, staring at my feet as I debated what to say, not willing to look her in the face, afraid that if I met the eyes I adored, I'd lose myself in them.

I'd never stopped loving her, had never stopped thinking about her. As ridiculous as it seemed, some part of me had always held out hope that she'd somehow miraculously return. And here she was, right before me. She said she didn't know what had happened to her, what had kept her away . . . And I wanted to believe it. My long-broken heart whispered bitter words, telling me to walk away and never look back, that that part of my life was over.

But it was a lie. That part of my life would never be over. She'd filled my heart in a way no woman ever had or would again. And I wasn't about to piss on that by turning her away when she clearly needed me.

"What trouble are y'in?" I asked, forcing my voice to be gentle.

"It's my concern," she said with a sniff, making me feel like an irredeemable jackass for bringing her to tears. "I didn't come here to beg you to help me or to drag you into my mess. I just . . . I just wanted to see you again. I dream of you, of us, every night, Gideon. When I close my eyes, your face is all I see. I know you don't believe me, but I *did* love you—I still do. I always will."

I felt my chest tighten at her words, wanting so desperately to believe her. I risked raising my gaze to hers, gauging her sincerity. To my surprise, she actually seemed to be telling the truth.

Damn me to hell, but I was gonna fall for her all over again. Even though I was furious and hurting and knew with certainty that I was bound for heartache again, I was powerless to stop it. But she didn't have to know that. And I'd make sure she didn't. I'd managed to keep my emotions in check all these years, had learned to maintain the stoic silence that was required of my servitude to the king. I never imagined I'd need those skills to guard my heart. And when she left again—as she'd already admitted she would—I'd at least be able to maintain my dignity.

In the meantime, I couldn't abandon her now any more than I could the day we'd met. What nobility remained a part of me forbade it. I'd be a friend to her. Just a friend. I owed it to what we'd once shared to at least try to accept that whatever had happened to her, whatever mysterious force had kept her from coming to me, she was here *now*. And she needed my help.

I smoothed my hand down her arm, drawing her closer, shoving aside all my feelings of anger and betrayal to focus on quieting the fear I saw in her eyes, on being the friend she needed me to be at this moment. "Tell me what's happened to you, lass. Let me help you. I'll talk to my king. I'll do whatever I can. You know I will. Just tell me what you've done."

The look she gave me was agonized, torn. Finally, she nodded and slipped her hand into mine, little sparks of desire firing off in my blood at the touch of her skin. "Let me show you."

Chapter 5

The "warehouse" to which Arabella directed me when we returned to Chicago was not a warehouse at all, but an abandoned theater, which, from the thick layer of dust that covered the seats and clung to the rotting grand drape hanging cockeyed above the stage, had been abandoned for quite some time. Random stage props were scattered about the building, along with chairs, lamps, tables, scraps of wood, racks of clothing, and rows of shoes from pretty much every possible era. There were stacks of bottles, dozens of hatboxes, shelves filled with a stunning variety of antique trinkets and baubles.

"You've been living here?" I asked, curious how she would find such a place habitable. The stench of mildew made my nose itch, and I sneezed twice before I added, "Where did all this stuff come from?"

She shrugged and strolled toward the steps leading up to the stage. "Here and there. Most of it was here already, but I've brought it out into the open to take an inventory."

I shook my head in confusion. "Inventory? Why do you care about cast-off props from a washed-up theater?"

She paused when she reached the stage and spread her arms, gesturing toward the vast collection. "Because these aren't all just props, Gideon. Many of them are relics. *Tale* relics. I've hidden them among the junk to avoid detection."

When I gaped at her, she snatched up an ancient-looking oil lamp and tossed it to me. The moment it hit my open palms, I could feel the magic infused in the metal. My nerve endings tingled and a barrage of images flashed through my thoughts, telling the entire story of the fabled lamp in three seconds flat. My gaze snapped up to hers. "This is Al Addin's lamp. The one that held his genie."

She nodded and picked up a shepherd's horn. "Little Boy Blue's horn." Next was a small red hooded cape. "Little Red's riding hood from when she was a child."

Now understanding the import of the collection she'd amassed, I turned a slow circle, surveying all the items again. "Where the hell did you get all this?" I breathed. "I didn't think anything came over with us. How're all these relics in the Here and Now?"

She jogged down the steps. "I have no idea. Someone has been either sending them here from Make Believe or drawing them in to the Here and Now. And they're from the entire timeline of Tale history, Gideon. Some are ancient. Others are only decades old."

"How did you even discover them?" I asked, dumbfounded.

"That morning at the falls, the item I liberated—"

"Stole."

Her mouth hitched up at one corner, giving me the saucy, mischievous smile that had first won my heart. "Semantics."

I grinned in spite of myself. "You were saying?"

"I had in my possession an item that had been given to my mother to keep as a memento of my father after he died. It was one of several of his possessions that were returned to her after he was killed. Just days later, soldiers came and looted our home, taking the items, hiding them by dispersing them far and wide. Just a few weeks before that morning at the falls, I learned that at least one of the treasures— a magical helm—was held by the fairy king. And I decided to get it back."

"What happened to it when you fell?" I asked.

She shook her head. "When I came to, it was gone, along with everything else I had. I was lying on a riverbank, completely naked, all my possessions gone."

A vision of her naked in the moonlight intruded upon my thoughts, a remembrance of our last night together. Heat flooded my body, and

I turned away to hide certain other effects, hoping she didn't notice when I covertly shifted to make myself a little more comfortable.

"I searched everywhere in Make Believe," she continued. "But there was no sign of it. Until I came here. I found the first relic by accident when I was doing a job in Rome—"

This brought me back around. "Rome?"

"Which made me start looking for other things, just out of curiosity, mind, but the more I looked the more I found. And two weeks ago, my informant discovered the helm was *right here* in Chicago. I mean to get it back."

"What the hell were you doing in Rome?" I demanded, remembering I'd heard about a trip my ol' pal Merlin had taken there just last year. With a lady friend.

She shrugged out of her jacket and tossed it over the back of one of the seats. "Jewelry heist. There was a shipment of diamonds—" She broke off suddenly, her eyes going wide with excitement. "Do you want to see it?"

I frowned, confused. "The diamond shipment?"

She waved away my words with a laugh. "No, not the diamonds! I sold those *ages* ago." She grimaced when she saw the look on my face. "You don't really want to know this, do you?" She sighed. "I had to make a living once I came over, Gideon. I couldn't expect Merlin to keep letting me freeload off of him."

I strode toward her, closing the gap between us in just a few steps. "You could've come to me," I insisted. "You *should've* come to me instead of relying on that egomaniacal bastard."

She tilted her head to one side, her brows drawn together in a pained expression. "Oh, Gideon . . . Don't you think I wanted to?" She rested her hand on my chest for a moment, an explanation hovering on her lips. I could feel her indecision, her desire to *protect* me, of all things. "Please, can we not argue any more about the past? Can we just hang on to the present?"

If I hadn't been able to feel the agony and regret she was experiencing because of the time we'd lost, I don't know that I could've forgiven her. But the ache at the center of her chest was making it hard for her to breathe; the weight of her remorse was so substantial she was crumbling beneath it. How could I not rescue her from such torment?

I took her face in my hands and pressed a lingering kiss to her brow, then rested my forehead against hers for a moment. When I pulled back and peered down at her beloved face, she was smiling again, the twinkle of excitement that was so contagious shining in her eyes once more.

"C'mon," she said, taking my hand. "I want to show you the first relic I found, the one that has helped me locate all the others."

I followed dutifully, my curiosity admittedly aroused. She took me to what must've once been a dressing room for the actors but had been converted into a bedroom, although aside from a bed there was little that made it so. The thought of her sleeping alone in this musty, rotting building night after night made my chest tight with sorrow. Of course, she hadn't been alone, had she? She'd been with Merlin. And he'd done a piss-poor job of looking after her, that was for damned sure. What kind of man let a woman stay in a place like this?

I clenched my fists at my sides. "That son of a bitch."

"What's that, love?" she called over her shoulder as she dragged aside several plastic storage containers packed full of books to get to a beat-up chest of drawers that was missing two of its four porcelain knobs. "Didn't catch that."

"Nothing," I muttered, stepping in to take over with the books. Through the clear plastic I could see quite an assortment of titles at a glance, most of them classic stories, fairytale anthologies, books on myths and legends. She'd been doing her homework.

When the books were finally moved aside and stacked out of the way, she pried open one of the drawers with a missing knob and rooted through a neatly folded stack of satiny undergarments. Feeling my cock growing hard again, I averted my eyes and tried to focus on a libido-dampening nineteenth-century painting of a bucolic landscape that hung on the wall.

Except instead of the effect I'd hoped, the painting brought to mind the number of times we'd tumbled to the ground in an intimate tangle in just such golden fields, our desire for one another too strong to deny until we could reach the cottage I'd built for us to share. Even as I stood there, I could once more feel the heat of the sun upon my skin as we lay naked together, our arms and legs entwined, basking in what I'd thought to be a perfect happiness.

How wrong I'd been.

"Gideon?"

I tore my eyes away from the painting and met her questioning gaze for a long moment. My God, I wanted to take her in my arms just then, prove that I could be everything she wanted, everything she needed. I wanted to whisper my love in her ear, hear her call my name in rapture. But I swallowed hard and pushed away such thoughts as she took a step toward me, cradling in her hands a beautifully crafted silver hand mirror.

"Here it is," she said, her voice thick with barely contained excitement as she held out her hands for me to take the mirror.

I took hold of the handle and held it up, startled to see my own reflection dissolve into a churning haze of mist and smoke. Then another face began to take form. One I didn't recognize.

"Bella, *dolcezza,*" came the heavily accented voice of the dark-haired man now visible in the mirror, "you really have *the* worst timing. The *contessa* was just about to do her little dance in front of the mirror again, and—*Dio mio!* You are not my little Bella."

"Clearly," I replied, sending a confused glance Arabella's way, mildly irritated to see her grinning. "I'm Gideon, representative of the fairy king."

Arabella came to my side, slipping her arm around my waist and turning her body into mine as she peered into the mirror. I stiffened at her closeness, her honeysuckle scent wafting to me as her hair fell over her shoulder.

"*Buongiorno, Fabrizio,*" she greeted. "I was just telling my friend how I found you."

The man in the mirror eyed me suspiciously. "A friend, you say? Well then, I will reserve judgment for the moment. But I will tell you truthfully, Bella, his hair is *far* too red for my liking. You would do better with a brunet, *dolcezza.*" He wagged his eyebrows at her with a grin that was more charming than I liked.

She laughed softly. "And I suppose you know just the brunet for me, do you?"

Fabrizio drew himself up proudly—well, as much as the confines of the mirror would allow. "I tell you, if I were out of this mirror, I would make love to you every night. You would never want for the . . . *Come si dice . . . ?* Ah, yes—the *multiple orgasms.*"

"Hey, hey, *hey,*" I interrupted, my angry tone making Arabella's cheeks flush when she cast a furtive glance my way. "That's *not* a problem, pal."

Fabrizio shrugged as if he sincerely doubted the veracity of my claim. "I have not seen our Bella take a lover since she found me, but I tell you—she deserves a real man—not an ignorant brute who does not know how to please his woman. *This* I know."

I felt my rage building, not sure which pissed me off more—his referring to Arabella as if he had some claim on her, or his implication that I'd be unable to please her. I had half a mind to throw her down on the bed and prove just how much pleasure I could give her. But instead, I jabbed a finger at the mirror. "Now, y'listen t'me, you little—"

Arabella pried the mirror from my grasp with a grin and held it against her chest. "You have to forgive Fabrizio," she whispered. "He hasn't been with a woman since he was trapped in this mirror. It makes him a little . . . petulant."

"Petulant?" I repeated. "He's a self-important prat."

"I heard that," came a muffled voice. "But do keep on talking. I quite enjoy being buried in Bella's cleavage. . . ."

Arabella laughed and pulled the mirror away from her chest, wagging a finger at the man in the mirror. "Aren't you a cheeky one today? Behave yourself, or I'll have to put you back in the drawer."

Fabrizio sighed and rolled his eyes. "You wound me, *dolcezza.* Truly, your words are like the arrows in my heart."

"Don't tempt her," I warned. "Her aim's legendary."

Arabella turned her face up to mine to offer me a grateful grin. For a long moment, our gazes locked together in a tense silence. My arm went around her, pulling her even closer until her body was pressed flat against mine. I could feel her heart thundering in her breast, echoed by my own. Her lips parted in a little gasp and her fingers tentatively came up to caress my cheek.

"Your eyes," she murmured. "All that time . . . How did I never notice the way they change?"

"It only happens when I'm reading the emotions of others," I explained, my voice growing deeper as I took her in, "discovering their desire before they even know it themselves."

I could not just see the heat and need that was building inside her, I could *feel* it. Most likely because I shared it. Her hand moved to the back of my neck, gently urging me down to her mouth. Lost in her eyes, in the feel of her, the scent of her, I only vaguely realized that I was bending forward, far too willing to comply.

"Ahem," Fabrizio coughed, making us both start guiltily. "If you would like to be alone . . ."

I took a step out of Arabella's arms, feeling suddenly cold. "No, that's not necessary." I chanced a glance at Arabella. "Why did you show me this mirror?"

She couldn't have hidden her disappointment had she tried. It was written all over her aura, making me feel like a stubborn ass for selfishly wanting to protect my heart from further damage.

She rallied quickly, though, taking a deep breath and shaking off the tension between us. "This is not just any mirror—"

"This is true," Fabrizio chimed in, with a shrug. "I am quite remarkable, as you can see."

"What I mean is this is *Snow White's* mirror," Arabella said with a reproving look at Fabrizio. "Fabrizio is able to move in between any and all reflective surfaces—mirrors, windows, chrome . . . It doesn't matter. He's the most valuable recon I could possibly wish for."

"This is how you've been breaking into places so easily?" I guessed. "He checks out all the security measures for you in advance."

Arabella quickly looked away. "That's part of it."

She went to a clothes rack that contained all manner of costumes and withdrew a long, dark green hooded cloak hidden among them. There was nothing remarkable about it. If I'd had to hazard a guess, I would've thought it nothing more than an old wool cloak from days gone by—or a decent reproduction. But then she draped it over her shoulders and a tiny cloud of fairy dust rose up in the air around her.

"That's an enchanted cloak," I announced. "It's fairy-made."

She nodded, grinning with barely contained excitement. "Not just that." She pulled the hood up over her head and winked. The next thing I knew, she was gone. No, not gone—I could still feel her in the room, but she had vanished from my sight. Then I felt a *whoosh* of air and I was jerked forward until I bent slightly at the waist. And then there was the fleeting pressure of her lips upon mine. When my eyes went wide with surprise, she shoved the hood from her head and became visible again, her own eyes dancing with delight.

"An invisibility cloak," she said, stating the obvious. "And not just *any* invisibility cloak—it's the one my mother made for my father, the one that was taken from her after he died and lost to the ages. But I found it, Gideon! I found it!"

With a little bounce of excitement, she threw her arms around my neck, hugging me tightly. I wrapped my arms around her and lifted her from her feet, happy to return the embrace, probably holding her longer than I should have.

"And there's more!" she said, taking my hands in hers when I set her back on her feet. "I've slowly been tracking down all of the things that were precious to him, the relics my mother had given him, had made for him, infusing them all with her love. I've retrieved nearly all of them."

"Are any of these items by chance among those you stole from the Met?" I asked.

Her excitement slowly faded from her face and her grip on my hands loosened, letting them drop out of her grasp. "I didn't take those."

"But—"

"Someone else got to them first," she interrupted. "When I got there, they were already gone."

"Arabella, those items belonged to Arthur Pendragon," I reminded her, my head spinning with the implications. "Are you telling me . . . ?"

"Yes," she replied, her chin going up a notch. "Arthur Pendragon was my father. And he didn't die because my half-brother Mordred killed him. He was murdered because he was in love with my mother, Nimue, the Lady of the Lake."

I thought of Guinevere and the vehemence with which she'd said how precious Arthur's relics were to her. Had she killed him in a jealous rage because of an affair? If so, why would she now be collecting evidence of that affair? None of it made any sense, least of all how Arabella came to be living as a thief in the forest if she'd been born to a fairy as powerful as the Lady of the Lake.

I took Arabella gently by the shoulders. "Lass, are y'sure about all this? Could there be some mistake about where y'came from? I know you felt adrift in Make Believe, like the forest was the only place y'belonged, but—"

"I'm absolutely certain, Gideon," she shot back. "I received the news from the most reliable source possible."

"Who? *Fabrizio?*" I heard Fabrizio's muttered words of indignation from where Arabella had placed him on top of the dresser.

"No, not Fabrizio," she huffed, taking off the cloak and casting it onto her bed. "It was the one man who knew Arthur best, who knew his most intimate secrets, helped him rise to glory and was there with him when it all fell apart."

Understanding dawned, bringing an unpleasant taste to my mouth when I realized whom she meant. "Merlin."

She slapped her hands on her hips and lifted her chin. "Exactly. And what reason would he have to lie to me?"

I could think of several, not the least of which being that Arabella was a beautiful woman and Merlin was an unrepentant womanizer.

"Not only that," she continued, "but he's been teaching me all kinds of things I didn't even know I could do—"

Oh, I bet he was . . .

"—abilities I must've inherited from my mother."

I eyed her skeptically, wondering what manner of nonsense Merlin had been filling her head with. "Arabella . . ."

"Don't believe me?" she retorted, that impish chin jutting up at me. "Well, watch this." She took a step backward and vanished again, this time without the benefit of the invisibility cloak. And I couldn't feel her presence any longer. It was as if all the light had gone out of the room.

Suddenly, she reappeared before me, holding a cup of coffee in each hand and a small bag of freshly baked scones, and grinning from ear to ear. "Wasn't sure if you were hungry, but I missed breakfast following you around."

"Where the hell did you go?"

"Café around the corner," she said with a shrug, handing me one of the coffees. "I'm still getting used to popping out of the rift unnoticed, though—nearly scared a poor old lady out of her knickers."

"You can shift," I marveled, somehow finding her even sexier now than ever. "Only fairy-born can do that."

She spread her arms and bowed with a wink. "It has become quite handy, I must say—especially when it comes to keeping up with you, love."

"Or spying on me," I added, lifting a brow pointedly.

She squirmed a little. "I wouldn't call it *spying* exactly."

"No?" I replied. "And what would *you* call what you were doing at the king's estate last night and then again this morning at the Met?"

She lifted her chin a notch. "Surveillance."

I grunted. She could call it what she liked. But the fact was, her ability to shift through time only increased her talent for stealth. And it certainly explained how she'd managed to pop in and out of places to nick the relics without getting caught. It also explained the magical residue left behind at the crime scenes, making her protestations of innocence less likely to be believed by the authorities—or my king.

"Okay, so how do the fairy dust thefts tie into this?" I asked, feeling the tingling at my wrists growing with urgency I wouldn't be able to ignore much longer.

Arabella heaved a sigh. "I can't tell you that," she insisted. "Not yet. Right now we need to go to Vegas."

"Vegas," I repeated, frowning. "Merlin's in Vegas."

She gave me a curt nod. "Precisely." When my expression grew stormy, she quickly added, "Merlin has some of the answers. It's best if you hear them from him. Please, Gideon. Just trust me. I promise, I'll reveal everything in time."

She was damned right she would . . . whether she liked it or not, unfortunately, once the king had his hands on her. The mere thought of what the king might do to her in his fury brought back the maddening panic that had gripped me in Central Park. Soon I'd have to make a choice. I just prayed I'd have the strength to make the right one. And be able to live with my betrayal.

Chapter 6

Arabella seemed a little twitchy as we came out of the time rift. She'd had trouble opening another portal so soon after her Starbucks run, but I chalked it up to her still learning how to pass through the folds of time. There were some extremely powerful fairy folk who never managed to master it with the ease with which I handled it. But when I noticed that some of the bounce had gone out of her step and that her cheeks had gone a little pale, it became clear that something else was at work.

As we walked the Vegas strip, she grew even more agitated, stripping off her jacket and tossing it onto the sidewalk with a groan. I snatched it off the ground and gently took her hand in mine, pulling her aside and into the shade of an awning marking the entrance to a midlevel casino.

"You're hungry," I told her, taking hold of her chin to look into her eyes, concerned to see the difficulty she had focusing.

She forced a smile. "Maybe I should've had more than a scone and a latte for breakfast."

I frowned down at her, not liking her growing pallor. "We're going back," I announced, grabbing her hand and heading back in the direction from which we'd come. "You're not well."

"Gideon, I'm fine!" she grumbled, digging in her heels. "I just need lunch. I'll get something from a food truck on our way to Merlin's hotel. Amazing invention, the food truck. Really, I've grown quite fond of them since I've been here."

I studied her for a moment, then glanced around before waving my hand and producing a chili dog with shredded cheese and mustard. Her eyes widened with delight. "How did you know...?" I peered over the top of my shades so she could see my eyes, making her chuckle. "Seriously? It works that well, does it?"

I shrugged. "Sometimes."

She took a huge bite of the chili dog as we walked, moaning a little as the flavors hit her tongue. "This is delicious," she said after she'd swallowed the bite. "My God—no wonder you're such an amazing lover if you know exactly what a girl is thinking, what she's wanting you to do for her...."

I kept my gaze straight ahead, trying to ignore the images her words brought to mind and wondering just where the hell Merlin's hotel was anyway. I wasn't exactly eager to see my old pal again now that I knew what he'd been up to with Arabella, but I'd kiss that bastard on the mouth if it'd get Arabella to change the subject. A subject that was torturing me with erotic images of us together that I had no business thinking about just then.

"Are you always this serious?" she asked, polishing off her chili dog. "You never used to have that perma-frown going."

She was right, of course. I hadn't been nearly as serious or severe when she'd known me. Not externally anyway. But what she didn't realize was that any lightheartedness she'd witnessed had been more *her* doing than any inherent trait of mine. Her smile, her fearlessness, her brash eagerness to embrace every experience as an adventure—it was contagious.

And I'd craved it. Arabella had been a breath of fresh air to a dying man. Quite literally. The path I'd been walking had had only one destination. But she had offered me a detour that led me away from certain damnation and into her arms, giving me a glimpse of what the Ordinaries would call heaven. The memories of that happiness and the pure hell I'd experienced after I thought she'd died came back to me in a painful rush, making me wince.

"Oh, and there's another scowl brewing, just there between your eyebrows," she teased, wagging her index finger at my forehead. When I frowned at her, fulfilling her prediction, she gave me a playful smile, genuine this time. "Although, I have to say, you're quite handsome when you're worried about me."

"Handsome?" I grumbled, letting her drag me along behind her. "I'd rather never have to worry about you and you think me repugnant."

She sent a flirty grin over her shoulder. "Never happen."

"You not giving me cause to worry? Oh, yes, I'm well aware that you take great delight in tormenting me with your antics. You always did."

She laughed. "I meant, you'd never be repugnant to me—even if you were old and grizzled and all those gorgeous red-gold curls fell out, I'd still think you were the most handsome man I'd ever seen." She abruptly stopped and spun around to face me to say something more, but having not anticipated her sudden halt, I slammed into her, my arms going around her to keep us both from stumbling. Laughing, she grabbed on to my jacket to steady herself.

I cursed under my breath and took a step back, putting her at arm's length. "Sorry, lass," I threw over my shoulder as I strode away, walking ahead of her now.

"Gideon!" she called, jogging to keep up with my long strides.

Fortunately, at that point we finally arrived at the hotel and casino where Merlin was staying and performing his act. I went into the lobby, making a beeline for the elevator. As luck would have it, the doors happened to open just as I pushed the up button. Not so fortunately, Arabella and I were the only passengers.

"I'm not gonna be just another one of yer games, Arabella," I muttered. "Not this time."

She pressed the button for the penthouse, then stepped directly in front of me, crossing her arms over her chest. "For the record, you were never a game to me. And you're not a game now."

I studied her for a long moment, wanting to believe her. "You have chili on your mouth," I told her, avoiding the conversation about *us*.

She swiped at the corner of her mouth. "Gideon—"

"You missed it," I said. "It's the other side."

"Bugger all . . ." She huffed and wiped the other corner. "Listen, I—"

"It's still there."

"Oh, for fuck's sake!" she grumbled, throwing her arms up in the air as we jolted to a stop and the doors opened. A man in a loud silk shirt started to get on, but Arabella threw a glare at him over her shoulder. "Take the next one."

The guy grunted and started to get on anyway, but Arabella blocked his path. "Oi!" she snapped, giving him a shove back into the hallway. "Hop it, mate!"

As soon as we were on our way again, she turned back to me, her lips pressed together in an angry line. But before she could take the piss out of me, I cupped her cheek and pulled her toward me, wiping the smudge from the corner of her mouth, letting my thumb pass over her lips more than was necessary.

"There," I said, my thumb now smoothing over her cheek as I marveled at the softness of her skin. "That should do it."

She shook her head. "No. I don't think so." With that, she grabbed my jacket and pulled me down to receive a hard, hungry kiss. I wanted to resist her. I knew I should push her away. But I was far too weak. I kissed her back, lost in the sweet taste of her. I snaked an arm around her waist and pulled her hard against me, lifting her up on her toes. When she released me and took a step out of my arms, she closed her eyes for a moment. "I'm sorry, Gideon. I shouldn't keep doing that, but—*bloody hell,* I've missed kissing you."

I wanted to tell her how much I'd missed kissing her, too. I wanted to drag her back into my arms and capture her mouth again, show her just what we'd missed out on all these years. But I didn't. I shoved my hands into my pockets to keep from peeling off her clothes right then and there and caressing every inch of her body, and took a step back, putting a safe bit of distance between us.

"All I want—" She suddenly grimaced, in visible pain, bracing her hand against the wall of the elevator. She swayed a little on her feet, and I was at her side in an instant.

"What is it, lass?" I asked, my arm going around her waist to steady her.

She gave me a shaky smile and patted me on the chest. "No worries. Just a bit knackered." When I gave her a disbelieving look, she laughed. "I'm fine!" She reached up and smoothed her index finger over the crease between my brows. "So serious!"

I wanted to press her to tell me what was going on. I knew she wasn't being honest with me and even as I gazed upon her, her aura thinned out, growing dimmer. Unfortunately, before I had the chance to urge her to tell me the truth, the elevator doors opened, granting us access to the penthouse level—and the most garish, ostentatious décor I'd seen since the Renaissance. Crystal chandeliers, gilt crown moldings, white shag carpet, antique furniture upholstered with luxurious crimson velvet . . . And in the center of it was a ridiculous white fountain overgrown with all manner of vines and flowers and complete with a fat little cherub playing a harp.

It had Merlin written all over it.

When I'd first met him, he'd been a bookish, scrawny lad I'd had to defend from trolls in a chance meeting on the road to Camelot. Who would've thought we'd cross paths again many years later and that we'd actually become friends?

Merlin had been a nobody then, an apprentice wizard still wet behind the ears, but with a great deal of talent and more than a little promise. But still unsure of his abilities, Merlin had allowed Uther Pendragon to take advantage of him, use his magic for purposes that were in direct conflict with Merlin's principles. It must've been a relief when the old king was murdered, leaving his noble son as heir. It was only after being given charge of the young king that Merlin was finally able to come into his own and realize his full potential.

Too bad that realization came along with a monster ego and overactive sex drive that turned him into an unrepentant attention whore the likes of which was only rivaled by our Shakespearean brethren, the Willies. God forbid they should ever find themselves in the same room together.

Merlin had come over just ten years before, but had immediately won over the Ordinaries with his elaborate magic shows and over-the-top special effects. The guy had taken Vegas by storm and was soon one of the most celebrated "illusionists" of the twenty-first century. Of course, it didn't hurt that the women thought him something of a rock star. And he lapped it up like milk from his mother's teat.

He'd completely bought into the rock star image, ditching his druid's robes and long beard for black leather pants, piercings, and tattoos.

"Fantasia, darling," came a voice from the other room but coming closer as he spoke. "I told you I needed the hot tub cleaned after last night's visitors. Not a single one of them swallowed. . . ."

I grunted in disgust. The thought of such an unapologetic philanderer looking after Arabella, keeping her from me all this time, filled me with rage.

"And, really, darling, I can't have tonight's guests—" His words cut off when he entered the foyer and saw us. He laughed a little nervously. "Gideon, my old friend . . ."

"Friend?" I growled, stalking toward him. "You son of a bitch!"

His heavily charcoaled eyes went wide just before my fist connected with his mouth, snapping his head back and knocking his top hat to the floor.

"Gideon!" Arabella cried, rushing forward and grabbing my arm in an attempt to hold me back.

"Bloody hell!" Merlin yelled, spitting blood onto his carpet before wiping a hand over his black goatee. "I have a show tonight, you wanker!"

I grabbed the lapels of his tuxedo jacket and slammed him up against the wall. "I don't give a flying *fuck* about your show, Merlin. How could you keep this from me? How could you keep *her* from me, knowing how I . . ."

I released him with a cry of rage and strode several paces away, trying to get a handle on my anger before I ripped his fucking throat out. Suddenly, Arabella was blocking my path, slipping her arms around my waist and resting her cheek against my chest.

"Hush now, love," she murmured, her voice calming me like nothing else could. "I'm here *now*. We have *now*."

"You just couldn't stay away from him, could you, Bella?" Merlin huffed.

Arabella turned her face up to mine, her eyes so full of sorrow it made my heart ache. "No," she said softly, her dark gaze locked with mine. "I couldn't. I tried, Merlin, I really did."

I wrapped my arms around my little love and held her against me, having her in my arms giving me the strength to rein in my temper and anger. When I finally raised my gaze to meet Merlin's, my expression must've been far less deadly for the wizard heaved a relieved sigh, his tension visibly diminishing.

"So," Merlin drawled, making another swipe at his mouth with his fist, "what brings you by, Bella? You've finally revealed yourself to our dear friend, after all. I'm surprised you're not off shagging your brains out while you can." When my expression went dark, Merlin held up his hands before I could fire off the retort that came to my lips. "Oh, come *on*! Don't tell me it hasn't crossed your mind."

"We didn't come here to discuss our relationship," Arabella assured him. "I need you to tell Gideon about the relics."

Merlin's eyes widened ever so slightly. His excitement was obvious, the prospect of sharing some of his arcane knowledge awakening the nerd the rock star tried to hide, but he snatched up his top hat and strolled casually toward us, spreading his arms wide and revealing the vast network of skulls, dragons, and other tattoos on his bare chest. "Well, I suppose I can take a few moments to impart a little of my vast wisdom. Come, let us away to the study, my darlings."

We followed him into an office that was even more garish and ostentatious than his foyer, but I had to give him credit for the floor-to-ceiling bookshelves that lined all four walls. And they weren't the kind of books you'd find in your average bookstore. These appeared to be a collection of archaic volumes of magic, mythology, herbology, and other ancient texts and scrolls written in pretty much every language imaginable and in every form of writing from cuneiform to runes to hieroglyphs to ancient Greek.

He bypassed them all and went to a heavy wooden pedestal that held a vase depicting a couple in the throes of passion. He knelt before the pedestal and lifted one of the panels to reveal a safe in the wall that was armed with not just a fingerprint scanner but a retinal scanner and a twelve-digit code. When he finally opened the safe, he withdrew the item inside and gingerly set it down on the table.

"What I am about to show you is known only to a few privileged individuals who have been trusted to keep its contents confidential—"

"So, why're you telling us about it?" I asked, wondering just how many people knew all about this supposedly secret tome. "I mean, if it's supposed to be a secret."

Merlin gave me an acerbic look. "I'm offended that you could even think I'd be so careless with this knowledge!"

"Oh no, Merlin, I know you're a great one for secrets." I sent a pointed glance Arabella's way.

He opened his mouth to protest, but then snapped it shut again and shrugged. "True. But this is different, Gideon. I share it with good reason. The secrets within this tome are of such great import—"

"Always so dramatic," Arabella muttered, rolling her eyes. "This isn't your show, Merlin. Get on with it."

Merlin opened the book where a red satin ribbon marked, revealing a text written in Early English. His eyes glimmering with excitement, he spun the book around for me to read. "Take a look . . . at *this*."

"Here, let me," Arabella said, moving to take the book and read it for me as she'd done in Make Believe, regaling me with the stories of our Tale brethren, laughing her way through the amusing bits and wiping the tears from her cheeks when their stories did not end with Happily Ever After.

I was tempted to let her read to me again, but I placed my hand on hers. "I've got it."

A slow smile curved her lips, and never had I been prouder of my education than when I saw the delight in her eyes as she realized I could read. When I pulled the book closer to me, she wrapped her arms around my bicep and leaned around to look at the text with me.

I took a deep breath, drawing in the honeysuckle scent of her, and then skimmed through the text quickly, my brows coming together in a frown. When I finished the passage, I looked up at Merlin, not surprised to see him watching us with a smug grin, his arms crossed over his chest.

"I've never heard any of this before," I told him.

He laughed and spread his arms wide. "Well, of course not! That's rather the point, old boy."

"But this is a full inventory of Arthur Pendragon's relics," I said. "There was only a handful known to the Ordinaries through his story here, Excalibur being the most famous, of course."

"That was by design," Arabella said, carefully turning the page so I could read the next passage.

I shook my head as I read, a horrible sinking feeling in my gut growing with each word. "This says that if one person possesses all of the relics, it will make him unstoppable, that he can never be vanquished, he can never die."

Merlin nodded. "Exactly so. Now you know why it's been kept a secret all this time. If the wrong person was to acquire all the objects..."

"But how did this knowledge come to the Here and Now?" I asked. "This text is hundreds of years old. It clearly wasn't written by a Tale since our relocation, Merlin. How did they know this? It's almost as if..."

"As if Arthur was real and not a Tale," Arabella finished for me.

I turned my head to her. "The Ordinaries have always theorized that Arthur was based on a real person in the Here and Now."

"He wasn't just *based* on a real person," Merlin explained. "He *was* a real person. He was an Ordinary. The Arthur who lived and died in the Here and Now is the same Arthur who lived and died in Make Believe. They were one and the same."

I began to pace, trying to process what Merlin was telling me and the implications of such an anomaly. "How is this possible?" I murmured. "How was an Ordinary able to actually exist in our world *and* this one?"

Merlin shook his head. "I have no idea. I practically raised the boy, Gideon, you know that. And I guarantee you, his father was a Tale. But this was before we even knew of such a place as the Here and Now, before we knew to look for a Tale aura. Who would've thought that there were those among us who weren't... *like* us?"

"So, when Arthur died..." I mused, not wanting to voice my conclusion.

"He died forever," Arabella said, her voice little more than a whisper. "But Merlin says the part about my mother sending Arthur to Avalon is true, so I like to think he's still alive there, as immortal as any Tale. And I hope my mother's there with him, that they're finally able to be together. That maybe there's a place where a Tale and an Ordinary can be happy after they're gone." She laughed, the sound a little shaky. "But maybe that's just the romantic in me."

I frowned at her, curious at her declaration. Arabella was many things, but a romantic wasn't one of them. She'd never believed in happily ever after; she'd told me so when we were in Make Believe. She only believed in *now*. She'd reiterated as much to me on more than one occasion even today.

But before I could respond, Merlin added, "You've yet to ask the most obvious question, old boy."

I turned my attention back to him, trying to focus on what I already knew. "I have a million questions."

Merlin gestured toward the book. "But the *big* one is . . . ?"

"Why did Arthur die?" I said, seeing what he was getting at. "If he had all of the relics Nimue made for him, and they are as powerful as you say, then he should've been immortal."

Merlin leaned over the desk and whispered conspiratorially to Arabella, "He always was a clever one."

Her grip on my arm tightened. "I've always thought so."

When he caught sight of my scowl, Merlin cleared his throat before continuing. "You are absolutely correct, old boy. I believe someone stole the actual relics and replaced them with fakes, leaving Arthur vulnerable. Unfortunately, I didn't discover the deception until it was too late. By then, there was nothing we could do except take his body to Nimue."

"But it wasn't just Arthur that was returned," I deduced. "It was the relics as well, all the tokens of her love for Arthur."

Merlin inclined his head, confirming his role in the tragedy. "I do have my moments. I'm not always the self-centered bastard you're so inclined to believe me to be."

The jury was still out on that one. I'd yet to know Merlin to do anything altruistic without an ulterior motive.

"Who sent the soldiers to steal them away from her?" I asked, getting back to the point.

"I've no idea," the wizard admitted on a sigh. "I had a vision of an attack, but it was unclear who was coming for Nimue." He paused, an uncharacteristically somber expression darkening his face. His voice was curiously tight with emotion when he continued, "I came as quickly as I could, but she was already gone, and the relics were nowhere to be found. Even her sweet child, who was but ten years old, had disappeared."

"The soldiers took Arabella?" I asked, covering Arabella's hand with mine. It felt cold, clammy. I glanced over at her, concerned to see her skin growing pale again, but she gave me a weak smile.

Merlin shrugged. "I assumed so, but it seems our brave girl struck out on her own, hid in the forest."

"I wouldn't call it brave," Arabella muttered, uncomfortable with the praise.

"I searched everywhere," Merlin continued, "but she was nowhere to be found. In fact, it wasn't until well after you'd gone into service with the king that I finally found her. She was so lost, confused after the falls. I took care of her for a time, helped her find her way again. Hardly surprising that when she came over, she sought me for help."

A deeply affectionate look passed between them, making my blood boil. I didn't like to think about how Merlin might've "taken care" of her in Make Believe, how he might've preyed upon her vulnerability. I snaked an arm around Arabella's waist, pulling her against me in a protective, possessive move that was no doubt the cause of the amused grin Merlin wore, but I didn't give a shit.

"What of the relics?" I asked, pointedly avoiding the topic of the nature of their history together. "How many have been located? How many remain missing?"

"I've retrieved all but seven," Arabella said, her voice taut, bringing my attention back to her pallor. "The three that were taken from the Met, Arthur's shield, his ring, and Excalibur. And, of course, the last one is the helm I had in Make Believe that vanished when I fell."

"And, aside from the helm, which you discovered is in Chicago, do we know where any of the remaining relics are?" I prompted.

"*We* don't know anything about their location," Merlin drawled, sweeping his hand toward Arabella and me, "but *I* have a lead on the ring, no thanks to that ridiculous Italian dandy who fancies himself a spy."

"Fabrizio, you mean?" I chuckled, finding Merlin's criticism a bit ironic, all things considered.

"They have a bit of a rivalry going," Arabella stage-whispered to me with a grin. "I think Merlin's jealous."

"Jealous of an idiot who got himself trapped in a mirror after screwing the wrong witch's daughter?" Merlin grunted. "Not bloody likely."

Arabella's eyes twinkled when she winked at me. "Well, Merlin, if you are so assured of your superiority, perhaps you should share this supposed lead on the ring?"

He did a little dance shuffle out from behind the desk and raised his arm, striking a theatrical pose. "The ring is . . ." He paused a beat for dramatic effect. "On the hand of fair Guinevere." With that, he knocked his top hat off his head onto his shoulder, popping it with his bicep and catching it in midair.

"Nice try," I told him.

He slapped his hat against his thigh with a huff. "Oh, come *on*! That was *brilliant*! Who else do you know who can do the thing with the hat?"

"I'm not talking about your little performance, Merlin," I drawled. "I'm saying I saw Guinevere just this morning and didn't notice a ring on any of her fingers. She made a point of assuring me she was single."

"I'll bet she did," Arabella mumbled.

Merlin blinked at me in a rare moment of astonishment, not used to being wrong. "But . . . I had it from a reliable source. I've had Rick Rumpelstiltskin on the lookout for a particular style of ring—of course, I didn't tell him why. Probably thinks I intend to give it to one of my ladybirds. He told me Guinevere brought the ring in to have it appraised when she came to Chicago on business a week or two ago."

Rick Rumplestiltskin ran one of the swankiest jewelry businesses in Chicago's Jewelers Row. If anyone could offer an expert opinion, it'd be the infamous imp.

"But Guinevere told me she didn't keep any of the relics with her," I insisted. "She said they were all on loan with museums because she thought they were better protected that way."

"Perhaps she lied to you," Arabella suggested, her tone clearly displaying her distrust of the erstwhile queen. She batted her lashes at me. "But, then, I suppose it *is* difficult to pick up on someone's obvious deception when you're completely mesmerized by the breasts she's shoving into your face."

I was jolted by the accusation, wondering how the hell Arabella possibly knew about Guinevere's advances. "How'd you—"

Yeah . . . I wasn't even going to finish that sentence. It was a no-win.

"The ring isn't particularly flashy," Merlin interjected, uncharacteristically coming to the rescue. "It's just a series of Celtic knots forged in silver. She could easily keep it in her jewel case and no one would be the wiser."

I scrubbed my jaw with my palm, mulling over the number of mysteries that were piling up. A soft gasp from Arabella snapped me out of my musings and I turned my attention to her. I lifted her chin with the edge of my hand, disturbed by how much trouble I was having getting a read on her. "Are you all right, lass?"

She nodded, forcing a weak smile. "Of course."

Merlin's grunt in response brought my gaze to him. "Bella, you need to tell him."

She glared at him. "Sod off, Merlin. This is my affair."

"What aren't you telling me?" I demanded.

"You haven't yet asked about the fairy dust," Merlin prompted, crossing his arms over his chest.

Arabella muttered a curse under her breath and sent Merlin a beseeching look.

At the mention of the fairy dust, the magic in the king's binding spell flared, searing my skin and making me wince, but I ignored the pain to ask, "What of it?"

Merlin dragged his gaze away from Arabella's and began, "She needs the fairy dust—"

"To shift," she interrupted, throwing her hands up in the air with a laugh. "You caught me! My magic is rubbish. However, shifting has become quite an asset to my relic liberation efforts, as you can imagine. And, unfortunately, it tends to take the piss out of a girl. I need a dose of dust now and then to combat the fatigue."

Merlin's expression was sour when he muttered, "Yes, quite."

I studied them both, knowing the bullshit they were feeding me was only half the truth. But I feigned ignorance to see how things would play out. "So you decided to steal the fairy dust you needed? You couldn't have just gone to a distribution center for a prescribed dosage?"

Arabella averted her eyes. "It's not that simple."

I took her hand and pulled her to me until our bodies were nearly touching, and captured her gaze, everything male in me smugly enjoying the way her chest rose and fell rapidly when we stood so close. My voice was a husky rasp when I added, "You could've come to me." She swallowed hard, her breath growing even shallower. Then a slow smile curved her lips. "Too right."

I conjured a handful of my own dust and blew gently across my palm, directing the silvery particles toward Arabella. She inhaled deeply, breathing it in, keeping her eyes closed as it hit her system and energized her again. When she opened her eyes a few moments later, she was visibly improved.

"Better?" I murmured, smoothing the back of my hand along her cheek.

Her lips parted in a little gasp at the contact and she pressed her cheek into my touch. I could feel the desire building within her, and I knew without a doubt what she wanted, what she *needed,* was more than a little fairy dust. And, my God, I wanted it too. Too much for my own damned good.

I took a step backward and gave myself a rough mental shake, bringing my own desires back under control.

"Well," Merlin drawled, spreading his arms wide and shepherding us out of his study. "As much as I'd love to continue hanging around to watch this little drama play out between the two of you, I have a show to do. You're welcome to make yourselves at home. *Mi casa . . .* and all that."

He gave me a pointed look and jerked his head a couple of times toward a door that led to what appeared to be a bedroom. When I frowned at him, he jerked his chin at Arabella and then pumped his fist.

Subtle.

When Arabella turned to see what was making me frown, Merlin darted forward to press a kiss to her cheek, then dashed away, calling over his shoulder. "G'bye, darling. Good luck with the adventures tonight. Don't do anything I wouldn't do. . . ." At this, he came to an abrupt halt and turned back to add, "On second thought, for once, *please* do something I would do. You're in *desperate* need of a good shagging."

After Merlin had gone, Arabella and I stood facing one another in awkward silence, the tension between us a palpable force in the room. The air sizzled with the undercurrent of desire, and suddenly it was a little hard to breathe. I stuck a finger under the collar of my shirt and pulled to see if that's what was choking the life out of me. It wasn't.

"So . . . what now?" I asked, simultaneously dreading and hoping like hell that she'd suggest we follow Merlin's advice.

"Now," she said, her hips swaying as she came closer, clearly enjoying my torment, "we go pay a visit to your not-so-secret admirer and retrieve Arthur's ring." She slipped one arm around my neck and then the other, pressing her body into mine. "But first, I think we should go back to my room at the theater."

I was barely able to suppress the groan that preceded my strangled response, "Oh, yeah?"

She nodded. "Mmm-hmm." She pulled back enough to give me that saucy, dimpled smile of hers, knowing damned well that she'd never needed any magic to enslave me. "If I'm going to go sneaking into the Queen of Camelot's bedroom, I'm going to need a change of wardrobe. And so are you."

Chapter 7

"I loved him, you know," Arabella called from behind the dressing screen.

My head snapped up at her words, jealousy spiking in my veins. "Say again?"

She peeked out from behind the screen, offering a tantalizing glimpse of her bare shoulder. "My father," she clarified. "I didn't see him very often. And I had no idea who he really was. I just knew he was the man who brought me the most beautiful dresses and baubles from his travels and that my mother loved him."

"And you didn't know your mother's true identity either?" I asked, trying very hard to concentrate on her words and not the shadow of her nude form behind the screen as she tried on yet another outfit for the job we were planning to pull off that night.

"Not a clue."

I watched her shadow hop around a little, then wiggle into whatever it was she'd chosen this time around. I'd offered to provide exactly the ensemble she needed, but she'd refused, preferring to go about it the hard way.

"Hmm," she muttered. "Nope, I don't think this one's going to work either."

Bored out of my mind after two hours of wardrobe changes, I fell back onto her bed with a groan. "Arabella, lass, I *beg* you to let me give you what you need."

I heard her go still, my words hanging heavy in the air between us, the double meaning not lost on either of us. I squeezed my eyes shut, grimacing at the war of emotions raging within me.

So much for keeping my true feelings under control, playing it cool. There was no doubt that the attraction was still there, that the intense desire we'd felt for one another hadn't been affected by time or distance. But my heart was another matter. I wasn't eager to let it take another beating. And yet here I was letting loose with double entendres that betrayed me. Freud would've had a friggin' party with all the shit running through my head. Especially after what I'd just said.

Let me give you what you need. . . .

These were the same words I'd spoken to her our first night together. I never could've forgotten them, not when that night was seared into my memory, as vivid today as when I'd first taken her into my arms. After I'd finally spoken the truth that had weighed heavily on my heart, Arabella and I had shared our first kiss. But one kiss hadn't been enough. It had never been enough. One kiss always led to hundreds, thousands. Too many moments of bliss to recount.

And that night . . .

I squeezed my eyes shut, willing away the remembering, but my will was no match for my heart. It wouldn't forget. And once more she was cradled gently in my arms . . .

I peered down into her dark eyes, made even darker by the intensity of her desire. She was so innocent, so inexperienced, but the apprehension she felt was gentled by her trust in me, her belief in me and my love. I wavered beneath the weight of it, averting my eyes, ashamed. I wasn't worthy of her high regard, didn't deserve her love. And I sure as hell didn't deserve the gift she was prepared to give me.

Her fingertips lightly caressed my cheek. "I want this," she whispered. "I want to be yours."

I shook my head. "You deserve so much more than me," I insisted. "What can I offer you? Trouble? Poverty?"

Her lips turned up in a slow smile. "You're all I want."

I grunted dismissively, wondering how long she'd feel that way

*after the winter set in and the travelers were fewer, offering less op-
portunity to steal their valuables and put food in our bellies. But she
grasped the nape of my neck and pulled me down to her, kissing me
soundly, her skill vastly improved with the amount of practice we'd
had since our first kiss. I groaned with need, my tongue slipping between her teeth to caress hers.*

*She hooked her heel around the back of my knee and rolled onto
her back, urging me along with her. I settled between her thighs,
breaking our kiss with another groan, somehow resisting the urge to
bury myself in her sweet heat. She gripped my shoulders, rolling her
hips upward until the tip of my cock slipped inside.*

*She gasped, her eyes going wide, her muscles tensing. But when I
retreated and would've rolled away, her grip on my shoulders tightened. "No, please," she said, breathless. "Don't stop." She closed her
eyes for a moment and I watched in fascination as the tension faded
from her lovely face, and her lips parted as she rolled her hips again
and began to move in rhythm with my slow, measured thrusts, a little
deeper each time.*

*I braced myself on my elbows, rising up so I could study her ex-
pression, watch her aura for even the slightest misgiving, but all I
saw was yearning, desire, love. As I thrust gently, she moved with
me, matching my pace.*

*"My God," she gasped, her nails digging into my skin. "Please,
John . . . I need you."*

*I'd never heard those words before, had never had anyone need
anything from me but the death and destruction I could deliver with
my sword, or a fleeting night's pleasure in my bed. But to know that
she needed me, needed my love . . . It touched me on a level I hadn't
even realized existed. And that cavernous emptiness that had threatened more than once to drag me down into its dark abyss was suddenly brimming with light.*

*My throat was tight with emotion when I whispered, "Then let me
give you what you need."*

"Gideon?" Arabella called softly, snapping me out of my bittersweet reverie, the sound of my name on her lips sending a shiver
down my spine that I had to work to repress.

I heard her come out from behind the screen but kept my eyes closed, not wanting to meet her gaze just then, afraid she'd somehow guess at what I'd been thinking. But realizing I was being a total fucking coward, I sighed and forced my eyes open. "Arabella, what I meant—"

The words died on my lips. She was wearing a black leather jumpsuit that hugged every tantalizing curve and zipped up the front from navel to the cleavage I'd often dreamed of nuzzling again. She'd pulled her hair up into a ponytail that hung down to her shoulders, the soft tip of it curling invitingly around the curve of her throat. I swallowed hard, my eyes fixed on her as she walked toward the bed, my gaze taking in every enticing movement.

My cell phone suddenly rang, jolting me out of my stupor and thankfully dampening the painfully hard erection pressing against my fly. I pulled my phone from my jacket pocket and glanced at the number, surprised to see it was the king. I held a finger to my lips, then answered the call. "I am at your service, sire."

"Gideon," came the king's booming voice, overloud as if he suspected the distance between us would interfere with my ability to hear him. "Where are you?"

I winced, holding the phone back from my ear. The man was a brilliant businessman and tactician, but when it came to technology, he was a total neophyte. It was rare he deigned to contact anyone via telephone or any other means of communication aside from the conjured mists through which only we fairies and our most trusted friends communicated. "I am investigating the fairy dust thefts as you requested, sire," I told him, my conscience cringing at the half-truth. "The lead you provided proved promising. However, the situation is a bit more complicated than we imagined."

Arabella's mouth hitched up in one corner and she lifted an eyebrow.

"Oh? How so?" the king asked.

"I believe there is more at play here than just the fairy dust thefts," I explained, wincing as my bonds flared again. "I'm going to need a little more time to sort things out, get to the bottom of everything."

"Of course, of course," the king replied. "What's a few more days, eh?"

"Were the additional security measures I suggested for the transports approved?" I asked, wanting to make sure that the other thief, whoever he was, didn't make an appearance before I could track his ass down and turn him in, hopefully before I was forced to hand over Arabella.

There was a moment of hesitation. "I trust your judgment completely, my boy. But you know Mab is not so easily persuaded of your incomparable value to us, I'm afraid. You understand."

Oh, I understood perfectly. Reginald had brought my ideas forward, had ridiculed them as only he could, and then had convinced the queen and the others to take his advice instead. The king would've no doubt argued—briefly. But if Mab had it in her head she wanted things a certain way, the king always caved. The only instance where I'd ever seen otherwise was when it came to the king's daughters and his insistence upon Mab's accepting them.

"Just bring me my thief by the end of the week," the king continued. "Then we won't have any concerns, true?"

"As you say, sire," I replied, my bonds flaring again. Arabella sat down beside me and took my hand, lifting it up to press a kiss to the inside of my wrist. I cleared my throat and shifted uncomfortably, trying desperately to will away the erection that was raging once more. "I'll be traveling back to New England this evening to have dinner with Guinevere Pendragon. I believe she knows more about the museum theft than she's admitting."

"Indeed?" said the king. "Then, by all means, you should return and see what else she can tell you." The king paused briefly before adding, "You know, there are quite a few attractive Tales in that area of the country, Gideon. Perhaps after you visit Guinevere you should take in some of the local sights, meet a nice young lady with whom to have breakfast, if you take my meaning."

"I'll take it under advisement," I replied, struggling to keep my tone even so that the king wouldn't notice any discomfiture in my voice.

"A man should not be too much alone," the king continued, his words ironically underpinning what my libido was roaring loud and clear.

"Thank you, sire." I swallowed hard as Arabella removed my shades, her dark eyes boring into mine. "I'll be in touch soon."

Her gaze still locked with mine, Arabella took the phone from my hand and disconnected the call, then tossed it aside. "Are you ready to go?"

Hell, yeah, I was . . .

It took me a moment to realize she was talking about the trip to Connecticut to visit Guinevere. "Oh. Oh, yeah." I shook my head in an effort to get my shit together. "Yes, I'm ready." I stood, pulling her to her feet.

She straightened my tie, then smoothed the shoulders of my jacket. "You are devastating, love," she murmured. "Guinevere won't be able to resist you. Just be sure to keep her busy long enough for me to go through the house and find the ring." She gave me a playful look from beneath her dark lashes. "And remember, this is a *dinner* date. Not dinner and breakfast, no matter what the king says."

I chuckled. "Fear not, lass. I have no intention of spending more time with Guinevere than absolutely necessary."

The smile that brought a dimple to her cheek was too much to resist and I bent forward, sweeping my lips across hers. Which was a mistake. Because then I had to kiss her again. And again. I wrapped my arms around her, keeping her from leaving my embrace until she'd been thoroughly kissed.

When I finally released her, she twirled out of my arms and snatched up the magic cloak, draping it over her shoulders with a flourish, a sparkle of excitement in her eyes. "Just like old times, eh? Robin Hood and Little John off on another adventure."

I nodded, remembering well our escapades—and how they always ended with us falling into bed together naked. My cock jumped a little at the thought as if it, too, was eager to skip to the end.

Forcing myself to focus on our mission, I offered Arabella my arm. "My lady, shall we away? Your carriage awaits."

Her brows shot up as she took my arm. "Carriage?" she repeated, snatching up her knapsack of tools as we left her room. "You plan to drive?"

I shook my head. "We won't shift on the way there because of the effect it has on you. So I have procured transportation that will have us there just in time for my dinner engagement."

She tilted her eyes to the sky, considering our options. "Hmm . . . Witch's broomstick?"

I chuckled. "We are, indeed, flying, but not by broomstick."

"Flying monkeys?"

"A plane awaits us at the airport," I explained.

"That'll take hours," she pointed out, her expression wary.

I peered over the top of my glasses and winked. "Not when I'm the pilot."

Chapter 8

"Well hello, handsome," Guinevere purred, striking a provocative pose in the doorway to the modest home she'd rented in a quiet Connecticut suburb. I'd expected her to have taken an apartment or even a swanky hotel room during her stay in New York City, so it was quite a surprise when the address she'd given me after accepting my invitation to dinner was in a sleepy little town that was a not inconsiderable train ride away from the big city.

The house was a two-story Colonial that could've passed for a typical middle-class family's home. It sat on a wooded lot surrounded by a proliferation of mature trees that had shed their leaves for the fall. Smoke curled from the chimney, lending the scene a quiet simplicity that was in direct odds with the woman in a bright red silk dress that was only long enough to be barely decent and which sported a neckline that plunged down to her navel. Her blond hair was swept up into a messy knot at the crown of her head, giving the illusion that she'd already had a tumble in bed that evening—or, hell, maybe she had.

"You're looking particularly lovely this evening," I told her, meaning every word of it, for she truly did—even though I found myself preferring a black leather pantsuit and ponytail to the *do me* dress Guinevere was modeling. I offered her my arm. "Shall we?"

But instead of taking my arm, she grabbed my tie and pulled me inside. "I thought we'd dine in tonight," she informed me, swinging the door shut and pressing her back to it, blocking my exit. I inclined my head politely. "If that is what you want, I'm happy to comply." Which couldn't have been further from the truth. Arabella had suggested that I take Guinevere out to dinner for a couple of hours so that she could have the freedom to move through the house swiftly without detection. "But are you certain you wouldn't prefer to dine in the city? A dress such as that is meant to be seen and admired—as is the woman wearing it."

"A dress like this," she replied with a sultry grin, "is meant to be seen and admired for only as long as it takes for a man to remove it." She glanced off to her right, where I could hear the rhythmic cadence of a grandfather clock. She raised a brow at me and stepped back from the door to allow me in. "Tick-tock, Mr. Montrose."

I inclined my head in a polite nod and stepped inside, hoping Arabella found that damned ring before the situation became too uncomfortable. Thanks to Fabrizio's reconnaissance, we'd been led to believe that Guinevere was alone this evening, most of her staff having been given the night off. Which made me wonder who had prepared the dinner I could smell from where I stood in the foyer. Having an unaccounted for servant certainly complicated our plan.

"This is a lovely home," I said as I followed her into a room that adjoined the foyer. It was a comfortable sitting room with rather generic furniture that could easily be accessorized to represent pretty much any decorating scheme from rustic to French country. Currently, it was very much a minimalist setting with sharp lines and angles, modern artwork with bright splashes of color, and not much other composition hanging on the walls.

I fought back a cringe at the artwork, not impressed in the least. I wasn't a fan of this particular school of art even on a good day, but the painting hanging to the left of the fireplace, little more than random circles of various colors and a few tread marks, was especially off-putting. There was something about it that made me uneasy—as if I should've seen through the kindergarten quality to something more profound, but it was completely lost on me.

The room's only redeeming quality was the fire that blazed in the hearth behind a glass screen. The soft pop and hiss of the flames soothed away a few of the room's harsh edges, but even the fire was more for décor and ambiance than for warming the room.

"Would you care for a drink?" Guinevere asked, sidling over to a sideboard cabinet that contained an assortment of crystal decanters and matching glasses. "You strike me as a man who would prefer a cognac on a crisp autumn night. Am I right?"

"You're very astute," I said with a smile.

When she turned her back to pour the drink, I sent a quick glance behind me, startled to see Arabella in the doorway, her mouth agape.

What the hell is she wearing? she mouthed, gesturing toward Guinevere's barely-there dress.

I gave her a stern look and gestured for her to get out of sight. She looked torn between storming into the room and snatching Guinevere bald and bolting up the stairs, but then her eyes went wide and she darted from the doorway, apparently deciding that the latter option was the better choice. Her cloak flared out behind her but vanished just as Guinevere turned back around.

"Here you are," Guinevere said, calling my attention back to her. She handed me one of the snifters, stepping closer as she took a sip from her own.

I sipped the amber liquid, enjoying the smooth warmth as it traveled down my throat. I immediately recognized the taste. The king's favorite—and not at all affordable to the average person. If it was the vintage I suspected, the bottle had fetched a price upward of several thousand dollars. Not exactly what one would expect on the income Guinevere claimed. "This is a fantastic Courvoisier L'Esprit—and well aged, if I'm not mistaken. How did you come by it?"

She laughed lightly. "Why am I wasting my money on expensive cognac on my modest income, you mean?" She didn't wait for me to respond before adding, "It was a gift. As was this home and everything in it. It's temporary, of course. I will be returning to London in a week if nothing else should keep me here."

"And you'll be taking the relics with you?" I reasoned.

She took another slow sip of the brandy, then replied, "All but those that were stolen, of course."

"Of course."

"Have you any leads on who might've taken them?" she asked, gliding gracefully to a small sofa just wide enough for two. She draped herself quite artfully upon it, turning her body to allow me a glimpse of the side of her breast.

"Not yet," I told her truthfully. Since Arabella had confirmed someone else had stolen the relics from the Met before she'd had a chance to get to them, I couldn't even guess at another suspect. All I could hope was that when I talked to Trish Muffet, she might have a lead from the information she'd gathered at the crime scene. "But, rest assured, I will continue to investigate the matter and do everything I can to ensure that the items are returned to their rightful owner."

Her lips curved into a tight smile. "I'm sure you will, Mr. Montrose. From what I hear, you are a man of your word."

I narrowed my eyes behind my shades, wondering whom she'd been talking to. And why the words, which were so sweetly said, nonetheless seemed tainted by distrust. "I certainly hope so. I always try to be."

She patted the couch beside her. "Please, join me. We have a few moments before dinner. I want to hear what it is you do for the king."

I glanced around the room for a viable alternative, but the larger sofa was far enough away that sitting there would've been such a pointed refusal to cozy up with Guinevere that I feared it would interfere with my ability to keep her attention on me and not on Arabella's mission upstairs. And the only chair in the room was a delicate thing that never would've stood up to my large build.

I moved to join her, sending my gaze toward the foyer once more. The moment I settled next to Guinevere, she turned toward me, placing her hand lightly on my thigh.

"So, tell me," she drawled, her voice going breathy, "what does your service to His Majesty entail?"

I cleared my throat, hoping she didn't move that lovely hand any higher, biological responses being what they were. "I am primarily his bodyguard and warden of the Seelie family. Their protection is my responsibility. I am also the master of the guards and personal assistant to the king. If there is anything he desires, I am charged with procuring it."

She arched a pale brow at me. "Indeed? And Queen Mab? Do you serve her as well?"

"She has very little use for me," I told her honestly.

Guinevere shook her head solemnly on a sigh. "What an idiot this queen must be. Were I in her place, I would have many uses for you, Mr. Montrose, I guarantee you."

I had no doubt of that. I'd heard enough stories about Guinevere to know that a number of Arthur's knights had been quite delighted to be at her beck and call and to perform whatever task she requested of them. The risk of Arthur discovering them performing such *service* to their queen apparently paled in comparison to the rewards the queen herself provided.

Not quite sure how to respond, I inclined my head. "I am delighted to know that my lady would think me equal to any task she required."

Guinevere shifted slightly so that her calf caressed mine as she crossed her legs, causing the hem of her dress to rise to a level that revealed she wore nothing beneath. "And I know exactly what task I would set you to first."

She slid her hand farther up my thigh, damn it all, her lips curling into a lascivious grin. Instinctively, my hand clamped down on hers, halting her progress. When I saw the look of offended pride come into her eyes, I offered her a smile. "My lady," I said mildly. "I believe dinner is ready."

She opened her mouth to refute me, but at that moment a lovely maid in an old-fashioned black-and-white uniform entered the room with a polite cough. "Your dinner awaits, m'lady."

I rose and offered my hand to Guinevere to help her rise.

"Oh, you *are* good," she breathed, letting her hand drift across my chest as she turned toward the doorway.

Relieved to have avoided offending Guinevere with a more pointed refusal of her advances, I blew out a quiet sigh and shook my head, wondering how Arabella was doing upstairs.

The dinner that had been prepared for us rivaled anything I'd eaten at the king's palace or elsewhere. Each dish was more delicious than the previous, and the wine that accompanied each course was beyond compare. I gathered that each of the bottles was also a gift from Guinevere's benefactor as the least expensive of them I knew to cost over 300 dollars.

As the wine continued to flow, Guinevere became less fixated on her intention to drag me to bed and more focused on the relics that had gone missing from her collection at the museum.

"I know everyone thinks that I didn't love Arthur," she mused over our filet mignon, "but I truly did. I loved him so desperately. All I ever wanted was for him to love me in return."

I frowned slightly at this, finding it a strange remark, considering the stories we'd all learned of their time together. "But I thought yours was a love match."

She laughed bitterly. "On my end, but to Arthur, I was merely an advantageous connection. I was beautiful, accomplished, and considered to be a proper queen for him. But he never loved me, never wanted me. My God, we only slept together once the entire marriage. Why do you think we had no children?"

I shook my head, surprised by the information she'd imparted. "I always assumed that it was because of Morgana. She was certainly powerful enough. Everyone has pretty much assumed that she placed a hex upon you to keep you barren."

Guinevere shook her head. "Poor Morgana. So misunderstood. I wish she'd come over to the Here and Now with us to make a fresh start instead of being trapped in her horrible story in Make Believe. You see, she held no malice toward me or toward Arthur. Yes, Arthur rejected Mordred as his son, but who wouldn't? I mean, the boy was born of incest. But neither Morgana nor Arthur realized they were brother and sister when they were together."

My brows shot up. "Indeed?"

"Arthur was the only one who mattered to Uther, you see," Guinevere explained. "He sent Morgana away to be raised by a witch in the village. His offspring grew up with no knowledge of their relation to one another. And Arthur was barely a man when he met Morgana and bedded her. Neither of them knew how to keep a child from being conceived and nature took its course. But when the truth became known, Arthur couldn't acknowledge such a child as heir to the throne. Morgana understood and accepted that."

"And so, the animosity between them?" I prompted.

Guinevere shrugged. "Nonexistent. Mordred knew his father, spent time with us at the castle, was raised as a nobleman. He died in battle, this is true, but it wasn't at Arthur's hand. And Arthur was quite devastated by his loss. As was I. I'd always craved a large family, and Mordred was the closest thing to a son I was ever to have."

"Unbelievable." I sat back in my chair, marveling at how the legend had been misrepresented. But I shouldn't have been surprised when this was the case for so many of us. Still, it made me wonder even more at Arthur's dual existence in Make Believe and the Here and Now and how he came to know Nimue.

"I know people think me a heartless trollop because of my relationship with Lancelot," Guinevere told me, her speech slurring just a little but not enough to hide the sorrow in her voice at the mention of her infamous lover. "But what would you have done? If you were living a lie and the person to whom you were wedded didn't return your affections? Would you have wallowed in loneliness forever, hoping by some miracle that person would one day grow to love you in return? Or would you accept the love and adoration that was so freely offered elsewhere?"

"I don't know that anyone would blame you if they knew the whole story," I told her. "Living without love isn't easy for anyone, let alone a Tale."

The look she gave me was so filled with gratitude it pained me. I felt sorry for Guinevere now that I understood her better. I saw through her advances. She wasn't just some oversexed siren. She was deeply, miserably lonely and longed to be loved and adored just as any other person would be. And like so many others of us Tales, she was a victim of her reputation, most of which was woefully misrepresented.

"You speak as if you understand what it's like to long for the one you love," she said on a sigh.

"I do," I admitted, raising my wineglass in salute.

Guinevere lifted her glass in response and opened her mouth to say more when a small thud sounded outside the dining room. She frowned, her gaze trained on the doorway. "What in the world was that?"

Apprehension shot through me, clenching my gut when I thought of Arabella, searching through all of Guinevere's things. When my hostess got to her feet, I rose along with her, and eased her back into her chair. "Please," I said with a grin. "Allow me."

I didn't wait for her response before striding out to the foyer and glancing around, searching for Arabella. The patter of light footsteps sounded down the hall, so I followed. Although I knew she had the cloak, I could sense her presence before I reached the door to the library. I eased it closed behind me. The moment it latched, Arabella shoved the hood from her head.

"You two are getting awfully cozy," she noted, an angry edge to her voice.

"Isn't that what I'm supposed to be doing?" I whispered. "I'll be the first to admit, I had Guinevere all wrong. She's really just terribly misunderstood."

Arabella rolled her eyes. "If you believe that . . ."

"How's the search for the ring going?" I asked, changing the subject.

She shook her head. "Not great. I've looked everywhere I can think of in her bedroom. I even checked the guest rooms. Nothing."

"So much for Merlin's 'in her jewel case' theory," I murmured. "Where next?"

She let out a sigh and glanced around the room in which we were standing. "Going to have to look down here. I'll start in this room. Try to keep her distracted."

"I thought you didn't want me to get too cozy with her," I teased with a grin.

Arabella narrowed her eyes at me and playfully smacked me on the arm. "Just keep her talking." She started to pull the hood back up over her head but paused and wagged a finger at me. "*Talking*. But nothing else."

I couldn't help smiling, enjoying the fact that she was feeling a little jealous. I was still grinning when I returned to the dining room. "All's well," I assured Guinevere. "Just the house settling."

"That's a relief." She chuckled a little. "I've been hearing all sorts of noises in here the last few days. I can't tell you how many times I thought someone was in the house, only to discover that there was no one there."

This brought me up short. "When did the noises start?" I asked, resuming my seat at the table. While I was gone, the dessert course had been laid out and yet another glass of wine poured.

She shrugged. "Right before the relics were stolen from the Met. I'd been a little jumpy about leaving them, and thought I was just imagining the sounds here because my nerves were already on edge. I'm glad to know it was nothing more than this old house's bones creaking."

I forced a smile, wondering if the same thief who'd stolen the items from the Met had also visited the house, looking for more—perhaps even searching for the very ring that was reported to be on the premises but Arabella couldn't seem to find.

"Have you noticed anything else strange about the house?" I asked. "Anything else give you cause for alarm?"

"Not until now," she said, her tone wary. "Why do you ask?"

I gave her a reassuring smile. "No reason. Just want to make sure you're safe here, that's all. This house is rather secluded, after all. I'm surprised that the friend who gifted it to you for your stay would leave you out here all alone."

"I'm not alone," Guinevere corrected, rising to her feet and coming toward me. "I have my maid and my manservant." She came around behind my chair, trailing a fingertip across my shoulders. "And now you're here." When she reached the other side of my chair, she slipped the straps of her dress from her shoulders, letting it slide down her slender form to pool at her feet. As I'd suspected, she'd been wearing nothing beneath.

Ah, hell . . .

I swallowed hard, hoping Arabella wouldn't choose this moment to come checking up on how my little chat was going. "Guinevere—"

She draped herself across my lap, but in her tipsy state, she lost her balance and fell backward. Instinctively, my arm went around her waist to keep her from tumbling off.

"My lady," I began, "please don't think—"

Suddenly, she was pressing her lips against mine. Before I could even react, an angry gasp from within the room brought Guinevere's head up, and she glanced around in confusion.

Well, shit. Arabella.

This visit was just going to all kinds of hell. Things couldn't have looked worse than they did at that moment with the former queen of Camelot draped across my lap, completely naked but for her stiletto heels. I took hold of her arms and gently but firmly eased her from my lap and onto her feet.

"You heard that, too, didn't you?" Guinevere asked, confused.

"I think you mistook the intention behind my invitation to dinner," I told her, picking up her dress from the floor and handing it to her. "And for that, I apologize."

But apparently my rebuff was the least of her concerns. Holding the dress against her breasts, she strode angrily from the room, calling out, "Who's there? Come out right now, damn you!"

I heaved a sigh of exasperation and made to follow her but Arabella was blocking my path, hands on her hips, *pissed-off* written all over her face. "What the hell was that?" she demanded in a fierce whisper. "You were supposed to be talking, not all—" She wrapped her arms around herself and made kissing noises while wiggling her hips back and forth.

I laughed in a loud burst before I could stop myself, but choked it back when her expression went from *pissed off* to *fucking furious*. I raised my hands before me. "I'm sorry," I whispered. "I had no idea she was going to throw herself at me like that."

Arabella gave me a wry look. "Really? The *shag me* vibes she's been throwing out at you all night didn't clue you in?"

"Did you get the ring?" I asked, glancing toward the doorway, pointedly changing the subject. I could still hear Guinevere calling out angrily as she marched through the house.

Arabella huffed and lifted her right hand, showing me the silver ring on her middle finger. I wasn't entirely shocked or offended by the fact that it was the only finger she raised. "Yeah, it was hidden in a cigar box in the sitting room. Seemed a little odd for a former queen to have a box of stogies sitting around, so I took a look inside while you were playing kissy-face with Guinevere."

I rolled my eyes. "I wasn't—"

A scream upstairs and a loud thud cut me off and brought both our gazes to the ceiling. I bolted for the doorway, taking the stairs two at a time. "Guinevere!"

A muffled cry at the end of the hallway was the only response. I crashed into the room just in time to catch a glimpse of a man in a hooded cloak not unlike Arabella's. He had Guinevere in a headlock, a knife to her throat. When he saw me, he flung Guinevere at me and darted toward the open French doors that led to the balcony. Before I could set Guinevere away from me, Arabella raced by, giving chase.

I took hold of Guinevere's shoulders. "Stay here," I ordered. "And lock the doors. Don't let anyone in." Sobbing hysterically, she didn't respond. I gave her a little shake, and bent my knees so that I was at eye level with her. "Guinevere, do you hear me? I'll be right back. Lock the doors."

This time she nodded.

Not waiting another instant, I bolted for the door and flung myself over the balcony railing, landing in a low crouch, my eyes scanning the darkness. All was still. I conjured a handful of fairy dust and blew across my palm, sending my searching spell out to look for Arabella. Instantly, her footsteps lit up, giving me a trail to follow.

I ran as fast as I could, not bothering to hide my movement, my only concern getting to Arabella before that bastard—whoever he was—could harm her. A moment later I heard someone panting. Then I saw him—the cloaked intruder. He was bent over slightly, catching his breath. I slowed my pace, now creeping forward.

But he must've sensed my presence. His head snapped up. I didn't realize he had a gun until he raised his arm and the moonlight glinted off the steel. I brought up a protective shield with my magic but before he could get a shot off, I heard the hiss of an arrow. The man howled in pain as the point struck home, going straight through his forearm. The gun fell to the ground with a soft *thud*.

I barreled forward, taking him down. He grunted a stream of curses but recovered quickly, his fist coming around and striking me in the temple.

I was stunned by the blow just long enough for him to squirm out of my grasp. But instead of running, he turned to kick me in the ribs. Which was a mistake. All it did was piss me off.

With a roar of rage, I grabbed his leg and pulled it out from under him. He landed flat on his back with a gasp as the air shot out of his lungs. I was on him in an instant, my fist slamming into his face twice, leaving his mouth bloody and his nose broken. I raised my fist again when he lifted his hands up in surrender.

"No, please!" he blubbered. "Stop! Gideon!"

The fact that he knew my name brought me up short more than his pleas for mercy. I grabbed him by the collar and jerked him up into a sitting position, then conjured a ball of silver light.

"Georgie?" I breathed. "What the hell are you doing here?"

"You know this guy?" Arabella asked, now standing beside me, her bow in hand. She must've grabbed it from her stash of tools outside Guinevere's house at some point during her pursuit.

I got to my feet, dragging Georgie up with me. "Yeah, I know him. He's a petty thief who's been dealing fairy dust."

Georgie held up his hands in front of his chest, taking a few hesitant steps back to put a little distance between him and me. "I swear, it wasn't what it looked like," Georgie stammered. "I wasn't gonna do nothin' to Guinevere. I was just supposed to take something. That's it. But she surprised me."

"What were you supposed to be stealing?" I demanded, with a glance at Arabella.

Georgie's frightened gaze darted back and forth between the two of us, probably trying to figure out which one posed the bigger threat. "Just jewelry," he insisted. "That's it. I was just supposed to grab some shit and get out. They told me I could keep whatever my employer didn't want."

"Who's your employer, Georgie?" I asked, taking a menacing step forward. "Is it the same asshole who's got you dealing D?"

Georgie's head bobbed up and down. "Yeah, yeah. Same guy. But he's just a messenger. None of us knows who the real boss is."

"Then who's the messenger?" I pressed. "Gimme a name, Georgie."

"Can't," Georgie insisted, shaking his head frantically.

Arabella nocked another arrow and drew back, this time aiming at his chest. "Can't," she asked, "or won't?"

Georgie whimpered. "*Can't,* I swear! You don't understand what'll happen to me if I give you a name."

I jerked my head toward Arabella. "I know what'll happen if you don't."

"Okay, okay!" Georgie glanced around, his nervous trembling visible even in semidarkness. "It's"—he lowered his voice, whispering—"the *Huntsman*."

"Bloody hell," Arabella breathed, just as horrified as I was to hear the name.

Bloody hell was right. No wonder Georgie was ready to piss himself for the second time in our association. The Huntsman was *the* Tale assassin. There was a reason Snow White's stepmother had sent him to do her dirty work. The Huntsman had no morals, no scruples. He was ruthless. That part of the story about his having a change of heart? Total bullshit. Snow got lucky, that's all. It was the one and only time the guy ever failed in his assignment that any of us was aware of. There were days that I deeply regretted the deeds I'd committed as a soldier and a thief and a servant to my king. But I seriously doubted that the Huntsman ever gave any of his crimes a second thought. He enjoyed the hunt . . . and the killing.

And for whatever reason, he'd set his sights on the same treasures we had. It didn't surprise me that he'd hired a little piss-ant like Georgie to do the shit work. He didn't have the time or the inclination to deal with petty jobs and recon work. He liked the big jobs—and if there was killing involved, even better. No, the real question was who the hell had hired *him*. Because no matter how much the Huntsman would get off on having all the relics of Arthur Pendragon and the power that went along with them, I found it hard to believe he'd be enterprising enough to come up with the scheme on his own.

"Where do you meet up with him?" I asked. "Have you ever seen him in person?"

Georgie nodded. "Yeah, yeah. He's a big-ass dude. Huge. About as big as you, Gideon. Got one of those military-style haircuts."

I ran a hand down my face. "Thanks, Georgie. You just described about a hundred different Tales in the U.S. alone." I sighed and decided to try a different line of questioning. "How's this all connected to the fairy dust thefts?"

Georgie shook his head. "Hell if I know. I'm a nobody, man. You know that. They don't tell me nothin'!"

I nodded. "Okay. Well, here's the way I see it, Georgie. Thanks to your little fuckup back at Guinevere's, I'm betting the FMA will be here in about five minutes. So, you can tell me what you know now and I'll tell them you were there to do a simple B & E job. Otherwise, I'll confirm whatever she tells them you were up to. And I can assure you, Georgie, you have a long record of assault charges on women. You think Al Addin—or Tess Little—is going to let you off with a slap on the wrist for another attempted sexual assault? You've only been out of FMA prison for a couple of years after doing all that time for the last ones."

"I didn't touch her!" Georgie cried. "I swear it! I was just there to get the jewelry."

"Then I suggest you fill me in on what else you know about the Huntsman and are clearly keeping from me," I replied with a shrug.

Georgie wiped his forehead with his sleeve, muttering a string of curses under his breath. "All right. He—"

Georgie's words were cut off suddenly as his head snapped backward. For a split second, I didn't realize what had happened, but then the report of the shot sounded just as Georgie fell, the top of his head blown away.

Arabella cried out at the same moment, ducking into a crouch and pulling me down with her, but not soon enough. White-hot pain seared my bicep where another of the assassin's bullets grazed my skin.

"Go!" I winced, holding my hand against my arm. "Shift!"

Her eyes were wide with concern for me, but she did as I asked and vanished in the next instant. I started to follow, instinct telling me she'd gone back to Chicago to the safety of her theater. But a sudden prickling of dread hit me at the back of my neck. Fearing the worst, I shifted back to Guinevere's house.

"Guinevere!" I called out when I found the bedroom empty. I thundered down the steps, calling for her again. As I made the foyer, I slipped on something thick and wet and slid across the tile, slamming into the wall. I cried out as the pain from the gunshot wound lanced up my arm and into my spine. When my vision refocused, I saw the source of the puddle.

Lying on the floor was Guinevere's maid, a deep gash across her throat, her eyes staring wide and sightless.

I scrambled to my feet and ran into the sitting room, still searching for Guinevere. But the room was empty. I called out again and stood still, silent, waiting for a response. To my relief, I heard a whimper not far off.

I rushed toward the sound, at last locating her in the dining room. She lay on the rug on her side. She'd put on a white bathrobe after Georgie's botched burglary, thank God. I dropped down beside her and rolled her over, cradling her in the crook of my arm. And had to bite back the gasp that rose to my lips.

Her face was covered in blood from a deep, jagged gash that ran from her forehead, across her brow, and down her cheek. Worse, though, was the blood that soaked the front of her bathrobe. Frantic to find the source, I pulled back the edge of the robe, revealing at least three stab wounds to the chest.

"Oh, shit," I breathed. "Hang in there, my lady. I'll get you some help. Just hang on." I reached into my suit pocket and dialed the FMA's emergency number, praying they would arrive in time, muttering, "Pick up, pick up, pick up, come on . . ."

"Fairytale Management Authority," the operator answered. "What's your emergency?"

I closed my eyes briefly and sighed with relief. "There's been an attack on several Tales," I explained in a rush. "Two are dead, one is still alive, but has at least three stab wounds." I rattled off the address, holding the phone between my shoulder and ear so I could use my free hand to put pressure on what looked like the worst of the injuries.

"We're sending a team right away," the dispatcher assured me. "Are you in danger where you are? Are you able to stay with the victim and keep me informed of the situation?"

I didn't immediately respond.

"Gideon," Guinevere gasped, grasping my hand. "Please, don't leave me."

My instinct was to run now that I knew help was on the way. I was afraid for Arabella, desperate to know if she was okay. My need to know that she was safe was on the verge of full-blown panic, a persistent itch just beneath my skin that was impossible to scratch. And I was wounded and covered in the blood of two of the victims. Not to mention, I had a questionable history that might not play out so well for me if I stayed. But I couldn't leave. Not when my staying might be the difference between Guinevere living and dying.

I swore under my breath and cursed my conscience, hoping it wasn't leading me down a path toward certain damnation. I cradled Guinevere closer and swallowed the fear and apprehension that rose in my throat, hoping like hell I was making the right choice, then ground out, "I'm not going anywhere."

Chapter 9

"So, I have two dead Tales, another on life support, and a wounded and bloody fairy bodyguard who thinks he can feed me a line of bullshit and that I'll be too stupid to notice he's lying out his ass."

I heaved a sigh, but didn't bother to lift my head to meet the accusing gaze of Tess "Red" Little, the Assistant Director of the FMA. It'd been a long flight from Guinevere's back to Chicago and I'd been in the holding cell at FMA headquarters for a couple of hours already. I couldn't even guess what time of morning it was at this point, but I knew it wasn't Red's typical hours. The cup of coffee she'd brought with her was about twice the size of her usual.

Definitely not the time to become confrontational with her. The fact that she and her husband were good friends of mine didn't make her any less pissed off with me for getting into this mess and for dragging her from her bed in the middle of the night to deal with the cleanup. Not to mention, the woman had proven on numerous occasions that she could take down creatures twice as dangerous as me without breaking a sweat—and I had no intention of making an enemy of her. I liked her. She was tough, intelligent, and funny as hell. And I could appreciate the fact that she didn't take shit from anyone—even if at that moment I was the one on the receiving end of her iron will.

"I didn't injure Guinevere," I assured her. "You know I wouldn't hurt an innocent person, Red."

I heard her take a deep breath and let it out slowly before she dragged a chair over and set it directly in front of me. She sat down and rested her forearms on her knees, clasping her hands. "Gideon," she said softly, "you're a good man. I know that you'd never do anything like this. But the Tribunal has been looking for a reason to bust your ass ever since you got off scot-free for your relationship with Lavender back in the day. They're gunning for you, big guy. And I can only do so much to protect you."

"The evidence will speak for itself," I insisted.

"Yeah, about that . . ." she began. "Here's the thing. Your signature is all over Georgie, and his blood's on you."

"We had an altercation," I replied. "I told you that."

"And he's dead now, Gid."

"But he was shot," I reminded her. "And there's no evidence that I fired a weapon. Your people checked me for that already."

"And you're a powerful fairy who's done a lot of dirty work for your employer over the centuries. You know how to hide shit like that, Gideon—either with the tricks the Ordinaries use or with your own magic. That's what Mary Smith is going to say if she has to prosecute you for this."

I closed my eyes, realizing how the circumstantial evidence was piling up. If anyone could build a case out of a lot of flimsy evidence and make it stick, it was Mary "Contrary" Smith, the FMA's prosecutor.

"You've *got* to give me something here," Red pleaded. "Please. Let me help you."

I lifted my head at this, touched by her friendship and willingness to put her own neck on the line. "I've told you everything I can."

"Give me the name of the person who was there with you," she said. She must've seen the wariness in my expression for she added, "Yeah, we know about her. Her magical signature is all over the house, too. And on the arrow that Georgie had sticking out of his arm. Is she the one who took them all out? Are you protecting her?"

"It's not like that," I assured her, shaking my head. "She shot Georgie with the arrow to protect *me*."

Red ran a hand through her thick black hair and let it fall onto her shoulders as she flounced back in her chair, muttering a string of curses. "You're killin' me here, guy. If you want to help yourself and your little girlfriend, you've got to tell me what you're holding back."

I wanted to. I wanted to let Red know that the Huntsman was to blame, but I couldn't prove it. All I had to go on was the information from a two-bit thief whose gray matter was scattered on the ground in the woods near Guinevere's home. Besides that, Red had a husband, kids, people who counted on her and loved her. I wasn't about to put her in danger by setting her on the trail of the Huntsman.

"I can take care of it," I told her. "Just let me out of here, and I'll bring whoever did this to justice. I swear to you."

She regarded me for a long moment, her blue eyes narrowed in scrutiny as she weighed her options. I could feel her coming to a decision about what to do with me, but a sudden pounding on the holding cell's door interrupted her thoughts.

She got up and patted me on the shoulder before stepping outside to see what was going on. I listened intently, trying to catch a bit of the quiet conversation outside the door, but the walls and door of the cell were thick lead and infused with magic that dampened the abilities of anyone held within.

A few minutes later, she came back in and unlocked the heavy shackles around my wrists. "Mary's agreed to let you go for now because we don't have quite enough evidence to formally charge you with anything. But I can't promise that'll be the case after Trish's team finishes going through the evidence." When she saw my questioning frown, she explained, "Trish had to take herself off the investigation. Everyone knows how close you two are. She didn't want there to be any question about the validity of the test results. But she'll be supervising to make sure there're no mishaps or tampering."

I nodded, understanding. "Thank you, Red."

"Don't thank me yet," she drawled. "You'd better bring me something I can work with before Mary finds something to stick you with. Otherwise, there's not much else I can do." She gestured to the door. "Now, go ahead and get outta here. Someone's already here to take you home."

When I'd reclaimed my things from the desk clerk, I expected to see one of the king's servants or perhaps one of the guards waiting for me. I frowned when I saw who it was that had actually come for me.

"What the hell are you doing here?" I grumbled.

"You're very welcome," Merlin shot back from where he was leaning against the wall. "Glad to see a night in the joint hasn't affected your good humor."

I sent a scathing look his way but said, "Thank you. I owe you one. How'd you even know I was here?"

Merlin glanced around casually before saying, "A little bird told me." *Robin.*

"She's safe then?" I asked, eager for confirmation.

Merlin nodded. "Not a scratch. She waited at the theater for you, but when you didn't return, she went back to the crime scene and saw them taking you away in handcuffs. She came to me straightaway and we hopped my private jet to Chicago."

"Where is she now? Back at the theater?"

Merlin shook his head. "No, considering what she told me, I thought perhaps it might be best for her not to return home. Who can say how much this"—Merlin glanced around again and lowered his voice—"*Huntsman* knows about you and about her."

"Take me to her," I demanded. "I have to see her, Merlin."

The moment we entered Merlin's Chicago loft, I could feel Arabella's presence, caught the honeysuckle scent of her made more potent by her anxiety. And if I'd missed any of that, the quick rhythm of her feet as she ran in from the other room at the sound of the door opening would've clued me in.

The moment I saw her sweet face, her dark eyes wide with tentative relief, my soul was at peace. She was safe. I rushed toward her, meeting her halfway as she ran to me, and gathered her into my arms, holding her so tightly it must've been difficult for her to breathe. But she didn't protest. She just clung to my neck made wet by her silent tears.

After several longs moments, I set her down on her feet and took her face in my hands, pressing kisses to her cheeks and lips, my resolution to keep my distance crumbling in an instant.

"I'll just let you two have some time to yourselves," Merlin called out from the doorway. "I have something . . . to . . . *do,* I guess. Yes, I'm sure I'll figure out something to occupy myself for a while."

As soon as the door shut behind him, Arabella pulled me down to her for a proper kiss that was slow and sweet and oh-so-inviting, but I drew back after a few moments, disgusted by the blood and grime that still covered my clothes and skin.

"I need to get out of these clothes," I told her.

She lifted an eyebrow, a slow grin curving her lips. "Aye, that you do, love."

She took my hand and led me toward the bathroom and turned on the water in the walk-in shower, positioning the multiple shower-heads. It was as she was bent over adjusting the temperature controls that I noticed she was still wearing the jumpsuit from the night be-fore. The sight of her perfectly rounded bottom wrapped in that tight black leather was almost more than I could stand.

A low groan of desire escaped me before I could stop it.

She slowly straightened at the sound and turned to face me. For a long moment we just stood there, our gazes locked, the tension in the air between us mounting to the point that I half-expected to see sparks of electricity popping all around us. Then she placed a booted foot on a low stool to her right and slowly unzipped it, tossing the boot aside before she unzipped the other boot, discarding it as well.

"What are you doing, Arabella?" I asked, more of a warning than an actual question. There was no doubt in my mind what she was doing— or that I desperately wanted to indulge her until she screamed my name.

"I'm not happy with this outfit anymore, Gideon," she whispered. "I think I'll let you give me what I want after all. . . ." She grasped the zipper of her jumpsuit and slowly pulled downward as she came to-ward me, baring her beautiful full breasts to me inch by enticing inch.

Ah, hell . . .

I might've had a chance before then. I probably could've contin-ued to hold fast to my resolve to not give in to my urges and keep my distance. But the moment I saw the soft swells of her breasts, the pink nipples going hard, darkening with desire even as I looked on, I was lost.

I grasped the nape of her neck and dragged her to me, capturing her mouth, my lips far too harsh, I knew, as they crushed hers. But her answering whimper was one of desire, not pain. Her kiss was as hungry as my own, her tongue eager and teasing as it swept across the seam of my mouth. I deepened the kiss, savoring the taste of her, determined to reacquaint myself with every mystery those sweet lips could unlock.

I peeled the jumpsuit off of her shoulders and down her arms, completely baring her to the waist. She made short work of my tie and jacket, and my button-down followed soon after. When she clawed at my T-shirt, I broke our kiss just long enough for her to pull it over my head and toss it aside before claiming her mouth once more.

I wrapped my arms around her, my hands smoothing over her back, my strokes commanding, demanding, just the way she wanted them to be at that moment. I pressed her into my body, reveling in the warmth of bare skin upon bare skin. When the tantalizing pressure of her breasts against my chest was too much to resist any longer, when the way they tingled, longing for my attention, made my mouth water, I grasped her shoulders and eased her away from me so that I could capture one of the tight little pebbles in my mouth.

She gasped with pleasure when I grazed it with my teeth, the sound heating my blood to a boil. Her arms went around my neck, her fingers twining in my hair, keeping me where I was as I teased and nipped at her skin, but I wasn't going anywhere. The way her pleasure buffeted my senses was intoxicating, increasing my own until I felt drunk on it. When I shifted my attention to the other breast, she moaned, arching upward toward me, urging me on.

I backed her toward the wall, allowing her to lean against it as I pressed kisses to the valley between her breasts, then made my way along her clavicle to her shoulder. My hand slid down her belly then around to the small of her back. When my hand traveled lower to smooth the roundness of her bottom, she mewled with pleasure, arching against my palm, her body telling me what she wanted when her voice failed. And I was more than happy to give it to her.

"*Dolcezza,* you will never believe—"

Arabella shrieked in surprise at the sudden intrusion—or perhaps it was the murderous look on my face and growl of frustration that rose up in my chest just before I turned to face the intruder who'd popped into the bathroom mirror unexpectedly.

"Fabrizio," I snarled, "this had better be seriously fucking important."

The man was staring off to his right, studiously trying to avoid getting a glimpse of Arabella as she worked to slip back into her jumpsuit from behind the shield of my body.

"A thousand apologies," Fabrizio said, his gaze briefly flicking our way. "I did not mean to interrupt. It never occurred to me that you would be having the passion so early in the morning. Perhaps I have misjudged you, yes?"

"What do you *want,* Fabrizio?" Arabella demanded through clenched teeth, zipping up her jumpsuit with an angry pull and stepping out from behind me.

"Ah, yes," he mused. "As I was to say, I have found the location of the shield of Arthur Pendragon."

Arabella and I shared a glance and said together, "Where?"

Chapter 10

"This is bollocks."

I grinned, adjusting my sword belt, surprised how comfortable the weight of it felt around my waist after all these years. "Just try to blend in, lass."

Arabella fidgeted irritably with her tunic. "Easy for you to say. You're all . . . *knightly* and sexy as hell. Is this how you looked when you were a warrior for your people?"

The similarities would've been much greater had I still been covered with the blood and grime from the night before. But the quick shower I'd taken—cursedly *alone*—before we left had somewhat diminished the authenticity.

I shrugged. "More or less."

Her gaze traveled up and down my body. "Not bad, love. Not bad at all." She nodded, agreeing with her own pronouncement. "The armor suits you. You're the very picture of a gallant knight, I must say. I've no doubt you stole the heart of many an unsuspecting maiden in Make Believe." She gave me a dimpled sidelong glance, the heat in her gaze warming the center of my chest. "I wish I'd known you then."

I was glad she hadn't.

I repressed a shiver as I thought of the person I'd been back then and of the images of war and loss that haunted me every day even still.

"I can't believe you had this already on hand," she further mused. She felt the chain mail of my hauberk with her fingers. "It feels authentic."

"It is," I told her. "My armor from when I was a warrior for my people was lost to me long before you and I met, of course. This is my king's livery. It was what I was wearing when we came over so it traveled with me. Unfortunately, it was a bit outdated for the early nineteenth century, so I've had it in storage. I've only had occasion to wear it when the king holds his annual tournament to celebrate Mab's birthday."

"I imagine you're a force to be reckoned with," she mused, her voice carrying a ferocity that made me glance her way.

I hadn't been wrong. There was a fierceness in her eyes as she met my gaze, her head held high. She was *proud* of me, I realized. Intensely *proud* of me. I squared my shoulders, her belief in me affecting me more than I could've imagined. I knew I'd served my commander well as a warrior, had served my king well as a bodyguard, had served my friends and family as well as I could as one who was devoted to them. But to know Arabella believed in me and thought there was something remarkable about me . . . That filled me with a joy that was indescribable.

"I, on the other hand," Arabella continued on a dramatic sigh, sweeping an arm down the length of her body, "look like a reject from a Disney theme-park casting call."

I laughed, unable to suppress it. She had a point. In the green tunic, brown leggings, and green suede knee boots she'd procured from her collection of costumes at the theater, Arabella was a caricature of her own story. At least the bow and arrow she carried were her own, a precaution we'd agreed upon before leaving for the Texas Renaissance Festival.

"Remind me again why we couldn't have just come in as attendees," she demanded, her eyes narrowing at me. "Why did we have to come in costume?"

I offered a courteous nod to a passing performer dressed as a pirate and his shockingly buxom barmaid companion. "Fabrizio said the shield is being used by the jousting troupe as part of their heavy arms demonstration and is kept in their tent during the joust. While they're preoccupied with the performance, we'll just slip into the tent and get the shield."

"We could do that in normal clothes," she grumbled.

"Yes," I conceded, "but if anyone witnesses us entering, they're less likely to think anything of it if we look like we belong there."

She gave me a doubtful look. "Because I look so knightly, dressed like a prepubescent boy?" she shot back, adjusting her feathered cap. "Why the hell do people think I wore so much freaking *green*, anyway?"

I chuckled. "You're the one who chose the costume. You could've dressed as a barmaid. Or a noblewoman."

She grunted. "I did the whole noblewoman thing once before, and—"

"You did?" I interrupted, the news halting me in my steps. "When was this?"

She turned back to face me, her mouth opening and closing as if she wasn't quite sure what to say in response to what seemed to me a completely innocuous question. The smile she donned was forced in its guilelessness. "It doesn't matter, does it, love?"

It shouldn't have, but it did. And I couldn't really understand why. There was something about the unexpected news that made me bristle, something in the way she'd immediately shuttered her emotions, trying to hide the truth from me. "Was it before we met?"

She heaved a sigh and pressed her lips together, clearly irritated. "Aye, it was."

"Why didn't you ever say anything about it?" I asked, following behind her as she turned and strode toward the arena where spectators were gathering for the jousting tournament. "The entire time we were together, I thought you'd been living in poverty, forced to steal in order to survive and help others in need."

"Do we really need to do this now, Gideon?" she huffed. "Besides, it's not like you weren't keeping any secrets of your own. I didn't realize you were a fairy until the day I fell."

With that she increased her pace as if trying to outrun the truth.

"Don't run away from me, lass," I said, closing the gap between us in a single stride and taking hold of her arm, gently pulling her to a stop. "Not from *me*." She glanced away, averting her eyes as she wrestled with indecision. I gently took hold of her chin and turned her face toward me. "You never need hide anything from *me*."

She raised her gaze to mine, her long dark lashes wet with tears. "I'm not hiding it, love. It just . . ."

I smoothed her chin with my thumb, realizing the memory that haunted her was a painful one. I, of all people, could understand that. "Then we won't speak of it, lass. There's no need."

I released her and started walking again. A moment later, I felt her at my side. Her emotions were twisting at her painfully, so I was surprised when she said, "After my mother died, I fled to the woods, hungry, afraid. A nobleman by the name of Locksley found me wandering and took me in. He and his lady wife loved me as another daughter. They became my new family and I loved them with all my heart. When I was sixteen years old, a Tale came to visit. A recent acquaintance of Lord Locksley, Sir Guy of Gisbourne was handsome, charming. Everyone believed him to be honorable and noble, but he took advantage of a young woman's naïveté then left her heartbroken— and with child."

I shook my head, confused. "But you were still a maiden when we met. I remember well our first night together."

Her expression softened and she placed a hand upon my cheek. "As do I," she said with a smile. "It wasn't I who was harmed. It was the one who'd been like a sister to me—Lady Marian."

"Maid Marian," I murmured as pieces of the Robin Hood story fell into place. I knew Arabella hadn't had another lover—man or woman—prior to me. But I'd never thought to ask who the source of the fabled Maid Marian was. "What happened to her?"

Arabella's eyes clouded with sadness. "Lord Locksley was determined to defend the honor of his daughter and wanted Gisbourne to care for her and the child. But Gisbourne refused. And, like the coward he was, he sent his men to answer Locksley's challenge. My adopted father fought valiantly, but he was outnumbered. And my lady mother . . ." She blinked away the tears and turned to resume our trek to the arena. When she felt my presence beside her, she continued, "Lady Locksley sent Marian and me into the woods to hide while she stayed behind to draw the men away and give us a chance to save ourselves."

I could well imagine the brutality that Lady Locksley must've suffered at the hands of Gisbourne's men. I'd seen far too many acts of such violence committed against my own people by thieves and raiders to have any illusions about her treatment. "I'm very sorry."

Arabella took a deep breath and let it out slowly before she said, "Marian and I were left with nothing and no one but ourselves. As she was with child, I took to stealing to keep us alive. I learned to fight out of necessity to keep the other thieves in the woods from harming us. Fortunately for us, there was still honor among thieves and some of the men came to our aid and we banded together. They looked on us as their little sisters and offered their protection—for a price, of course. It turned out I was rather adept at thievery and damned good with a bow, so I planned the jobs, kept us off the gallows, and let them keep a share of the haul. But because I'd been left with nothing twice in my life before I'd even seen eighteen years, I insisted that part of what we stole had to be given to the needy. Eventually, I became the leader of my ragtag band, my so-called *merry men*."

"And Marian?" I prompted.

Arabella lifted her chin a little as if attempting to defy the sadness threatening to overcome her. "Marian was not meant for such a life," she said after a moment. "She was fragile. She didn't survive the birth of her daughter. I took the baby to a couple in the nearby village who I knew had been unable to have a child of their own."

Arabella's sorrow was so intense in spite of her efforts to rein it in that it struck me in the chest, making my own heart ache. I wanted nothing more than to take her in my arms, hold her until the pain eased. But I knew that kind of pain would never go away—I'd lost enough of those I'd loved to know that for fact. Even so, I wanted to give her my love, lend her my strength, soothe her wounded heart. But when I reached for her hand, she increased her pace, her fingers slipping from my grasp.

"The tournament is about to start," she said, nodding toward the arena where the performers were preparing for their demonstrations. "Now's our chance."

"Arabella," I called after her, the rebuff stinging more than I cared to admit.

She turned and spread her arms as she continued to walk backward, forcing a smile that was laced with mischief as only hers could be, bringing that adorable dimple to the corner of her mouth. But her smile lacked its usual carelessness. "Coming?"

I caught up to her just as she reached the tent opening and pulled back the flap to enter. It was at that moment that I felt the prickling of danger at the back of my neck. My hand shot out to grasp her wrist and roll her out of the way, blocking her with my body.

Pain exploded in my side as the assailant's dagger struck my surcoat and hauberk but the ache in my kidney was immediately dulled by the adrenaline that blazed in my veins. I dove into the tent in time to see a hooded figure dressed as an Old World executioner ripping through the canvas on the other side, a heavy shield under his arm.

As I charged after him, I heard Arabella calling my name, her voice heavy with fear, but I wasn't about to let the bastard get away with the shield. My legs pumped, the chausses I wore adding extra weight and slowing me down, but I gained quickly, pouring on a burst of speed to close the last couple of yards between us, diving forward to take him down to the ground.

Quick to recover, the bastard brought up his elbow, cracking me in the cheek hard enough to make me loosen my hold on his jacket, giving him just enough room to swing the heavy shield around as we rolled and smash it into my head. Thank God the mail coif I wore kept the edge of the shield from cracking open my skull.

The Executioner quickly scrambled to his feet and made for the tree line, but I was on him again in an instant, drawing my sword as I gave chase. Realizing the futility of trying to outrun me, the Executioner suddenly halted and whirled around to face me, swinging a heavy axe as he turned.

I saw the blow coming just in time to leap back. With a roar of rage, I attacked. He managed to bring up the axe and block the downswing of my sword, but it sent him staggering backward. I offered no quarter. I brought my sword down in a savage arc, only to be blocked by the shield the Executioner carried. Undaunted, I delivered another blow and another, each time knocking him further off-balance and weakening his defense.

But the man in the mask was no amateur and was certainly no Renaissance festival performer who'd only met an enemy in the carefully choreographed arena of a mock battle. He was a seasoned warrior, his defense against my attack skilled and patient. I could see in every movement that he was biding his time, waiting for me to reveal a weakness, to leave a vulnerable area unprotected.

And just when I began to think his strength was failing, the powerful blows of my sword nearly forcing him to his knees, he surged upward with his shield, deflecting my attack at the last second and swinging his axe with the other arm. With no shield to defend myself, the blade of his axe landed in my side; the chain mail held against the axe's sharp edge, but the force of the blow sent a wave of agony through my entire body and brought me down to one knee with a guttural cry.

Before I could rise or return the attack, the Executioner tossed his shield aside and snatched the coif from my head to grab a fistful of my hair. But the smirk I could feel lurking behind his mask died when he jerked my head back and got a good look at me.

"Fuck me," he cried out.

I snatched the dagger from my boot and drove it up into his abdomen in one quick motion. He immediately released me and staggered back, clutching at his belly, blood dripping through his fingers. The axe he'd carried slipped from his other hand to fall, unheeded, onto the grass.

My grip on the hilt of my sword tightened as I got to my feet and rushed forward to finish him off, but sudden applause brought me to a halt. I'd been so intent on reclaiming the shield and taking out the Executioner, I hadn't even noticed that a crowd had gathered around us as we'd fought, no doubt thinking our engagement was another mock battle for their entertainment.

Arabella stood among them, her lovely face twisted with horror. I spared her only a glance, though, before turning back to face my foe. But to my astonishment, he had vanished, leaving the shield behind in his haste to retreat and tend to his wound.

I cursed under my breath, furious with myself for letting him get away. I wanted to believe that the masked Executioner and the Huntsman were one and the same, but the man today didn't quite fit the description Georgie had given me. Georgie had said the Huntsman was similar to me in height and build, but this man had been several inches shorter and of an athletic frame. And why he had balked at the sight of my Unseelie eyes was beyond me. Did I know the man? Had we met in battle before?

Pondering the man's identity would have to wait though. Right now, we had to get the hell out of there before we drew any more attention and the jousting troupe returned from their demonstrations. I grabbed up the discarded shield and axe and limped toward Arabella, the pain in my side growing with each step now that my adrenaline was ebbing.

She rushed to me, pulling my arm around her shoulders and slipping her arm around my waist, offering me her strength. "Come on, love," she murmured as we made our way from the makeshift battleground, offering smiles and nods of acknowledgment to the spectators and their continued applause. "Let's get you home."

I groaned as I attempted to remove my hauberk, the bruises from my battle with the Executioner still healing. Arabella took hold of the mail and helped pull it off.

"I thought these would've healed by now," I mumbled. "Damn, that bastard was good. I've encountered few with that kind of training since coming to the Here and Now."

"Who was he, do you think?" Arabella asked, tossing her cap aside as she threw herself down upon the bed.

I sat down to remove my boots, wincing at the movement. *God, was I actually getting old?* "Not sure."

"The Huntsman?"

"I've no idea. I've never met the Huntsman; I know only of his story. And without seeing his face, there's no way to be sure. And the Executioner had finesse, battle experience. From what I know of the Huntsman, he's more about stealth. He kills from afar, never getting close enough for hand-to-hand combat."

I paused and took a deep breath, letting it out slowly as I mulled over the facts. There were so many unknowns. And I didn't like it one damned bit.

"Regardless of the Executioner's true identity," I continued, "this is the second time someone's shown up where we were looking for one of the relics." I shook my head, frowning as I mentally went through the events of the last two days. "I get that someone else is looking for the relics and has hired henchmen. But I want to know how the hell we keep winding up in the same place at the same time."

"At least no one died this time," Arabella soothed me.

I grimaced as I pulled off the sweat-soaked T-shirt I'd been wearing and got to my feet to head to the shower, but Arabella's sharp intake of breath brought me to an abrupt halt.

"Bloody hell," she breathed.

It was at that moment I caught sight of myself in the dresser mirror. A massive bruise covered my lower back just over my kidney, a mottled, angry mess of blue and green and yellow. Hardly surprising considering the blows the Executioner had landed there, but what *was* surprising was the fact that it was still there. Even though it hadn't been that long since my confrontation, the bruise at least should've begun to fade by now, thanks to my Tale metabolism.

But even though the bruise was surprisingly slow to heal, that wasn't what was most troubling. Radiating outward from the mass of the bruise were numerous black and blue tendrils. And as we watched, they continued to spread, stretching toward my spine, wrapping around my ribs.

"What the fuck?" I muttered.

Arabella came to me, pressing gently upon my skin and wringing a cry of agony from me before I could check it. "Dear God," she breathed. "What would do this?"

"Poison," I informed her, my muscles growing weak even as I spoke, the tendrils now wrapping around my spine. I staggered back to the bed, falling onto it as my strength gave out.

Arabella was at my side in an instant. "Poison?" she repeated, her voice edged with panic as she knelt on the bed beside me. "But his weapons never penetrated your armor." Her hands roamed my chest, unsure how to help me.

"Damned good thing," I ground out, perspiration beading on my forehead with the effort to bite back the rapidly increasing pain. "I probably wouldn't have lasted more than a couple of minutes if I'd been without the hauberk." I groaned and rolled onto my side, a fresh wave of agony surging through my body as the poison dug its claws into me.

"What can I do?" Arabella asked, her voice breaking. "Tell me what to do to help you."

I shook my head frantically as I rolled onto my back, searching for relief and finding none. "Nothing," I said through clenched teeth. "Just have to wait it out."

She made a little sound in the back of her throat that was something between a groan and a sob. "Oh, God. For how long?"

The tendrils of torment had now worked their way up and down my spine and shot through my nervous system, making me arch off the bed. I panted for a moment, blinking away the involuntary tears that blurred my vision. "As long as it takes," I gasped. "This is powerful magic. It might take a—" My words broke off on an anguished roar. My hands fisted around the bedclothes as I tried desperately to keep it together, to fight back against the pain, but it was a battle I couldn't win. When that wave of pain finally ebbed, giving me a moment of respite, I dragged in a deep breath and took hold of her wrist. I could feel another wave of pain building rapidly. "Arabella."

She placed her cool hand upon my forehead. "Shh, quiet now, Gideon," she murmured. "I'm here." As the wave of pain crashed over me, wringing a guttural cry from me, she stretched out beside me, curling into me and resting her head on my shoulder, smoothing her hand over my chest. "I've got you, love. Just hold on to me. I'm right here. . . ."

Chapter 11

"I'm right here."

I heard her laughter, but still couldn't see her from her hiding place in the woods. I was tempted to let my senses drift, trace her by the honeysuckle scent that was so intoxicating. Or depend upon my empathic ability, track her by the emotions she allowed so close to the surface but tried to hide behind laughter and lightheartedness. But it was far more amusing to allow her to play her games, let her think I was like all of her other merry men. There was no need to divulge my unsavory past or the truth of my heritage.

I crept through the underbrush, my eyes narrowed as I searched for movement among the thick brambles and overgrowth and in the trees overhead. In the year I'd been part of her band of thieves, I'd learned that no place was off-limits.

"Oh, come now, Little John," she taunted, her voice coming to me now from far to my right. "Really, you disappoint me."

"Do I now, lass?" I called back, stepping onto the trunk of a fallen tree to get a different vantage point. "I'll have to see what I can do about that, now won't I?"

She chuckled, the game we played a well-worn one now. "I'll look forward to your attempts."

This exercise was supposed to be practice for our ambushes of wealthy travelers, but over the months I'd been part of her band of thieves, we'd taken to sneaking off into the woods together for training more and more often.

I didn't bother to suppress the grin that came to my lips as I moved toward the sound of her voice. I could picture her dark eyes shining with mischief, anticipating the moment when I would find her—or she would surprise me. The sparring that would then ensue was the best foreplay I'd ever experienced, but had yet to result in consummation. It was the sweetest torture.

I was so lost in my thoughts of her cheeky grin and sparkling dark eyes, I didn't sense the danger lying in wait. Suddenly, the edge of a sword at my neck brought me up short.

"Another step and I'll cut you down."

I cast my gaze toward the brigand who'd ambushed me. He was ragged and filthy and had spent more than his fair share of time in the bottom of a bottle from the stench of him. "I wouldn't try it, if I were you, friend," I warned as a courtesy. It was one I wasn't likely to repeat.

The bandit laughed. "Says you. But seems to me I've got you by the balls, friend.*"*

A slow grin spread across my face.

The edge of the sword dug deeper, the dull blade scraping against my skin. "What're you smilin' at?"

"I was just thinkin' it's been far too long since I split a man from gut to gullet. But I think you'll do nicely, friend."

Before he could respond, I twisted inward and took a step back, grabbing his sword arm on either side, then pushed, breaking his elbow. The man howled in agony, dropping his sword. At the same moment, I heard his associates crashing through the brush, cries of rage filling the forest as they raced to aid their leader.

I snatched up the man's sword, cutting short his cries of anguish and pivoting just in time to meet the first of his associates to arrive. I dispatched him within two parries of his unskilled attack and turned to meet the next. He, too, met the edge of the borrowed sword and joined his companions on the forest floor.

The next leaped from the fallen log I'd stepped on moments before, slamming into my back, sending me staggering forward, but I threw him off with a shrug and spun in time to meet his sword and knock it from his hand before slicing open his stomach.

I heard a soft swoosh *near my head and twisted around to see an arrow strike home in the eye of another would-be assailant. Another* swoosh *and the next arrow lodged in the chest of the man behind him.*

"John! Behind you!"

I flipped the hilt of the sword in my hand, adjusted my grip, and dropped to one knee, thrusting the sword up behind me, driving it deep into the belly of my attacker. He was still groaning from the initial strike when I launched to my feet, twisting my body as I rose, using my momentum to rip open his gut, spilling his innards at his feet.

The snapping of a twig behind me brought me around again ready for the next kill, the rage of warfare hot in my blood, but the intoxicating aroma of honeysuckle brought me up short, staying my sword.

My darling lass stood there with an arrow at the ready; her eyes widened for the briefest moment as she surveyed the carnage at my feet, but she immediately turned away to scrutinize the surrounding area, searching for any other assailants lying in wait. Every muscle in her body was tense and ready to fight.

"Are you hurt?" she asked, too intent to spare me a glance.

I tossed the bloody sword aside. "I'm unharmed," I assured her, then added, "thanks to you."

At this she lowered her bow and turned to face me, her lips curving into a slow smile. "Oh, something tells me you would've been just fine without my assistance. It just might've required you to break into a sweat."

I chuckled softly but didn't confirm that she was most likely correct.

"Come, lass," I said instead, holding out my hand. "Let's be on our way before anyone else shows up spoilin' for a fight."

She replaced her arrow in its quiver and pulled one from the center of the man's chest. When she reclaimed the arrow lodged in the thief's eye, she had to give the arrow a good shake, attempting to dislodge the eyeball that had come out with it. Finally, with a huff, she grabbed the offending orb and pulled it off, tossing it out into the woods.

"Where'd you learn to fight like that?" she asked as we made our way back through the woods toward our current camp. "I knew you were well versed in hand-to-hand combat when you bested me that day on the bridge, but I've never seen a man fight that way, move that fast. You don't strike me as one of the mercenaries the local lords hire or one of their degenerate knights who'd just as soon rape a damsel in distress as help her."

I shook my head, glad she hadn't lumped me in with either group. "I'm not originally from this area of Make Believe, 'tis true. When I was a boy, raiders burned down our village and we were forced to find a home elsewhere. My mother was killed trying to protect me. Then my father was killed during a retribution raid."

"I'm so sorry," she said. "How old were you?"

I cleared my throat, uncomfortable reliving those horrible days. "I was eleven years old. Old enough to wield a sword. So I took my father's place representing our family and became a warrior for my people."

"A warrior?" she echoed. "With warriors like you, I imagine your people are quite a formidable force."

The sorrow I fought to repress surfaced before I could stop it. "We were," I agreed. "But we are no more."

"You're no longer warriors?" she asked.

"We're no longer a people," I told her. "I am the last."

To my surprise, her fingers curled around mine, giving my hand a comforting squeeze. When I turned my head to send a startled look her way, she lifted those beautiful dark eyes to mine, her gaze a little uncertain. But then she swallowed hard and twined her fingers with mine, ensuring they were clasped tightly together.

Warmth spread through the center of my chest and radiated out through my body. My God, the way this woman made me feel was like nothing I'd ever experienced. I'd shut down my emotions when my family was murdered, had vowed never to let another into my heart. And yet here was the lovely lass at my side, defeating me at every turn.

I needed her in a way that went far beyond the physical. I needed her lightheartedness, her enthusiasm, her gentleness. In my eyes, she was everything good and pure—my antithesis. She soothed my soul in a way I never could've anticipated. And I wanted her with a desperation that frightened me.

"Will you teach me?" she asked after several peaceful moments of walking hand-in-hand together through the forest.

"Teach y'what?" I asked, hoping like hell that her thoughts were tending the same direction as mine.

"How to fight."

My eyes went wide. This was decidedly different from what I'd been hoping. "You know how to fight," I reminded her. "You've done just fine for yourself."

"Yes, but I want to fight like you," she insisted.

"No, you don't, lass," I assured her, shaking my head.

"Why not?"

"Because right now y'still have a conscience. You don't enjoy the killin'."

Her grip on my hand loosened ever so slightly. "And you do?"

I halted and turned toward her, hating the sudden wariness in her eyes. "More than I should," I admitted. "But not as much as I used to before—" I bit back my words, thinking of the rage that had fueled me for so long, had driven me to seek retribution for all that had been stolen from me. But some of that rage had dissipated, replaced by a new emotion that I'd never expected to feel.

"Before what?" she prompted.

My heart began to pound, uncertainty making my tongue heavy when I confessed, "Before you."

She blinked at me, her breath going shallow. And her voice was little more than a whisper when she asked, "What are you saying?"

I swallowed hard, trying to hold back the words, but the truth I'd tried to deny would be contained no more. "I'm sayin' I love you, lass."

She gaped at me in disbelief, rendered uncharacteristically speechless. My heart sank.

Damn me to hell.

Humiliated, I turned without a word and strode away, not wanting to prolong my embarrassment and concerned that my confession had irreparably destroyed the easiness between us, that the friendship and laughter we'd enjoyed would never be the same, that—

"John!"

I halted midstride, but couldn't bring myself to face her.

There was a slight hesitation and time seemed to have slowed to a crawl, but then I heard her hurried footsteps and turned around just in time for her to throw her arms around my neck. Gathering her into my embrace, I lifted her from her feet and buried my face in her hair, breathing in the scent of her, my heart nearly bursting at the feel of her in my arms. I closed my eyes, not sure I should trust this moment, knowing damned well I didn't deserve it.

And then she spoke. "I love you, too."

My breath caught in my chest, and, for a moment, I was certain my heart had stopped. I slowly lowered her to her feet and took her face in my hands, marveling at the emotion in her eyes as she gazed up at me, emotion that she'd somehow hidden from me. But it was hidden no longer. The full force of what I saw, what I felt, was more than I'd ever dared to dream possible. It slammed into my senses, wrapped around me, filled me, making me whole.

And then I kissed her.

Her response was tentative, inexperienced. It was obvious she'd never kissed a man before, but that knowledge made our first kiss all the sweeter. And as my lips brushed over hers again, she followed my lead, her arms coming up to encircle my neck as she leaned into me. And when I deepened the kiss, she met me eagerly, a quick study in the lessons I was more than willing to teach.

When I finally pulled back far enough to look down at her smiling face and peered into that bright, intelligent, fearless gaze of hers, I realized I was lost—completely and blissfully lost. And I knew just as surely that I'd never find my way back. . . .

I awoke to the sound of sniffling. I had to blink a few times to orient myself to my surroundings. It took a few moments for the haze of pain to dissipate before I recalled that I was staying in Merlin's Chicago flat—and that Arabella was with me.

I turned my head toward the sniffling and saw her sitting beside me, her back against the headboard, her knees drawn up to her chest. "Aww . . . what's this now?" I muttered, my mouth feeling like it was stuffed full of cotton. "You're far too fair to be cryin', lass."

She gave a little gasp and scrambled to my side, her cheeks still wet with tears. "You're awake," she said on a sob. Then she laughed, the sound more relief than mirth. "Oh, thank God! You scared the *shit* out of me, Gideon! I thought I was losing you."

I reached up and cupped her cheek, attempting a reassuring grin, guessing it looked as weak as it felt. "Nah... I'm not going any-where. It'd take a little more than a couple of cursed weapons to do me in."

She shook her head. "Cursed weapons? I thought you said it was poison."

"Aye, it was," I confirmed. Still weak from the hours of mind-numbing pain I'd experienced until the poison had worked its way out of my system, I pushed up until I was sitting against the headboard, my head swimming more than a little. "The poison was caused by a curse."

"Who would have magic that powerful?" she asked, her lovely brows furrowed in a frown.

I pulled my hand down my face, sorting through my jumbled, poison-addled thoughts. "Unfortunately, I could probably give you a dozen. Witches, sorcerers, jinn, other fairies... Hell, even your garden-variety gnome can manage to curse a weapon. The curses are cake. The strength of this curse, though... That tells me it was someone with serious experience."

"Could it have been the Huntsman?" Arabella asked.

I shook my head. "I've never sensed any magic in him—nor who-ever it was under the mask at the festival. The magic was attached only to the weapons, not the man."

We sat in pensive silence for several moments, each of us lost in our thoughts. Whoever the man had been, he'd been prepared for a confrontation. Your average thief would never bother to carry an ar-senal of cursed weapons for a simple heist. Although after what I'd just been through, I was seriously considering adding a few curses to my own weapons and to Arabella's arrows, just to be on the safe side. I'd be damned if that bastard was going to get the drop on me again. The next time that fucker and I met, he'd find out just how brutal a warrior I could be.

"I've never been so scared in all my life," Arabella finally said, her voice little more than a whisper but enough to break into my very graphic plans for retribution. "I sat here, watching you writhe in pain, Gideon, and I . . ." She swiped at her eyes. "I couldn't do anything to help you. All I could do was watch you suffer."

I looked away, sorry for what I'd put her through. I reached for her hand, giving her fingers a squeeze.

"Was that what it was like for you?" she whispered. "When we were at the falls?"

A sudden lump lodged in my throat, the fear, pain, helplessness of that day returning in a heartrending rush. "Probably so."

She took a deep, shaky breath. "I'm sorry."

"Arabella—"

"I'm *so* sorry, Gideon," she interrupted, "for all the hell that I put you through. I never meant to hurt you, you must know that."

I brought her hand to my lips and pressed a kiss to her palm. "Of course I do, lass."

That simple kiss sparked between us, and the heat that'd been simmering and had nearly come blazing forth earlier raged once more. Arabella lifted her eyes to mine, her pupils dilating with desire as her gaze met and held mine.

Without a word, she moved to straddle my lap, settling in easily where we'd joined together so often before in Make Believe, and took my face in her hands. "I promise, I will *never* put you through that again."

I frowned at her. "I should hope not," I said, examining her face, searching the emotions that were raging through her. There was such a jumble, I couldn't make out what was going through her head. But I knew what was weighing on *my* heart, what I'd been longing to say since the moment I saw her. And after the close call with the poison, I wasn't about to keep it in check another moment. "Stay with me, Arabella."

Her eyes grew sorrowful, and she tilted her head to the side, the excuses to leave, her insistence upon the *now*, rising to her lips. But before she could utter a word of refusal, I grasped her nape and dragged her to me, stopping her words with a brief, harsh kiss.

"Deny me," I ground out when the kiss ended, my lips still hovering near hers. "Tell me y'don't want me, that y'don't want to lie in my arms again, and I'll let y'go right now and ne'er bother y'more."

For a long moment she didn't respond. Then, without a word, she rolled off of my lap and got to her feet beside the bed. My heart sank as I watched her walk toward the doorway. But then she paused, her fingers gripping the doorframe, and turned back to face me.

"Oh, love," she drawled, shaking her head slowly. "You of all people should know what I want. . . ."

As I watched her walk away, the wake of her emotions buffeted against my senses, drawing me to my feet to follow. I entered the bathroom just as she was adjusting the water for a shower. Sensing my presence, she turned to face me and offered me a saucy grin. "I think we have some unfinished business, don't you?" Before I could respond, she grabbed the hem of her tunic and pulled it over her head, baring her breasts.

I needed no further encouragement. I strode into the bathroom and kicked the door shut, dragging her into my arms in the next instant, my mouth crashing down on hers. One hand grasped a tight fist of her silky hair while the other slid down her back to press her tighter against me. She met my kiss with her own, our hunger for one another too desperate to be denied any longer. She moaned softly, grinding her hips against mine, driving me wild.

It was hard to tear myself away from the bliss of her kiss, but I had to feel more of her, taste more of her. I pressed kisses along the curve of her throat, her shoulder, gently nipping at her skin with my teeth.

"My God, I want you," she murmured, fumbling with the button of my breeches. Seconds later, her hand slid down between us.

The air burst from my lungs when her slender fingers gently grasped my cock. I hissed a curse and squeezed my eyes shut for a moment, focusing on the mind-numbingly perfect stroke of her hand on my shaft. Her touch was gentle, loving, and it set my mind reeling.

As reluctant as I was to pull away, I could feel her growing anticipation in the way her aura flared, growing brighter with need, the heat of her own desires bringing an alluring flush to her skin. And I knew what she wanted, what she needed at that moment, what she'd craved for far too long. And I was more than happy to comply.

I stepped back and knelt before her, grasping the edges of the tights and easing them down her legs, revealing the tiny scrap of pale pink satin she wore beneath, somehow restraining myself from tearing those damned tights to shreds and ravaging her like I was some overeager brute. But I didn't want our first time together again to be over too quickly. I wanted to savor each moment, draw out her pleasure—and my own—until our *only* option was to surrender to it.

She lifted one foot to let me slide the tights down her calf, gasping when I nipped at her knee with my teeth. And when she lifted the other foot, I slipped off the tights and tossed them aside. But before she could set her foot back down, I caught her leg behind her knee and draped it over my shoulder.

When I pressed a kiss to the triangle of satin, Arabella's gasp ended on a moan that made my cock jump, eager for some action, but I ignored my own needs for the moment, preferring to focus on hers. I could've thrown her down right there on the floor and relieved both our suffering, but when I turned my eyes up to her face, made all the more beautiful in the throes of passion, the intensity of her building pleasure was far more intoxicating than any primal release I could've experienced from a quick orgasm. This was more than just the typical biological response. So much more.

I slipped my index finger under her panties, very slowly caressing along the edge, teasing, building her anticipation of my touch. And when I journeyed farther, my fingertip brushing against her clit, she cried out with a shudder.

I couldn't help the self-satisfied grin on my face when I hooked my finger around the panties and slid them out of the way. I'd intended to just tease with a kiss, but the moment my tongue met the sweet taste of her, I moaned with need and pressed farther in, delving deeper. My God, I couldn't get enough of her. She writhed against my mouth, her breath coming in short, shallow gasps.

"Oh, dear God," she groaned, arching back against the wall.

When her muscles began to tense, I braced her hips and eased back just a little, flicking my tongue, drawing out the buildup. When she whimpered, her pleasure at its peak, I let her come, driving her through it, my teeth grazing her clit and making her cry out as another release washed over her.

"Gideon," she panted. "Please . . ."

I lifted her leg from my shoulder, then slowly rose, kissing the inside of her thighs, her belly, between her breasts, as I went. When I was standing again, she ran her hands over my chest and down my abdomen until she reached my waistband. She pushed my breeches over my hips, sliding them down as I had done for her, her hands gliding up my legs as she slowly rose. She then wrapped her arms around my waist, pulling me against her.

When she turned her face up to mine, I bent forward, brushing my lips over hers in a tender kiss. This time the kiss was slow, languid. And where that kiss ended another began.

When the steam from the shower began to fill the room, I drew the kiss to a close and opened the shower door. I stepped inside, pulling her in after me and gathering her into my arms. For several long moments, we just stood there, our bodies pressed together as the water sluiced over us. My hands roamed lightly up and down her back, over the swell of her bottom. Reading her emotions at that moment, waiting until her body gave me the cue I was looking for.

And when Arabella tipped her head back to wet her hair, the movement was so erotic, I grinned.

Oh, yeah . . . There it was.

I couldn't help pressing a kiss to her throat. She was smiling when I pulled back to run my hands over her hair. The smile was so sweet, so contented, I wondered if perhaps she was remembering the many times we'd bathed together in Make Believe, how much pleasure we'd taken in ministering to one another. I'd dreamed of those moments together so often, for a moment, I wondered if perhaps this was yet a dream, that I was actually still trapped in the coma, fighting off the poison that ravaged my body. Afraid I'd wake up at any moment, I took my time caring for her, washing her hair, her body, relishing the feel of her lathered skin beneath my hands.

At some point, Arabella took the soap from me and began to lather my body with it, running her hands along my back and shoulders, down my arms, across my chest. When she journeyed between my legs, my cock strained toward her, so hard that there was no doubt where my thoughts were tending.

When she knelt before me and took me into her mouth, my arms shot out to brace myself against the shower walls, the wicked glint in her eyes alerting me to what was coming next. Still, I hissed a strangled curse as her tongue swirled around the tip, and ground my teeth, holding it together for as long as possible. But when she took me in deep and slowly withdrew, those soft pink lips were devastating.

I abruptly pulled away and drew her to her feet, chuckling at the self-satisfied smirk on her face. I was still smiling when I pressed my lips to hers again. The gentle kiss soon grew deeper. Her arms went around my neck, keeping me from drawing away. But I had no intention of backing out this time.

I lifted her into my arms, wrapping her legs around me, and pressed her back against the wall of the shower. I thrust into her without hesitation, groaning as her warmth enveloped me. It was almost more pleasure than I could stand—I knew it was more than I deserved. It took every ounce of willpower I had to move slowly, to not pound into her and race toward the release that would grant me mercy from the sweet torment building inside.

But with each thrust she grew tighter and tighter, her pleasure building along with my own. I kissed along the curve of her throat, teasing the juncture between neck and shoulder that drove her wild. When she couldn't take any more, she dragged my face up to hers and kissed me tenderly, her hands cupping my face and keeping me there as her lips passed over mine, lingering longer each time, until her tongue pressed against my lips.

She shattered apart then, her kiss becoming more frenzied with each shuddering aftershock. And still I drove her through it and on to the next peak. This time, her nails dug into my back as she gasped my name.

And it was too much for me to bear. I poured into her with a hard thrust, groaning with the intensity. My hips continued to move as if of their own accord, driving into her again and again, the friction where we were joined too pleasurable to break away from just yet.

Arabella's breath was hot in my ear as we both raced toward another release. When I felt the pressure building in the base of my spine, the tempo increased, and this time when Arabella shattered apart, I didn't even bother to try to keep quiet.

For some time after, I couldn't move, I couldn't speak. I could barely breathe. My head hung down, my eyes closed as my breath sawed in and out of my lungs. But I finally managed to lift my head and kiss her long and hard.

When the kiss ended, she grinned at me, her eyes half closed in blissful satiation. She smoothed my hair from my face, kissed me, ran her hands over my shoulders. And when I finally set her down on her feet, she slipped her arms around my waist and pressed her cheek against my chest.

There were so many things I wanted to say at that moment, but my emotions choked me, keeping me from uttering a single word. All I could do was hold her close, keep her tight against me, and hope that this time I'd have the strength not to let go.

"Gideon?"

Her soft entreaty drew me out of my dark thoughts in an instant. I peered down at her and attempted a comforting smile, but I wasn't fooling her any more than I was fooling myself.

"Are you all right?" she asked, pulling back enough to study me with that shrewd gaze of hers.

I bent and pressed a kiss to her forehead. "Better than I've been in a long while."

"Are you sure?" she pressed.

"I suppose I'm still having a hard time believing that you're here in my arms," I admitted.

A slow, sultry smile curved her lips as she wrapped her arms around my neck and pulled me down to receive her kiss. "Take me to bed, Gideon," she murmured against my lips. "Let me show you just how real I am."

Chapter 12

I was awakened by Arabella's tender kiss upon my back. Grinning, I rolled over and snaked my arm around her, curling her in against my body. After our escapades in the shower, we'd moved to Merlin's guest room where we explored each other again, making love until we were both too exhausted to go on. We'd fallen asleep wrapped in each other's arms and had slept like the dead.

I lifted my head just enough to see the clock on the bedside table behind her. Seven-ten. The room's blackout shades prevented me from knowing if it was morning or evening. But I didn't care. I could've slept for hours more, especially with Arabella in my arms.

"Hi," she said, resting her chin on my chest and smiling up at me.

I smoothed her hair. "Hi."

"How did you sleep?"

I grinned wickedly. "Far too well. I would much rather have continued making love to you."

She chuckled and propped herself up on one elbow, scooting up the bed to press a kiss to my lips. When she pulled back I realized she looked tired, dark circles hanging heavily beneath her beautiful eyes.

I cupped her cheek, languidly smoothing her skin with my thumb. "What about you, lass?"

She kissed me again before responding. "I haven't slept that well since the last night we were together in Make Believe. I've missed being in your arms."

The sweetness of her words filled me with warmth I'd thought I'd never feel again, but I sensed she hadn't slept quite as well as she'd have me believe. "Well, then," I drawled, pulling her back to me, "let me hold you a while longer."

She curled into my body, sighing contentedly, draping one leg over mine, her hand slowly smoothing over my chest. "I wish we could stay here all day," she murmured with a sigh. "Could you make the world stop for a while, Gideon? I need more time. Just put everything on hold so we could make up for the time we've lost. Could you do that for me, love?"

I trailed my fingertips lazily along her spine, perplexed by her wistfulness. There was more to it than just a lover's romantic musings. "Would that I could," I said. "But we'll make up for lost time, lass. I promise. You'll never go another day without me at your side, if that's what you want."

She scooted up until she was peering down at me and caressed my cheek, her eyes so full of sorrow that I felt her sadness like a fist constricting my heart. "Oh, love, there's so much that I wanted for us. . . ."

"We can still have it," I assured her.

At this, she leaned in and brushed her lips lightly over mine. As tender and sweet as the kiss was, it felt wrong. Like a good-bye. When she started to draw away she had a look in her eyes I'd seen before—the one that told me she was on the verge of bolting. I rolled her onto her back, caging her in with my arms.

"Do y'doubt me?" I pressed.

She shook her head. "Never. Not you."

I brushed a lock of hair off her brow and let my fingertips drift down her cheek, picking up her inner turmoil, her indecision. But before I could determine the source of her disquiet, she shifted beneath me, wrapping her legs around me and bringing me into the cradle of her hips. And then pulled me down to receive her hungry kiss.

And there was no "good-bye" in this one. Whatever it was about the future that frightened her, it was far from her mind now. There was an immediacy in her kiss that put a stranglehold on the *now*. But before the kiss could lead to more, my phone began to vibrate on the bedside table, drawing my attention away from the far more pleasurable possibilities that waited in Arabella's arms. With a frustrated groan, I pulled back from the warmth of her embrace, intent on silencing the damned phone for good.

"You should probably answer it," Arabella said, grimacing guiltily. "Someone's been ringing you about every thirty minutes since early this morning."

Instead of chucking the offending device across the room, I glanced down at the display. My brows came together in a frown when I saw the number of missed calls that had come in during my battle with the poison. There were few who knew the number and fewer still who actually used it. Considering all the shit that had recently gone down, getting a call from any one of those parties probably wasn't a good thing.

I quickly paged through the list of missed calls, my stomach lurching with uneasiness when I saw that the majority were the number that worried me most.

"Shit."

She winced. "I'm sorry, Gideon. You were sleeping so soundly, I didn't want to wake you."

I gave her a quick kiss and then rose from the bed, already missing the feel of her arms around me. "I'll only be a moment. Don't go anywhere."

She gave me a mock salute, then fell back upon the bed, her hair splayed upon the pillow to create a striking contrast to the stark white of the linens. She was so lovely, her creamy skin so inviting, it took all my willpower to turn away and tend to my duties.

Groaning with frustration, I reached through a rift to grab a fresh set of clothes and pulled on my jeans before leaving the bedroom and dialing my king. The number rang several times before someone finally answered. "Hello?"

I drew the phone away from my ear and looked at the number, making sure I had dialed the correct one. When I saw the familiar set of numbers, I put it back to my ear. "Lily? Where's your father?"

The king's daughter cleared her throat. "Um, hey, Gideon. Dad's not here at the moment."

I could tell she was lying even without the benefit of being able to read her. "Lily, I know he's there," I told her evenly. "I need to speak with him, please."

She paused and I could hear a conversation going on, the speakers whispering urgently. Lily cleared her throat again before coming back on the line with, "I'm supposed to tell you you've been disavowed."

I went completely still, in shock at what I was hearing. "I'm afraid I must not have heard you correctly," I said at last, my voice hoarse.

Lily swallowed hard. "We heard about what happened at Guinevere Pendragon's house in Connecticut, that you were taken in for questioning and that you may be charged with her attempted murder. Dad says that he has to keep his distance for a while until the mess with the FMA is ironed out. He can't allow his alliance with Al Addin to be jeopardized, especially right now when there's a rather sensitive matter concerning the fairy dust transports that needs to be dealt with."

I pulled a hand down my face, surprised to find so much stubble there. "I'm aware of that matter, Lily," I told her. "I'm looking into it. Please let me talk to your father."

I heard her curse softly under her breath. "I'm really sorry, Gid. But Dad says you have three days to turn over the thief or he'll be— and I quote—'very displeased.' "

"He told me I could have until the end of the week," I replied. "I need more than three days. Lily—"

"I'm sorry, Gideon," she said. "I really am."

The call was disconnected before I could utter another word. "Fucking hell."

"What's going on?"

I turned to see Arabella standing in the doorway of the guest room with a sheet wrapped around her, her hair in an alluring tangle. "I need to go."

She nodded. "Okay. I'll get dressed."

I followed her into the room and grabbed my shirt. "You're staying here," I told her. Before she could protest, I added, "No one knows you're here, Arabella. You're safe. I don't want you out and about with me."

I don't know why I was surprised that instead of actually listening to what I said and agreeing to what made the most sense, she put her hands on her hips, not bothering to hold the sheet in place, and gave me a stubborn glare.

"I'm coming with you," she insisted. "So, either help me find some clothes or I'll tag along naked. Either way, I'm going. It's not safe for you out there either, and who'll have your back if I'm not with you?"

It was really hard to argue with her when she was standing there, indignant and regal and looking like a goddess, but I gave it a go. "Arabella, I have only three days to figure out who the other fairy dust thief is before the king calls me in. And now that I've been disavowed—"

"What?" she cried. "Why?"

I quickly relayed my conversation with Lily.

"You must be joking," Arabella scoffed. "The king must know that you're not guilty of what happened at Guinevere's!"

I pulled on my T-shirt and sat down to put on my boots. "I'd like to think so. But the king's reputation is essential to the success of his business. He can't be associated with me until this is cleared up. I understand that."

"Well, I'm glad you do because I certainly don't," she huffed as I reached into the rift and extracted clothes for her. "It's rubbish!"

I sighed and ran my hands through my curls, then came to her, taking her by the shoulders and pressing a kiss to her forehead. "We'll get it all sorted. I'm going to go home, see if he'll grant me an audience to find out just how bad this is."

She gave me a skeptical look. "All right, but—" Her words cut off as she swayed a little on her feet.

"Are you all right, lass?" I asked, bending so that I could look into her eyes.

She forced a smile. "Oh, yeah," she assured me with a shrug. "Brilliant. Just a bit exhausted from all the fun we've had, love. Heists, battles, mind-blowing sex . . . You have a way of taking it out of a girl."

I saw through her attempt at humor in an instant. Even if I wasn't an empath, I could've sensed her holding back on me. I wanted to stay and look after her, discover exactly what it was she was still hiding from me, spend more time lying in her arms, forgetting about the danger and death that lay in wait just outside. But the longer I waited to approach the king and gauge his true feelings on the accusations against me, the worse it would be for everyone concerned. Still, I couldn't leave Arabella in such a state.

"Do you need a little fairy dust from me?" I asked. "I don't want to dose you too often; you'll become addicted to me."

She chuckled and slipped her arms around my waist, lifting her smiling face to mine. "I'm already addicted to you, love, but not because of your fairy dust. I can't get enough of you—I never could."

After that kind of statement, I really had no choice but to kiss her. Which was a mistake. I couldn't just give her a quick kiss and walk away. There was no going back now that I'd had her in my arms again, had made love to her again after all those years of longing for her, dreaming of her.

My hands roamed over her skin as I walked her back toward the bed, tripping over the discarded sheet and falling onto the mattress with her in a tangle. We both chuckled, but her laughter died on her lips as my hand slipped between us. She arched into me with a very feminine moan.

My God, she was enthralling in the throes of passion. I could've stayed there all day watching bliss play over her features again and again as her climax built.

"Please, Gideon," she whispered, clutching my shirt as she pressed kisses to my chest, the side of my neck. "I want to be with you. I want to feel you inside me one last time."

I instantly stilled at her words, my heart clenching painfully in my chest. I laughed in a short, bitter burst and withdrew from her. "One last time," I repeated, shaking my head as I swung my legs over the side of the bed and sat up.

I heard her inhale sharply as if she'd just realized what she'd said. She knelt beside me on the bed and placed a hand tentatively on my shoulder. "Oh, Gideon, that's not—"

I shook her off and got to my feet, snatching up my jacket from the end of the bed. "Just hoping for a quick tumble, were you? Thought I'd welcome y'back in my bed without a second thought? The poor pathetic jackass who was idiot enough to fall for yer lies before would certainly fall for 'em again. Well, I won't be just a body to warm yer bed for a time, Arabella. I'm sure Merlin'll be back soon if you want someone to bed you without any strings attached."

I strode from the room, slamming the door behind me, this new hurt just reinforcing the heartbreak and anger that I'd felt before. I'd been weak, had let my defenses down, had played along with her flirting, added a little of my own, had believed that what had happened between us the night before signaled a new start for our life together.

God, what I fool I'd been.

Well, her slipup and the king's decision to disown me were the eye-openers I needed. I was done fucking around with my life, living only to serve another and not be true to who I was, true to the man I realized I *could* be. I needed more, and goddamn it, I *deserved* more. I hadn't always thought so. I'd spent centuries doubting my worth, believing that my servitude was just and fitting penance for my inability to save the woman I loved. But I knew better now.

I knew all that. And yet there I stood in the living room of Merlin's loft apartment, my feet rooted to the floor. Unable to move forward, unwilling to turn back.

By the time Arabella joined me in the living room, I'd resumed my carefully schooled aloofness, determined not to let my guard down again. But, damn it all, when I saw her in the little blue dress, tights, and biker boots I'd pulled from the rift, she looked so goddamned adorable, it was all I could do not to sweep her into my arms and make another visit to that sweet valley between her breasts, then slowly explore the rest of her delicious body with my lips and tongue— to hell with every resolution I'd just made.

But in spite of the intensity of my desire, I held firm, hardening my heart and steeling myself to resist.

I can only imagine my expression. Whatever it was, it brought her up short, making her footsteps falter momentarily. But then she pressed her lips together in a determined line and strode toward me. Her ponytail swayed gently as she walked across the room, a silky pendulum that seemed to be marking our time together with the slow beat of a funeral dirge.

I frowned at the downturn of her mouth, the puffiness around her eyes where she'd been crying. But even more troubling was the faintness of her aura. She was even more exhausted than I'd realized; her emotions were all over the place. And when her eyes lifted and met mine, I felt another emotion—one that was so strong it overpowered the others.

Love.

But it wasn't folded in happiness; it was tinged with pain and regret and sorrow . . . and fear.

I closed my eyes for a moment, feeling out her wants and desires. She loved me still. I knew it beyond a doubt, just as sure as I knew that my love for her had never faded. So why did she see things coming to an end between us before we'd even given them a chance?

She heaved a sigh, preparing herself for whatever it was she intended to impart. "I was afraid to come to you," she announced after a long pause.

I shook my head, not understanding. "What?"

"When I came to the Here and Now," she explained. "I was afraid you would hate me for breaking your heart. That you'd never forgive me. But there's another reason I didn't find you sooner, Gideon—" She swayed again on her feet, but held out her hand, stopping me when I instinctively stepped forward. "No. Let me finish what I have to say."

"Arabella, lass," I said gently, my concern for her overriding my own hurt. "I just—"

She suddenly cried out, cutting off my words as she doubled over in pain, clutching her stomach.

My heart seized in panic at the sight of her in such misery, and I closed the gap between us in an instant. "What's wrong, lass? Tell me the truth this time."

"What the hell is going on?"

I cast a glance over my shoulder to see Merlin walking in the door, reeking of booze and sex after his long night of carousing. "Don't worry about it," I barked. "I've got this."

"Oh, clearly," Merlin drawled. "She looks like shit, Gideon! What the hell have you done to her?"

Arabella cried out again and her knees buckled, but I caught her up in my arms before she hit the ground. When the wave of anguish passed, her gaze met mine. Her face was pale, clammy, and her lips were turning blue, her Tale aura thinning and growing dimmer even as I watched. My stomach plummeted when a terrifying thought struck me, and I feared I knew what mysterious ailment plagued her.

"Ah, God, no," I moaned, emotion strangling the words, my knees nearly giving out in my sudden despondency. "No. Not that, lass. Please not that . . ."

Merlin came toward us, holding out his arms. "Let me take her, Gideon."

I clutched her closer, the sympathy seeping into the air around Merlin serving only to fill me with rage-fueled denial. "Touch her, Merlin, and it'll be the last thing you do."

He took a hasty step back, lifting his hands. "Your call, old boy," he said, more pitying than offended. "But she needs medical attention."

I ripped open a time rift in my desperation. "Then I know just where to take her."

Chapter 13

I kicked the door of the French Provincial-style home with the toe of my boot, grateful that the secluded Highland Park estate prevented nosy neighbors from seeing me standing on the doorstep with a limp woman in my arms. I shifted Arabella up a little farther so that her head was resting more comfortably against my shoulder. She mumbled something incoherent in response. "It's all right, lass," I soothed. "I've got y'now."

I was preparing to kick the door again when it swung open. Trish Muffet's dark green gaze widened when she saw me standing there. "Gideon? Good Lord—what's happened?" She didn't wait for an answer before pulling me into the foyer of her home. She immediately took hold of Arabella's wrist, checking her pulse.

Trish was the FMA's Director of Forensics, but I knew she'd practiced medicine prior to joining the FMA and held multiple medical degrees from both the Ordinaries and the Tales. And I trusted her more than anyone else I knew. If anyone could figure out what was wrong with Arabella, I knew Trish could. She *had* to.

"Can you help her?" I demanded, panic fluttering around in my chest, making it hard to breathe.

"Bring her to the guest room." She motioned for me to follow as she hurried down the hall toward the grand staircase that led upstairs. "I need to examine her more closely."

"Her aura's weak, Trish," I informed her, fear seeping into my words. My throat was tight as I almost outpaced the petite blonde in my haste to get upstairs. "If this is what I think it is . . ."

"We don't know what this is, Gideon," she assured me, taking me to the first room at the top of the stairs. "Let's not jump to conclusions before I have a chance to examine her. I'll do everything I can for her, but you're going to have to help me, okay? I need you to answer some questions."

I set Arabella gently on the huge four-poster bed and stepped away, making room for Trish to get to her. She sat down next to Arabella and placed a tender hand to my dear one's forehead.

"How long's she been like this?" Trish asked, lifting Arabella's lids to check her eyes briefly. She looked away before her ability to see into someone's thoughts could kick in, never one to use her talent on the living without their permission if she could help it.

I shook my head. "Dunno. I hadn't seen her in a long time. She's had a few episodes, but she blamed exhaustion . . . and then she just collapsed this morning. Shit, Trish, I didn't know where else to take her."

Trish caught the edge in my voice and twisted around to peg me with an inquisitive look. "She should be at the FMA hospital," she said mildly, although her eyes asked a thousand questions. "They're better equipped, Gideon. I haven't practiced this kind of medicine on the living in decades."

I ran a hand down my face, scrubbing at the stubble along my jaw, then shook my head. "Can't take her there." When Trish's eyes narrowed at me, I borrowed a phrase from Arabella herself: "It's complicated."

"What's doin', doll? I thought you were joining me."

Trish and I both turned toward the bedroom door, where Trish's husband, Nicky Blue, stood wearing nothing but a towel, his hair still wet from a shower. It was then that I realized Trish was dressed in only a bathrobe. Obviously, my unexpected arrival had derailed some rather personal plans.

Nicky jerked his chin at me. " 'Sup, Tiny?"

"My apologies for dropping in unexpectedly," I muttered. "But I needed Trish."

Nicky's brows shot up. "That so?"

"This woman—" Trish sent a glance my way.

"Arabella," I filled in.

"Arabella is a *friend* of Gideon's, Nicky, and she needs my help."

Nicky gave a curt nod. "Good enough for me." He strolled in and peered down at Arabella, then turned a concerned frown on his wife. "You okay to take this on, though, doll?"

Trish's hand instinctively went to her belly, and belatedly I realized the reason for Nicky's worry.

Trish nodded, her lips curving into a smile as Nicky pressed a kiss to her forehead. "I'll be fine; the morning sickness isn't bad today. Besides, Gideon can't take Arabella to the hospital. And we can't turn him away."

Nicky lifted his eyes, his knowing gaze meeting mine. Having made his fortune as head of a very lucrative Tale crime syndicate, Nicky certainly understood the occasional need for discretion. "You let me know if there's anything you need, Tiny. We'll do everything we can to help your friend. You know that."

I nodded, grateful as always for the friendship I'd managed to form with the couple. They were as much a part of my family now as the Seelies. I would've laid down my life for either of them without hesitation, and I had no doubt they would've done the same for me.

Nicky gave me a reassuring clap on the shoulder before bending down to murmur in his wife's ear and press a kiss to her cheek. The look she gave him in return was so filled with love that I had to glance away, my heart constricting with the knowledge that one of the only women who'd ever looked at me that way now lay unconscious.

I took a few steps back, giving Trish plenty of room to conduct her examination, assisting only when Trish needed to remove Arabella's boots. The process seemed to take forever but was most likely less than five minutes. Still, I waited anxiously, chewing on the edge of my thumb as the seconds ticked by far too slowly.

Finally, Trish smoothed the hair away from Arabella's brow with a tenderness that would've won Trish to my heart if she hadn't already been as dear as a sister to me. "Is it what I think it is?" I asked, my voice little more than a dry rasp. "Is she *fading?*"

Fading was a mysterious wasting illness and one of the most agonizing ways for a Tale to die. We'd never discovered why it happened, although we suspected it had something to do with the Ordinaries' waning interest in our stories. But that couldn't be the case with Arabella. The Robin Hood story was alive and well in the Here and Now, spawning several movies and TV series just within the last couple of decades.

Trish heaved a sigh and came over to stand before me, placing a hand on my forearm. "It looks that way," she said softly. "But maybe it's reversible if we can find the reason behind it . . . She's fighting hard."

I brought my hands up to my face, pulling them down my features, then balled my hands into fists, rage and helplessness filling me to the point of desperation. I strode a few steps away then back again, my movements aimless. Dread pressed in upon me so heavily, I feared I might suffocate under the weight of it.

"Did you *see* anything?" I asked of Trish, desperate to know what secrets might've been revealed. "Did you find out . . ." I let my words trail off, not sure what to ask about. I didn't know Arabella anymore, not really. She'd attempted to hide her illness from me. I'd known something was wrong even before her first episode, but I'd chalked up her evasiveness to her desire to shield me from her illegal activities. Hell—who knew what else she might be hiding.

"I didn't look," Trish told me. "I think whatever it is that lies between you should be yours alone to sort out. When she wakes up, I'll let you ask her the questions that are weighing heavy on your heart."

I met my friend's knowing gaze. Arabella wasn't the only one hiding things. If I was going to be completely honest with myself, I'd been hiding a great deal from those who were nearest and dearest to me. Who the hell was I to judge?

"There's a lot about me you don't know, Trish," I said, "things about my past that I've never shared with you."

She gave me a knowing grin. "Oh, I don't know . . . I've probably figured out more than you realize."

My eyes narrowed, trying to read her, wondering if she'd used her ability on me at some point in the years we'd known each other, but before I could get more than a glimpse of her emotions, she held up her index finger, giving me a look that I'm sure would serve her well in motherhood.

"No, I've not used my ability on you," she assured me. "And I'll thank you not to use yours on *me,* Gideon Montrose. That was our agreement. Unless you sense that I'm craving double-fudge chocolate ice cream with whipped cream and caramel drizzle. Then bring it on."

I laughed a little and inclined my head, grateful for her attempt to distract me from my worry and help me bring my emotions back to heel. "As you wish."

"Now, I'll leave you two alone for a little while so I can get dressed," she continued. "Arabella would benefit from some fairy dust to slow the *fading* process and help with the fatigue and pain she's experiencing. If you're willing to share until I can get a licensed distributor here—"

"I'll give her every bit of mine if it'll help," I interrupted, "but we're not calling in anybody else."

Trish frowned at me in exasperation. "Gideon, you're an Unseelie. Yes, I'm well aware of that fact—don't look so surprised. I also know that your fairy dust isn't as powerful as a Seelie's. I'll just call in Lavender's sister Poppy."

"No!" I barked more harshly than I'd intended. "Trish . . ." I hesitated, but my new vow to be completely honest with my friend pressed on my conscience. I heaved a sigh and continued, "I've been disavowed. The king has distanced himself from me because of the trouble at Guinevere's. I can't ask one of his offspring to help me right now."

Trish put her hands on her hips in a huff, her brows furrowing in frustration. "Your fairy dust will give her some of her strength back, Gid," she said. "But we need time to figure out how to *save* her, and if you want the effect to last, we need a Seelie's fairy dust. That's probably why Arabella's been stealing it."

My eyes widened in surprise. "How'd you know . . . ?"

Trish cocked her head to one side and looked at me like I was an idiot for even asking the question. And I was. *Of course* Trish had been the one investigating the crime scenes and would've been very familiar with the evidence on the case. "Her magical signature is the same as one of those at the crime scenes."

"*One* of the signatures?" I repeated. "Then you've identified the others?"

She nodded. "There are at least three distinct signatures—maybe more. Unfortunately, several of the crime scenes were contaminated by your king's guards. No offense, Gid, but some of them are bumbling idiots. It's no wonder the transports were stolen with those guys guarding them! Now go ahead and lie down with Arabella, lend her your strength. But think over what I've said. Poppy's the best fairy dust therapist in Chicago. Perhaps she could come here on the sly without her father finding out." She paused at the door and turned back to me, weighing her words for a moment before adding, "You know, we all have our secrets, Gideon. But trust me when I tell you, living in the past will do nothing but bring you misery. *Now* is all that matters."

I was struck dumb by Trish's pronouncement, which so closely echoed Arabella's own insistence. For several moments, all I could do was stare at the closed bedroom door. They were right, of course. I'd denied myself a great deal by dwelling in the past, clinging to what *was* instead of focusing on what *is,* and completely denying there was even the possibility of a what *could be* until last night. And when Arabella had intimated this morning that things between us were only temporary, I'd immediately closed off my heart again to keep her at arm's length. But in guarding my heart, I could be denying myself one of the greatest joys of my life—a joy that now might be fleeting at best.

A shaky sigh behind me brought my attention back to my little love, so beautiful even though some of her vibrancy had been robbed by this horrible illness. I stretched out on the bed beside her and pulled her into my arms, cradling her head in the crook of my elbow. She moaned softly, her brow furrowed.

"Hush now," I crooned, smoothing her hair, conjuring a sprinkling of my silver fairy dust and letting it drift down upon her. "I've gotcha, lass."

She inhaled, pulling the dust into her lungs. I offered another dose, marveling at how the silver clung to her skin, her hair, her lips, instead of instantly dissolving as it did on most Tales. After a third dose, she began to look like the winter fairies I'd watched as a child as they skimmed the surface of the ponds, freezing the water little by little. I'd marveled at their beauty, the way their skin sparkled in the moonlight.

I tenderly smoothed her hair away from her brow, still finding it hard to believe that she was alive and in my arms. But as soon as the happiness began to creep into my heart, the knowledge that she was dying stabbed through it. Now I understood everything—the reason for the fairy dust thefts, why she'd been stealing the purest form of the dust in hopes of controlling her symptoms, her need to find the remaining relics that her mother had created for her father to keep him alive . . .

The panic and desperate need to *fix* what was wrong with her, to find a cure for this horrible wasting illness that would take her from me yet again, clawed at my guts, squirmed under my skin, making me restless, anxious. Never in my life had I felt this kind of helplessness.

I was a warrior—a man of action. My instinct was to fight and destroy, conquer my enemy. Since coming into the king's service I'd learned patience, self-control, but I was still a guardian, a protector to all those I cared about. And yet I felt completely helpless to save the one person who had meant more to me than anyone else in my life. I'd take her place in a heartbeat, trade my life for hers without question. But not even my fairy dust was potent enough to relieve her symptoms for more than a little while. For that she needed a Seelie's magic.

There was naught else I could do for her besides hold her at this point, let her take from me what little strength was mine to give, what little comfort I could offer.

I lay back with my arm behind my head, staring up at the ceiling, and curled Arabella into me so that her head was resting on my chest. She whimpered a little, but it was faint, the pain seeming to lessen thanks to the effects of my fairy dust.

And as I lay there, a long-forgotten lullaby from my childhood drifted into my thoughts. I remembered it from those nights when I couldn't sleep, when fear and worry for my people and my warrior father kept me from closing my eyes.

My mother would sit beside me, her long red curls falling over her shoulder as she smiled down at me and whispered, "What's the worry, wee'un? Yer father'll come home t'us, sure's the mornin'." Then she would stretch out beside me on the bed and cuddle me close, her own worry far too easily read by an empathic child.

When I tried to argue against her assurances, I would always get "Hush now, Gideon. What'll happen'll happen. But we've got to be strong for yer *dadaidh*. He needs t'know ye're his wee warrior." It was then she would sing to me, her gentle voice flowing over me, wrapping me in her love.

It was that song I sang softly now as I held Arabella in my arms, hoping she could feel the love I'd carried with me all these years, the memories that had sustained me in my darkest days. The love that would sustain me in the days to come, which promised to be darker still.

Chapter 14

I didn't realize I'd fallen asleep next to Arabella until a shuffle of movement in the semidarkness of the room jolted me awake. When I didn't feel her in my arms, panic gripped me. I shot to my feet, calling out her name on a gasp. "Arabella?"

As soon as the word crossed my lips, I saw her sitting in a nearby chair, tying her boots. She paused, her eyes trained on me, and I felt her sigh more than heard it. She was running away again, I knew, even before I asked, "Going somewhere?"

She held my gaze for a moment, wavering between truth and lie. "Gideon . . ."

I shook my head. "You've got to be fucking kidding me," I said on a bitter laugh. "You're still running? After what happened earlier today? After what we *just* went through? For chrissake, Arabella! Do you even realize what's happening to you?"

She turned her head away, unable to look me in the eyes. "You know then."

"Aye, I do *now*," I said, raising my arms to my sides, exasperated. "You should've told me!"

Her head whipped around, her anger rolling off her as she leapt to her feet. "Why?" she demanded. "What good would it have done?"

I closed the distance between us in one stride, taking hold of her shoulders. "I can *help* you."

"Can you?" she shot back. "Really? You have the secret cure for *fading* then? You've found the answer where all the best medical minds among the Tales have failed?"

I closed my eyes for a moment, not willing to admit she was right. I shook my head. "Of course not," I said. "But there are ways to slow the process. The fairy dust—"

"Is just delaying the inevitable," she interrupted, her tone more pitying than angry. When I opened my mouth to argue, she took my face in her hands. "You know it as well as I do."

I shook my head vehemently, not willing to admit defeat. "No, I refuse to believe—"

She pulled me down to her, silencing my protest with a kiss, and another. When the kiss ended, I pressed my forehead to hers, closing my eyes against the blur gathering there.

"I'm dying, Gideon," she said, putting the horrible truth into words. "We have to face that."

"Trish thinks she can reverse it if we figure out the reason you're *fading*," I assured her. "We can beat this."

She stepped back and turned away from me, wrapping her arms around herself. "There won't be a *we,* Gideon," she said after a moment. "I'm not staying."

"Don't be daft, lass," I reasoned, trying to keep my voice calm even though my heart was racing at the prospect of her running away again. "Of course, you're staying. You need *treatment*, Arabella."

"I never should've come to you in the first place," she sighed, running a hand through her hair. "It was selfish of me. I had no right to do this to you."

I went to her and turned her around to face me. "Do *what* to me?"

She lifted her hand and caressed my cheek, her eyes filling with sorrow. "I won't let you watch me die again, Gideon," she insisted, her voice breaking. "I *won't*. I refuse to put you through that hell."

I huffed, exasperated. "Bella—"

"Gideon!" she snapped. "Why do you think I stayed away in the first place? When I came to the Here and Now, it became apparent almost immediately that something was wrong. And when I discovered what was happening, I swore Merlin to secrecy. It was to protect you."

"Don't you think you should've left it up to me as to whether or not I could go through losing you again?" I demanded. "Don't you think perhaps *I* should've had a say in it?"

Her chin trembled as she met and held my gaze, her eyes filling with tears. "Then perhaps I was the one who couldn't handle it," she said, her voice catching on a choked sob. "That day at the falls, Gideon, I saw the pain and sorrow in your eyes just before I fell. I could see your heart breaking, and it tore me apart."

A single tear slid down her cheek. I bent forward and kissed it away, then brushed a kiss to her mouth. "My sweet little love," I murmured against her lips, "I would never be parted from you—in life or in death. My heart is yours. Do y'not *see* that, lass?"

A sob shook her, and her voice was thick with tears when she said, "I see it all too clearly, love. That's why I would rather have suffered a thousand heartbreaks before letting you know I was here." When I opened my mouth to protest, she placed her finger on my lips. "I love you, Gideon. I love you with all my heart. And when I fade away, it will be that love alone that brings me comfort. Call me a coward, if you like, but I can't bear to see that pain in your eyes again."

"You're anything but a coward," I protested. "But it's time to stop runnin', lass. You've been runnin' yer entire life. Y'don't have to run anymore. Not unless you're runnin' to me."

She shook her head slowly, her eyes so filled with sorrow it was almost more than I could bear. "When I swore to you earlier today that I'd never put you through hell again, I meant it."

I pulled her to me and wrapped my arms around her, holding her close as I rested my cheek upon her hair. "The only hell is life without you, lass," I whispered. "And I am not about to let you go."

She heaved a sorrowful sigh. "Gideon—"

"We'll find the rest of the relics," I promised her, smoothing her hair. "That's why you were hunting them, wasn't it? To try to save yourself? It wasn't just sentimental value."

She nodded against my chest. "But it's just a hunch. There's no guarantee."

"A hunch is enough for me," I said, setting my jaw. "We were robbed of our happily ever after in Make Believe. I will make sure we have it now."

She gave me a pained look. "Gideon—"

"Do y'doubt I could make you happy?"

She shook her head. "It's not the 'happily' part that's the problem. It's the 'ever after' bit, love."

"Fate wouldn't have brought us together again just to tear us apart," I argued. "I'll save you, Arabella. I swear it."

She laid her hand upon my cheek, her lips curving with a hint of a smile. "Ah, love . . . When you say it, I almost believe it."

After extracting a promise from Arabella that she would rest a while longer, I left her to find Trish and thank her and Nicky for their hospitality. But as I made my way downstairs, I heard several voices in the kitchen, one of which was singing the latest annoyingly trite ditty from *The Pinocchio Show,* the most popular children's television program on the Tale TV network, and what I imagined was the source of endless irritation for the long-suffering parents who got to hear their tots sing the simple songs over and over and over again.

I cringed when I realized who must be visiting the Blues and had just pivoted to go back upstairs when I heard a curt "Get your ass in here, Gideon. We need to chat."

I heaved a sigh, knowing well the hell I'd catch if I took off. Sometimes it was just better to go along with Red's will than to fight it. Slipping on my shades, I strode into the kitchen, offering a slight bow to Nicky Blue, who stood at the island in the center of room, chopping vegetables. "Good afternoon."

He jerked his chin at me in greeting. "Hey there, Tiny. Come on in."

I glanced toward the dinette, where Trish and Red sat with Red's young son Max. The boy lifted his dark eyes from his coloring book and smiled, waving his hand in cheery greeting.

"Hi, Uncle Gideon," he chirped. "Look what I can do." Suddenly his adorable, cherubic face became a horrifying skeleton amid swirling smoke and shadow.

When I jerked in surprise, the smoke faded and he threw his head back, laughing so hard in delight at the effect of his newfound skill that his entire body shook with mirth. The boy's laughter was so uninhibited and contagious, I couldn't help chuckling.

"Yeah, that's new," Tess told me.

"Max," his father, Nate Grimm, scolded mildly from his place at the stove, "don't make faces."

Max was still giggling, his eyes still twinkling with mischief, when he turned his attention back to coloring and to his Pinocchio song.

Red rose from the table and strode toward me, her irritation unmistakable even without my ability to read her anger. "Okay, you have thirty seconds to spill it," she announced, slapping one hand on her hip, the other hip already occupied by her infant son, Rowan, who was busy gumming a chubby fist and blinking at me with wide, robin's egg blue eyes as if he knew I was about to catch hell and couldn't wait to see what was going to happen next.

"I beg your pardon, Red," I replied, feigning ignorance. "But I've no idea of what you speak."

"The hell you don't!" she charged.

Nate was busy preparing something that smelled delicious, but managed to send an apologetic look at me over his shoulder. "Nicky and Trish told us your friend isn't well, Gideon. I'm sorry."

I gave him a nod, unable to speak for the sudden knot in my throat.

"They also told us that Arabella's the fairy dust thief," Red continued. "Is she the one you were protecting after the cluster fuck at Guinevere's? What the hell is going on with you, Gideon? Are you trying to get yourself thrown in prison—or worse?"

I glanced at Trish, who grimaced in apology. Ah, well. Trish was a bad liar even on a good day, bless her. And Red had a way of getting what she wanted from even the toughest Tales, which was why she'd been made Assistant Director of the Fairytale Management Authority. Hardly surprising that Red had an axe to grind with me if Trish had filled her in on the situation with Arabella.

"It's a little more complicated than that," I told her, keeping my voice level.

She lifted her brows, waiting. When I remained silent, she took another step forward, going toe-to-toe with me. "Okay, so let me put it this way. You have thirty seconds to convince me why I shouldn't arrest your girlfriend for crimes that Trish assures me are considerable." Here her voice softened and she said gently, "She's looking at fifty years in the FMA prison at least, Gid. And God knows what kind of sentence you'd get, all things considered."

I shared a glance with Trish again. It seemed the head of forensics hadn't shared *all* of the facts about Arabella's condition, the big one being that she didn't have fifty years. I gestured toward the dinette. "Please, have a seat."

I quickly brought them all up to speed on my relationship with Arabella in Make Believe, how she'd resurfaced to me just the other day, how we'd seemingly picked up right where we'd left off. When I explained that Arabella was *fading,* Red cursed under her breath, but I barreled on, not able to dwell on the truth of her condition for fear I wouldn't be able to finish my tale.

When I stopped talking, they all gaped at me in silence, Trish dabbing at her eyes with a handkerchief. "I'm sorry," she murmured. "It's the pregnancy hormones."

"Bullshit it is," Red replied, making a covert swipe at her own eyes. "That fucking sucks, Gideon."

"What can we do to help?" Nate asked, cradling his and Red's youngest in his arms, the boy's tufts of black hair tickling his chin. I could tell by Nate's expression that he was the one taking my news the hardest. As Reaper to us Tales, he'd be the one to have to gather Arabella's soul when she died, and that weighed heavily on him. Nate did his job efficiently and effectively from everything I'd seen, but he didn't enjoy it.

"I guess the first thing you can do is not take Arabella in," I told him. "The king has demanded I bring her to him."

"Screw that," Red scoffed. "He has no jurisdiction on this."

I grinned at her naïveté. "Jurisdiction or no, he has commanded it, and I must obey."

"Is there anyone capable of breaking the king's spell on you to buy us more time?" Nicky asked. "Anyone whose magic is strong enough?"

I shifted uncomfortably in my chair. There was only person I could think of, but it was out of the question. "No."

"Gideon," Trish chastised, knowing better. "You need to think of Arabella . . ."

"I *am* thinking of Arabella!" I shot back, my temper flaring. When Nicky straightened defensively, ready to defend his wife, I held my hands up before me. "Forgive me. I know you mean well, Trish, but calling in Lavender would be a bad idea for many reasons, not the least of which would be that I'd be asking her to defy the father she adores and who has forbidden all contact with me."

But even as we spoke, I could feel the pain from the magic in my bindings growing more intense, my continued denial of my duty causing the bindings to become more insistent that I follow my orders.

"And there's more," I told them, having saved the worst of it for last. "We're not the only ones searching for the relics. There's another who's been hired to retrieve them. The Huntsman."

"Son of a bitch," Nicky muttered, glancing between Red and Nate. "Who the hell hired that bastard?"

Red shook her head, worry creasing her brow. "No clue. Haven't heard his name in quite a while."

"He's the one who murdered Georgie Porgie and Guinevere's maid," I explained. "That's what I was keeping from you last night, Red, what I'd hope to handle on my own. I didn't want to put any of you in his crosshairs."

"I wish I'd received the call about the killings sooner," Nate said. "Maybe it would've made a difference."

"He's fast," I told him. "And I have my doubts that he committed the murders alone. We ran into someone else yesterday down in Texas while trying to acquire one of the relics. This guy was too good, too seasoned a fighter to have been the Huntsman. For all I know, he could've been at Guinevere's, too. Maybe he was taking out the people in the house while the Huntsman was bringing down Georgie."

Trish nodded. "There's a lot to sort through, a lot of signatures throughout the house. Guinevere liked to . . . uh, *entertain*. But you might be right, Gideon. The person who stabbed Guinevere was right-handed. From anything I've ever seen of his handiwork, the Huntsman is left-handed. I'll run through the evidence again and see what else I can nail down. Unfortunately, by the time I could get to the victims, I wasn't able to get anything from their final thoughts. They were too far gone by then."

"I appreciate all your help, but I can't ask you all to ally yourselves with me," I told them sincerely. "It's too dangerous. I'd never be able to live with myself if anything happened to any of you because you were trying to help me."

"You're family, Gideon," Trish informed me. "We love you, and we'll do whatever we can to help you, no matter what."

I shook my head. "I appreciate it, but—"

I was surprised when Red reached across the table and covered my hand with hers. "You love this woman, Gideon. And you have a second chance with her if we can reverse the *fading* and get these relics she needs. Trust me, no one appreciates second chances more than I do." She sent a meaningful glance her husband's way, receiving a nod in return. "Let us help you."

At that moment, little Max wandered over to me and climbed up in my lap, rubbing his eyes with a yawn. He shifted around, finally finding a comfortable spot after wrapping his arms around my neck and resting his wee head upon my shoulder.

My throat grew tight as I held him, wondering if I'd ever have the chance to have a wee one of my own, a son or daughter who'd worry for me when I was out doing my duty, protecting my family with my last breath. And this extended family of mine was offering me the opportunity to take that chance, to claim the love and happiness that was almost within reach.

I heard a polite cough behind me and turned around in my chair, my heart immediately lifting at the sight of my little love standing there, still pale but smiling shyly at the roomful of strangers. "Hello, all," she said with a little wave.

I got to my feet, little Max in my arms, and went to her, caressing her cheek with the back of my fingers. "How are ye, lass?"

She nodded, her lips trembling a little as she gazed at me. "Better." But in spite of her words, her eyes filled with tears as she lifted a hand and tenderly smoothed Max's hair. When her gaze returned to mine, I saw a tentative spark of hope and such longing that my decision was made.

I took a deep breath and let it out slowly, hoping I would be able to live with what I was about to do. "Very well," I said. "Call Lavender."

Chapter 15

With Lavender being well into her pregnancy, shifting wasn't an option, and the soonest she and Seth could get to Chicago in response to Trish's urgent—and intentionally vague—request for her help was the following afternoon.

My friends went out of their way to make Arabella feel welcome during our dinner at the Blues' home, keeping conversation as light as possible. But when dinner ended, I could tell Arabella's strength was waning again. And so could Trish.

"You should stay here," she insisted as we prepared to leave. "I can monitor your condition much better that way."

"I appreciate the offer," Arabella assured her. "But . . . I have a home. Of sorts. I don't want to impose upon you and Nicky."

"Forget about it," Nicky drawled. "You're a friend now. It's no imposition. You need anything, we're here for you."

Arabella gave each of them a big hug. When she turned to Red and Nate to offer the same, I cringed, but to my surprise, the normally standoffish Assistant Director of the FMA accepted—and even returned—Arabella's hug, however briefly.

"Take care of yourself," she said, sending a glance my way. "And stay out of trouble. I'm gonna keep things as quiet as I can, but . . ."

I gave her a cockeyed grin. "We'll be sure to stay off your shit list."

Red gave me an *I'll believe it when I see it* look, but her words were solemn. "I really hope so, Gid."

"Come on," Nicky said, clapping me on the shoulder. "Let's get you a ride home."

When Nicky offered to arrange a ride home, I thought he meant calling us a cab. But when he took us into his massive warehouse of a garage, I found out he had something else in mind. With his trademark half-grin, he swept his arm toward the fleet of cars—classic and new—that were his pride and joy. "Take your pick, Arabella."

Her eyes went wide. "Seriously?" When he nodded, she said, "But I can't drive. I've never bothered learning. I mean, I never thought . . ." She glanced over at me, then cleared her throat. "I never thought I'd have time."

"Yeah, well, as soon as we get you through this, kid, I'll teach you myself—unless Gideon prefers to do the honors." He leaned toward her and added in a stage whisper, "But I've seen him drive . . . You're better off with me."

Arabella laughed, the sound music to my ears. "Good to know."

When she hurried off to inspect the fleet, I extended my hand to Nicky. "Thank you."

Nicky gave me a terse nod as he shook my hand. "She's good people. I like her." He gave me a grin. "And who'd have thought you and me would've had a . . . *colorful* past in common, what with us both bein' all respectable now?" He chuckled. "Fuckin' poetic."

"Yeah, well, I'm persona non grata at the moment," I reminded him as we started down the aisles in search of Arabella. "Not much respect in that. There's a shitload of circumstantial evidence from Guinevere's case that points to me."

"Trish has good people on her team," Nicky assured me. "They'll find out who's really to blame." He shoved his hands into his pockets, strolling nonchalantly beside me. "And, you know, if that doesn't come out roses, then there's other ways to handle it."

I glanced over at him, gauging his thoughts. Nicky had gone legit with his business since marrying Trish, but he still had his connections, his sway in all the right places. I knew for a fact that he'd pull whatever strings he had to if a friend was in trouble and needed a hand. I also knew that such an act of kindness on his part wouldn't come for free. It'd cost him a favor to that connection at some point, and I didn't want to be the one to put him in a position to have to settle on a debt that should be wholly mine.

"I appreciate that, Nicky," I told him, "but I'm not letting you put your neck on the line for me. No offense."

Nicky turned his mouth down in the equivalent of a shrug. "I can respect that. But the offer stands. You need anything, Tiny, all you gotta do is ask."

"I found it!"

Nicky and I both turned toward the sound of Arabella's voice. She was standing a few yards down the aisle from us, her face pale and wan but beaming with excitement. I couldn't help grinning, the smile on her face lifting my heart like nothing else could.

Nicky whistled in appreciation when he saw the car she'd chosen. "I knew I liked this gal," he said with a chuckle. "She's got an eye for *badass*."

"That I do," Arabella said with a wink at me. She then turned with a bounce in her step and ran her palm along the long sleek fender of the black 1967 Chevy Impala. "I think this will do quite nicely."

A few minutes later, we said our good-byes to Nicky and I started up the engine, loving the way it growled to life. Badass was right. I rarely drove because it was unnecessary and time-consuming when I could easily shift to where I wanted or needed to go. But with Arabella still trying to regain her strength after her latest episode, shifting was the last thing she needed to be doing. Plus, I had to admit, being behind the wheel of this beautiful, powerful machine with Arabella in the seat next to me was almost enough to make me forget that she was *fading,* that our days together were numbered unless I managed to find the relics of Arthur Pendragon, and unless, by some miracle, our theory about them actually proved true.

"I'm sorry about earlier," Arabella said, breaking the silence and bringing me out of my fantasy of a normal, boring life with the woman I loved. She turned her head toward the window, frowning. I sensed that she had more to say, so I waited, giving her the time she needed to put into words what was weighing so heavily upon her. At last she took a deep, shaky breath and said, "I'm afraid, Gideon."

I reached over and took her hand, giving it a squeeze. "I know y'are, lass."

Her mouth twitched at the corners in the hint of a smile. "Of course you do. How was it that I was ever able to hide anything from you before?"

Hell if I knew. Maybe it was because deception had been her livelihood. Maybe it was because I'd only seen what I wanted to see. But the fact that she was even asking made me sift through her motivations and desires, searching for what was behind her question. I hated that I mistrusted her, that I saw an ulterior motive in what might've been just an innocent question, nothing more than curiosity.

I forced a smile to hide my uneasiness. "A person's personality gives him away within seconds. And what I can't determine immediately, I can discern from feeling out his emotions. I'm an empath—I can feel what others are feeling . . . kind of like a ripple in the cosmos that buffets against my senses. The more time I spend with someone, the quicker I can respond to their needs. It's easier with Tales whose needs are predictable." I cast a grin her way. "But, Arabella, lass, you're *anything* but predictable."

"That's why you fell in love with me, isn't it?" she guessed, giving me her sauciest grin. "Because you can't always get in my head."

I chuckled. "Wasn't your *head* I was tryin' to get into."

She threw her head back with a laugh that would've convinced me she wasn't sick at all if I hadn't known better. "Ah, now the truth comes out."

On an impulse, I steered the car off the road and onto the shoulder and threw it into park. I twisted in my seat to face her. "You want to know why I fell in love with you?" I asked, reaching up to caress her cheek with the back of my hand. "Here y'are then. It was because you're beautiful and daring and brilliant and, yes, unpredictable. And your laugh makes me want to be near you, just for the chance to hear it again. And your smile . . ." I took a deep breath and blew it out on a sharp sigh. "I've never known another quite like it. Nothing gives me more pleasure than seeing y'smile."

She arched an eyebrow at me, her grin growing. "Nothing?"

My cock went hard in an instant, ready to call me a liar. "Well," I drawled, my heart beginning to race as she undid her seatbelt to slide across the seat toward me, "perhaps there's one or two other things I can think of."

I scooted out from behind the wheel and pulled her onto my lap, taking hold of her hips when she straddled me.

"Hmm," she taunted, "I wonder what those 'one or two other things' might be. . . ." She was still grinning when she took my face in her hands and pressed her lips to mine in a lingering kiss. "Is that one of them?"

I turned my eyes upward, mulling it over. "I'm not entirely certain. Perhaps you should give it another go. Just t'be sure."

She kissed me again, longer this time. "And now?" she asked, pulling back and lifting an eyebrow at me. "What say you?"

I closed my eyes for a moment, groaning with frustration. My voice was deeper than usual when I ground out, "I say it's time to get y'home."

With a wicked grin, she scrambled back to her seat, and I threw the car into drive, buckling my seatbelt as I drove. Considering I was confined to two tons of steel, I made remarkable time and my heart was pounding with anticipation when I pulled into the deserted parking lot outside the theater. Arabella was giggling when I pulled open her door and swept her out of the car, carrying her up the steps to the theater's entrance. I sent out a sharp word of magic, tripping the locks and swinging open the door.

Arabella kicked the door shut as I swung her inside and threw her head back with a laugh at my urgency. But the moment we entered the auditorium, the laughter died on her lips, and I slowly lowered her to her feet as I surveyed the room, my senses immediately on alert.

"Oh, my God," Arabella breathed, her hand going to her mouth as she sank down into the nearest seat.

The place had been ransacked. Arabella's meticulously arranged collection of props and Tale relics were strewn about the room as if a tornado had ripped through the confines of the theater. The clothes were in tatters. The furniture destroyed. The shelves of antiques tipped over, their contents shattered.

As my initial shock wore off, another, more urgent emotion washed over me. "How the hell did someone get by your protection spell?"

"I didn't have a protection spell," she admitted, her voice shaking. "I didn't know I could do such a thing."

I tore my gaze away from the mess in the theater to turn my frown toward her. "Merlin didn't teach you one?"

She shook her head. "We hadn't really gotten to such complicated spells yet."

"Where are Arthur's relics?" I asked. "Were any of them in here with the other items you'd located?"

She shook her head. "No, they were all hidden in my room. Except for the ring." She held up her hand to show me it was still safely on her finger. "And the shield and cloak that we left at Merlin's. We're still only missing five."

I took off through the debris field before she'd even finished her sentence, anxious to see if the items that were critical to her survival had been spared. I heard Arabella calling after me but didn't slow my pace. More familiar with the theater, she caught up quickly and was holding my hand when we reached her bedroom. The door stood ajar, the light from the hallway spilling inside to illuminate the pile of items that littered the floor.

I gently nudged her back against the wall with one arm, then, with my free hand, slowly pushed open the door. As it swung inward, I scanned the darkness, preparing for a fight, but whoever had tossed the place was long gone. Satisfied that there was no danger lurking in the darkness, I snapped my fingers, my magic flipping on the lights.

I should've left them off.

From behind me, Arabella choked on a gasp of horror and anger. She barreled by me into the room and began to frantically sift through the clothes and other items that littered the floor. She lifted up floorboards, false bottoms in drawers, cleverly disguised cubbies, quickly gathering together the relics she'd amassed. When she'd finished, she surveyed the pile of items.

"Nothing's missing," she murmured, her brow furrowed in confusion. "Whoever did this didn't manage to find any of my father's relics."

"Perhaps we interrupted his search," I suggested The thought that he could've been there when we arrived, waiting to attack when we entered, put me on edge. Hell, for all we knew, he could still be there somewhere, watching us right now. My muscles tensed, preparing for a battle that might or might not come. I slowly scanned the room, searching now with new intent. I was so focused, I didn't realize Arabella had resumed her search through the debris.

"Where is it?" she muttered. "Where the hell is it?"

Unfortunately, I didn't need to ask what she was looking for. The moment she asked the question, I sensed the item's absence. "Gone," I told her, hating to have to deliver the news and wishing I was mistaken.

She shook her head vehemently. "No!" she cried, her voice tight with emotion. "It can't be."

"Arabella—"

She dropped to her hands and knees, shoving aside books. "It has to be here, Gideon."

I went to her and knelt down beside her, taking hold of her shoulders and bringing her up to her knees, forcing her to stop her panicked search. "Arabella, lass—"

"They took the mirror." Her entire body sagged under the weight of the truth. "They took Fabrizio."

"Not to worry," I assured her. "I'll just send out a search spell."

She shook her head, staring blankly at me. "I don't know what that is."

I lifted my brows. "Merlin didn't teach you how to use a search spell either?" Before she could answer, though, I added, "Well, no, I guess he wouldn't have. He would've had to use the fairy dust necessary for it to stave off your symptoms."

I got to my feet and pulled her up with me, then brought up a handful of my silvery fairy dust and blew across my palm.

"What does the fairy dust do?" she whispered as if the sound of her voice might make the spell go awry.

I smothered a grin, looking forward to all the wonders of magic that I could teach her. I jerked my chin. "Look there as the dust settles."

The dust scattered about the room, searching for a trace of the one I sought. But, to my consternation, instead of lighting upon the footsteps of the intruder or a trail in the air that would mark the mirror's journey from the room, the dust merely settled upon the carpet and the debris that littered the floor.

"Was something supposed to happen?" Arabella asked, casting a searching glance about the room.

I nodded, narrowing my eyes. "The dust should've illuminated the trail of the person I indicated. But there's nothing. No trace of Fabrizio or our thief."

"Try again," she prompted. "Maybe you didn't do it right."

I gave her a slightly annoyed look. "I've been doing search spells since I was at my mother's knee," I groused. "I did it right." I took a slow turn about the room, searching the ground for any sign of the trail. "Even though Fabrizio is trapped in a mirror, it should've worked."

"What does his being in a mirror have to do with it?" Arabella asked, confused.

"The spell only works on individuals, not objects," I muttered. "But even if Fabrizio's imprisonment were an issue, the spell should've picked up on the thief."

"What would cause it to fail?" she asked, her dejection returning.

I clenched my jaw, knowing only one reason. "Whoever stole Fabrizio knew we'd use the spell and covered his tracks."

Her shoulders sagged. "Who could've managed that?"

Good question.

When I didn't respond, she dropped down on the bed, her hands lying limp between her knees.

I sat down and pulled her into my lap, wrapping my arms around her. "It'll be all right," I promised. "We'll figure out another way to locate the relics."

She lifted sorrowful eyes to me. "I'm not just worried about finding the other relics, Gideon. Fabrizio's a friend."

I pressed a kiss to the top of her head, then tucked her under my chin. "We'll get him back, lass."

She snuggled in closer, resting her cheek against my chest. "Who would've taken him, do you think? The Huntsman?"

That was the logical assumption, considering he'd been turning up at all the same places, but how he'd traced Arabella to the theater was a mystery. And how he'd managed to hide his tracks from my search spell an even bigger one. "It doesn't make any sense," I muttered, completing my thought aloud. "The Huntsman has known where the relics are each time without the benefit of Fabrizio's recon. Why steal the mirror now?"

She frowned in thought. "Maybe the Huntsman doesn't know where the final two relics are any more than we do. I mean, Fabrizio hasn't revealed the location of the helm—just that he's found it here in Chicago and that we'll go after it as soon as it's safe. Even I don't know the exact location yet."

"Maybe," I conceded. "But even if that's the case, how'd he know about Fabrizio? Who else knew you had the mirror?"

She shook her head. "No one but you and Merlin."

I cursed under my breath and pulled my hand down my face, not liking where my thoughts were headed. Apparently, Arabella knew exactly what I was thinking.

"No," she said, her chin jutting out at that defiant angle I knew all too well. "Not possible. Don't even suggest it."

"How do you know what I'm suggesting unless you're thinking it too?" I shot back. "Whoever was involved here had to either be magic or have access to it. No nonmagical Tale could've hidden his tracks."

She shoved to her feet, taking a few angry strides away from me before turning and crossing her arms over her chest. "Merlin isn't behind this," she insisted. "There's no way. He wouldn't steal the mirror from me when he knows that's the only way I've been able to track down the other relics."

"You give Merlin too much credit," I charged, getting up but planting my feet where I stood. "He's always been too arrogant and self-serving for his own good. God knows what kind of scheme he's cooked up."

Arabella shook her head slowly and gave me a look that clearly conveyed her disappointment. "Of all people, I figured you'd be the least likely to judge another before you have all the facts."

"What's that supposed to mean?" I demanded.

She put her hands on her hips, her expression reproachful. "Considering the kind of prejudice you've faced in your life, and how quickly the FMA accused you of the murders at Guinevere's with nothing but circumstantial evidence, I would've thought that you would give Merlin the benefit of the doubt."

"Merlin's reputation is his own doing," I argued. "Trust me, lass, he has a past just like any man. He might've been an able and worthy adviser to your father, but power like that has a way of going to a man's head."

She lifted her arms to her sides. "Very well, then. Shall we go ask him if he took the mirror? I believe he was planning to stay in Chicago for the rest of the week."

"Very well." I snatched up a knapsack from among the items strewn around the floor and began gathering up the relics and shoving them inside. "But we're taking these with us."

Chapter 16

I sensed something was wrong at Merlin's flat the moment we pulled up. I grabbed the knapsack out of the backseat and locked it in the trunk, then placed my hand upon the car and murmured a spell that would prevent anyone but me from reclaiming what was inside. Satisfied that the relics were safe, I turned to Arabella. "Stay here."

Her irritation hit me like a smack in the face. Which was probably what she was hoping for. "Like hell I will," she informed me, hands on her hips. "You know better."

I shook my head with a chuckle. "Aye, that I do, lass. That I do." I snaked an arm around her waist and pressed a brief kiss to her lips, then reached into a rift and dragged out a set of throwing knives.

Arabella's eyes went side. "Well, hello, my lovelies."

I slipped the holster over her shoulders and adjusted it for her. "Mind you only use these on the enemy."

"It's the enemy that'd better mind me." She gave me a saucy grin, then snatched one from its sheath, turning it over in the moonlight, whistling low at the craftsmanship. "These are magnificent. Where'd you find them?"

"Didn't," I said, starting for Merlin's flat. "I made them."

"Made them?" she echoed. "You're joking!"

"Nope."

She jogged quietly beside me, her footfalls nearly silent as we made our way up the back stairs. Unfortunately, her talent for silent approach apparently was confined only to her footsteps.

"When did you make them?"

"Ages ago."

"Where did they come from?"

"Storage."

"Storage?" she repeated, that insatiable curiosity I found so endearing making her eyes sparkle in the darkness as she fired off questions. "What kind of storage? Where is it?"

I held my finger to my lips, shushing her with a chuckle.

She sighed, exasperated, but was grinning. "Fine," she whispered. "Keep your secrets."

With that, she sprinted forward and took a running leap, grasping the bottom rung of the fire escape, pulling down the ladder and scaling it with ease. She reached the first landing, then leaped up to grab the railing above her and flipped up over it like an acrobat in the Cirque du Soleil.

I couldn't help the pride that swelled in my chest as I was flooded with memories of the many times we'd sneaked into the home of some tyrannical lord to nick a pair of candlesticks or plate of gold that would feed a nearby village for a good month.

I glanced over at her as I made the landing, not bothering to suppress the smile that curved my lips. My God, how I'd missed her. I'd mourned the love we'd shared, the intimacy that was our solace in the darkest and coldest of nights. But I hadn't realized how much I'd missed our adventures together.

Feeling the weight of my gaze upon her back, she paused in opening the door that led into the hallway and turned back to me. "What is it?" she mouthed. "Is something wrong?"

Was something wrong? Hell, pretty much everything was wrong. My life was falling apart in ways I'd never anticipated. She had finally been returned to me, our love for one another was as beautiful and breathtaking as it had always been—perhaps more so after so long apart. And there was every likelihood that she'd soon be taken from me again by a cruel disease. This was what my head told me, what I should've believed. But all I could think of at that moment was how for the first time in centuries, everything felt right. Because Arabella was at my side.

I shook my head in answer to her question and chucked her on the chin. Then I stepped forward, putting myself ahead of her. I pulled the door open wider, slipping into the dim hallway. The only lights were at either end of the hallway in keeping with the stark, industrial feel Merlin had cultivated for his Chicago flat. Unfortunately, the intentionally poorly lit hallway might look all dark and mysterious, but came at the cost of Merlin's security setup. Hell, he didn't even have a protection spell on the door, no doubt thinking no one would ever dare to cross such a fabled wizard as he.

Arrogant git.

When I reached the door to his apartment, I wasn't surprised to see that it was slightly ajar. I slowly pushed it open, grimacing as its heavy steel hinges creaked. I let my senses drift out. There was someone else in the apartment. What I couldn't immediately tell was whether or not that someone was Merlin.

I motioned for Arabella to stay by the door to prevent whoever was there from making a hasty retreat. She gave me a tight nod and moved her hands to the throwing knives hanging at her sides, silently unsheathing them.

Unlike Arabella's theater, Merlin's home hadn't been ransacked. Which either meant we'd gotten there before the thief could do his worst or that the intruder had come for some other purpose than finding the relics we'd left behind.

A soft shuffle in the bedroom that Arabella and I had used made me snap to attention. I turned back to Arabella and motioned toward the bedroom door, alerting her to where I was heading. With each step, my senses sharpened, my apprehension growing. The danger waiting in the darkness was menacing, there was no doubt, the intruder's purpose far more sinister than just making off with a few relics.

I pressed my back against the wall just outside the bedroom, peeking around the doorjamb into the room, trying to get a read on where the intruder was lurking. I squinted into the darkness, searching for even the slightest movement within the shadows.

I darted to the other side of the doorway, attempting to get a look at the other side of the room from that vantage point.

Shit. Nothing.

Only one thing left to do. I tensed, crouching at the ready, and shifted into the room. And brought my arm up to ward off the heavy battle-axe swinging toward my head. I caught the handle just in the nick of time, the deadly blade coming within inches of splitting open my skull.

The assailant grunted in frustration and tried to break away but not soon enough. I shoved, throwing him back hard enough to knock him off balance. He crashed into the dresser, crying out when the wood slammed into his spine. He reflexively released his hold on the battle-axe and rolled away, drawing a spiked mace from God knows where in one deft movement—with his left hand. In that split second I sized up the hulking shadow in the darkness, his height and build equal to mine, and suddenly realized just who I was dealing with.

The Huntsman.

He charged forward, bringing the mace down toward me in a powerful arc. I snatched up the axe just in time to block his strike, not about to let the head of the mace make contact and possibly infect me with another curse. Even though I was certain this wasn't the same man who'd attacked me at the Renaissance festival, I wasn't going to take any chances.

I twisted, driving my shoulder into him and sweeping his leg to knock him off balance. He landed flat on his back, the mace still in his grasp, but the bastard was fast, rolling out of the way before the sharp spell I spat could ensnare him.

I charged at him again, cursing the fact that I'd cornered him in a bedroom, of all places. The space to maneuver was almost nonexistent in the confines of the room, the furniture creating a half-visible obstacle course that threatened to trip me up at any moment and give the Huntsman the advantage. I needed to draw him out of the damnable room, get him somewhere more open.

I pivoted and bolted from the room and heard his harsh, sadistic chuckle as he clearly mistook my reason for retreating. His footfalls were heavy as he gave chase, not bothering to hide his pursuit now that he thought he had me scared as hell and on the run.

I pressed my back to the wall outside the room, waiting. When he came charging through, I brought my elbow up and drove it into his face, shattering his nose. He roared with pain and rage, only momentarily stunned by the blow. But the pain made him sloppy as he swung his mace in wild arcs, his attack no longer strategic. I could sense his fury—and his desperation. He was afraid. Not of me, clearly. He didn't see me as a foe at all—at least, not a worthy one. No . . . there was someone else. His employer.

Interesting.

One particularly savage blow caught the head of my axe, wrenching it from my hands and sending it sailing through the air toward the door where I'd left Arabella. I cried out, sending out my magic in a frantic burst, halting the axe's path in midair, then releasing it, letting it drop.

It was enough of a distraction that the Huntsman barreled into me before I knew what was coming, sending us both crashing into Merlin's coffee table. The wood broke apart beneath us, painfully digging into my side. Before I could extricate myself from the rubble, the Huntsman's fist connected with my jaw once, but it was a glancing blow that only served to piss me off.

When he came at me a second time, I grabbed his fist and twisted, snapping his wrist. He roared, pulling back enough that I was able to land a punch of my own and throw him off of me and into a nearby bookshelf. The shelf shuddered with the impact, sending several of the books tumbling off. The Huntsman lunged for his mace, ready to have another go.

Enough of this bullshit. I was done fucking around.

I brought up a ball of my silver magic and lobbed it at the Huntsman. It slammed into him, throwing him back against the wall and knocking one of Merlin's Picassos to the floor. Realizing the work of art was in peril, I snapped my fingers, transporting it to the pocket of time I used for storage barely in time to avoid the Huntsman's next charge.

Damn, the guy was persistent!

Suddenly, the lights flicked on, momentarily blinding both the Huntsman and me. I blinked away the spots before my eyes, and when they adjusted to the light, I found him training a red laser sight on the center of my chest.

"Well, well, well," the Huntsman drawled, his voice nasal and thick with blood from his broken nose. "What 'ave we here? If it isn't the infamous Gideon Montrose. Never thought I'd be the one to get the drop on you. Guess it's just my lucky day, mate."

"Guess again, *mate.*"

My pulse spiked at the sound of Arabella's voice, but I couldn't see her. Neither could the Huntsman. He glanced around, searching for the source of the voice, giving me the chance I needed. I sent out another burst of magic in the form of a lightning bolt, nailing him in the center of the chest and sending him flying off his feet. He landed with a grunt and slid across the floor before coming to a hard stop when he smashed into a heavy bronze statue that was part of Merlin's extensive, if eclectic, art collection.

Arabella shoved the hood from her head, becoming visible again just a few feet from where the Huntsman lay, an arrow at the ready and trained on the man's chest. At some point during my altercation with the assassin, Arabella must've completely disregarded my instructions to stay where she was and slipped away to retrieve the invisibility cloak and bow she'd left at Merlin's.

"Will you *ever* listen to a word I say, lass?" I chastised, shaking my head as I strode to where she stood over the Huntsman.

She gave me that saucy, dimpled grin of hers. "Not likely."

I winked at her. "Good thing."

"Seems a pity to waste an arrow on this worthless pile of shit when I could use these magnificent knives instead," she said on a dramatic sigh. "Shall I let him run, love, give 'em a try?"

I shrugged. "Up to the Huntsman here." I snapped my fingers, dissipating the magic I'd used to immobilize him and jerked my chin at him. "What do you say, *mate?* Want to take your chances? See if you can outrun one of her knives?" I flicked my hand, sweeping the edge of Arabella's cloak back over her shoulder to reveal the silver knives in their holster. "You might be able to do it. I'd give you . . . What odds do you think, lass? Thirty percent?"

Her eyes narrowed with deadly menace. "Ten."

I whistled at the dire odds. "Well, better than nothing, I suppose,"

I conceded. "I can feel you tensing, Huntsman, getting ready to bolt and test your ten percent odds of escape, take your chance on whether or not my associate will use those lovely, cursed knives of hers." When I saw his eyes widen a bit I added, "Oh, yes, *cursed*. Didn't I mention that before?"

"I think you left out that part, love," Arabella chimed in.

"Ah, well, no matter," I said, offering him a tight smile. "She'd only be switching to the knives to make things a bit more interesting."

Arabella *tsked*. "Too right."

"The thing is, Huntsman, my darling lass here's already got the drop on you with her bow, and I know for a fact you can't outrun that arrow. She's a deadly shot, this one."

"I'd say he's exaggerating," Arabella told him with a casual shrug. "But he's not."

"Enough of your little games," the Huntsman snarled. "If you're going to kill me, get on with it."

I shook my head. "I have no intention of killing you—unless I have to. I just want information. And then I'll let the FMA deal with you."

He chuckled darkly. "The FMA? Do you really think they can hold me? My services are too valuable to too many people for me to be locked up, rotting in a prison."

I dropped down, then grabbed him by the front of his shirt and pulled him half off the floor, my face close to his as I snarled, "They're not important to *me*. And they sure as hell aren't important to Guinevere's maid and Georgie Porgie, you son of a bitch."

The bastard merely grinned at me, not perturbed by my anger in the least. "They were important to the Tale who hired me to kill them. Maybe you should take this up with him."

I shoved him away and got to my feet. "Happy to. Who is it?"

"Did you really think you could just ask and I'd tell you?" the Huntsman growled. "I 'ave a reputation, mate."

I nodded. "So do I." I reached out and snatched one of the knives from Arabella's belt and sliced open the Huntsman's thigh before he could even flinch. It was a shallow wound, little more than a scratch, but he howled in pain as the curse hit his bloodstream. "You have five minutes until the curse paralyzes your heart," I told him evenly. "Start talking and I'll consider retracting it."

"You can do that?" Arabella whispered.

I threw a glance her way. "My curse. My call."

The Huntsman's back suddenly arched off the ground, the curse wringing a raw cry from him.

"Looks like five minutes was a bit off," I corrected. "Probably more like three. Start talking."

The man glared at me through the haze of his agony, sweat beginning to bead on his forehead. "Bugger off."

"Where are the other relics?" I demanded. "The ones you stole from the Met. Where are they?"

He shook his head and attempted to force a smile through clenched teeth. "Up your ass."

I made another slash with the knife, this time cutting across his chest. "I just cut your time in half," I informed him. "Better get on with it."

His muscles were beginning to twitch uncontrollably, his legs bending and extending in rapid succession, but still he refused to say a word.

"Where are the relics from the Met?" I asked again, speaking slowly.

"Eat shit."

"Where is the magic mirror you stole?"

"What mirror?"

"Nice try," I snapped. "It's *the* magic mirror—Fabrizio."

He laughed, a dark sound that squirmed along my skin.

"Who is your employer?" I demanded, trying another tack.

He spit toward my face, missing. "Go fuck yourself."

I sent a casual glance at the spittle that fell short.

"This isn't working," Arabella said softly.

I made another slash across his chest, my desperation to save Arabella sending me to that dark place where I'd once dwelled. "Answer any *one* of the questions, Huntsman, and I'll stop the curse."

"Gideon," Arabella admonished, "he's not going to talk."

The Huntsman clenched his teeth tighter, groaning with pain, the veins in his neck bulging. His face was turning purple now, his time rapidly running out. And I didn't give a shit. All that mattered to me was getting the information that would save the woman I loved.

I heard Arabella's soft curse and glanced up at her, the wary look in her eyes when she gazed at me giving me pause. I turned away from the confusion I saw there, somehow knowing that my torture of the Huntsman, worthless asshole that he was, had irreparably damaged her image of me.

The weight of that realization sat like a rock in the center of my gut, weighing down my hope of ever reclaiming what we'd had before. But if it meant Arabella would live, it was a risk I was willing to take.

"Last chance, Huntsman," I ground out, my voice as deadly as my resolve. "Tell me—"

"They're at Guinevere's!"

I held up my hand at the Huntsman's sudden outburst, closing my fist and halting the progress of the curse. "What's at Guinevere's?"

He was panting, dragging in great gulps of air, wisely unsure of how long the reprieve would last. "The relics from the Met," he wheezed. "Guinevere's had them all along. She took them and reported them stolen to get the insurance money."

I pulled my free hand down my face. "You've got to be fucking kidding me," I muttered. "So, you were at her house not just for the ring, but for the other relics as well."

"If they were there the whole time, where were they hidden?" Arabella asked, clearly skeptical of the Huntsman's story. "I searched the house from top to bottom looking for the ring."

The Huntsman chuckled. "That you did. I enjoyed watching your little drama play out."

I opened my hand, giving him just a hint of the curse. "Answer the question."

He turned furious eyes on me. "There's a safe behind a piece-of-shit painting in the sitting room."

I knew exactly which one he meant. *Damn it!* I'd been staring right at it. I'd known something was off about the painting that looked like a preschooler's art project. I'd been drawn to it for reasons I couldn't comprehend, even though the painting itself was far from interesting or exceptional. Now I knew why. But I kept my expression blank, not about to let on that I knew what he was talking about it.

"And the mirror?" I asked, not about to let up on him now that he'd broken his silence. "Where's Fabrizio?"

"Not my handiwork," he spat. "I know Fabrizio of old. I'd sooner pay someone *else* to steal it than have to put up with that arrogant pain in the ass."

I shrugged, conceding the point. "Fair enough. Who else knows about it? Your employer? Did he take it?"

He eyed me askance. "You'll have to ask him."

"Love to," I shot back. "Where can I find him?"

The Huntsman laughed again. "Right under your nose."

"What the hell is that supposed to mean?" I demanded.

A smirk tugged at the corner of his mouth. "Ask your king."

I slowly straightened, not sure whether I should strangle the son of a bitch for what he was implying or save that dubious honor for my king. Disbelief and confusion crashed over me in one great wave. And for a moment, I was so stunned I forgot to halt the curse infecting the Huntsman. But his anguished scream snapped me out of my stupor.

With one hissed word, I waved my hand, immediately relinquishing him from the magic's grasp. Exhausted from this last onslaught, the Huntsman slumped over in a heap, unconscious.

"Dear Lord," Arabella breathed, her eyes wide when she turned her head to look at me.

I sent a dark glance her way, but didn't say a word in defense of what I'd done. I had the answers I needed. And I didn't regret for a moment the means I'd had to employ to obtain them.

But Arabella's unasked questions weighed so heavily on my conscience, I turned away and dialed Red Little's cell.

"You miss me already?" she drawled by way of greeting.

"What can I say," I quipped, "it must be your sunshiny disposition."

She laughed. "I get that a lot. Let me guess—calling about Guinevere?"

I frowned. "No. What about her?"

"Just got word she's awake," Red explained. "Thought that was why you were calling. As soon as she's feeling up to it, we'll question her about what happened and get everything sorted out."

"I'm glad to hear she's conscious," I told her. "I'm certain she'll be able to clear my name."

"That's the plan," Red assured me. "So, if you weren't calling about our lovely Lady of Camelot, what's doin'?"

I glanced at the Huntsman, still lying in an unconscious heap on the ground. "I have a present for you."

"Aww, for me? You're gonna make Nate jealous."

"Yeah, well, a few more seconds and I would've been giving this present to him. But this one's all for you."

"Color me intrigued," she said. "Let me hand off the boys to Gran and we'll be on our way."

As soon as she disconnected the call, I texted the address for Merlin's flat, then turned my attention back to the Huntsman. He was beginning to stir. I crouched down beside him and placed my hand on his arm, sending out a binding spell to keep him from getting too friendly when he came to.

"What the *bloody hell* happened here?"

Arabella and I spun around to see Merlin standing in the doorway to his flat, a tall, leggy blonde under one arm and an equally statuesque redhead under the other.

"You two have *got* to be the worst houseguests in the *history* of . . . of *houseguests!*" he sputtered. "Look what you've done to my furniture! And—*blimey!*—my shelves! Do you have any idea what those books are *worth?* And—" His words broke off when he finally noticed the Huntsman lying on the floor. "Hel-lo . . . Who's *this?*"

I glanced toward Merlin's visitors. "Perhaps you should ask your lady friends to depart."

Merlin blinked at me in dismay. "My what . . . ? Oh, yes, yes." He plastered on a smile and turned toward the door, his arms spread. "Seems our plans have changed, my darlings."

The women pouted in almost perfect unison, simpering in disappointment as Merlin ushered them out.

"But you *promised,*" the blonde sulked.

"Oh, I know, I know, ducky," Merlin soothed. "I was looking forward to our little party too."

"I thought we were going to play with your magic wand," the redhead moped.

Arabella grunted in disgust and rolled her eyes. "You and everybody else," she muttered.

I smothered a smile, wondering how I'd ever mistakenly believed that she and Merlin could've been romantically involved. My darling lass had no doubt seen through his advances in a heartbeat and put him in his place with a wry look or an acerbic word.

When the women were gone, Merlin turned back to us, his devil-may-care attitude gone in an instant. His expression was stormy, his anger a palpable force in the room as he strode toward us. And for a moment, I thought he might actually unleash that infamous, phenomenal power I'd witnessed on more than one occasion in our days in Make Believe, the same power that had made him an almost unstoppable force when he was adviser to the kings of Camelot but which had taken a regrettable backseat to illusions and parlor tricks. But before he could give us a glimpse of the Merlin of old, he turned that furious gaze upon the awaking Huntsman.

"Who *the fuck* are you?" he demanded of the assassin, his voice deeper and deadlier than I'd ever heard it. "And what the hell are you doing in my home?"

"He came to steal the relics," Arabella explained before the visibly rattled Huntsman could respond.

Merlin grabbed the Huntsman by the collar and jerked him upright. "I don't take kindly to someone stealing from me or my friends," he snarled. "Those who cross me tend to suffer *most* grievously."

"Red Little's on her way," I assured Merlin. "She's going to take him into custody."

Merlin put his face close to the Huntsman's and hissed, "It's a damned good thing." He shoved the man away and straightened, taking a deep, centering breath and letting it out slowly before turning his attention back to Arabella and me and coming forward, his arms spread wide. "Are you all right? This bastard didn't harm either of you?"

I shook my head. "Not to worry. And he won't be any trouble for a while. I've bound him until Red can get here and put him in shackles."

"Did he manage to get what he came for?" Merlin asked.

Arabella shook her head. "No, all the relics are safe. And he told us that the three stolen from the Met are at Guinevere's."

Merlin's eyes narrowed on me. "I'm guessing that's not all he imparted."

I met his gaze, not missing the shrewd intelligence there. Merlin might pretend to be an irresponsible reprobate, but he was far more discerning and perceptive than even I'd given him credit for. I had a feeling I'd grossly underestimated my old friend. I would not make that mistake again.

"Fabrizio has been taken," I told him. "Arabella's theater was in shambles and the mirror was gone. No one besides the three of us knew about the mirror."

Merlin took a step back, suddenly wary. "I assure you I had no hand in his disappearance. As much as I despise that annoying prat, I bear him no ill will. Nor would I ever do anything that would cause my darling Bella any grief. You must look elsewhere for your thief."

"I hope so," I told him. "I would never want us to be unfriendly, Merlin."

Merlin inclined his head, acknowledging the warning in my voice, his steely gaze offering a warning of his own. "Nor would I."

I reached for Arabella's hand. "We're going to Guinevere's to gather the other three relics there. I trust you will guard the Huntsman until Red arrives?"

Merlin sent a glance toward the man in question. "My pleasure. I'm sure he and I will have a *lovely* time together until Ms. Little arrives."

Chapter 17

In the interest of saving time, I took a chance and shifted us to Guinevere's home, but it was clear that the journey had taken a toll on Arabella from the moment we got there. She didn't complain, though, instead offering me a bright smile.

"Well, here we are again," she mused, trudging toward the front door. "Shall we?"

I darted forward, reaching the door just before she did, blocking the entrance. "I'll go first," I insisted, my skin prickling in warning.

She started to protest but must've caught the wary watchfulness in my gaze as I surveyed the surrounding area. There was danger lurking nearby, waiting for the opportunity to attack. She nodded her understanding and slipped her hand in mine.

I eased open the front door, peering uneasily into the darkness. The light switch was just inside the front door from what I recalled of my earlier visit, but I didn't want to flip it on and alert anyone who was watching the house. Instead, I called up a small ball of magic and shined it into the foyer, peeling away the shadows, gauging if it was safe to enter. When I felt certain we weren't in any immediate danger, I stepped inside, my grip on Arabella's hand tightening.

I didn't waste any time before heading for the sitting room where the Huntsman had indicated the treasures were stored. I went immediately to where the painting hung on the wall. Even in the semidarkness, I could see that the painting was slightly askew.

We weren't the first to come looking for the relics. I just hoped the previous visitor hadn't been successful in getting inside the safe that was hidden behind the monstrosity of a painting.

I slipped it from its hook and set it aside, relieved to find the safe behind it as the Huntsman had indicated. Fortunately, the lock was undamaged and there was no magical residue upon it to indicate that anyone had attempted to break in. I studied the edges of the safe, searching for any booby traps that might set off a curse like those I'd already encountered. But it seemed clean.

I glanced at Arabella and shrugged. "It looks like just a regular safe."

Her brows came together. "Are you sure?"

I took one last look, smoothing my fingertips over the edges of the safe. "I don't sense anything. I think we're good."

"Now if we only knew the combination," Arabella mumbled. "How are you at safecracking, love?"

I gave her a sidelong smirk, then winked. At the same instant, the lock popped and the safe door swung open with a quiet creak.

Her eyes sparkled with delight. "Is there anything you *can't* do?"

"I'll let you know when I find out," I teased.

I was still grinning when I turned my attention to the contents of the safe, relieved to find all three relics there as we'd hoped. I quickly fished out the goblet, the broken dagger, and the penannular brooch with Arthur's dragon's head seal, and handed them off to Arabella. Three more relics safely in my little love's possession, leaving only two to secure: Arthur's helm and Excalibur.

I was just about to swing the door shut when I noticed something else in the safe. "What the hell?"

"What is it?" Arabella asked, going up on her toes to peer around me to get a peek at what had captured my attention.

Still too stunned to answer, I produced a handkerchief and reached inside again to take hold of the silver chain and pendant that lay tucked in the very back corner of the safe, nearly hidden by the other mementos and a few carefully folded documents. I held the chain up before my eyes, studying the design.

"It's lovely," Arabella breathed. "I've never seen such intricately crafted designs on a pendant. But the symbols look familiar."

I sighed. "It's because you've seen them before." I held my wrist before her eyes, revealing the king's bonds upon me. "These symbols constitute the Seelies' family crest. They are the symbols of my king's house."

"Why would Guinevere have a necklace that bore your king's crest?" Arabella asked.

"Perhaps we should go ask her."

"How are you holding up?" I asked Arabella as we made our way down the hallway toward Guinevere's room at the Tale hospital.

She gripped my hand and offered me a smile that was far weaker than the last time I'd asked. "Peachy. You?"

I brought her hand to my lips and pressed a kiss to her knuckles. "Worried about you. I shouldn't have taken you with me to Guinevere's house. The travel has worn on you."

"Sorry, love," she said, lifting her chin a bit higher. "I'm not about to let you have all the fun. What if someone dark and deadly had been skulking about in the shadows? What would you have done without me there to protect you?"

I chuckled. "What would I have done, indeed?"

When we reached Guinevere's door, I glanced up and down the hallway to gauge how much interest our visit had caused, but at this time of night, the doctors and nurses were scarce and those who were present seemed preoccupied with keeping up with the duties that were normally handled by twice as many staff during the day.

I pushed open the door and slipped inside, pulling Arabella in after me. The room was lit by only one small lamp in the corner so as not to disturb Guinevere, whose blonde hair was in a tangle upon her pillow, evidence that although she slept, her rest wasn't peaceful. When I took a step toward the bed, her eyes snapped open on a gasp.

"It's all right," I assured her quickly, keeping my voice low, soothing. "You're safe, my lady."

"Gideon," she sighed, her lids closing in relief. "I was worried you might be . . ."

"The Huntsman?" I prompted. "Or the other assailant?"

Her lids lifted again with more than a little effort. "You saw them then?"

I shared a glance with Arabella. "Something like that."

Guinevere's lips trembled, and her chest began to heave with emotion. "I tried to stop him," she said. "I tried to keep him from hurting the others, but—"

"Hush now," Arabella soothed, coming forward and placing her hand on Guinevere's arm. "There's nothing you could've done."

Guinevere's eyes snapped. "Who the hell are *you*? How would you know?"

"This is Arabella Locksley," I introduced, conveniently leaving out the part about Arabella being the offspring of Guinevere's unfaithful husband. "She's a friend."

Guinevere's eyes lit with understanding. "Ah, so *this* is the reason you didn't accept my . . . invitation?"

I inclined my head. "Indeed she is."

"Well, I suppose I shouldn't be *too* insulted. She's pretty enough." Guinevere closed her eyes again, sinking down into her pillows. Her strength was failing, her recovery still not certain. It was this fact, no doubt, that kept Arabella's retort from slipping past her lips. That and the fact that I had pulled her slightly behind me, putting myself in the line of fire between the two women before any additional exchanges could take place.

"Guinevere," I said gently, "we just wanted to assure ourselves that you were recovering as reported. I am delighted beyond measure to see that the reports were, in fact, true. I also wanted to assure you that we have the Huntsman in custody."

"Thank heaven for that," she murmured. "I hope that bastard gets what's coming to him."

So did I—especially considering his declaration that he'd be out of FMA prison in no time thanks to the influence of those who required his services.

"And what of the other one?" she asked.

I hesitated before admitting, "Still unaccounted for. But we're doing everything we can to find him. Do you think you'd be able to give a description?"

She shook her head. "No. It all happened too fast. He was wearing a mask. I never saw his face."

"But you did see the Huntsman?" I pressed gently. "You could identify him as one of the attackers?"

She nodded. "Yes. The other man even called him 'Huntsman' when he sent him after you and the man who attacked me upstairs."

At least my theories of multiple attackers could be proved. Now we just needed to figure out who the hell the mystery man was.

"We won't take up much more of your time," I assured her. "I'm sure the FMA will send people along later to question you more extensively."

She nodded.

"Before we go, though, I wanted to return something of yours." I took the necklace from my pocket with a handkerchief and draped it across her palm.

The moment the silver hit her skin, her eyes snapped open on a gasp. "Where the hell did you get this?" she demanded, her voice breaking.

"It was taken from your safe," I told her, watching her closely to see if the half-truth would play as well as I'd hoped.

She closed her fingers around the pendant, squeezing it so tightly that she would no doubt have an imprint of the symbols embedded in her palm when she finally released it. "Thank you for returning it," she said, her words clipped.

"I know the value of such a piece," I told her, intentionally keeping my tone conversational. "These pendants are quite rare and not often relinquished by the owner. I'm curious how you came by it."

She laughed bitterly. "Did I steal it, you mean?" Before I could answer, she placed her closed fist upon her chest, clutching the pendant to her heart. "It was given to me, if you must know. I thought it was a token of great affection, a promise. But I was mistaken."

"Do you mind if I ask who gave it to you?" I pressed.

"Yes, I mind!" she snapped, her eyes brimming with tears. "I mind a great deal. I thought—" She took a deep, shaky breath and glanced away, clearly not wanting us to see the emotional response she had to the necklace.

Arabella took my arm and nodded toward the door, signaling that it was time for us to go.

Dissatisfied with the answers I'd received, I wanted to press further, make Guinevere tell me which Seelie had given her the token of love and devotion she clutched in her hand, but the sorrow I could feel in her was enough to keep my questions at bay.

I let Arabella lead me to the door, but before we exited, I paused and turned back to Guinevere. "Whoever he was," I told her, "he loved you a great deal. Those pendants bind one to another when a Seelie shares it with his beloved. And that bond is unbreakable unless the one who forged the necklace destroys it. No matter what has happened since you received this token, the heart that loved you once loves you still."

Guinevere turned her eyes up to me, the tears brimming there finally making their way to her cheeks. Without a word, she brought the pendant to her lips, a single sob shaking her shoulders.

I closed the door behind me and walked in silence beside Arabella as we made our way out of the hospital.

"Was that true?" she asked after several moments. When I glanced down at her but remained silent, she asked again, "What you told Guinevere about the pendant. Was it true?"

I nodded. "The magical bond is embedded in the silver when it's forged. I've created several of them in my time with the king, most recently the one Lavender shared with her husband. Each one is unique, specifically designed to represent the beauty of two people's love for one another."

Arabella tugged me to a halt and grasped the silver chain around my neck, bringing my own pendant out from beneath my shirt. "And this?" she prompted. "Is this the same kind of pendant?"

I nodded, taking it gently from her grasp and tucking it back under my collar. "It's a Seelie custom. And being an Unseelie slave, I didn't have the right to bestow my heart where I pleased. It was only after our relocation to the Here and Now . . . after everything . . . that I was allowed to possess one. A small freedom granted as a gift by my king as a token of his gratitude for risking my life to protect his daughter."

Arabella walked in silence for several moments, but I could feel the questions pressing upon her, her curiosity itching to be scratched. Finally, she said in a burst, "If Lavender hadn't left you when you came over, would you have bound yourself to her?"

The question brought me up short. I turned to face Arabella and shoved my hands deep into my jeans pockets. "Does it matter?"

Her face went through a variety of contortions as it revealed many emotions within the span of a few seconds. "No, of course not," she finally said. "But, I mean . . . um, well, yeah, actually, it does matter."

I narrowed my eyes at her, wondering what kind of answer she wanted. I had a bad feeling that no matter what I responded to this particular question, it was going to be wrong. But avoiding it altogether wouldn't have been helpful either. *Christ.* I was centuries old, had lived through wars, famine, pestilence, and gruesome violence the likes of which still haunted my nightmares. And yet nothing frightened me quite as much as the wrath of this angry woman.

I squared my shoulders and rallied my courage, deciding to just stick with the truth and then deal with whatever fallout might occur. "I was already bound to Lavender when we came over," I admitted. "She gave me her pendant in Make Believe."

Arabella's eyes went wide and she blinked at me for several seconds, her expression impossible to read. Finally she swallowed hard and her mouth opened and closed several times as if she was trying to form the appropriate words. But all that came out was a quiet, "Oh."

I waited, not sure what was coming next. In fact, I waited with such tension that the muscles in my shoulders began to ache. Unable to take the suspense any longer, I continued, "Our pendant was destroyed after our relationship was discovered and she agreed to release me from our bond to protect me. I won't lie to you, Arabella—it was a difficult time. For the second time in my life, I'd lost a woman I loved."

"Why didn't you try to rekindle things with Lavender later?" she asked. "I mean, if she meant so much to you, why didn't you fight for that love?"

I sighed. "Every good warrior knows when to make a strategic retreat, when to admit when he's beaten, and when to stand and fight to the death. I loved Lavender, but she'd made her choice and I had to respect that. And, after a little while, I realized she'd made the right decision. As much as we cared for one another, the truth was, I wasn't the right man for her, and she wasn't the right woman for me."

"How do you know that?" Arabella pressed.

I took her by the shoulders and peered down at her, emotion making my throat tight when I said, "Because she wasn't you."

Arabella's expression went through another series of rapid transformations, but this time of a very different sort. And when she finally settled on one, it was so full of happiness, I couldn't help smiling back. And I was still grinning when she pulled me down to receive her kiss.

"So who do you think gave Guinevere the pendant?" Arabella asked as we made our way back to the car, leaning on my arm a little more than she would've ever admitted.

I frowned at the question. "There aren't too many possibilities. Most of my king's offspring are daughters. His only son is Puck, but he's just bestowed his pendant within the last few months. I've never been asked to forge another for him."

"Could the king have another son that you're not aware of?" she asked cautiously, studying me closely as she waited for a response.

Curious.

I shook my head. "Not likely. The Tales the king has been with know exactly what they'd be missing out on if they didn't claim his paternity. None of his children want for anything—nor do their mothers. My king is extremely devoted to all of his children. I see to it personally. Even when he and Puck were estranged, I secretly watched out for Puck, making sure he never got into too much trouble, that all his debts were paid, that his business interests were secure. Secretly, of course. Mab would've been furious had she known as she was the one who turned Puck out in the first place."

"The queen turned out her own son?" Arabella asked, aghast. "I can't imagine a mother completely cutting herself off that way."

"Mab's never been particularly maternal," I explained. "She only bore three of the king's children and never cared for them. They were her pretty little baubles, playthings, status symbols. She and Lavender are only friendly again because Lavender managed to redeem herself with her recent heroics."

"Well, that's *something*, I guess," Arabella said.

I grunted. "Yeah, except Mab hasn't restored Lav's true identity within folklore. The Ordinaries only know of her as Cinderella's fairy godmother. And Puck's identity has been wiped clean, sanitized as much as Mab could manage. He has a story through his association with the Willies, which she can't control, but that's pretty much all that anyone remembers about him. And good luck finding Mab's youngest daughter *anywhere*."

Arabella's brows shot up. "There's another daughter?"

"Precisely my point," I replied. "Poppy has unfortunate taste in men, but she's a good girl—a kind and gentle soul, generous and trusting to a fault. But she was never powerful enough or ambitious enough to suit Mab. The queen has refused to have her good name tarnished by the exploits of her offspring."

"Good Lord," Arabella said, shaking her head in disbelief. "To think of a mother being so callous to her own children."

"It irks Mab to no end that the king demands she accept his illegitimate children," I told Arabella. "In this one thing, the king will not allow himself to be ruled by his wife."

Arabella fell silent again for a moment before asking, "So, what if the king *did* have children he wasn't aware of?" she pressed. "What if there are children whose mothers didn't realize who he really was. Or *what* he was?"

"What are you getting at?" I asked.

"What if the king had children with Ordinaries?"

This brought me to an abrupt halt. "I'm not aware of any."

She shrugged. "Hypothetically speaking."

"Very well then," I said, willing to play along even though the conversation was making me angry for reasons I couldn't even begin to understand. "*Hypothetically speaking,* how would someone *else* know that the king had children with Ordinaries if he himself wasn't aware of any?"

Arabella pursed her lips and I could practically see the wheels turning in her mind. "What time is it?"

Frowning at the sudden change in topic, I glanced up at the night sky. "Edging on midnight. Why?"

"Then we have to hurry," she said, grabbing my hand and dragging me behind her. "There's a shipment of fairy dust coming through tonight. I know a shortcut that will get us there in time to intercept the drop."

"Arabella!" I barked, bringing her up short. "What the hell are you talking about? I'm not going to knock over the king's shipment of fairy dust. I'm already in deep shit. The *last* thing I need to do is add robbery to my list of offenses."

She huffed, frustrated with my resistance. "Gideon, if you want answers, this is the place to start."

"How about you give me a few answers right now," I insisted, standing firm. "I'm not taking another step until you come clean."

She closed her eyes for a moment, then heaved a sharp sigh. "When I was stealing the fairy dust from the transports, it wasn't just for me."

"What?" I said, shaking my head. "What do you mean?"

"There are nearly a dozen others *fading*, Gideon," she told me. "And every single one of them is only half-Tale. Like me. But unlike me, it's their *father* who is Tale—and that father is your king."

Chapter 18

I sat gripping the steering wheel of the Impala, my knuckles white, fury blazing through my veins as we waited at the airfield for the shipment of fairy dust to arrive. The information Arabella had shared with me on the drive to the drop location still buzzed in my head. The "children" ranged in age from infants to a man in his fifties who still looked like he was a strapping lad of twenty-five—or, at least, he *had* until he'd begun to *fade*.

The first case had surfaced just a couple of months after Arabella arrived, right around the same time she began to *fade*. It was a nine-year-old boy who had been healthy, happy, living a decent life with his adopted family in Oak Park. Then he suddenly began to waste away from a mysterious illness, and no matter how many specialists were consulted, no reason for his failing health could be identified. Then a similar case cropped up not far away in Glen Ellyn. A five-year-old little girl living in foster care. And then a fifteen-year-old set of twin boys in Schaumburg. The list grew rapidly.

Eventually, the National Institutes of Health was called in to investigate. There were three main commonalities linking all victims. They'd all been adopted or were living in foster care. Their mothers had either died under suspicious circumstances or had disappeared without a trace. And all the children had a blood type that no one had ever seen. And it was this last one that had raised the big red flag that had brought the Agency running.

"All of the children were taken to a medical facility in the Agency's Chicago headquarters for observation," Arabella told me as I stared straight ahead, trying to take in all she was telling me.

Having been acquainted with the Agency for many years now, I could only imagine what they meant by "observation." God knows what those kids had endured.

"It was only when Merlin made inquiries in his efforts to help me that the rumors of these lost and forgotten children came to his attention," she continued. "And when it became clear that the small amount of fairy dust Merlin was able to procure was staving off my symptoms—at least temporarily—I made it my mission to help the children being held at the Agency."

"And so what did y'do?" I demanded, well acquainted with her iron will. "March right up the steps and demand t'see the person in charge?"

I felt her shrug next to me. "Something like that."

I smothered a smile, pride in my brave lass momentarily breaking through my fury and concern.

"Fortunately," she went on, "the new director of the Agency didn't toss me into one of their holding cells or demand that Al Addin lock me away in FMA prison for barging in and threatening some damned treaty between the FMA and the Agency. How in the hell was I supposed to know there was a treaty anyway? I'd only been here a few bleeding months!"

I turned my gaze toward her at this, not surprised to see her aura growing weaker with the level of her frustration.

"The Agency refused to let the children leave, of course," I filled in for her. There was no need for her to say it. These children were exactly the kind of chance to study our kind that the Agency had been looking for, even if the children were only half-Tale. They never would've walked away from that kind of opportunity just because some random—albeit adorably spunky—Tale asked them nicely. Or not so nicely. I can only imagine my brave lass barging in and demanding the children's release.

She grunted. "They gave me some cocked-up excuse about being responsible for the children's medical care and not wanting to take the risk of discharging them without a guarantee of the proper care."

"The Ordinaries are good at fabricating 'cocked-up' excuses to hide their fuckups," I muttered. "Trust me."

"Yeah, well, their attitude toward me changed when I assured them that fairy dust could slow the *fading*," she said. "They agreed not to turn me over to the FMA for trespassing and all the other bullshit charges if I helped them gather the mass quantities of fairy dust they'd need for the children. It all had to be kept hush-hush, of course, so as not to jeopardize the agreement."

I huffed. "Wouldn't have expected any less of 'em."

"I enlisted Merlin's assistance," she admitted. "I told him if he helped me, he'd get the chance to dive into pages and pages of medical records and other documents to help find an answer to save us all. He couldn't resist." She sighed, growing visibly weary. "Merlin's search was futile, as it turned out. But he did make an important discovery about the children's shared blood type: it perfectly matched that of your king, which was on file with the FMA's database."

I pulled a hand down my face. *Fucking hell.* The king had managed to keep himself out of all the Tale databases for nearly two centuries. But thanks to his unexpected sojourn in the hospital a few years earlier, his rather unique medical profile was now public.

"You should've informed the FMA," I told her, diverting the topic slightly. "Al Addin wouldn't have let this go on had he known."

"No one is supposed to know about it," Arabella insisted. "They said they would kill the children if we interfered. Or if I stopped delivering fairy dust. They have them booby-trapped in some way. Something about a 'kill switch' microchip embedded in their skin. If the kids leave the premises, it will trigger the switch and stop their hearts."

"Jesus Christ," I muttered, scrubbing the stubble along my jaw. "There's got to be a way. We can't leave those children—old or young—in there for the Agency to experiment on."

"We'll get them out," Arabella assured me. "As soon as we figure out a way to save them, we'll do what we have to."

My chest was growing increasingly tight the more I thought about what was happening. If these were, in fact, the king's offspring, I was duty-bound to protect them at any cost. And I'd be damned if anyone could keep me from doing my duty.

I wished Arabella had come to me sooner, had enlisted *my* help instead of Merlin's. Perhaps we already would've had a resolution to the dilemma—and she wouldn't be slowly dying, sacrificing what little vitality she had to try to save these children she'd only heard about in rumors.

"The search for the relics," I said, a gut-wrenching thought suddenly occurring to me. "It was never about saving you, was it, Arabella?"

She didn't immediately answer, but her silence told me what I needed to know before she said, "No."

"It won't work," I snapped, fear sparking my temper. "The legend states that a person has to possess them all to be immortal. They can't be spread out among the children. You can't save them all."

"I know!" she shouted. Then she took a deep breath and let it out slowly before adding, "But maybe I can save *one*. If I can save even *one* . . ."

I took her hand in mine, holding it gently, knowing the kind of hell that was weighing on her shoulders. I'd been there. "But which *one*, lass?"

"I don't know. Right now, I'm not even sure I can save *any* of them. Once I have all the relics, if the *fading* stops, then I'll figure it out. I'll figure out some way . . ." Her face fell, sorrow and hopelessness overwhelming her and swamping my senses. "My God, Gideon . . . How can I possibly *choose*? They're children!"

I pulled her into my arms, holding her against my chest. Smoothing her hair, kissing the top of her head, murmuring what words of comfort I could. Knowing damned well that it wasn't enough.

"I'll go to the king," I told her. "I'll persuade him to help. He will not refuse."

She pushed against my chest, pulling out of my embrace, her eyes wide. "But, Gideon, if you go now while you're disavowed—"

"Hush, now," I soothed, wiping tears from her cheeks. "Let me worry about that."

"If you insist upon going, I won't let you go alone," she vowed, stubborn as ever. "I'll go with you."

I scoffed. "Don't be daft, lass. I'm not about to let you stroll in there and risk the king's wrath."

"Oh, but it's fine for you to face his wrath alone?" she huffed. "You have no problem waltzing headlong into danger and leaving me at home to fret and worry and be the good little helpless woman, wringing her hands until your return, is that it?"

I sighed, savoring the taste of the foot I'd firmly lodged in my own mouth. "That's not what I meant—"

"Then I'm going and we'll not have another word about it," she spat, lifting her chin at that stubborn angle, ever defiant.

I shook my head, marveling at the iron will of my darling girl. She'd never been one to hide in the shadows and wait until danger had passed. Not my little love. I should've known better than to even suggest such a thing. "Then we'll have to be strategic about it," I relented, smothering a proud grin. "It won't do me any good if you're captured along with me."

A satisfied smile curved her lips and lit her eyes. "That's more like it."

I had just leaned forward to brush a playful kiss to her lips when she abruptly straightened, suddenly on alert. Regrettably, my kiss missed the mark, landing on her cheek instead. But before I could even groan in frustration, she was scrambling out of the car.

I threw open the door and joined her behind the shipping container where she'd taken cover. "There they are," she whispered, nodding toward the nondescript black armored truck from the fleet that the king used for all his shipments.

I narrowed my gaze, taking in the scene before me. Two of the king's guards got out of the truck and went around to the back to unload the cases of fairy dust that would be neatly stacked inside.

I knew from the incident reports I'd read that every time one of our transports had been attacked, the thefts had taken place sometime between when they were unloaded from the truck and when they were transferred to whatever was the next mode of transport. Hardly surprising. Tonight, the crates were to be loaded onto a plane that would be flying the shipment to the fairy clinic that served our kind in Alaska and half of Canada. Because of its remote location, that clinic only received shipments three times a year, as opposed to the monthly shipments most of our other North American clinics received, so it was even more imperative that this shipment make it.

"Have you ever seen the other thief?" I asked.

She shook her head. "I never take more than one crate," she assured me. "The person who steals the rest of it must come in after I'm already gone."

As I watched the guards moving the crates from the truck to the plane, I couldn't help grunting in disgust. It was no wonder that the transports were regularly attacked. The lackadaisical way in which the guards unloaded the crates made me want to march over there and crack some heads. Knowing full well the problems we'd been having, they should've had at least two guards on watch, keeping an eye on things as the others moved the crates. And there was no protective barrier, no spells shielding the transports or the guards.

"This is bullshit," I grumbled. "Incompetent idiot."

"Who do you mean?" Arabella asked.

"That bastard Reginald Mann," I spat. "I gave him specific instructions about how to improve security for the transports. He's disregarded every single one of them."

"I'm going to go down and have a closer look," Arabella whispered, gesturing toward the truck. Before I could respond, she had draped her invisibility cloak around her shoulders and was tiptoeing in the guards' direction.

I cursed under my breath, wishing I knew what spell her mother had used on that damned cloak so I could replicate it. Instead, all I could do was hold my position and wait. And hope that Arabella wouldn't do something foolish and give herself away.

Fortunately, I didn't have to wait long.

The guard had only managed to move about half the supply to the plane when a sleek, silver Porsche came racing toward them. The driver braked too fast, sending the car skidding and throwing up a cloud of dust. But the little maneuver was controlled, all for show.

I grunted, knowing who the driver was even before he got out.

Reginald strolled toward the guards, one hand nonchalantly tucked in the pocket of his slacks. The guards immediately halted and came to attention, treating the asshole like he was their commander instead of the queen's glorified errand boy.

Arrogant son of a bitch.

I could hear the murmurings of a conversation taking place between him and the guards, but even with my enhanced hearing ability, they were too far away for me to make out what they were saying. No doubt Reginald had decided to drop in on the guards unannounced to check their progress and make sure they didn't fuck up another transport. If the nervous expressions they wore were any indication, they'd been given one hell of a warning about what might happen to them if they failed.

Of course, if Reginald had wanted to ensure a night without incident, he would've chosen two more capable and experienced guards— not the two men who stood before him, shaking in their boots. These two had only been hired two months before, having been recruited from new arrivals in Make Believe at the behest of the queen. She'd felt our current guards were growing lazy and incompetent and insisted that we needed to increase our numbers to ensure the Seelie interests were adequately protected.

In that one regard we had agreed, but instead of leaving the hiring to me, she had once again depended upon Reginald's opinion. And here before me was the proof of his impeccable judge of character. Instead of hiring fierce warriors who would be loyal to the crown, he'd managed to find two of the most nervous, cowardly recruits I'd ever seen.

I shook my head, disgusted. Unfortunately, I was so intent on what was happening between Reginald and the guards that I didn't immediately see the two black SUVs until they were within a few yards of the transport.

I cursed under my breath, torn between holding back to watch how the scene played out so I could gather the intel I needed, or bolting forward to defend that which belonged to my king—protecting even that prick Reginald, if necessary.

But before I could do more than make note of my options, my course of action was decided for me when the SUVs came to a screeching halt and four armed gunmen in black suits leaped from the vehicles. A spray of bullets peppered the king's armored car, mowing down the guards before they'd even had time to register what'd happened.

My heart seizing with concern for Arabella's safety, I shifted, coming out within inches of one of the gunmen. Before he did more than register a startled look, I snatched his weapon from his loosened grasp and slammed the butt of the gun against his skull, then turned the weapon upon the two gunmen behind him, firing a single round into the forehead of each, dropping them before they had a chance to fire upon me.

The fourth gunman got lucky.

The bullet caught me in my left shoulder. I dimly registered the bone shattering as the pain exploded, momentarily clouding my vision. I raised the gun I held in my right hand, planning to put an end to the asshole, but his eyes suddenly bulged and he dropped to his knees.

Standing behind him was my darling girl, her eyes fierce and deadly, a bloodied knife still clutched in her hand. The moment our gazes met, she rushed toward me, pulling my uninjured arm over her shoulders, lending me her strength.

We walked over to the closest body, that of one of the armed men. With the toe of my boot, I rolled him over, getting a good look at him.

"These guys look like they're from the Agency," Arabella said. "Why the hell would they need to steal more dust when I've been stealing it for them?"

I sighed, beginning to understand what was going on. "They aren't from the Agency," I told her. "Someone just wanted it to look that way."

"Someone's trying to compromise the truce between the FMA and the Agency," she guessed.

I stepped away from her and crouched down beside the man at my feet, my heart sinking when I recognized his face. "Maybe," I told her. "But maybe they're just trying to cover their own asses and the Agency is a believable red herring."

"You know who's behind this," Arabella surmised.

I hated to admit it, but I was beginning to think I did. "This man is one of the king's guards. The traitor is within the king's household." I reached out and closed his eyelids, rage making my hand shake. I stood, cradling my injured arm as my gaze searched the field. "Where's Reginald?"

As if on cue, Reginald's Porsche roared to life. He gunned it in reverse, then whipped the car around and sped off, leaving another cloud of dust in his wake.

"Son of a bitch!" I growled. "I knew that bastard was dirty."

Arabella glanced at the departing car and then back at me. "That's Reginald?" she asked, gaping. "That's who you think is behind this?" When I nodded warily, she let out a bitter laugh. "I knew I should've shanked that asshole when I first saw him!"

I blinked at her, surprised by her vehemence. "You know Reginald Mann—the queen's attaché?"

"The queen's attaché, is he now?" She laughed again, shaking her head. "His name's not Reginald Mann, Gideon." She clenched her fists at her sides and hissed, "*That* sorry excuse for a Tale is Sir Guy of Gisbourne."

Chapter 19

"You're healing nicely," Arabella informed me, inspecting the exit wound on my back with gentle fingers while I sat dutifully on the edge of the vanity in Merlin's bathroom. "I don't think you'll even have a scar. But maybe we should take you to a clinic—or Trish—just to be sure."

I suppressed a smile. My Tale metabolism would've knitted the bones together and healed my wound within a day or two, most likely, but my fairy blood made me heal even more quickly than the average Tale. I wasn't surprised at all to hear that the bones were completely mended and my flesh now nearly unmarred.

"I'm sure it'll be fine. It hardly aches at all." When she set aside the bloodied washcloth, I took her hand and pulled her around from where she stood beside me and then drew her toward me until she was standing between my thighs. "Thank you for caring for me."

"*Thank you?*" she repeated, incredulous. "Don't be ridiculous. You never need thank me for caring for you." She took my face in her hands. "I *love* you, Gideon."

I bent forward and pressed my lips to hers, intending only to give her a tender kiss, but I should've known better. The moment I captured her mouth, I gathered her into my arms, luxuriating in the sweet honeysuckle scent of her as it swamped my senses.

She slipped her arms around my neck, pulling me closer, her lips parting to draw my kiss in deeper. It was several minutes before she gently pulled away and took my hand. "Come on, love, let's get you to bed."

I let her lead me into the bedroom, trailing behind enough that I could get a read on her. She was exhausted, her aura flickering and *fading* alarmingly. She desperately needed to rest, to let her body do its best to heal her. She put on a good show, could've fooled perhaps anyone else but me.

"You're the one that needs to be in bed," I told her gently, not wanting to offend by rebuffing her tender care of me.

She whirled around with a forced smile, intending to argue, but when she saw my eyes, she slapped her hands on her hips. "You're not playing fair. Can you not just take my word that I'm fine?"

"I could," I replied, taking her by the shoulders. "But what good would that do?"

She closed her eyes for a moment and heaved a sigh. "It would let me pretend that I'll *be* fine, that we have all the time in the world. I can't bear the thought of being parted from you again, Gideon, but the thought of the pain you'll feel when I go . . . It breaks my heart."

I pulled her close and wrapped my arms around her. "Very well, then," I relented. "For tonight, we have forever."

She lifted her face, her eyes glistening with unshed tears. "Tell me what forever will be like."

"We'll have a home nestled in the woods with enough land for us to go exploring together and never tire of the adventures we'll share," I told her. "We'll have an archery range and perhaps I'll eventually become a decent shot."

She chuckled, knowing well my lack of skill with a bow and arrow. "There may be hope for you yet."

I smoothed her hair. "Perhaps."

A single tear made its way to her cheek. "And will there be children?"

I wiped the tear away with my thumb and nodded. "As many as y'like. They'll be our pride and joy. We'll fill our home with laughter and love, Arabella, and our wee ones will want for nothing. They'll always know how much their parents adore them. And when they have nightmares, we'll hold them in our arms and sing them lullabies until they nod off again, secure in the knowledge that they've nothing t'fear."

"Will we grow old together?"

I somehow managed a smile. "If you like. But it'll take centuries. And every night, we'll curl up by the fire together and just enjoy the warmth and light we share. I'll hold you in my arms until you fall asleep, and then I'll carry you to our bed where I'll guard you through the night and keep you safe with my very last breath."

"That sounds perfect," she said, her voice tight with emotion. She reached up to lightly caress my cheek. "But you forgot one thing."

I lifted a single brow. "Did I now? And what was that?"

Her fingertips trailed down the edge of my jaw, along my throat to my bare chest. "We'll make love every night until, too exhausted to go on, we'll collapse in each other's arms."

My hand slid up her back until I reached the zipper on her dress. I pulled it down slowly, my gaze holding hers. "I didn't forget."

The dress slipped from her shoulders and pooled at her feet. A moment later, the rest of her clothes followed. Her hands roamed over my back as I pressed kisses to her shoulder, the curve of her neck.

"You should be resting," I murmured against her skin as I pressed kisses down the valley between her breasts, my knowledge of what she *wanted* at war with my concern for what she *needed.*

Her fingers slid into my curls as I took one of her rosy nipples into my mouth. "This is all I need," she said, breathless.

I took my time, lavishing my attention upon one breast before moving to the other. When she moaned softly, needing more, I eased her down onto the bed, now pressing a line of kisses down her belly, along her ribs, the curve of her hips. When I reached her thighs, I kissed the soft skin there, loving the way it made her writhe in antic- ipation, but I moved lower until I reached her knee, nipping at it gen- tly with my teeth. She gasped my name and reflexively tried to draw away from the unexpected intensity of the pleasure that little nip caused.

I smiled as I shifted to the other thigh, working my way back to- ward the center of her. When I reached the heat of her sex, I flicked my tongue, teasing, testing. She arched toward me with a moan, clutching my hair in both fists.

This time, I sank farther in, my tongue caressing, exploring, loving how she gasped and panted, writhing against my mouth, her body begging me for what she needed when her voice was struck mute.

Again, I took my time, drawing out the pleasure until she had no choice but to give in to it. Her loud cry of release was the sweetest music to my ears. I grasped her hips, driving her through the climax and not letting up until she collapsed. I drew away just long enough to kick off my jeans, then settled atop her. Her muscles were still contracting when I gently joined our bodies.

She hooked her legs around the back of my thighs and grasped my hips, moving with me in slow, languid rhythm. I braced myself on my elbows, peering down the length of her body to watch as we moved together, my chest growing tight with emotion. But then Arabella grasped the nape of my neck and pulled me down to receive her kiss and I sank into her arms, losing myself in the *now* and pushing from my mind the horrible, gut-wrenching realization of what my life was going to be like without her.

I disconnected the call and let my head fall back against the headboard, frustration creeping under my skin until I wanted to claw at it.

Arabella stirred on the bed next to me, having finally curled up beside me to rest after making love for most of the night. She hadn't been eager to sleep, instead wanting to take advantage of every moment we had together, but she'd been exhausted, pale and wan, and even the fairy dust I'd given her hadn't improved her situation, so she'd at last relented, but only when I'd promised to stay at her side.

I smoothed her hair tenderly, not wanting to wake her but unable to resist touching her, reminding myself that she was indeed by my side again. For now. The knowledge that she was *fading* faster and faster weighed heavily on my heart, crushing me to the point I couldn't breathe when I thought on it too much.

I squeezed my eyes shut and forced the panic and hopelessness away, shaking my head in denial. I *would not* lose her. I would find a way. I refused to accept the fact that she could slip away from me again at any moment. There were only two relics remaining. We'd find them.

And then she would be mine forever—if she would have me. And whether that was with the benefit of a formal union between us, or merely an understanding that we would never be apart, didn't matter a damn to me. All that mattered was that she would never again want for anything, and she would know the strength and depth of my love in every word, in every glance we shared.

She grimaced in her sleep, rolling onto her back as the pain of *fading* gripped her. It was worse when she slept, when her guard was down. I bent forward and pressed a kiss to her forehead.

When she seemed to quiet a little, I turned my attention back to the phone, dialing the king's number once more. This time it rang twice before being sent to voice mail.

I sighed and sat up, swinging my legs over the side of the bed and resting my head in my hands. I had to reach him, had to warn him of the treachery under his roof. If I couldn't get him to talk to me by phone, I'd have to figure out another way to get the information to him.

My phone rang, the sudden sound startling me. I glanced at Arabella, relieved to see the ringtone hadn't woken her. "This is Gideon," I whispered, quickly slipping from the room and into Merlin's living room.

"Why the hell are you whispering?"

I grinned. "Well, good morning, Red, to what do I owe the pleasure of this call?"

She hesitated for a beat. "I wish I could say I was calling to give you some good news."

I ran a hand through my hair and strolled toward the picture window that opened out into a view of the wooded park across the street. "It must be pretty bad if you're calling *this* early. Might as well give it to me straight."

"The Huntsman's gone."

I squinted into the early morning sun, finding it hard to believe I'd heard her right. I cursed soundly under my breath, then said with a huff, "So soon?"

"Sorry, Gideon," she replied. "Last time I saw him, he was safely locked away in an FMA holding cell. Someone broke into the cell in the middle of the night—blew a hole in the freakin' wall."

"And no one heard anything?" I demanded, finding it hard to believe an explosion large enough to blow a hole in a wall of concrete and steel wouldn't have raised a couple of eyebrows.

She cleared her throat. "The guards at the jail heard the explosion and went to investigate," she said, her voice monotone, calm—as if she was delivering an update to the press and not to an old friend. "From what we can surmise, there was a brief struggle—so brief that none of the guards was able to send up an alarm. We found their ashes this morning when the next shift came in to relieve them."

"Fucking hell," I breathed.

"Yeah."

I pulled a hand down my face, feeling responsible for the Tales who'd lost their lives guarding a prisoner I'd handed them, a prisoner who'd assured me we couldn't hold him. I'd signed the death warrants of those men as surely as if I'd put my signature on paper.

"Did they have families?" I asked, my voice tight.

"One did," Red told me, her tone sympathetic. I could tell she knew what was going through my head. "The others were alone in the Here and Now. The FMA was pretty much all they had."

I walked toward a nearby easy chair and dropped down into it, covering my eyes with my hand as guilt washed over me anew. "He told me he'd be out in no time," I said. "I thought he was just blowing me shit, trying to sound tough. I never thought . . ."

"I know," Red assured me. "We're gonna catch the bastard, Gid. Count on it."

"Any idea who aided him?" I questioned, wondering if Reginald would be brash enough to go bust the Huntsman out of FMA jail after the fairy dust theft had gone down so badly. "The Huntsman didn't have any magic. Who do you think broke him out?"

"No clue," she said on a sigh, as frustrated as I was. "The security footage was completely jacked up."

Shit.

If I was going to go to the king and inform him that the queen's most trusted confidant was a traitor, it would've been helpful to have something more than my word to go on. Making such an accusation was a step below accusing the queen herself. And I sure as shit didn't want to get anything going with my lady. She'd have no qualms about sending me to the Tribunal for another go-around.

"I'll see what I can find," I finally told Red. "I can visit the jail, send out a search spell. Maybe we can track him down that way."

"Already tried. One of our Investigators on the scene used a spell that should've lit up his tracks like a neon sign. But it was no good. If not for the big-ass hole in my holding cell, it would've looked like the guy just vanished into thin air."

Better and better.

Once again someone had known how to cover their tracks to throw us off their trail. And it was seriously pissing me off.

"Let me know if you get any leads," I told her.

"You got it."

"And hey, Red?"

"Yeah?"

I paused, hating that I needed to ask yet another favor of a friend. "While I've got you on the phone, could you see what you can find out about a Tale named Reginald Mann?"

"Yeah, sure," she said. I could hear her typing as she spoke. "Who is this Reginald guy anyway?"

"One of the king's employees," I told her, my tone clipped.

"Here we go," she said. "Search results coming up now. Hang on a sec." There was a pause. "Huh. That's weird."

"Did you find him?"

"You could say that," she muttered. More clacking on her keyboard and then, "When did this guy work for the king?"

"He's currently employed by him," I explained. "He's been there for about three years, I guess."

"Yeah, well, your king might want to do a better background check next time," she said. "Unless he's into hiring ghosts."

I straightened in my chair. "What?"

"Reginald A. Mann," she read. "Arrived in the Here and Now on October first, nineteen-twelve. Rhyme. Candlestick maker by trade. Went missing three years ago when his candle shop in the mall was broken into and ransacked. Crime scene evidence pointed to a robbery gone bad, although employees were not able to identify anything that was stolen and no money was taken. There was no blood found at the scene, no trace of the perp. Mann never resurfaced and is presumed dead."

"Is there a picture of him on the file?"

"Yep," she said. "I'll text it to you, but you didn't get it from me, you feel me?"

"Understood."

"Okay, it's on its way," she informed me. "So, you and Arabella gonna be at Trish's this afternoon? Lavender's flight should be in around four o'clock."

I glanced at the steampunk-style clock hanging from the ceiling in Merlin's living room. It was seven o'clock in the morning now. If I could get in to see the king shortly after darkness fell and get the hell out, we'd be there in time for a late dinner.

"Yeah, we'll be there sometime this evening."

"Evening?" Red asked, her tone edged with suspicion.

"I'm sure Lav will want to rest," I told her. Even though Red had sent the FMA's private jet to pick up Lavender and Seth, it was still a few hours' flight. Considering I was going to ask Lav to perform magic that would be difficult even for her, giving her some time to get settled seemed like the gentlemanly thing to do even if I hadn't needed the extra time to try to get an audience with the king.

"Okay, I'll buy that," Red said, although her tone still held a hint of doubt.

My phone chimed in my ear, alerting me I had a text. "Hey Red, if for any reason I don't make it, though, look after Arabella for me, will you?"

Before she could ask any questions of me, I hung up and checked the text, pulling up the photo of Reginald Mann. I wasn't entirely surprised when the photo revealed a pudgy, middle-aged man with a receding hairline and a jolly smile. He looked more like somebody's favorite uncle than a silver-tongued lothario who'd managed to worm his way into the royal household.

"You're up early."

I glanced up to see Merlin strolling into the room, already showered and dressed in jeans, a Metallica T-shirt, and Converse sneakers.

His hair had returned to its natural brown and was newly shorn but still disheveled. I had to do a double take, almost not recognizing him.

"So are you," I replied. "What's with the getup?"

He shoved his hands in his pockets as he came toward me. "It was time for a new look," he said with a shrug. "Boring, I know, but those leather pants chafe my dangly bits."

I chuckled. "I'll take your word for it."

He jerked his head toward the phone in my hand. "Who were you talking to? Didn't sound like good news."

I ran a hand over my hair. "The Huntsman escaped last night."

Merlin blew out a frustrated sigh. "You should've killed him when you had the chance."

"I'm not a murderer, Merlin," I snapped. "If I'd killed the Huntsman, I wouldn't have been any better than the bastard himself."

He shrugged. "Perhaps. But does that really matter at this point, Gideon?"

I narrowed my eyes at him. "What are you getting at?"

He dropped down on the sofa and propped his feet up on the coffee table I'd magically restored when I'd returned from the debacle at the air strip. He regarded me solemnly for a long moment before folding his hands across his abdomen. "You and I have a great deal of blood upon our hands, old friend. And, really, what's one more insignificant drop upon the stain of your conscience?"

I met his gaze and held it for a long moment. "Every drop is significant, Merlin. You once believed that as well."

He nodded. "That I did. And maybe someday I'll believe it again. But that would require a measure of hope I most certainly lack at present."

It had been a very long time since Merlin and I had had a serious conversation. I had buried my emotions in duty; Merlin had buried his by shirking it.

"What would restore that hope, Merlin?" I asked.

He gave me a sardonic grin. "Well, I have no Arabella to magically reappear and save me from myself, if that's what you're getting at," he drawled. "The only woman I ever loved didn't give a whit about me. I'd say we can pretty much take love off the table, eh? So maybe someday I'll find an actual *purpose* again—beyond levitating half-naked assistants and making white tigers disappear in obscenely overpriced venues, that is."

"I may have a job for you then," I told him. "And, believe me, my friend, it's one of the most important duties with which I can entrust you."

Merlin pulled a face. "Best get someone else to do it then."

I chuckled. "I believe this will be right up your alley." When he gave me a wary look, I grinned. "I need a diversion."

His brows lifted, and I knew I had him. "What kind of diversion?"

"I need to sneak into the king's house to warn him about a traitor in his midst and explain everything about Arabella," I said. "I can't reach him, but I might be able to persuade one of his daughters to let me in."

His feet dropped to the ground and he leaned forward, light dancing in his eyes. "Daughters? How many daughters?"

"There are two visiting at the moment."

"Are they pretty?" he asked, regarding me out of the corner of his eye. "Or is this one of those *take one for the team* moments?"

"They're quite beautiful," I assured him. "And one of them is rather . . . bookish."

At this he straightened, a broad smile growing on his face. "Well then, when do we leave?"

I gave him a curt nod, glad to have his help. "As soon as night falls."

"Like hell I'm staying here!"

"Arabella, please," I begged, following along behind her as she paced angrily around Merlin's flat that evening after having slept most of the day. "I need you to stay with Trish and Nicky."

She suddenly whirled around, advancing on me with her index finger aimed at my face. "You promised you wouldn't go without me!" she raged. "We agreed to do this together!"

I stood my ground, refusing to retreat. "Things have changed—"

"Oh, they certainly have!" she spat, crossing her arms over her chest and turning her head away at that stubborn angle I knew so well.

Frustrated, I took her face in my hands and forced her to look up at me. "The Huntsman has escaped," I informed her through clenched teeth. "And I could very well be going to my execution. I need to know you're safe."

She pressed her lips together in an angry line. "I won't let you do this alone."

"I won't be alone," I assured her. "I'll have Merlin."

She made a noise of disgust in the back of her throat and tried to turn away again, but I kept her where she was, determined to make my reasons known.

"Arabella," I said, my voice stern. "I would walk through the flames of hell with you, lass. There's no one in this world or any other that I trust more. And that's why I need you here." When she opened her mouth to protest again, I interrupted, "Because who else can I count on to come to my rescue if I get into trouble?"

She narrowed her eyes at me, wondering if I was playing her. "Well, you *are* taking Merlin with you, so the odds of your getting into trouble *will* increase exponentially. . . ."

"Hey!" Merlin called out from the other room. "I resent that!"

Arabella gave me a pointed look and raised her brows expectantly.

I heaved a sigh. "Fine. You can come along with us to help create a diversion, but you *are not* going inside with me. Is that clear?"

She gave me a sharp nod. "Fair enough." She then grinned and batted her long, dark lashes at me. "As you said, who'll swoop in and save your ass when Merlin mucks it up?"

"And you're up to it?" I asked, my pleasure at seeing the rosiness of excitement in her cheeks dissipating when I realized her skin was hot to the touch. I smoothed my thumbs over her cheeks. "You've got a fever now, lass."

She blinked at me, her eyes glassier than they'd been the night before. "I feel fine. Just a bit warm is all. Now, stop your worrying." She flashed her dimpled grin and bounded away, excited for our impending adventure. As she passed through the doorway she paused and peeked around the doorjamb at me, her smile growing. "Coming, love?"

I sighed and rubbed the back of my neck, hoping like hell that I was making the right decision.

Chapter 20

Arabella's eyes narrowed as she scrutinized the wall that surrounded the king's property. "They've no doubt doubled the protection along the wall since the last time I was here," she murmured. "Do you sense anything that would keep me out, Gideon?"

To my surprise, the protection spell to guard against those who would harm the king and his family had not been altered since my departure, but the barrier that would specifically keep *me* from entering was new. I'd called both Ivy and Lily on the drive over, hoping that I could reach one of them and try to persuade them to let me in, but hadn't been able to get in contact with either. A shitload of good it was going to do me to have Arabella and Merlin causing a diversion if I couldn't make it past the fucking gates.

"I can't sense anything at all," I admitted, much to my chagrin. "The spell to keep me out blocks *everything* from my senses. Whoever put it in place did one hell of a job."

"Well," Merlin mused, "it's been a few centuries since I walked into an ambush. About time for another cock-up."

I sent an acerbic glance his way. "If you have any better ideas, I'm open to them."

He held up his hands and shook his head.

Arabella adjusted her quiver and tossed her bow to Merlin. "Hold this."

"Where are you off to?" Merlin questioned.

Arabella motioned me forward. "Come on, love, give us a boost."

I didn't even bother trying to suppress my grin as I linked my fingers together and lunged forward.

"Just like old times, eh?" she said with a wink. Then she ran toward me, leaping up onto my thigh at the last moment and placing her other foot in my hands. The moment her foot hit my palms, I pitched her into the air. Even in her weakened state, she flipped gracefully in the air, her cloak flaring out around her, and nailed a perfect landing on the top of the wall. She swept a dramatic bow, then motioned to Merlin.

He chuckled softly and tossed her bow up to her, receiving a playful salute in response. She pulled her hood up over her head and in the next moment she was gone, having dropped down on the other side of the wall.

"Now what?" Merlin whispered.

I shrugged. "Now we wait. It should only take a few minutes for her to do a quick check of the perimeter and determine how many guards we're up against."

Merlin gave me an irritated look. "Well, *obviously*. Give me a *bit* of credit, will you? I meant, what are we planning after she returns?" He rubbed his hands together in anticipation. "When do I meet the lovely ladies of the house?"

I cleared my throat. "About that . . ."

He advanced on me, wagging his finger in my face. "Oh, no you don't. Don't you dare go back on our arrangement. The only reason I came is because you promised I'd get a crack at the king's daughters."

"I promised no such thing," I shot back. "And if you touch either one of them, the only crack you'll get is one in your skull when I give you a sound thumping."

Merlin shook his head. "False pretenses. I would like the record to reflect that I was brought here under false pretenses."

"What record?" I asked. "There's no record."

"The record of our friendship," he explained.

"No one keeps a record like that, Merlin."

"Well, they should," he grumbled, crossing his arms over his chest. "You could be interfering with my ability to meet the love of my life, Gideon. This is the ultimate cock block, mate."

I took a few steps back and regarded the top of the wall, distracted from Merlin's continued bellyaching by my concern for Arabella. She rarely needed more than a moment to get the lay of the land. "What's taking so long?"

"Patience, patience, love."

I spun around to see Arabella leaning against the wall, arms crossed, her eyes sparkling with amusement. "You're lucky the guards took off to deal with some kind of commotion at the house. You two squabble like an old married couple."

"What commotion at the house?" I asked, ignoring her comment and Merlin's indignant protest. "What's going on?"

She shoved off the wall and sauntered toward us. "Oh, just a little message for an old friend."

I regarded her out of the corner of my eye, having no doubt which "old friend" she meant. "Arabella . . . What did you do?"

"Old friend?" Merlin demanded. "What old friend?"

Ignoring us both, Arabella continued, "Only a handful of guards are positioned along the wall. They've concentrated most of their protection on the house itself. The only way you're going to get into the house is either by shifting in or sneaking in when Merlin and I draw them away."

I cursed under my breath. Neither of those options was any good if I couldn't make it past the security at the wall. I'd worry about the rest once I got inside. "Did you find any weakness in the protection spell at all? Was there any way of getting me beyond the wall?"

She shook her head. "None that I could see."

"Damn it," I hissed, running a hand through my hair. "I've got to—" My head snapped up as I suddenly caught the scent of lilies of the valley.

"Gideon?" Arabella asked, picking up on my wariness. "What is it?"

I pressed my lips together and shook my head, tamping down my irritation. Then before our intruder could react, I shifted, wrapping my arms around her and shifting us back to where I'd stood a split second before.

Dressed in a long black form-fitting dress and platform boots, the woman had hidden easily among the shadows, but a flower fairy's scent was not so easy to disguise, especially from another fairy. "Let me go!" she demanded, throwing her head back in an effort to connect with my nose. Fortunately, I was tall enough that she missed and only managed to nail my chest.

"Who the hell is this?" Arabella demanded, gesturing toward the struggling woman in my arms.

I winced as I caught a kick to the shin. "This," I groaned, "is Lily Seelie."

Lily sagged against my hold. "Gideon," she said on a relieved sigh. "It's you." But her relief was short-lived. In the next moment, she turned to look over her shoulder and peg me with an angry look. "For shit's sake, Gid, you didn't have to jump me. You could've just asked me to come out."

"And you could've answered your phone, my lady," I ground out, still pissed about the kick in the shins.

"And risk my stepmother's wrath?" she replied. "I think not. That woman's a raging bitch."

I heard Merlin chuckle. "Oh, I like this one, Gideon."

Lily turned her leaf-green eyes on Merlin. "Yeah, pretty boy? Who the fuck are you? And why should I give a shit?"

"And such a pretty mouth," Merlin teased with a cockeyed grin. He then turned that grin on me and gestured toward Lily. "*Please* tell me this is the 'bookish' one, Gideon. I think I'm in love."

"Dream on, half-wit," Lily muttered.

"Half-wit?" Merlin scoffed. "I'll have you know—"

"Behave, Lily," I interrupted, wrapping a quick binding spell around her and setting her gently away from me, "and I'll release you momentarily. I just need to talk to you."

She lifted her chin and shook back her long, black-streaked white hair, giving Merlin the once-over before turning her gaze back to me. "You don't need to talk to me," she shot back. "You just need me to let you in. So what do you say we cut the bullshit?"

I grinned, having always liked the king's defiant daughter. "Fair enough. How'd you know?"

"I didn't," she admitted, flapping her hands as much as the binding spell would allow her to move. "But as you've been blowing up my phone all day, I was hoping you had something bat-shit crazy in mind. So, what's the plan?"

"Just let me in," I told her. "That's it. Then I'll slip in and see if I can reason with your father."

Lily gave me a bored look. "You've got to be kidding me. You're a total badass, and all you've got planned is a little chat with Dad? Seriously? There's not going to be a battle or *anything*?"

"I'm going to cause a diversion," Merlin chimed in, bouncing a little on his toes and grinning at Lily like a love-struck schoolboy.

She sent an annoyed glance his way. "Good for you, skippy." She turned her attention back to me. "Now, if you don't mind—"

"There will most likely be explosions," Merlin interrupted.

Lily's head snapped back toward him, clearly intrigued by the possibility. "Really?"

"No!" I interjected, wagging my finger at Merlin. "There *won't* be any explosions! Summon up some dragon's breath or something. But don't blow up *anything*, is that clear?"

Merlin peeked around me at Lily and shrugged an apology. "It was worth a shot."

"What about you?" Lily said, jerking her chin at Arabella, her gaze softening, no doubt picking up on Arabella's waning aura. Her voice was gentle, slightly pitying even, when she asked, "What are you planning?"

Arabella forced a smile. "Whatever it takes to make sure my man gets inside."

I extended my hand to Arabella and drew her toward me, pressing a kiss to her forehead, alarmed to find it was burning to the touch. "Bella," I murmured, "if you want—"

Arabella pushed away and strode to Lily's side. "What do you say we get this party started, eh? Gideon, love, would you mind releasing my lady?"

Lily cast a look toward me, her eyes filled with sympathy. I glanced away, not willing to admit that Arabella's situation was as dire as I knew it to be. I refused to mourn her again before I'd even lost her. For as long as I still drew breath, there was hope. We were two items away from having all of Arthur Pendragon's relics restored to Arabella's possession. I had to believe that once we had those in hand, we'd find a way to keep her—and my king's children—alive. We had to.

The four of us stood in the center of my sitting room, looking at the map of the grounds that I'd produced from my temporal cache. Lily tapped a room at the center of the house. "This is where I saw Dad last," she told me. "That was earlier today when you called him and got me instead. He's been keeping to himself a lot lately and rarely leaves the room, not even to dine. When you called, I'd just brought him a tray of food to try to persuade him to eat *something*. Anyway, I'm sure if you can get that far, you'll find him there."

I nodded then turned my attention to Arabella and Merlin. "Once you've drawn the guards away, I'll slip inside to see the king. You two take the car and get the hell out of here. Lily can make sure you get away safely."

Arabella shook her head. "No way I'm leaving you here."

I took hold of her shoulders. "Even if I insist upon it and extract your solemn vow that you'll let Merlin take you to Trish, you'll stay anyway, won't you?"

She shrugged. "Odds are."

I sighed, wishing that just *once* the stubborn woman I loved so well would do what I asked. "Fine. Come back here to my home, then. I'll block all but you three from entering. You should at least be safe here. But if I'm not back within the hour, promise me you'll leave without me."

"If you're not back within the hour, we're going to come in after you," Arabella insisted.

My gaze flicked to Merlin, understanding passing between us. He gave me an almost imperceptible nod, assuring me he'd look after Arabella in my absence.

When we stepped out into the darkness, Merlin took a deep

breath, pulling the night air into his lungs and letting it out with a satisfied grin. After years of performing parlor tricks on stage for his audience, he was about to unleash the true power he had mastered.

It was about damned time.

"Stand back, darling," he said to Lily as he spread his arms. "Prepare to be amazed."

"Dazzle me, oh great one," she drawled, rolling her eyes.

Merlin began an incantation, his voice deep, guttural, as the spell built from within him. As he spoke, the mists began to roll in, wispy tendrils of fog gathering along the grass, churning as they traveled over the lawn, growing thicker with each word. At first I thought Merlin was merely calling forth a veil of fog to shield their activities as they prepared for a larger diversion, but then a sound like rolling thunder rumbled in the distance.

I sent a startled glance his way. "You're joking."

Merlin's brows shot up. "You wanted a diversion. Well, I can't think of a better diversion than a dragon."

As if on cue, the beast swept low over our heads, the downdraft from its massive wings nearly knocking us off our feet.

Lily whirled around to face Merlin, her eyes wide, a broad grin curving her lips. "You've called an *actual* dragon?"

Merlin shrugged. "Well, not an *actual* dragon. The only real one is about an hour away, as the dragon flies. You see, they're rather in short supply in the Here and Now, darling." He leaned toward her conspiratorially. "But it's a smashing illusion, wouldn't you say?"

"My stepmother is going to lose her freaking mind," Lily murmured. Then she laughed—one of the only laughs I'd ever heard from her in the many years of our association. "Well, come on," she said, grabbing Merlin's hand and dragging him after her. "This I've *got* to see."

I tilted my head to one side, watching the two of them disappear into the fog. *Interesting.*

"I guess I'll head to the house and cause a bit of mischief," Arabella said with forced cheerfulness.

I pulled her into my arms for a brief kiss. "Be careful."

She patted me on the chest. "Come now, love, you know me."

Before I could respond, she gave me a playful swat on the ass and pulled her hood over her hair, vanishing once more. In the distance I heard the chaos coming from the house as the guards burst into the yard to defend their king's home from the dragon they believed to be attacking.

I crept through the fog toward the great house, not trusting myself to shift inside just yet. A few moments later, I heard car alarms going off in the garage and the shouts of the house staff as they rushed to see what in the hell else was going on.

Apparently, Arabella had struck again.

"That's my girl," I muttered. And then I shifted, hoping like hell I wasn't heading straight to my doom.

Chapter 21

When I slipped into the king's study, I was surprised to see the man I'd thought to be imperturbable slumped in his chair, his forehead resting on the palm of his hand, eyes squeezed shut in a grimace of pain and sorrow that I'd only seen on his face twice before in our long association. Although the cacophony outside was faint in this part of the house, the chaos could still be heard, and yet it didn't seem to register with my lord.

I cleared my throat, politely announcing my arrival. Startled out of his thoughts, he snapped up his head, his expression morphing from fury at being disturbed to what I can only describe as relief.

"Gideon, my boy," he breathed, his voice tight. "How did you get in?"

I took a hesitant step forward. "I persuaded Lily that I must speak with you and she let me beyond the barrier."

The king got to his feet and strode toward me. My heart pounded as I prepared to meet his wrath. But, to my astonishment, instead of striking me dead for disobeying his order to stay away, the king gathered me into his embrace for a brief, fatherly hug. He then set me at arm's length, searching my face with eyes that brimmed with emotion. "Is it really you? Have you returned, my boy, even upon pain of death?"

I nodded, concerned that he'd perhaps lost his mind in my absence. "Yes, sire."

A smile broke over his face. "Loyal to the last," he said, his pride in me so powerful, the intensity of it warmed my skin where he still grasped my arms. "I knew you'd return. I *knew* it."

I frowned at him, utterly confused. "Sire, if you'd wished me to return, all you had to do was command it. I never would've stayed away at all had you not wished it."

At this, he heaved a mournful sigh. "Oh, my boy. My dear boy. I never wished you to stay away. I had to keep you away from here for your own safety."

My brows shot up. "Pardon?"

He released me and went back to his chair, his feet dragging with each step. "Gideon, it is time you and I had a conversation. It's one I should've had with you long ago, but have put off for my own reasons—mostly selfish ones." He gestured toward the chair across from his desk. "Please."

"I'm afraid I have no idea what you're talking about, sire," I informed him, taking the seat he'd indicated. "Why would I need protecting?"

He smiled, rather sadly. "Oh, dear boy. *Everything* I've done where you're concerned was to protect you." When I opened my mouth to question him, he held up a hand to silence me. "Do you remember the day we met at the falls?"

I nodded. "How could I forget? You placed your bonds upon me, forced me into servitude."

The king's head tilted to one side as he regarded me for a moment. "And what would you have done had my men not apprehended you?"

"I would've followed my love to her death," I told him, knowing even as I said it that such an impulsive move would've been foolish and melodramatic, but we were Tales. Melodrama was rather a requirement.

"Precisely so," the king concurred. "And I simply could not allow that. I saw something extraordinary in you, Gideon—something you failed to see in yourself. I was not about to let you throw that away, especially as you were the last of your kind. I owed it to you, to your people, to protect you from yourself."

I blinked at him, astonished by his arrogance. Although his intention was noble, to presume that he was the one to decide my fate infuriated me. I had to avert my gaze, hide the anger no doubt raging there. But my king knew me all too well.

"It might not have been my place," he said as if I'd spoken my thoughts aloud, "but I had other reasons as well."

I sat back, spreading my hands and trying unsuccessfully to keep the edge of anger out of my voice. "Do tell."

"Let us go back a bit then, shall we?" the king said. "To my own youth."

I gestured for him to continue.

"I once had a sister I adored," he began. "She was beautiful, kind, intelligent—and her gift for magic was extraordinary. We were quite close, inseparable. As she was younger than I by two years, I felt it my duty to protect her. Never was there a more doting brother. But then one day she mysteriously fell ill. Desperate to find a cure to save her, I cast a spell upon her that changed her world forever, kept her from living a normal life. I didn't see the harm in such a solution— after all, I'd saved her life. But she was furious and refused to forgive me. She would rather have had a normal life for whatever time she had left than to be forced into a life she hated. She left home and never returned."

"I'm terribly sorry," I told him sincerely. I certainly knew the pain of losing those closest to me.

He offered me a grateful smile. "I kept watch over her from afar over the years, determined to continue protecting her whether she wanted my help or no. But she hardly needed me. She was quite powerful in her own right."

He fell quiet for a long moment, prompting me to say, "And yet . . ."

"Well, it seems my love for my sister led me to compound my original mistake by making yet another," he replied, his smile masking the pain I could feel emanating from him. "One day, an old friend came to me, requesting a favor. And, instead of granting his request myself, I sent him to seek my sister's assistance, knowing her magic bent more toward the elegant than mine. I thought perhaps sending my friend to her would help her see how much I still thought of her, how much I loved her."

My brows lifted. "And your friend harmed her?"

"Oh, no," the king informed me. "He fell in love with her."

"But you didn't approve?" I guessed.

The king leaned back in his chair, folding his hands over his abdomen. "It wasn't a matter of my approving or disapproving. He was certainly a man worthy of her love. And she was deeply in love with him in return. But so was his wife."

"Ah." I nodded. "I can see how that would be problematic."

"Too right." The king pulled a hand down his face. "There were other complications as well . . . My sister bore a daughter. A beautiful girl, so like her mother. I managed to slip in one night while they were sleeping and sneak a peek at the child." He smiled wistfully. "My own little Poppy wasn't much older than the wee slip of a thing I cooed over in her cradle. They would've been playmates under different circumstances, I think."

"What happened?" I asked, bringing him out of his musings. "Were your sister and her lover ever able to be together as a family?"

Sorrow clouded the king's eyes. "No. My sister's lover visited as often as he was able, but he had great responsibilities elsewhere that kept him away."

The king rose to his feet and poured himself a drink, knocking it back and pouring another before he returned to his seat. His scowl deepened as the memories of what he'd done pressed heavily upon him.

"Sire?" I prompted after several moments of silence. "Would you prefer to be alone?"

The king shook his head. "No, my boy. It's time you knew the whole of it. I've kept too much to myself for far too long."

I waited patiently for him to continue, curious how any of this story affected me.

He took a swig of his drink and set the glass down too hard, sloshing the amber liquid onto the desk. "In my arrogance, Gideon, I assumed I could fix everything, engineer a solution that would bring happiness to all. What an idiot I was! I assured my friend that I could clear the way for him to be with my sister. I would simply assume a name and identity and woo his wife, convince her that she didn't love him, that she loved only me."

"But you were already married to Mab," I pointed out.

He laid a finger aside his nose. "Aye, there's the rub. I doted on Mab at that point in spite of her rather . . . difficult temperament, but she had not enjoyed bearing my children and could barely tolerate the thought of me in her bed. Even back then she encouraged me to seek pleasure elsewhere. And so I did. For this reason, I saw no difficulty in spending time away for a while, especially if that time was spent in the arms of a beautiful woman. Unfortunately, I hadn't anticipated the strength of that woman's love for me. Or that I would fall in love with her in return."

"And so the plot thickens," I murmured.

He chuckled bitterly. "To say the least." He drained off the rest of his cognac and sighed. "I decided I would leave Mab, would take my children with me and start a new life with my love, give up all my power, my throne. Mab had only married me to be queen, to be wor-shiped and adored—ah, do not look upon me with such pity, Gideon. I've known it all along. To my mind, she could keep her throne. Love and family were all that mattered to me."

I could sense the impending tragedy even before I said, "But it wasn't to be."

The king shook his head. "Before I could inform Mab of my deci-sion, my friend's kingdom was invaded and we were called to action. As I prepared to ride into battle, my lover presented me with a gift— a beautiful helm, so finely crafted, I had never seen its equal except among those worn by my friend, the king. This helm resembled his favorite, the one I'd seen him wear to battle on several occasions and knew to be a gift from my sister as a talisman against harm. I had publicly remarked on its beauty many times, so I assumed my lover had commissioned a copy as a gift to me."

At this bit of news, I straightened, my heart pounding as the pieces of my king's story began to fall into place.

When I stared at him in astonished silence, he continued his story. "I gratefully accepted the gift, wore it proudly into battle. And, fortu-nately, I came out of the conflict completely unscathed. Yet my friend, my sister's lover, was slain. We, his faithful knights, had grown so accustomed to his imperviousness to harm, we paid little attention to his safety, left him egregiously unguarded."

"The helm was no replica," I guessed.

He narrowed his eyes in a remorseful grimace. "No, indeed. I'd failed to recognize the helm for what it truly was. Or perhaps I chose not to see the magic it held, for had I known the helm's importance, I would've been honor-bound to reject my lover's gift and offend her. But in my blindness, I'd accepted the helm my lover had taken from her husband's armory and presented to me, thereby leaving him vulnerable. His blood is upon my hands as surely as if I'd slain him myself."

"No," I breathed, shaking my head in disbelief. "It can't be."

My king gave me a tight smile. "You know the rest then, do you?

"You're talking about the helm of Arthur Pendragon," I posited. I pushed to my feet and began to pace, trying to make sense of it all. "Which means your sister is Nimue, the Lady of the Lake."

He inclined his head. "The spell I used to save her bound her to the healing waters of Avalon. She could only be away from them for short periods of time—days at most."

"And the woman you fell in love with must've been Guinevere."

The king winced upon my utterance of Guinevere's name, the pain of her loss a palpable emotion that buffeted my senses.

I stared at him, wide-eyed. "And the name you chose . . ."

He spread his arms and inclined his head slightly in introduction. "Was Lancelot."

"*You're* the one who gave Guinevere the pendant," I accused, not bothering to hide my disappointment at his selfishness. "You bound her to you without her even knowing what it meant."

The king closed his eyes briefly. "I had intended to return to her, but after Arthur died . . . I couldn't face her. She had loved him once. Cared for him still. And she took his death particularly hard. I was too cowardly to admit the truth of my role in her sorrow. And in my cowardice, I compounded it."

"You're the one who went with Merlin to deliver Arthur's body to Nimue instead of letting him be buried in Camelot?" I asked.

The king gave a curt nod. "I am. We ushered him on to Avalon, to wait for Nimue until such time as she could join him."

"And their child . . ." I said, unable to complete the thought.

"Was my niece," he said. "Arabella."

My knees suddenly went weak. I managed to stagger over to the chair I'd recently vacated, the implications of what I was hearing shaking me to my foundation. "But you were going to kill her for stealing the helm back in Make Believe," I charged, shaking my head.

"I wasn't going to kill her," the king insisted, clearly offended at the thought. "I was the one who tipped her off that I had it. I wanted to draw her to me, to talk to her, to try to be the uncle I should've been all along. She was understandably distrustful after all she'd been through. And she got spooked and ran. I sent my soldiers after her for fear that she'd go underground and that I'd lose her forever."

"And yet that's exactly what happened," I reminded him, forcing the anger from my tone.

"Believe me," he said, "I would've loved nothing more than to welcome her into my family, give her the home she deserved."

I lifted my gaze, blinking at him, not understanding. "But she was a grown woman by then. Why hadn't you stepped in before? Where was your benevolence when she wandered lonely and afraid in the woods after Nimue's death?"

The king dragged a hand through his curls. "I didn't realize Mab knew as much as she did about my affair. I never should've underestimated my wife—or her wrath. She was determined to destroy everything connecting me to Arthur, including his offspring. I rescued the relics I could, secretly scattered them across Make Believe to hide them and keep them from falling into the wrong person's hands. And as much as I wanted to bring Arabella home, Mab forbade it, refused to allow our home to be 'polluted' by the blood of a non-Tale such as Arthur Pendragon. I tried to resist, to argue with her, but I . . . I *couldn't*."

The king's shoulders sagged as he relived his failure to control the situation to his satisfaction. Once again, I wondered at Mab's control over the man whose strength I knew to be extraordinary. His will was unbreakable—except against his wife. Hearing the whole of their story now, it was even clearer to me that any love that had been there once had faded.

Although he still outwardly appeared to dote upon her, fawn over her, it was more the habit of a charming man who would fill his home with amity than any true fondness for the woman who shared his throne. And I was more convinced than ever that Mab's hold on the king was a product of her magic. How to rescue him from that hold, however, was beyond me.

The king heaved a sigh before he lamented, "Unable to bring my niece into my home after Nimue's death, I instead ensured that Arabella found her way into the home of a kind nobleman and his family. And she was happy there."

"Until the mess with that bastard Gisbourne," I told him, my tone harsher than he'd ever heard from me. I bit back the truth of just how far Gisbourne's treachery extended, waiting to find out just how much the king knew.

"That son of a bitch deserved to be drawn and quartered for what he did," the king spat, his agitation bringing him to his feet to assume the pacing I'd left off. "And I would've been happy to do the honors, but 'Sir Guy of Gisbourne' was just an alias . . . one of many, as it turned out. I lost his trail and was never able to inflict the punishment he so deserved."

"You may get your chance yet," I informed him, closely observing his reaction.

"Do you mean he's in the Here and Now?" the king asked, his eyes going a steely blue.

"Not just in the Here and Now, sire," I explained. "He's here in this very house. For the past three years, Sir Guy of Gisbourne has been masquerading as Reginald Mann."

"In *my* house?" he bellowed, his face twisting with rage. When I nodded, he had to visibly work at composing himself. "He dared to infiltrate this home, ingratiate himself with my wife . . ." He unleashed a roar of fury, his hand balled into a white-knuckled fist. "I'll have that son of a bitch in my dungeons by morning. I'll do right by Arabella and the others Gisbourne has harmed, I assure you."

"You could've done right by Arabella long ago," I told him, knowing very well that pushing him when he was so enraged was risky but unwilling to hold my tongue. "All the time she was living her life as Robin Hood . . . Why didn't you step in then?"

"I did," the king snapped. "Who do you think her 'merry men' were? Curiously honorable thieves who happened to leave a beautiful young woman untouched and unharmed? They were my own men, disguised as common brigands. They were charged with watching over her, protecting her."

"But she lived in the woods with next to nothing!" I shot back. "You couldn't have offered a cottage? The means to live comfortably without putting herself at risk?"

The king gave me a mildly chastising look. "Dear boy, you know my niece better than anyone, I imagine. Do you think she would've been content living such a prosaic life?"

I had to concede the point. She would've managed to find trouble and adventure, no matter what her circumstances. It was that spirit and zest for life that I loved so much about her.

"My men reported back to me regularly," the king continued. "Had she truly been in jeopardy, I would've stepped in."

"You must've known about me joining her band of thieves then," I said.

The king shrugged. "I did. But I didn't know who—or what—you were. I knew only that you were a man my niece fancied. I had no idea of the true depth of your affection for one another until that day at the falls." He came to me and laid a hand upon my shoulder. "I could see it in your eyes, my boy. I did not need your empathic ability to sense the love—and grief—that was so akin to my own."

"But you could've saved her!" I charged, my voice breaking. "You could've intervened when she fell! And we never would've been apart! We never—" I broke off, emotion choking me and preventing me from continuing.

"But I did intervene, Gideon," he assured me. "I was not in time to prevent her fall, but I was in time to prevent her death. My spell grasped her at the last moment. My intent was to send her to Avalon to be with her parents." The king's grip on my shoulder tightened. "But it seems she would not go."

I lifted my gaze to his, astonished. "What?"

He grinned at me. "She fought against it," he explained. "I believe her love for you was so strong, it kept her in a . . . sort of magical limbo. And, eventually, she made her way back to you."

I blinked, clearing the blur that obscured my vision. "Did you know all along then?" I asked. "Were you aware that she'd return?"

The king shook his head. "No. I only discovered that she'd returned to Make Believe when Merlin brought it to my attention. He was one of the only Tales who knew my true identity when I masqueraded as Lancelot, you see, so he was aware of the history we shared. But by then . . ."

"I was with Lavender," I filled in. "You knew about us?"

The king puffed up his chest, offended that I could even suggest his lack of knowledge about such goings-on in his house. "Of course I did. Did you really think you could keep such a thing from my notice?" I chose to keep silent on his lack of knowledge regarding the presence of a traitorous, power-grabbing bastard in his house for the past three years. Instead, I let him continue, "The trick was keeping it from Mab's. When we came over in the relocation and you came to Lavender's defense, there was nothing more I could do to hide your relationship."

I shook my head. "Why?" I asked. "Why do all of this for me?"

The king grasped the nape of my neck. "You are as dear to me as one of my own children, Gideon. What *wouldn't* I do for any of you?"

I swallowed past the lump in my throat, my emotions at war. "You could've released me from my bondage. Once you were assured of my safety, you could've let me go."

He patted my cheek. "I released you centuries ago, Gideon. The bonds were merely an illusion. You could've disobeyed me at any time, shirked your responsibility to me, to my family. It was your own noble heart that kept you here."

My gaze shifted to my wrists as I brought them up before my eyes. "But you commanded me to bring Arabella to you . . . I could *feel* the command. My bonds responded."

"All part of the illusion. I had to be sure that it was truly Arabella who had come to the Here and Now," he explained, turning away and drifting slowly back to his chair as he spoke. "Merlin did not come to me this time, he had kept the knowledge of her arrival from me. I cannot understand why he would prevent me from seeing my niece. Why steal from me instead?"

I sighed, preparing myself to deliver news I knew would bring him pain. "I imagine for the same reason he kept her arrival from me—to protect us." When the king frowned in confusion, I add gently, "Arabella is *fading,* sire."

Had the king been standing, he would've dropped into his chair. As it was, the sorrow and heartbreak that washed over him were almost more than I could bear. "That cannot be true. We only just got her back."

I shook my head. "We have no idea why it's happening, sire. There's no discernible cause—unless it's because she's half-Tale."

"But her fairy blood should protect her against such a thing as *fading,*" the king insisted. "In all our time here, none of the Seelies has ever fallen victim to the ailment."

I leaned forward in my chair, bracing my forearms on my thighs, and clasping my hands. "That's not all, sire. There are others *fading.* They are half-Tales as well."

"Surely our physicians are doing all they can to save them," the king insisted. "Right now, our concern is Arabella."

"I wish that were true," I said gently. "But these others aren't just any Tales, sire." I paused and took a deep, bracing breath before adding, "They are your children."

He gaped at me for a full minute at least, disbelief and denial making him mute. I grabbed his empty glass from the desk and filled it, wrapping his fingers around the glass when he blindly reached out.

"How is that possible?" he said at last. "How could I not know I had children with the Ordinaries?"

"I believe they were kept from you, sire," I said. "All of their mothers vanished or died mysteriously. Most were adopted by loving families or taken into foster care."

He was visibly shaken by the news, his heart aching at the thought of any of his offspring suffering. "How many are there?"

"Nearly a dozen, sire."

Something suddenly shifted in his emotions, a hard resolve bracing him as he slammed his glass down on the desk and got to his feet.

"I must go to them immediately," he informed me. "Take me to them, Gideon."

"I'm afraid it's not that simple, sire," I said.

"Of course it is!" he scoffed, waving a hand and producing his overcoat. "We will away at once."

I grasped his arm as he strode past me, bringing him to a halt. "Sire, they are in the custody of the Agency."

His face twisted with outrage. "Those conniving bastards! We've a treaty! They dare hold *my* children captive?"

"I have reason to believe that they were *offered* the children, sire," I told him as gently as I could. "I think whoever hid them from you offered them up to the Agency when they became ill."

"Another Tale?" he breathed, horrified.

I nodded. "I don't know who else it could be. Arabella has been stealing fairy dust to give it to the Agency in hopes of staving off the *fading* long enough to find a cure."

"Brave girl," the king murmured. "She truly is a Seelie."

"This gets to why I came, sire," I said, helping him to remove his overcoat and transporting it back to his closet with a sharp snap of my wrist. "We think the magic in Arthur's relics could grant a Tale immortality."

The king nodded. "That's why I hid them away. Should such power fall into the wrong hands . . ."

"Arabella has been gathering them—now with my aid—to test the theory," I told him. "But we're not the only ones looking for them. Someone has hired the Huntsman. And I believe this person is also behind the bulk of the fairy dust thefts."

"Dear God," the king muttered. "The Huntsman mustn't be allowed to have the relics. Do you have any idea who hired him?"

I shook my head. "Nothing definitive. I had the Huntsman in my grasp but turned him over to the FMA for questioning. Unfortunately, he escaped—or, more accurately, someone with powerful magical abilities infiltrated the FMA's jail and broke him out."

"So we know nothing of this Tale's connection to the relics?" the king said.

I thought back on what the Huntsman had imparted to me in Merlin's apartment. "He did tell me that his employer was right under my nose and that to determine who it is I should ask my king."

"How dare that butcher insinuate that I would hire him!" the king fumed. "The very idea!"

"That was my immediate reaction as well, sire," I assured him. "But I believe he was perhaps making reference to someone close to you, perhaps someone among us . . . a traitor."

"Gisbourne."

"It would stand to reason, knowing Gisbourne's past treachery," I confirmed. "But I have no proof."

"But why?" the king mused. "He has no reason to want them."

"Perhaps for the power they would afford him, the invincibility they would provide," I suggested. "You said you'd split up the relics to keep them from falling into the wrong person's hands. Gisbourne would certainly qualify as the wrong person."

"Well, then," the king said with a resolute nod, "we must ensure he does not succeed in reclaiming them."

"We possess all but two relics," I explained. "We've been using Snow White's mirror to locate them, but we're running out of time. And now the mirror has been stolen, its inhabitant, Fabrizio, kidnapped.

"We must find this mirror at once," the king insisted.

"I agree," I said gently. "But, sire, even if we find all the relics, their power may only be enough to save one person."

"Only one?" the king asked, his voice tight with sorrow. *"One?"* He shook his head vehemently. "No. That's unacceptable."

I ran a hand through my curls. "Arabella by rights should have the relics, but she refuses to save herself. She would save one of the children instead. But she grows weaker and weaker, sire. I don't know how much longer fairy dust can sustain her as we search for the relics. And now that our main source of information has been kidnapped, we have no idea where to find the final relics. I don't know what else to do. I beg you to help us."

The king nodded. "You know I will, my boy. I will do whatever you ask."

"Tell me where the other relics are," I said. "Help me find them."

The king held my gaze for a moment. Then, with a resigned sigh, he nodded and waved a hand with a flourish, producing a bundle wrapped in an aged, dirty burlap cloth.

My brows lifted, not daring to believe my eyes. "Is that what I think it is?"

In answer, he peeled back the burlap, revealing the tarnished helm. "I found it after Arabella's fall and kept it hidden all the long years after my parting with Guinevere. Then, suddenly, it surfaced in the Here and Now. I imagine it has to do with the overlapping of Arthur the man and Arthur the myth."

I frowned. "Sire?"

He turned his eyes up to the ceiling for a moment, searching for the words to explain. "Every great once in a while, there is an Ordinary who is a legend in his own time. For such a person, the story begins to grow, take on a life of its own. And, eventually, it becomes so powerful as to create the legend while he's still alive. Arthur was such a man. That's why no one is quite able to separate fact from fiction in his case. His story in Make Believe ran concurrent with the truth, evolving, becoming more dramatic and elaborate as time wore on. It's really quite fascinating."

"And so you think the relics Nimue created for Arthur in Make Believe were so powerful, their twins emerged here?" I guessed.

The king nodded. "Perhaps. I cannot say. All I know is that when I learned the helm was here, I was determined to have it again. You can imagine my surprise when I discovered that Guinevere had it in her possession." His mouth lifted at one corner in a wistful smile. "She was quite astonished to see me when I visited her in London."

"*You* are her patron," I realized. "You're the one providing the house in Connecticut—and an ample allowance, from what I can tell."

He nodded. "I offered more, but she refused. I would have her living in a palace with servants to tend to her every need. But she only accepted what she did as a favor to an old friend—which, I'm afraid, is all she considers me now."

I lifted a brow at him, recalling the cognac and cigars Guinevere had offered me during my visit. She certainly hadn't seemed attached to anyone in particular at that time, but I understood now that her advances were more to get back at the king than out of any true interest in me.

"She's as beautiful as ever." He grinned, a little sadly. "But she would not be wooed by me again. Her heart is no longer mine—she made that very clear."

I had a feeling he had misread her resistance to his charms. The look on her face when I'd returned her pendant spoke volumes about the truth of her feelings. She was just as much in love with him as ever, but hurt had clearly ruled her actions upon seeing her lost love again.

The king sighed and waved away his own moroseness. "No matter. I've made my bed and must lie in it, as they say."

I shook my head. "Sire—"

He held up a hand, silencing me. "We will speak no more of Guinevere."

"But—"

"I beg you, Gideon," he interrupted. "No more." He held the helm out to me. "Please, take it. Give it to Arabella. And tell her . . . Tell her it is from an uncle who loves her. And that I hope someday she will forgive me all my mistakes."

I took the helm and tore a small rift in time, tucking the treasure away in my temporal cache to be reclaimed when I returned to Arabella. "I will, sire."

"What remains then?" he asked.

"Only one," I told him. "Excalibur."

Chapter 22

"Well, that is a prize, indeed."

The king and I both turned toward the speaker, our magic instantly at the ready, prepared to unleash hell upon the intruder. To my astonishment, Mab and her ever-present toady, Reginald, stood in the doorway to the king's study. And gathered behind them were the king's guards. Even as we gaped at them, other guards shifted into the room, surrounding us.

"What is the meaning of this intrusion?" the king demanded, waving his hands absently to diffuse the magic he'd gathered.

Mab swept into the room, whipping the train of her evening gown behind her and sending up a cloud of glittering gold fairy dust that those around us greedily inhaled.

"We had quite a spectacle outside—a lovely diversion to allow this Unseelie filth back into our home," Mab drawled, her golden eyes trained menacingly on me. She then turned to the king and gave him her pretty pout. "I was concerned for your safety, my love."

When she took another step forward, I stepped in front of my king, putting myself between them. My magic popped and sizzled, bolts of silver sparking in warning. "That's close enough, my lady."

Mab chuckled, not intimidated in the least. "You think to threaten *me*, you insignificant fool! I could snap your neck with a flick of my wrist."

I met and held her gaze, no longer willing to back down—not when my king was at risk. "You could try."

"He's hardly worth the trouble, my lady," Reginald sneered. "Allow me to do the honors."

Mab smiled. "In good time." She then turned her attention to her husband. "I fear your servant has worked a spell upon you, my love. I thought we were in agreement about his being unwelcome in our home."

The king peered down his nose at her, the heat of his rising anger singeing my back. "We agreed upon nothing. And I guarantee that I am under no spell . . . not any longer. But I fear it is *you* who have been deceived, my queen."

A single golden brow arched. "Indeed? By whom, pray tell?"

"By the one calling himself Reginald Mann," I ground out. "He is not who you think."

She gasped in feigned alarm, a hand dramatically fluttering to her breast. "You mean . . . He's not really a devoted and faithful servant who never questions my orders and performs every duty with unyielding loyalty?"

Reginald rushed forward and rescued my lady's hand and brought it to his lips, pressing a kiss to her fingertips. "Never doubt me, my queen," he murmured against her skin.

She smiled, her cheeks blushing prettily. "What do I care if his name is Reginald Mann or"—she turned a hard gaze on me—"Sir Guy of Gisbourne?"

"You knew?" the king roared, his voice thunderous in the confines of the room. "You knew I had a score to settle with Gisbourne and you brought him into our house under false pretenses? Let him insinuate himself into every matter of our family, our business, for the past three years, knowing damned well that I'd put his head on a pike if I knew who he was?"

"Of *course* I did!" she hissed. "I've always known who he was!"

"Seize that man," the king ordered, gesturing toward Reginald.

The guards sprang forward to obey, but Mab held up her hand, staying them. "You'll do no such thing!" Mab's smile this time was rather sinister as she eyed the man next to her, the lust and greed pouring off of her making my stomach turn until I was forced to choke down my rising bile. "This man is under my protection."

And suddenly, I realized I'd been an idiot. When I'd come upon Reginald in the hallway a few nights prior, I'd assumed that he'd been out with Ivy and had insinuated himself into her bed. How wrong I'd been. He'd been coming in separately from his lover so as not to raise suspicion, that part was true enough. But that lover hadn't been the king's daughter. And the queen's next words confirmed it.

"You *dare* defy me to stand with some opportunistic, sycophantic bootlicker that you've only known for a few years?" the king raged.

"Reginald was my lover back in Make Believe while you were off *bedding* that royal whore Guinevere!" Mab spat, advancing on her husband. "And when I discovered where your pretty little half-Tale niece was living, I sent him to put her in her place once and for all, ruin any chances she had of ever being recognized as an equal, but— incomprehensibly—she was resistant to his charms. But it mattered not. Everything worked out perfectly in the end."

The king's fury was at war with his disbelief that the woman he'd been married to for centuries upon centuries could stoop to such depths. "You traitorous bitch."

I glanced at Reginald, his smirk more than I could bear. Without thinking, I charged him, fully prepared to knock that fucking smile from his face and rip out his heart for good measure. But before I reached him, a powerful blow sent white-hot pain through my back and knocked me from my feet, sending me slamming into the king's bookshelves.

"Remove that filth from my house," Mab sneered, jerking her chin toward me.

"Mab," the king thundered, "I will not be ruled in this! I have given you leave to do as you wish, to amuse yourself as you would. But Gideon will always be welcome here." At this he stepped forward to meet her, the power of his magic bringing a blue glow to his skin. "And I *will* accept all of my children into this family. Including the ones you have hidden from me."

Mab flinched ever so slightly at the accusation, but she lifted her chin a notch in defiance. "I have no idea what you mean."

"Do you not?" the king ground out through clenched teeth. "You tell me you had nothing to do with my children being held captive by the Agency?"

Her answering smile was tight and dripping with falsehood even before she said ever so sweetly, "Of course not. How can you think me guilty of such a thing?" When the king narrowed his eyes at her, Mab came toward him, her steps cautious. "Really, my darling, must we always argue so? Let us put all of this . . . *ugliness* behind us, shall we? There's no need to even recall this little spat today. . . ."

"Your honeyed words will not persuade me of your innocence, Mab," the king told her, his tone icy. "Nor will it ensure that you and I have a future together."

Her pretty mouth lifted at one corner as her fingertips lightly caressed the king's chest, sending up a tiny cloud of her fairy dust, threatening to enshroud my king and no doubt make him forget everything that had just occurred. I lunged to my feet and sent out a blast of my magic that scattered her dust, disintegrating it before it could infect the king and bring him back under her spell.

The king shook his head, trying to free his mind of what little of Mab's fairy dust had made its way into his system, but he was clearly disoriented. "What the hell . . . ?"

Mab turned her furious, now-glowing gaze on me, enraged at my interference. Without thinking, I released a silver lightning bolt, nailing her in the chest. She flew through the air with a sharp cry, slamming into the guards at the door.

The queen was immediately on her feet again. A bolt of her magic flashed from her fingertips, accompanied by a roar of rage that ripped from her throat. I instinctively brought up my arms, shielding myself with my magic, but the impact still knocked me from my feet. The guards were upon me in an instant, clamping shackles around my wrists before I could react.

Mab charged toward me, her face twisted in hatred and rage. A massive lightning bolt of magic rent the air with a deafening crack of power. Defenseless to block the deathblow this time, I braced myself.

And in that moment, I felt no terror, no anger. Just sorrow. And guilt. It seemed I was about to fail my darling lass yet again. But this time *I* was the one headed for a fall.

"No!"

I didn't at first realize what had happened. There was no impact, no pain. For a moment, I thought perhaps death had taken me so quickly that it hadn't yet sunk in. But then the truth hit me and brought me to my knees more surely than if Mab's magic had actually struck me. The guards' hold on me was all that kept me on my feet.

"Oh, my God," I heard Mab breathe. "What have I done?"

"Go," Reginald told her gently. "I'll take care of this."

I fought back through the haze of grief and disbelief and threw off the guards with a cry of sorrow as I dropped down beside my king. "Sire," I cried, grasping fistfuls of his shirt in my hands and giving him a shake. "Sire, can you hear me?"

To my immense relief, his eyelids fluttered. "Gideon," he whispered, his voice little more than a dry rasp. "You're safe."

I nodded, blinking away the sudden blur in my eyes. "Yes, I'm safe, sire. Thanks to you."

The king's hand patted blindly until he found mine. He grasped it to the point of pain. "Take care of them," he pleaded. "Take care of my family."

"I will," I vowed. "Always."

He offered me a weak smile. "You were wrong, you know," he said.

The guards had recovered from being thrown off me and made to take hold of me again, but I shook free, determined not to leave my king. "Wrong about what, sire?"

His grin grew. "I've never once been sorry to know you." And then his eyes fluttered shut.

Before I could fully register what had just occurred, the guards were dragging me to my feet and toward the door. Too stunned to put up a fight, I let them lead me away. My mind raced as I replayed the scene in the king's study—from the various details of our conversation to Mab and Reginald's intrusion and the battle between the king and queen. My throat grew tight when I realized that once more the king had saved me, had intervened because he saw something of value in me.

And I'd be damned if I was going to betray that faith by giving up now.

I kept my head down but lifted my eyes, taking in my captors at a glance. Four guards. And Reginald Mann. My gaze then flicked to my shackles. They were enchanted with the queen's own magic, too powerful for me to break. But the moment the guards released me, they'd be lucky if I broke only their arms.

The dungeon in the king's mansion was as dank and dismal as any dungeon I'd ever seen in Make Believe. It was built into the home mostly for show, a visible deterrent to any among the king's staff who would consider betraying him. But apparently the promise of such a punishment was not nearly as effective as it'd once been.

There'd been a time when every one of the guards now holding me captive would've laid down his life to protect the king or his family. Their lack of loyalty made me sick, physically ill. I suppressed a groan as my stomach rolled in disgust. I didn't give a shit if they'd been under Mab's spell the entire time they plotted to ruin my king. If they'd been truly loyal, they would've sooner died than give in to her treacherous magic. And now they would most likely die for it.

"Put him in that one," Reginald drawled, casually waving toward one of the cells. The guards shoved me inside and slammed the cell door. There was little more than a few bars keeping me from wrapping my hands around Reginald's throat and crushing his windpipe, but it was enough. I could feel the enchantments emanating from the steel and knew that they would prevent the use of my magic.

Reginald sauntered toward my prison, his ever present smirk draped across his lips. "Well, well, well. Whoever would've thought you'd end up here?" he taunted. "Gideon Montrose, the celebrated warrior of old, the king's ever faithful servant and loyal bodyguard."

"Fuck off, Reginald," I spat. "Or should I call you Gisbourne?"

He shrugged. "Makes no difference to me. The queen has her own name for me when she's fucking me—that's the only one that truly matters. She's a sweet piece of ass, don't you think?" He sucked in a sharp breath and shivered with pleasure. "I can hit that all night long."

"You'll burn for this," I assured him. "You may have fooled the queen into thinking that you care for her, deceived her into going along with your plans—"

Reginald's laughter cut me off. "*Deceived* her?" he repeated.

"You've got it all wrong. None of this was *my* plan. I'm just along for the ride, if you'll pardon the pun. And now that the king is out of the way, she and I will do quite nicely together. The fairy dust business is going to have quite the boom now that I'm in control. The Ordinaries are going to be *clamoring* for a little taste of Vitamin D."

I had to work to keep the concern out of my voice when I said, "Fairy dust doesn't affect them the same way it does us. It's dangerous for an Ordinary."

Reginald shrugged. "What the fuck do I care? Soon there will be only *one* drug lord in the Here and Now. Those two-bit thugs who fancy themselves gangsters will be lining up to kiss my ass to get a piece of the action. And if there are a few Ordinaries who can't handle it . . . well, it'll just thin the herd."

"And all this was worth raping a young woman, killing her family, betraying those who trusted you—and God knows what else?" I said evenly, my gaze deadly.

Reginald shrugged. "Your hands aren't without stain, Gideon," he reminded me. "And what the hell were you getting from the king in return for the sins you've committed? Okay, yeah, so you fucked his daughter—and, as it turns out, his niece. Hey, gotta give you credit—at least you're keepin' it in the family. But we all know how those relationships turned out. I suppose you might've actually had a chance with that little bitch from Sherwood, but I guess you'll never know, will you? What with her *fading* and all."

"What the hell do you know about it?" I snarled.

He shoved his hands deep into his slacks pockets and rocked a little on his heels. "Enough to know she's been trying to gather the relics of Arthur Pendragon to try to save herself. But Mab will see to it that never happens." When my brows twitched together in a frown, he explained, "Why do you think the queen wanted them? It isn't like *Mab* needs them. She's already immortal and all-powerful. She just didn't want your uppity little whore to have them."

Enraged, I charged the bars with a furious cry, fully intent on ripping out that cocksucker's throat for disrespecting Arabella, enchanted bars or not. But the coward stumbled back, his eyes wide with fear. When he realized he was out of my reach, he chuckled—albeit nervously.

"Well, it'll all be resolved soon enough, eh?" Reginald said. "Your pretty little bitch will be dead in another day or two—if she lasts that long. When we captured her a few minutes ago, she looked like she was at death's door."

Terror gripped my heart, squeezing so hard I couldn't breathe.

"Aww..." Reginald taunted, feigning a pitying pout. "Were you expecting her to pop by and rescue you? Maybe break you out of prison like Mab did the Huntsman?" When I just glared at him, he chuckled and turned to go, motioning for the guards to follow. But before going up the stone steps, he paused and turned to add, "Oh, and don't count on your other pal either. We captured Merlin skulking about in the garden. Nice touch with the dragon, by the way. Damned fine illusion."

When the bastard left, I dropped down on the stone bench and put my head in my shackled hands, trying to figure out how the hell I was going to escape and free Arabella and Merlin.

"I would wish you *buona sera,* but I have not the idea if it is really evening at all."

My head snapped up at the now-familiar voice. "Fabrizio? Is that you?"

"Regrettably, yes, it is I, Fabrizio," he said on a mournful sigh. "I was taken from my Bella's room and locked away in this—*Come si dice...?*—in this *shit-hole* dungeon. It is beyond insulting."

I glanced around, searching the other empty cells until I saw the faint glint of light upon the hand mirror that held Fabrizio captive. "What happened? Are you all right? Have you seen Arabella? Or Merlin? Did—"

"Please to ask the questions one at a time," Fabrizio interrupted, clearly irritated. "I have been kidnapped, after all. I am dealing with the trauma."

I rolled my eyes and tried not to sound too exasperated when I said, "My apologies. Have you seen Arabella? Did they bring her here at some point?"

"No," he answered. "I have not seen my *dolcezza.* Or the wizard, I might as well to tell you before you ask. Again."

I got to my feet and began to pace the confines of my cell, frowning so intensely that my head began to ache. I cursed roundly under my breath, frustration and concern making my thoughts race. Of course they wouldn't bring Arabella and Merlin here. They would want to keep us separated so we couldn't plot. There were few other places in the mansion that would dampen Merlin's magic, but a spell could be placed upon him that would prevent him from escaping. As for Arabella . . .

I could only hope that they didn't realize she had inherited some of her mother's fairy magic and would treat her as just another Tale. But even if they made that mistake, she might not be strong enough at this point to make use of her abilities. . . .

I needed intel. I needed someone who could assess the situation for me, let me know where they were being held. "Are you hurt, Fabrizio?" I asked. "Could you travel to other mirrors in the estate and tell me where Arabella and Merlin are?"

I heard him sigh. "Alas, no. I have tried. But that *bastardo* Mann had his patroness bind me to his bidding."

This brought me up short. "For how long?"

"Since before I came to my Bella," he admitted. "They wanted me to find the relics for the queen in exchange for freeing me from the mirror, but Bella found me. And how could I not help a damsel in distress?" I could feel his rationalization even from the cell where I was imprisoned. "I cooperate with the queen and her lover and am finally released from my curse. And if I tell my *dolcezza* the locations as well, she can get there before they do and steal the relics first."

That certainly solved the mystery of how the Huntsman kept showing up at the same place. The arrogant jackass had been playing both sides.

"You double-crossing son of a bitch," I snarled. "Arabella considers you a *friend*."

"Would I have continued to help her reach the relics first if I was not a friend?" Fabrizio countered.

"You could've told her what was going on!" I shot back. "You put her life in danger on more than one occasion by keeping her in the dark."

"I put *my* life in jeopardy *every* time," Fabrizio said. "It does not matter now. The *bastardo* will not release me—from my bond in this cell *or* from this cursed mirror."

"You idiot," I seethed, "he *never* had the power to release you from the mirror. Only the one who cursed you can lift the curse—that's how it works. Either that, or you fulfill your end of the bargain that breaks the spell."

I heard Fabrizio mumble a string of what I assumed were some extremely potent Italian obscenities. I couldn't be sure as my Italian was extremely limited, but I *thought* I caught something in there about Fabrizio encouraging Reginald to go fuck his own sister, mother, grandmother, and possibly a lame goat—and to choke on his own testicles.

When he'd finished his rather colorful and passionate rant, he took a deep breath and let it out slowly. "We must find my Bella and help her locate the final relic before the *bastardo* gets to it."

My brows shot up. "Do you know where Excalibur is?"

"*Naturalmente*," Fabrizio replied, his arrogance quickly returning. "I am finding all the relics, yes? How could I not know where the most important piece resides?"

I waited for him to tell me, but when he remained silent, I prompted, "And . . . ?"

"Release me from the cell and take me with you when you escape, and I will tell you," Fabrizio insisted. "Not a moment sooner."

I gripped the cell bars so hard in my frustration, I half-expected them to bend and allow me the freedom I desired, but they remained regrettably unaffected. "Fine," I hissed through my teeth. "I will release you—provided I can figure out a way to get the hell out of here."

"Leave that to me, love."

I gasped when Arabella suddenly appeared before me on the other side of the bars, her cocky, dimpled grin the most beautiful sight I'd ever seen. In spite of the shackles, I managed to grasp the edge of her cloak and pull her to me for a hard kiss.

"Getting into trouble again, I see," she said with a chuckle when I released her.

"How did you escape from Reginald?" I asked when she produced an old-fashioned skeleton key on an enormous ring.

"I didn't," she replied, quickly unlocking the door and pulling me out of the cell and unlocking the shackles. "I was never captured."

I shook my head, confused. "But, Reginald said he had you and Merlin."

Arabella's gaze briefly flicked up to mine and I could feel the guilt she was experiencing. "It wasn't me—it was Lily. The guards unleashed hellhounds and they caught my scent in spite of the invisibility cloak. Lily used a glamour on herself to mimic me and draw them away."

I ran my hand through my hair, my own guilt now mixing with what I was picking up from Arabella. I had promised my king that I'd take care of his family and now one of his daughters was experiencing who knew what kind of hell because she'd been trying to protect the woman I love.

"We have to find them," I muttered, grasping Arabella's hand and pulling her with me as I strode toward the stairs.

"Ahem."

Arabella dug her heels in and pulled me to a stop. "Fabrizio?"

"*Sì, dolcezza,* you have found me," Fabrizio called, his jubilant tone making my stomach roll in disgust. "I am rescued!"

Arabella rushed to the cell where the mirror lay and cast a surprised look at me over her shoulder. She immediately unlocked the cell and rushed in, snatching up the mirror to give it a quick hug before hurrying back to me.

I sighed, then pressed my lips together to keep from telling her about Fabrizio's double cross just yet.

"Can you find them, Fabrizio?" Arabella asked, breathless from just that little bit of exertion.

The man's gaze flicked toward me briefly, but then he smiled at Arabella and swept a gallant bow. "Anything for you, *dolcezza.*"

That lying son of a bitch . . .

As soon as he'd vanished from the mirror, Arabella turned to face me, her cheeks blazing with fever, her eyes glassy. "I was worried about you."

I pulled her into the safety of my arms, my throat tight with emotion at seeing the rapid acceleration of her *fading*. We were running out of time. If I didn't get Excalibur soon . . .

"And, apparently, with good cause," she added. "What happened?"

I tucked her in closer, holding her as much for my comfort as hers. "I'll tell you as soon as we're safely away from here."

"I have them," Fabrizio suddenly piped up from the confines of his mirror. "They are in the king's chambers."

I gave a resolute nod and then turned my gaze on Arabella. "Go to the car and wait for me there." When her expression warned of an impending argument, I interrupted, "I need you to have the car ready to go when I bring them. Can you get there unnoticed, do you think?"

She gave me a curt nod and pulled her hood up over her head. Then she and Fabrizio vanished from my sight.

I bolted up the dungeon stairs and then slowly opened the door at the top, peering down the hall to make sure the coast was clear before motioning to Arabella. I felt her brush a kiss on my cheek before she slipped out beside me and headed toward the safety beyond the estate's walls.

Chapter 23

Wishing I had an invisibility cloak of my own, I crept along the corridors, pausing periodically to listen for any pursuing footsteps. Luckily for me, it appeared that the queen in her inimitable arrogance had doubted my ability to escape and had left the house lightly guarded. The king's chambers were another matter, however. Two of the best-trained guards I'd had the privilege to command stood watch at the chamber door.

It pained me to think I might have to hurt them. Or kill them.

I took a deep breath and stepped out into the open, my arms raised slightly at my sides to show I meant them no harm. "Good evening, gentlemen."

The men immediately drew their swords and dropped to the ready. "How the hell did you escape?" one of the guards, Langdon, demanded.

"I will have the prisoners from you," I told them, my tone even. I could feel their fear rising with each step I took. Even if they were, in fact, under Mab's spell, forced to do her will against their own judgment, they knew that they were no match for me and dreaded the force of my wrath should they disobey *my* orders.

"We cannot release them," the second guard informed me through clenched teeth, as if it pained him to say the words. "Gideon, please—go now while you can."

I shook my head. "You know I can't, Seamus. I won't abandon my friends any more than I would abandon you. Release them to me, fight against the evil that binds you, and I will return to free you all from Mab's treachery."

"Gideon, *please*," Seamus pleaded, the veins in his neck bulging with the effort it took to resist whatever orders he'd been given. "Don't come any closer!" But before he could even get out the last word, Seamus charged, his sword raised over his head.

My heart filled with sorrow as I shifted to meet him, attacking first, grabbing his sword arm when I appeared before him and snapping it, wrenching his sword from his grasp when he screamed in pain. He dropped to the floor, groaning, his eyes wide with terror at the sight of his bones protruding from his skin.

Langdon was already charging me as I took Seamus's sword. Without time to do more than defend myself, I swept the sword around me, slicing open his stomach before he'd even realized I was armed.

I caught him under the arms as he fell, sinking down to the ground with him. "I'm so sorry, my friend," I whispered, damning Mab to hell for forcing their hands—and mine.

Langdon blinked up at me, his eyes wide with shock, clearing now from the spell. "Gideon," he gasped, coughing in an attempt to clear the blood pooling in his lungs.

Blood sprayed on my face and shirt, but I didn't flinch. Instead, I laid my hand over his wound, trying to stanch the flow of his blood. "I'm here."

"Mab," he managed to croak out.

"I know," I told him, quickly shedding my jacket and stripping off my shirt. I wrapped it around Langdon's abdomen, using it as a makeshift bandage. "Just save your strength, Langdon, let your body heal."

I glanced up and down the corridor, fully expecting more guards to arrive at any moment to investigate the reason for Seamus's screams. Hopefully, when they arrived they'd be cognizant enough in spite of Mab's spell to actually assist their brothers-in-arms and not leave them to die. But I couldn't wait around to find out. I had to move fast to rescue Merlin and Lily before there was more bloodshed.

I grabbed the sword and rammed the door with my shoulder. The wood splintered and the door burst inward, slamming into the wall. The king lay on his bed, his daughter Ivy at his side, clutching his hand while tears streamed down her cheeks.

"Thank God!" she cried, leaping to her feet.

"Ivy? What the hell are *you* doing here?" I sent a frantic glance around the room, then rushed forward, grasping Ivy's hand. "We have to get you out of here."

"What the hell is going on, Gideon?" She dug in her heels and pulled against my hold. "I'm not leaving my father when he's defenseless like this."

For the first time, I really looked at the king and saw that his chest was rising and falling in a slow rhythm. "He's not dead."

"Of course he's not," Ivy assured me, throwing her head back defiantly, clearly offended at the very idea. "Do you think that bitch could actually kill my *father*?"

As elated as I was to learn that my king was still alive, that meant I had one more Tale to get to safety. And in the distance, I could hear the footsteps of guards rushing to the aid of Seamus and Langdon.

Shit.

"Where are Merlin and Lily?" I demanded, grasping the king's wrist and pulling him up into a sitting position so I could heft him over my shoulder.

"That asshole Reginald dragged them away a few minutes before you got here," she said, taking the sword I held out to her and holding it with her fingertips as if I'd asked her to take a dead rat. "I have no idea where he took them."

"Can you shift?" I asked, grunting a little as I accepted the king's dead weight onto my shoulder, his height making him an awkward carry.

Ivy shook her head. "Mab made damned sure of that when she threw us in here," she spat. "We can shift within the house but can't get out. So, if we're leaving, we're going out the front door."

I adjusted the king slightly on my shoulder and took the sword back from Ivy. "Well, then, we'd better get going."

Ivy was close on my heels as we rushed from the room and hurried down the hall in the opposite direction from the advancing guards.

"Halt!" I heard just before a bolt of magic zipped by my head, searing some of my hair just before it blasted one of the many topiaries that lined the corridor. The small tree exploded, sending projectiles of wood flying. I heard Ivy cry out in pain as the shrapnel sliced through her skin.

I turned back and wrapped my sword arm around her waist, pulling her forward as she limped along, trying to protect her as best I could from the onslaught of magic that assaulted us. I threw out a wall of magic behind us, relieved when I heard the blasts crashing into it.

"Oh, God," Ivy moaned, her knees buckling under her, nearly taking me down with her.

It was then I noticed the jagged piece of wood embedded in her thigh. Her hands shook as she reached to pull it out.

"No!" I cried. "Leave it there."

She lifted terrified eyes to me. "What? I have a fucking branch sticking out of my leg!"

My mind raced, trying to figure out how I was going to drag her out as well now that she was wounded. If only Merlin was around to levitate her out of there.

Then a thought came to me. On a hunch, I ripped open the seam to my temporal cache, the pocket of time and space that was mine alone. To my relief, it seemed unaffected by Mab's spell. She had thought to block our exit from the mansion by prohibiting our ability to shift, but my temporal cache traveled with me, was part of my time stream and no one else's.

I unceremoniously dumped the king inside, muttering an apology for my lack of gentleness, then grabbed Ivy's wrist to shove her inside as well.

"What the hell are you doing?" she shrieked, her fear and pain causing her to fight against me.

"Ivy, listen to me," I snapped, sending a glance behind me as I heard my magic shield begin to give way under the guards' onslaught. "I can't get you out of here right now, but I can hide you. Just stay with your father and I'll come for you both as soon as I can."

She sent a frantic look in the direction of the guards, then nodded. "Gideon," she said, grabbing my hand before I could seal the seam, "find my sister."

I nodded, then sealed them inside just as the shield exploded behind me with a blinding flash of silver light, the heat of the explosion making me groan as it slammed into my bare back. I lunged to my feet, sword in hand, and turned to face the guards.

This was exactly what I'd wanted to avoid, but there was no choice. Running wasn't an option. If I wanted to get out of there, get back to Arabella, find the others, rescue my king and his daughter who were now hidden where only I could reach them, fighting my way out was the only choice.

I gripped the hilt of the sword, doing a quick head-count. Ten guards, all seasoned warriors. Although the hall was nearly twenty feet across, the room to maneuver was both a blessing and curse. If I wasn't careful, they'd flank me, surround me in a matter of moments.

Then I swung my sword in a figure eight, limbering up my wrist. "This is yer last chance, lads," I told them calmly. "And you'll only get but one."

Their fear and regret buffeted my senses, nearly knocking me over with the strength of it, but the spell upon them kept them rooted where they were, their shoulders hunched over, preparing to attack.

I took a deep breath and blew it out on a sharp sigh. Then I sprinted forward, sending out a blast of magic to stun and blind the guards. Too late, they blocked against it, three of them knocked unconscious before I even reached them. They were the lucky ones.

I swung my sword in an arc, slicing off the sword arm of the first guard and opening the gullet of another on the upswing, catching sight of his innards spilling onto the Persian rug as I swung to meet the sword of a third. I shoved, disengaging and making him stumble over the body of one of the unconscious guards. I spun around just in time to block the fourth guard's attack, our swords connecting with a grating clang of steel upon steel. Sensing a fifth guard at my back, I brought up my elbow, slamming it into his face and shattering his nose with a sickening crunch. When he howled in pain, I pivoted and grabbed his arm, throwing him into the fourth.

By now the third was back on his feet. I drove my sword into his belly to the hilt and swung around in time for another guard's down-swing to cut through his back instead of mine.

I tossed aside the body of my comrade and jerked my sword free, cursing under my breath as the unconscious guards began to rouse. I threw out another blast of magic, but the remaining guards were better prepared this time, easily dodging the full impact and covering their eyes to prevent temporary blindness from the flash.

I blew out a harsh breath and crouched with a thunderous cry, ready to plunge once more into the fray. But a quiet *whoosh* near my ear brought me up short as an arrow nailed one of the guards in the chest. A second struck before the incident had even registered.

I spun around, to see Arabella standing at the end of the hall, already firing off another arrow. It hit one of the remaining guards in the eye before I could even turn back to assess the situation.

"Come on!" she called, snatching another arrow from her quiver and letting it fly.

I didn't wait for another invitation, bolting toward her as she gave me cover. "What the hell are you doing here?" I growled, grabbing her and dragging her through a set of double doors that led to the drawing room and then on to the adjoining music room.

"I couldn't leave you," she panted, struggling to keep up with my long strides.

Feeling her strength waning, I grabbed her around the waist and threw her over my shoulder, ignoring her protests as she bounced with each stride. "Obstinate lass," I muttered, my heart swelling with love nonetheless. "You're gonna get yerself killed!"

"You're one to talk, love," she shot back. "Taking on a dozen guards? What were you thinking?"

"There were only ten," I assured her, glancing around for an escape route as I heard the heavy footsteps of more guards coming to avenge their fallen brethren. I tried the French doors that led to the gardens, but they were securely locked. I hurled a blast of magic at the locks, hoping to disengage them, but they'd been enchanted, making them impervious to my spell.

Damn. Mab had thought of everything.

"Oh, well, *ten . . .*" Arabella teased as I set her on her feet, taking a moment to steady her. "That's different then."

"I've fought more," I assured her, sending another glance about the room. Mab had thought of every means of blocking my magic to prevent our escape, but perhaps she'd overlooked more mundane methods. . . .

I grabbed a gilded straight-back chair and smashed it against the doors, shattering the glass. Another blow broke apart the wooden lattices as well as the chair, but made a hole big enough for us to fit through.

I turned back to Arabella and grabbed her hand, dragging her along with me. But we'd only gone a few yards outside when she stumbled, falling to her knees with a quiet grunt. I instantly dropped down beside her, gathering her into my arms. Her skin was ablaze with fever, her cheeks bright red. But even more alarming was the wheezing as she fought to draw breath.

I dropped down beside her. "Can y'go on, lass?" I asked, searching her face.

She nodded, grasping my arm, trying valiantly to get to her feet and failing. I needed to get Arabella to Trish immediately, but that would mean leaving Merlin and Lily behind. I squeezed my eyes shut, hearing the shouts of the guards as they discovered the smashed music room doors.

"Up y'go, lass," I said, scooping her into my arms and getting to my feet. "I'm gonna shift y'now."

Arabella shook her head frantically. "No," she gasped. "Merlin."

"I'll come back for him, lass," I vowed. "I swear it."

"Will you now?"

Every muscle in my body tensed at the sound of Reginald's voice. I ground my back teeth together as I slowly turned to face him. To my horror, he held Lily in his arms, a dagger to her throat. Her glamour had slipped away, revealing her true identity—as well as her bruised cheek and split lip. She sagged against Reginald, looking as if she could barely stand, giving the impression she'd been completely subdued by whatever harsh treatment he'd delivered. But I knew better.

Merlin, on the other hand, had fared much worse. He knelt next to

Reginald, his hands shackled. One eye was completely swollen shut and the other was nothing more than a small slit. His face was barely recognizable for all the bruises. From what I could feel of his pain, I sensed a few broken ribs as well. A guard had his sword point pressed to Merlin's throat, ready to plunge it deep should I refuse to cooperate.

"You have quite the dilemma before you, Montrose," Reginald drawled. "Surrender to save your friends, or take the coward's way out and run away." His smirk grew as he nodded toward Arabella. "Either way, that whore from Sherwood is going to snuff it."

I glared at him, weighing my choices, desperately searching for another option—my favorite one being throat-punching the arrogant dickhead and ripping out his larynx. But I glanced down at Merlin, catching his gaze, such as it was.

To my surprise, the wizard's mouth hitched up at one corner. "Lily, darling. Now that we're outdoors, would you be a dear?"

In the next instant, Lily shifted out of Reginald's hold and reappeared behind Merlin. She wrapped her arms around him, and they vanished before I could even blink.

Reginald's expression quickly morphed from shock to fury. Enraged at being deprived of his prisoners, he drew his sword and rushed me, murderous intent twisting his countenance into a gruesome mask. But it wasn't so much his expression that drew my attention but the beautifully crafted sword in his hand. It was exquisite, elegant. Fit for a king.

"Excalibur," I breathed. As Reginald took the hilt in both hands and brought it down toward Arabella and me, I dropped, curving my body around hers to protect her, then pivoted on my knees, coming up behind him when the momentum of his strike made him stumble past us.

I gripped the sword I still carried, preparing to meet Reginald even as I held onto Arabella, determined to have the final relic.

"Go," Arabella whispered, bringing my attack up short.

I sent a questioning glance down at her. She nodded and let her eyes close. Cursing in frustration, I shifted away just in time to avoid the next swipe of Reginald's sword. When I emerged on the other side of the shift, I was jolted by the numerous anxious faces that awaited my arrival—Merlin and Lily among them.

Nicky immediately rushed forward and attempted to take Arabella from my arms, but I clutched her closer. "No," I snarled, causing him to jerk his hands back.

But Nicky reached out again, tentatively this time. "Let me help ya out there, Tiny," he said, his tone cautious. "We'll let Lav have a look at her, see what she can do while Trish fixes that up for ya."

It was only then that I felt the warm trickle of blood down my arm. Apparently, I hadn't avoided Reginald's attack completely. Luckily, there were no poison curses attached to Excalibur. Otherwise, I would've been in a world of hurt. A flesh wound I could deal with. I shook my head. "I'll be fine. I've got others for Trish to tend to."

Confused glances passed among them. I jerked my head and uttered a sharp command, opening my temporal cache. "There."

Trish, Red, and Nate immediately rushed inside.

I found Lavender's face among the others, my heart lifting at the sight of her. Her husband, Seth, stood slightly behind her, his hands resting lightly on her shoulders. He gave me a solemn nod in greeting.

"Can you help her?" I pleaded, forcing the words past the lump in my throat.

Lav came forward and placed a tender hand upon Arabella's brow, then she raised her eyes to me. I could sense the doubt in her heart even as she vowed, "I'll do everything I can, Gideon. I swear it."

Chapter 24

I paced a tight line next to Arabella's bed as Lavender continued to infuse my darling lass with her healing light. Lavender was growing weary from the exertion, but she stood strong, determined to help Arabella. The *Book of the Ancients*, a collection of spells so powerful they were known only to their chosen guardian, lay open across her lap, the words glowing softly, infusing Lavender with the magic they held.

Seth stood nearby, ever watchful, his concern for the safety of his wife and unborn child clearly visible in the tension that pervaded every muscle in his body. "You doing okay, princess?" he asked, his tone gentle, soothing.

Lavender sighed and let her light slowly fade, then reached her hand out to Seth with a smile. "I'm fine, honey. Really."

He came forward immediately and sat down next to her, pressing a kiss to her temple and placing a hand upon her rounded belly. "You need a break."

She smoothed Arabella's hair. "Is this the woman you told me about, Gideon? The one who died the day Daddy found you?"

I cleared my throat, feeling guilty for putting Lavender through such strain. "Yes."

Lav turned her eyes up to me. "And she has returned to you?"

I nodded.

"Well then," she said with a sad smile, "I guess taking a break isn't an option."

A low growl rumbled deep in Seth's chest, reminding me that although he was generally a mild-mannered chef who could work magic of his own variety in the kitchen, he was also a werewolf who was intensely protective of the beautiful fairy godmother he loved. "Lavender—"

She placed a hand on his cheek and leaned in to brush a kiss to his lips, instantly quieting him. "Could you check on Daddy and my sisters for me?"

Seth returned her kiss, then pressed his forehead to hers for a moment. "As long as you're sure you're okay." When she nodded, he sighed and got to his feet, but when he sent a glance my way, his green eyes glowed in warning, his wolf still on alert.

As soon as Seth closed the door behind him, I pulled my hands down my face, then heaved a weary sigh. "Tell me the truth, Lavender."

She averted her eyes, turning her gaze back to Arabella. My darling love's wheezing had greatly decreased, thanks to Lavender's tender ministrations, but her fever still raged. She'd been sleeping peacefully while Lavender infused her with magic, but she was becoming restless again.

Lavender smoothed the back of her hand along Arabella's cheek. "She's lovely, Gideon. Truly lovely. And strong. She's fighting harder than anyone else might've been able to in such circumstances. I see why you never truly got over her."

I felt a twinge of guilt, knowing that as much as I'd loved Lavender once upon a time, I'd held back on that love. And she knew it. As well as the reason why.

"But I don't know that anything I can do will be enough," she continued. She looked back at me, frowning. "Do you really think the relics are the key to saving her?"

Between Lavender's sessions with Arabella over the course of the past several hours, I'd managed to bring everyone quickly up to speed on our pursuits and the information I'd gathered from the king.

I shook my head on a sigh. "I don't know, Lav. But it's all I have."

Lavender's brows came together. "And do you know where Reginald and . . ." She paused and cleared her throat of choking emotion before adding, "Where Reginald and *my mother* may have gone?"

I crossed my arms, the black T-shirt I'd borrowed from Nicky stretching tight across my back. "I can't even guess."

Lavender's frown deepened. "What of Fabrizio? Has he returned to the mirror?"

After a few pressing questions and one very pointed threat, Fabrizio had admitted that he'd known all along that Reginald had Excalibur but had withheld the information, knowing that if Arabella came for the sword, his double-dealing would be laid bare and his chances of offering any further information would be impossible. At least, that was his story. However, I had my doubts that his motives were entirely altruistic.

Still, I needed his help. If he'd found the sword's location once before, I hoped he'd be able to find it again. I glanced at the bedside table where we'd placed the hand mirror, frustrated to see it still empty.

"No," I told Lavender. "He's not back yet. Mab bound him to Reginald's will; for all we know that asshole has called Fabrizio back to him."

I began pacing again, torn between my need to go after the sword and my desire to stay at Arabella's side. I needed the sword to complete the collection of relics and hopefully save her life. Yet I couldn't leave her, not when she was like this, not when she was in danger of—I shook my head, refusing to articulate the words even in my head.

"Gideon," Lavender said softly, "you're going to wear a hole in Trish's carpet." When I came to an abrupt halt and sent a confused look her way, she offered me a smile. "Pacing isn't going to help Arabella. Why don't you go see how Red's coming along with everything?"

I went to Arabella's side and knelt next to the bed, smoothing her hair. Then I bent and pressed a lingering kiss to her forehead. I peered down at her for a long moment, reluctant to leave. But Lavender was right—all I was doing was distracting her from her efforts to help Arabella. "You'll call me immediately if there's a change." It wasn't a question.

Lavender placed her hand lightly on my shoulder. "Of course. She'll want to see you the moment she awakens, I've no doubt."

I squared my shoulders and gave a terse nod, then pushed up from the bed and strode from the room before I could change my mind. There was no doubt where the others were. The animated conversations were easy to hear as soon as I made my way downstairs. Red and Nate were both on their phones, barking out orders and giving instructions to their subordinates. Maps of what looked like an office complex were rolled out on the dining room table, with Nicky, Trish, and Merlin hunched over them, trying to determine where the king's children were most likely being kept.

"This is the area where we were taken three years ago," Trish said, pointing at a subbasement comprised of numerous maximum-security cells. "If they're trying to hide Tale children, this would be the best place to do it."

"I'll be there in thirty," Red barked into her phone, motioning me into the room as she hung up. "How's Arabella?"

I shook my head as everyone's gazes darted my way, eager for an update. "No change. Lavender is doing her best, but . . ."

"You need the sword," Merlin filled in.

"I have to return to the king's estate," I told them, "to see if I can pick up on Reginald's trail. Fabrizio has not yet returned and I've already delayed too long."

"They'll be waiting for you," Nicky said. "You know that, yeah?"

I nodded. "I have no other choice. Arabella's life hangs in the balance. I'd give my very last breath to save her."

"If you go in there alone, that's exactly what will happen," Trish informed me, her forehead lined with concern.

"He won't be alone." I turned to see Seth leaning against the doorway, his arms crossed. "I'm going with him."

"This isn't your fight," I insisted.

He gave me an offended look. "That bitch Mab made this our fight when she attacked Lav's dad."

"I'm going too," Merlin assured me, clapping me on the shoulder.

"Count me in," Nicky said, giving me a terse nod. "Nate?"

Nate glanced at his wife, clearly torn between wanting to assist and his duty to the FMA. Red pursed her lips and grabbed the blueprints from the table. Muttering under her breath, she rolled up the plans and returned them to the cardboard tube that Nicky's informant had used to smuggle them to us. But then she sighed, "Fine. You boys have your fun while I go play bureaucrat."

When I sent a questioning look her way, she waggled the cardboard tube a little. "I'm meeting Al Addin at the Agency's headquarters to have a little chat with their director so he can give us some bullshit about not knowing where the king's kids are." She grinned, her eyes taking on a reckless glint I was beginning to recognize. "Then I'll have a little fun of my own."

"On second thought, maybe I *should* go with you, sweetheart," Nate said. "Keep you out of trouble."

She winked at him, her grin growing. "Ah, come on, Spooky. Me? Get into trouble?"

Nate crossed his arms over his chest, returning her grin with one of his own. "My point exactly."

"Gideon!"

Lavender's urgent call from upstairs sent me bolting from the dining room and bounding up the steps to the balcony where she stood waiting. "Arabella?" I panted, my heart pounding.

Lavender gave me a tentative smile. "She's awake."

I rushed into the room, dropping down at Arabella's side, unable to hold back the tears that stung my eyes when I saw her weak smile. I took her hand in both of mine and pressed several kisses to it before I could manage to speak past the emotion that was choking me.

"Well, there y'are, lass," I whispered, attempting a comforting smile.

"Hello, love," she managed, her voice a dry croak.

I reached for the glass of water on the nightstand, then slid my other arm beneath her shoulders and lifted her up enough to accept a drink. She closed her eyes as she swallowed, then forced her lids open again to meet my gaze.

"You look like hell," she observed, reaching up to brush her fingertips to my cheek.

I chuckled. Although my wounds had healed, my hasty effort at cleaning the blood and grime from our adventures at the king's estate had most likely left something to be desired.

I peered down at her, alarmed at the increasing translucency of her skin, but managed to force a smile. "*You* look beautiful."

The corner of her mouth turned up in a barely perceptible grin. "Liar."

The *fading* was increasing rapidly, now affecting her actual presence, her hold on the world of the Here and Now. But I refused to voice my fears, not when she needed to keep fighting, not when she needed to believe there was still hope.

"I'm going back for Excalibur," I told her, abruptly changing the subject. I averted my gaze as I set the water glass aside, then gathered her into my arms and sat down on the bed, cradling her in my lap.

"You can't go there alone," she murmured, resting her cheek against my chest.

"I won't be alone," I assured her. "I'm getting the band back together." When she turned her face up to me to give me a questioning look, I grinned. "Seth, Nicky, and Merlin are going with me."

She chuckled. "That's quite a band of merry men." Here she sighed, her sorrow washing over me. "But I'm afraid you'll have to do without your Robin Hood."

My arms tightened around her. "Ah now, don't y'worry, lass, you and I'll have many adventures together once you're well."

She closed her eyes. "Gideon—"

"Ah, we've certainly had our fair share, haven't we?" I interrupted. "Do y'remember the tournament? The one where y'disguised yerself to sneak in? The look on Prince John's face when you split his arrow right down the middle!"

"Gideon, love—"

"And when we broke in to the sheriff's house to steal back the silver candlesticks he'd taken from the monastery as payment for taxes?" I said. "That was a night! We very nearly got ourselves shot full of arrows."

"That *was* a close one," she admitted on a sigh. "Good thing I was there to keep you out of trouble."

I kissed the top of her head and pressed her closer to my chest so she couldn't see the tears in my eyes. "Aye, that it was. You've saved me more times, in more ways, than y'know. I'm not sure how I've managed—" My voice broke, forcing me to bite back the words.

Arabella's arms slid around my waist, her embrace weak as she attempted to comfort me. "You've managed just fine without me," she rasped. "And you will again."

I shook my head, grinding my back teeth together to keep from roaring my frustration. "No," I ground out through clenched teeth. "No, I'm not letting you go this time, lass. I won't."

"I'm so sorry," she breathed, tears in her voice. "I know I promised not to put you through this again. Please forgive me."

My lips trembled when I said, "There's nothing to forgive. If anything, I'm the one who needs forgiveness. I've certainly never forgiven myself for letting you go that day at the falls, for failing you."

"Oh, Gideon," she admonished. "It wasn't your fault. You didn't let me go. I was the one who couldn't hold on."

I gathered her closer, not bothering to check the tears that were scalding my cheeks. "You have to hold on now, lass. Promise me."

Her hand came up to grip my bicep as she clung to me, and she nodded. "I swear it."

I held her close for a long while, needing to feel her in my arms, reluctant to part from her but knowing that if I was to save her—if there was to be any hope—I'd have to leave her side.

"You know, you were wrong, lass," I told her, at last breaking the silence.

"About what?" she asked, her brief rally beginning to diminish again.

"When you said I never needed anything back in Make Believe," I explained. I put my finger under her chin and gently lifted her face to mine. "I needed *you*. I still do."

The kiss we shared then was filled with longing, both of us knowing it could be our last.

Chapter 25

Lavender finished tying the lock of her enchanted hair around my wrist. "There. That should get you past any of Mother's spells on the estate." She blew out a frustrated sigh. "I should be going with all of you. My power is the only one she fears."

"Not for long," I assured her, squaring my shoulders, invigorated by the weight of my armor and weapons, my adrenaline spiking at the promise of impending battle. Dressed once more in the king's livery—more as a statement than a necessity—I was eager to be on our way.

I let my gaze take in my ragtag group in a glance, hoping like hell I'd be bringing them all back with me unharmed—or sending them all home safely without me.

Nicky was geared up in all black and loaded to the gills with guns, knives, a small crossbow, and night-vision goggles. He looked more like some sort of Special Forces operative than the leader of a crime syndicate turned legit businessman. Merlin had donned his druid robe, his expression fierce. The warrior wizard he'd once been to Arthur Pendragon had replaced the Las Vegas showman. To my surprise, Ivy and Lily had insisted upon joining our party and wore their magic like armor, their fairy light enshrouding them with a ferocity I'd never witnessed. They were their father's daughters and planned to prove it.

And Seth . . . He accepted a lingering kiss and an enchanted walking stick from his wife, murmuring quiet words that only she could hear, but the lavender glow they brought to her skin caused the rest of us to avert our eyes and give them a moment together.

I should've been going in without them, putting only my own life at risk. But I needed them, as much as I hated to admit it. And the seasoned warrior in me knew that every battle had casualties, and some of them were friends, family. As I took in each of them in turn, a horrible sinking feeling in my gut warned me that one or more of them might not make it back.

Trish strode into the foyer, trying valiantly to hide her concern for the group. "The king's coming around," she said, going to Nicky and slipping easily into his embrace despite all his gear. "But I haven't told him anything about this little expedition you've planned."

"Don't," I told her. "Keep him ignorant of what we're doing for as long as possible. Otherwise he'll insist upon confronting Mab. And I'll not risk his safety again." My gaze traveled once more over the faces of my friends. "I have enough to worry about."

"Remember," Lavender said, "Mother tends toward the dramatic."

Seth grunted. "How could we forget?"

"She leads each strike with a flourish," Lavender continued, ignoring her husband's acerbic comment. "She uses her reputation and authority to intimidate, but she's not all-powerful, Gideon. And she tends to leave her left side exposed."

I nodded, her grief over the situation compounding my own. "Lavender, I—"

"You've been lied to, you know," she interrupted, her brows coming together.

I glanced at the others before shaking my head in confusion. "Sorry?"

She sighed. "You were brought up believing that your kind—the Unseelies—were inferior to us, that your magic was less potent. If you tell someone they are inferior for long enough, eventually they begin to believe it. But it was a lie, Gid. Your people were subjugated in the ancient times because they were *feared* by the Seelies."

"I don't understand," I admitted. "Why tell me this now?"

"Because you need to believe that you can defeat my mother," she told me. "You are exceptional, Gideon. My father saw that the moment he met you. He knew you were destined for more than what you'd been led to believe. Those who know and love you see it in you. And Arabella is counting on you to see it in yourself. If you are to be the man you were born to be, you must believe that you're as extraordinary as all of us know you to be."

Her words weighed heavily upon me, the truth of my people's history difficult to accept. I gave her a terse nod by way of thanks, then tore open a rift in time. "Let's go."

We emerged near the lake that butted up against the Seelie estate, twilight casting thick shadows as we crept along the tree line toward the house. A fine misting rain had begun to fall, cooling the air and creating a dense fog that hovered close to the ground. Although the fog provided much needed cover, it also could provide the same for any approaching guards.

We'd just reached the edge of the lake when I felt the wall of magic Mab had placed around the estate. The power of the spell made my skin buzz with electricity. I felt Ivy's and Lily's gazes upon me, their hesitation understandable. As much as they disliked their stepmother, they still feared her and the power she wielded. I took a deep breath and let it out slowly with a glance down at the lock of Lavender's enchanted hair tied around my wrist.

Now or never.

I stepped forward, the spell squeezing the air from my lungs as I passed through it. When I emerged on the other side, I heaved a sigh of relief, grateful for Lavender's talisman against her mother's malice. I turned and motioned for the others to follow. They too managed to pass through without any ill effects. I could only hope that Mab hadn't accounted for such assistance from her daughter and that even now a warning bell wasn't going off somewhere to alert her to our presence.

When we were all together again, Merlin cast a glance my way, asking a silent question. When I gave him a curt nod, he muttered a spell sotto voce, then swept his hand in a gentle arc. The fog began to grow thicker, swirling now of its own accord.

Nicky lowered his field glasses and motioned toward the guard tower in the distance, then held up four fingers. He then gestured at either side of the mansion and held up his hand. Five guards at each of the back entrances. I knew there'd be at least that many manning the front as well. The house was surrounded. And with the guard tower fully manned, they'd have the advantage of the high ground. The best option was to take the tower guards out first and as quietly as possible to maintain the element of surprise.

I nodded toward Nicky and Seth. Their heads dipped in unison, knowing the plan we'd agreed upon before leaving. They each headed off in separate directions, Lily and Ivy in tow, ready to move in as soon as I took out the guards in the tower.

When they were out of sight, I turned to Merlin. He grinned and raised his arms and began to murmur under his breath, his voice little more than a whisper on the wind, but it was enough. The spell he wove drifted upon the fog, winding its way toward the house. I crept forward along with the spell, keeping to the shadows.

The first guard to fall under Merlin's power merely slumped forward, half-draped across the demi-wall of the tower. His companions only had time to frown in confusion before the spell ensnared them as well, and they dropped as if in slow motion, sinking out of my sight. With the night watch snoring softly, Merlin turned the spell on those guarding the back entrances. The men began to yawn in turn and nod off. Some of them slowly drifted to the ground, curling up contentedly. Others merely slumped against the house, sleeping where they stood.

Within moments, all of the guards at the back of the house were asleep. I heaved a sigh of relief, glad that the spell would most likely keep them alive if we were able to get in and out again before it wore off. It was a quick and effective spell—but, unfortunately, it wasn't long-lived. And it wasn't one Merlin could just re-up when it wore off. After that, the victim's brain wouldn't be lulled again so easily. He'd explained that very clearly when I'd expressed my desire to move in on the estate without any further casualties. But it was our best option for now, and so I was willing to give it a try. Of course, just to be on the safe side, Merlin had a backup plan. One that I wasn't exactly privy to, which worried me more than a little . . .

When we reached the ruined music room doors, still in disrepair after my earlier escape, I let my senses drift, searching for any emotions lingering nearby. But the room was completely empty. I frowned, not trusting the ease of entry. There should've been some kind of barrier erected to keep out the cold night air at least, but none existed.

"It's quiet," Merlin murmured. "Too—"

I sent a warning look his way, cutting him off.

His brows lifted and he shrugged his shoulders. "Well, it *is*."

As much as I hated to admit it, he had a point. There was a stillness in the air that I didn't trust. I moved deeper into the room, glass crunching under my boots with each step. I would've expected the house to be dark, but to my surprise, light from the hallway spilled into the room.

I made my way to the doorway and peeked around the doorframe. When I saw that the hall was empty, I motioned for Merlin to follow. My stomach sank as we crept down the corridor, the evidence of my confrontation with the guards still staining the walls and rugs, a gruesome reminder of what had transpired.

"You'd think if they knew we were coming they would've cleaned up the place," Merlin drawled.

I shook my head, my skin beginning to prickle with warning. "No," I told him, my voice low. "They'd want me to see this again, remember what my betrayal has cost."

As I spoke, the light in the adjoining hallway gradually grew brighter, as though luring us on.

"Hel-lo," Merlin murmured, his eyes narrowing. "What's this?"

My grip tightened around the hilt of my sword. "Drawing the moth to the flame."

Merlin grunted. "More like the lamb to the slaughter."

"You should get out of here, Merlin," I tossed over my shoulder as I strode toward the light.

"Are you completely mental?" Merlin hissed, jogging to catch up with me. He grabbed my arm. "It's a trap. You must realize that."

I clenched my jaw and reined in my temper to keep from wrenching my arm away from his grasp. "That's why you should go."

"Don't be a bloody idiot," he snapped. "You can't help Arabella if you're dead, Gideon."

"Neither can you, my friend." I rested my hand on his shoulder.

"Now, go keep an eye on the others. They'll need your assistance should the guards awaken."

Merlin drew himself up to his full height, clearly torn. But then he gave me a curt nod and hurried back the way we'd come, leaving me to face my fate on my own. I turned back toward the light and focused on an image of Arabella's dimpled smile, the glint of mischief in her dark eyes, the soft glow of love that surrounded her when she was lying in my arms, and I went forward, ready to move heaven and earth to see that face again.

I followed the corridor, and as that light faded another light drew me on, pulling me deeper into the bowels of the mansion. I wasn't in the least surprised when I eventually came to the intricately carved doors that led into the throne room that Mab had insisted upon adding to the mansion when the king designed it.

I stared at the doors for a long moment, feeling out what might be waiting for me on the other side, ready to unleash all hell the moment I went inside. There were several people on the other side of the door, I knew. I could sense the weight of their presence in the air. Reginald was among them, his thick, nauseating jumble of disgust, maliciousness, and disdain making me reel.

And Mab was there, haughty and aloof. Yet for all her coldness, her hatred for me burned so hot I half-expected the door between us to burst into flame. I'd always known of her dislike, her anger over the king's insistence that I be treated differently from all the other servants, her resentment at her advances toward me being rebuffed. She had buried her emotions deep for all these years, but finally was letting them come to the surface now that all other truths had been laid bare.

I swallowed hard, then took a deep breath and shoved open the doors with such force, they swung open in a massive arc, slamming into the walls. I strode in, my shoulders hunched forward, ready to cut down anyone who got in my way. But no one intercepted me. The guards that stood at equal intervals along the wall stared straight ahead, their eyes glazed over, seeing nothing but what Mab willed them to see.

The queen sat on her gilded throne upon a raised dais, imperiously peering down her nose at me as I prowled toward her. Her fairy

light burned so brightly in her rage, her skin was luminescent, emanating a soft golden light.

"Where is my husband?" she demanded, her voice echoing omi-
nously in the great hall, her eyes glowing golden orbs.

"Safe," I replied. "Protected."

"So you say," she hissed. "But you must forgive me if I find it difficult to trust the word of a slave. Tell me where he is being held or
suffer the consequences."

"He's in Lavender's care," I admitted, knowing that truth would
infuriate her even more than my reticence.

She narrowed her eyes at me, her entire body trembling with rage.
"You *dare* to turn my own daughter against me?"

"You needed no assistance from me in that regard," I assured her.
"I believe you've done well enough on your own."

Mab rose, drawing herself up in indignation. "You will bring him
to me immediately."

"To what end?" I retorted. "So you can finish him off? Not satisfied with just grievously wounding him?"

"That's none of your concern," she insisted. "Now, do as you are
bid or I will be *most* displeased."

"My apologies, my lady," I replied, inclining my head. A satisfied
smile curved her lips but it faltered when I added, "But I serve the
king and his family. And you are no longer counted among them."

Mab moved so fast, she was a blur of motion. In an instant, she
was standing mere inches from me, her fingers grasping my windpipe, the heat of her fury searing my skin. But I didn't flinch. I turned
my unconcerned gaze down to hers, towering over her slight frame.

"You are a fool if you think you can defy me," she spat.

"You're a fool if you think you can control me," I countered.

With a cry of rage, she shoved me from her, surprisingly strong
for such a petite woman. But the strength of the magic that blasted
from her fingertips in the next instant was no surprise at all. Even
with Lavender's warnings of her mother's tells before casting a spell,
I only saw it coming a split second before the golden lightning bolt
shot toward the center of my chest. I instinctively brought up my
sword. The bolt of magic struck the blade, knocking it from my hand,
and ricocheted, blasting a hole the size of a Prius in the wall.

I dove for my sword, snatching it up and rolling just in time to avoid another strike.

"Take him!" she roared, outraged at my evasion.

The guards immediately snapped to attention and came at me, unleashing hell as they did. I cursed under my breath as I defended myself, damning Mab for making me fight the very men I'd commanded. But there was no way around it. If I fell, Arabella would die. And that simply was not an option.

As I fought them off with sword and magic, I advanced toward Mab's dais, where she'd once more taken refuge, her eyes gleaming with maniacal intensity as she watched me throw off three guards who'd tried to jump me and physically take me down. As soon as they hit the ground, I dropped to one knee, driving my sword into the marble floor, sending out a blast of energy and knocking the remaining guards on their asses.

Now covered in blood and sweat, I slowly rose, turning my gaze upon Mab. "Enough of this, Mab. It's over."

"I've called more guards," she informed me. "They'll be here any moment."

I said evenly, "And I'll dispatch them as I did the others."

She lifted her chin defiantly. "You really think you can stop me? *You*, of all people . . ."

"I know I can," I assured her, prowling forward. "And I will. For the woman I love. For my king. For all who have fallen here today."

"I know you Unseelies of old," she sneered. "You're nothing but the refuse of the fae world. You're not fit to lick the shite from my boots."

"You didn't always think so," I reminded her.

Her eyes widened in outrage at the reminder that she'd once tried to tempt me to her bed. And that I'd refused. But before she could do more than gasp at the breach of etiquette in a slave reminding his mistress that he had rejected her, a lazy drawl announced, "Allow me, my lady."

I kept my gaze locked with Mab's, watching for the slightest hint of an impending attack. I didn't need to look at the speaker to recognize that smarmy voice. "Finally decide to come out of hiding, Reginald?"

"Let me deal with him, Mab," Reginald continued, feigning a yawn and ignoring my comment.

Mab tilted her head to one side, regarding me with such contempt, it was staggering. "I would not put you in danger, my love."

"Is that why you gave him cursed weapons when he came to steal Arthur's shield?" I asked. "Because you know he's not good enough—or brave enough—to face his opponent unassisted? He has to cheat? Is that it?"

"Figured out that was me at the Renaissance festival, did you?" Reginald chuckled. When I merely flicked an annoyed glance his way, he strolled toward us nonchalantly. "I admit, I was a bit surprised to see you and Arabella there. I could understand your running into the Huntsman at Guinevere's. Chalked it up to mere coincidence. But then you showed up looking for the shield, too, and I realized I'd been betrayed. Ah, well, that won't happen again, I assure you."

"What have you done with Fabrizio?" I demanded.

"Oh, he's found a new home in a lovely mirror in an Ordinary's antique shop somewhere in Middle of Nowhere, Indiana. No more of this hopping around with Tales business, making bargains to barter for his escape." Reginald *tsked* on a sigh. "Terribly sad, really. I can't imagine how he'll *ever* break his curse now . . . But such is the price of treachery."

"And you two would know all about that, wouldn't you?" I said.

Mab made a noise of disgust. "You of all people know what I've endured being married to the king, how many mistresses have shared his bed, the *children* I've been forced to welcome into my home."

"You encouraged him to seek his pleasure elsewhere," I reminded her.

Her eyes sparked with anger, but she didn't deny it. "Do with him what you will, Reginald," she called over her shoulder. "But I expect you to discover where my husband is being kept. He and I have unfinished business."

Reginald eyed me up and down, his arrogant grin growing. "Shall we have a rematch, Gideon?" he suggested. "See who really is the better swordsman?"

"I don't have time for your bullshit games," I sneered. "I only came for Excalibur."

Reginald sent an amused glance toward Mab. "Indeed? Well, you are welcome to it." He drew the sword from its scabbard and held it out to me. But when I made a wary step forward to accept it, he snatched it out of my reach. "If you can take it from me."

"With pleasure," I ground out, my sword at the ready. I lunged forward, ready to pummel the bastard and take the sword, but a blast of magic shattered the marble floor, bringing me up short.

"Without magic," Mab informed me. "If you want Excalibur, you will have to win it fairly."

Yeah, right. I'm sure good sportsmanship was exactly *what Reginald had in mind. . . .*

"*Win* it?" I glanced between the two of them. "What are you suggesting?"

Mab waved her hand at the guards who'd just come rushing into the throne room to aid their queen, swords drawn. She batted her golden lashes innocently, sending up a fine sprinkle of fairy dust. "Why, you must reach him first."

Reginald came to her side, positioning himself next to her throne, and smirked at me. "Come take it from me," he taunted. "If you dare."

I shook my head. "There has been enough bloodshed among the king's guards. Let these men live. If you want to have your little sport, I will take on Reginald right now, without my magic. I won't need it."

Mab lifted her brows in challenge. "Indeed?"

The panicked shouts elsewhere in the mansion brought Mab's head up. From outside, the shouts continued amidst the rapid staccato of gunfire and the low rumble of a heated skirmish. She turned to one of her guards. "What is the meaning of this? I didn't give a command to any of the other guards. What the hell is going on?"

"I imagine that sound is your guards getting their asses kicked by my friends," I informed her. "Your son-in-law and two of your stepdaughters are among them."

An explosion shook the entire mansion, making the ground quake beneath our feet. Paint and drywall from the ceiling showered down upon us.

I grinned at the queen. "And that," I said, "would be Merlin."

Her face twisted in disgust; then she waved to the guards. "Go. Deal with the wizard instead. I will not have that idiot blowing up my home with me in it."

The guards bolted immediately in response to Mab's command. A situation Reginald did not care for one bit. He sent a furious gaze Mab's way. "That wasn't the plan."

She rolled her eyes. "Oh please, Reginald. Don't be such a simpering child," she admonished. "Finish off the Unseelie trash and be done with it. I tire of this game."

Reginald gaped at her. "My lady?"

"Oh for God's sake," she said, laughing lightly. "He's just a *slave*. Have done with him already, Reginald. Your cowardice is beginning to bore me."

"*Bore* you . . . ?" Reginald repeated, his voice thick with offense. His expression grew dark, his eyes blazing with a fury that alarmed me.

Before I even realized what was happening, he'd snatched a dagger from his belt. A cry of warning ripped from my throat too late as Reginald slashed the blade across the queen's throat, glaring down at her as blood poured from the wound. As she grasped her neck, gurgling and sputtering, her eyes wide in startled bewilderment, he turned with scornful dispassion and strode away, his steps unhurried in his arrogance.

I bolted to the dais in time to catch Mab in my arms as she tumbled from the throne. I pressed my hand to the gash across her throat, attempting to stanch the flow of blood, but her life slipped between my fingers, spilling into a crimson puddle upon the marble and spreading until it trickled down the steps. Seconds later she went still, her eyes staring sightlessly over my shoulder.

I gently laid her down upon the dais, knowing that Nate Grimm would soon be visiting to collect her soul and offer her the final care she required. I looked down at the blood on my hands, my shock turning to rage. Then my grip tightened around the hilt of my sword and I shifted, zeroing in on Reginald.

He stumbled back, falling on his ass when I emerged directly in front of him in the path leading to the garage where his car was parked. His eyes widened when he saw me standing there. Bloodied and furious, eyes blazing with rage, I must've been a terrifying sight, for he scuttled backward quickly in an attempt to get out of my reach and onto his feet. He managed it only a split second before my sword swung down at him.

He brought up Excalibur just in time to block the blow. My sword arm hummed with the vibration from contact with the fabled blade. But my surprise at the strength of the weapon vanished as vengeance took its place. I struck again and again, hammering at him with every ounce of my strength, repeatedly driving him back to the ground when he tried to regain his footing, my speed and determination making up for what my blade lacked in enchantments.

But Reginald wasn't going down so easily, his talent for self-preservation a powerful motivator. He finally managed to spin away at the last second, rolling to his feet, immediately at the ready. Then it was his turn to move in. He was skilled, graceful in spite of the weight of the sword he wielded. If I'd had any doubts that Reginald had been the masked executioner at the Renaissance festival, the way he moved, the ruthlessness with which he fought, would've removed them. But his weaknesses were laid bare within a few moves.

Shorter than I by several inches, he ducked under my arm, slamming Excalibur's hilt into my back near my kidney as he dodged behind me. I grunted, cursing the lucky blow he'd landed as I stumbled forward a step. But with a roar of rage, I spun around, switching my sword to my left hand as I turned, and knocking his blade off target before it sliced across my gut.

Reginald's brows twitched together in confusion just before I swung my right arm, my fist catching him in the jaw. Blood and teeth sprayed onto the grass. Reginald stumbled a few quick steps, using Excalibur as a crutch to keep himself upright, but the blow had cost him. His eyes were unfocused and he swung sloppily. I easily side-stepped his attack and sliced my sword across his abdomen in the same motion.

Reginald dropped to his knees with a startled gasp, Excalibur falling from his grasp to land on the grass beside him.

I slid the toe of my boot under the sword near the hilt and pitched it into the air, catching it as it flipped, the moonlight glinting off the blade. I moved to stand directly before Reginald and pointed the tip of Excalibur at his chest. "Do you yield?" I ground out.

Reginald knelt before me, panting, his intestines slipping between his fingers as he gripped his belly. "Go to hell."

"It's over, Reginald," I assured him. "Excalibur is mine."

He laughed, spraying blood onto his shirt. "Take the fucking sword," he snarled. "It won't do a damned bit of good."

"What are you talking about?" I demanded. "It's the final relic."

He chuckled again. "Doesn't matter." He shook his head, blinking rapidly to clear his blurring vision. "Your little whore wasn't *fading* because she was sick. She was *cursed*. Mab cursed her because she was half-Tale. She thought they were an abomination. She cursed them all. Arabella. The king's bastards with the Ordinaries. All of them." He tittered with maniacal glee. "Mab was the only one who could save her by lifting the curse. And I *killed* her."

Reginald's laughter died abruptly. And as I turned to walk away I heard the dull thud of his severed head when it hit the ground.

Chapter 26

As I came around the house in search of my friends, I slowly became aware of the battle that raged around me. All the guards had awakened from Merlin's sleep spell but whether still under the vestiges of Mab's spell, confused by the presence of intruders, or true traitors at heart, they still fought against Merlin and the others, filling the darkness with bursts of fairy magic that lit up the sky like fireworks. Fire blazed on the lawn, ignited by the dragon Merlin had called. Merlin's backup plan, apparently, the beast stood guard near its master, steam curling from its nostrils as it snorted, impatiently waiting for the command to attack again.

I fought my way through the melee and to Ivy first where she was huddled within a bubble of magic, arms over her head as three of the guards blasted her shield in an attempt to get at her. My instincts to protect the king's family overrode my resolve not to harm anyone, if at all possible. With a cry of fury, silver bolts flashed from my fingertips, knocking each of them from their feet as if they truly had been struck by lightning. Ivy's head came up, her shock and fear quickly morphing to relief.

"Go!" I cried, waving my arm. Instantly, she shifted, taking herself far from the fray and out of harm's way.

I quickly glanced around, searching the darkness for the others.

Several of the guards already lay wounded, though I could not tell if they had already succumbed. In the distance, Nicky was locked in hand-to-hand combat with one of my finest guards, their skills evenly matched. I was hurrying toward him to intervene when a great white wolf suddenly leapt out of the darkness, tackling the guard and landing on his chest, teeth bared. *Seth.* His coat was matted with blood, but he appeared to be only slightly injured.

When I reached them, I wrapped a quick binding spell around the guard, noting the look of confusion and apology in his eyes.

"Gideon?" the burly guard muttered. "What the hell is going on?"

I traded a glance with Nicky before answering, "The queen is dead."

"Nate should be on the way," Seth said, rising to his feet, human once more. He laid a hand on my shoulder.

I nodded, and then let my gaze travel over the estate, my heart sickened by the devastation. The south wing of the mansion had caught fire now, the flames rising higher and higher, licking at the night sky. Several guards were emerging from the various exits, dragging their fallen comrades out with them.

Movement out of the corner of my eye drew my attention. The dragon had taken wing and was flying back to its roost. And against the backdrop of the flames, Merlin and Lily came toward us, bedraggled and exhausted, but seemingly unharmed.

"We'll need some help here," I murmured. "These men will need medical attention."

"Already on it," Nicky assured me, his cell phone up to his ear. "The FMA's sending a few teams out now. They should be here soon."

I nodded. "Thank you," I told them softly. "Thank you all. I . . ." I didn't have the words to continue. I'd asked them to do battle alongside me, to take up arms to help me save the woman I loved, and they'd fought valiantly, asking nothing in return.

"Gideon."

I turned at the sound of the voice behind me to see Nate standing there, a forlorn look on his face. My heart stopped beating as fear constricted my chest. "Arabella?" I gasped.

His dark brows drew together, the shadows that lingered around him growing darker. "We've found the children," he told me, his raspy voice rougher than usual. "Arabella and your king both insisted upon going."

"What?" I cried. "How the hell could you let either of them go anywhere? Neither of them has any business being out of bed!"

Nate held up his hands in front of his chest. "When we sent a car for Trish to bring her to the scene, the king had rallied and was in a rage, demanding to know what was going on, where his daughters were, where you were."

Having seen the king in an imperious rage, I could only imagine the scene at Trish's house.

"When he discovered that we'd found the children," Nate continued, "he demanded to go with Trish to the scene. Trish wasn't about to tell him he couldn't come along to liberate his own children. Gideon, this facility . . ." He took a deep, bracing breath, going visibly pale at the thought of what he'd witnessed there, and ran a hand down his face. "Fuck. I thought we were going to have to cuff Al Addin to keep him from beating the shit out of the Agency guards when we stormed the place."

As much as the news pained me and as heartbreaking as the scene must've been, there was one Tale whose well-being Nate still hadn't divulged. "And Arabella?" I prompted. My heart, having resumed beating, was now pounding painfully in my chest. "She must be doing better if she could go with Trish and the king. Lavender's treatments are helping?"

The look on Nate's face told me the answer even before he said, "Lavender was able to give Arabella enough strength to get her to Agency headquarters to see the children, but . . ." He placed a hand on my shoulder, his brows furrowing in sorrow. "I just got a heads-up call on her, Gideon. It won't be long. Go. I'll help handle things here."

I cast a glance at the others, but they nodded. "Go on," Merlin said, his voice tight with emotion. "We'll be fine."

I didn't wait another moment. I ripped open a rift and stepped through, zeroing in on Arabella. When I emerged on the other side of the temporal passage, I found myself standing in front of the Agency's headquarters. Several ambulances and FMA vehicles were parked in front of the building. FMA agents were milling about, escorting the Agency's agents to an area of the concrete steps where they were detaining them for further questioning. Those agents who were Tales working as liaisons in the Ordinaries' organization were handcuffed, their heads hanging low in shame.

And then I saw them, the children as they were being escorted from the building, their slight forms gray and nearly translucent, their muscles atrophied from their extended stay in the Agency's headquarters. They were walking skeletons, their cheeks sunken and hollow, their eyes haunted.

My king, still recovering from Mab's attack, was pale with horror as he took in the state of his offspring. "Come to me, my little darlings," he called, opening his arms wide and drawing them all close to him. "Come, little ones."

Even the oldest of the children, adults, allowed themselves to be led forward. They didn't know the man who called to them, but it was as if they instinctively could feel the love of their father as he drew each of them close, pressing kisses to the tops of their heads, murmuring softly to them.

I slowly came forward through the bustle as Tale paramedics encircled the king, eager to help, but he gave them a harsh look, making them take a few steps back. Then the king knelt in front of one of his children, a little girl of perhaps seven years old. He brought her hand to his lips and pressed a kiss to her skin. "I bind you to me, little one. I forbid you to *fade*." He then took the hand of the boy next to her, murmuring the same words.

The screech of tires made my head snap around toward the sound. A man with carefully coiffed blond hair emerged from the car that had come to an abrupt halt and strode angrily toward the building.

"What the hell is going on?" he demanded. "These children are the property of the Agency!"

I hadn't seen Al Addin until he burst from the crowd to grab the man by the throat and throw him up against the wall. "They are no one's *property*, you son of a bitch," the formidable director of the FMA growled. "They are children. And thanks to your scientists, who had the good sense to release them to us, they will be returned to their families."

"You're making a mistake by interfering, Director Addin," the blond man warned. "You'll pay for this."

Al shoved the guy away from him. "We'll see about that."

I dragged my gaze away from their confrontation and continued to search the crowd for the one face I craved most. Arabella was there somewhere, I could feel her, but her signature, her essence, was growing fainter.

Then I saw Red coming down the steps, cradling a small bundle in her arms. When she saw me, she held my gaze for a moment, her sorrow and heartache twisting her emotions into a knot.

I hurried toward her, my heart beating frantically. "Where's Arabella?" I asked in a rush.

Red jerked her chin toward a pretty little fountain in a walled courtyard adjacent to the building. I hurried toward it, my heart pounding with joy when I saw Arabella sitting on the edge of the fountain. But my elation vanished when she lifted her face.

Her skin was ashen except for her cheeks, which raged with fever. Dark shadows surrounded her eyes, giving them that same sunken look I'd seen on the faces of the king's children. When she saw me, she blinked slowly as if the effort to do even that much had cost her.

I hurried to her and dropped down on my knees, laying Excalibur across her lap. "I have the sword," I told her, gently taking her hand and placing it on the hilt. "There y'are, lass. You've the final relic now."

"They found the children," she murmured, her eyes unfocused.

"Aye, that they have," I assured her, smoothing her hair. "They're with the king."

She attempted to focus on my face, but her eyes soon clouded over again.

"You'll be fine soon, lass," I told her, placing her other hand on the flat of the blade. "You've all yer father's relics now. All will be well again."

She shook her head, staring over my shoulder. "I don't feel any different."

I cupped her face, the heat of her skin sending an adrenaline-infused spike of panic through my veins. Not knowing what else to do, I scooped her into my arms and stepped over the side of the fountain. I sank down into the water with her, the chill stealing my breath, but it seemed to soothe her.

Shivering, I cupped the water in my hand and poured it over her head. "There y'are, lass," I whispered. "There now."

As I held her, wetting her hair to cool her fever, I remembered that day so long ago when I'd pulled her from the river and laughed with her upon the bank. I'd been so enchanted by the way her hair had clung to cheeks, how her smile had first captured my heart. Little could I have known how deep my love for her would run, how it would define me from that point forward, how no other woman could ever fill my heart the way she did.

But as I sensed her slipping from my grasp, the thought of her hanging over the falls as the waters raged around us assaulted my memory. Once more I felt powerless to stop her from falling away from me and disappearing into the mists forever.

My lips trembled as I bent and pressed a kiss to her forehead.

"I'm slipping," she told me, her voice breaking. "Don't let me fall, Gideon."

"Hold on, lass," I breathed, feeling as helpless at that moment as I had the day in Make Believe. "Don't let go this time. I cannot lose y'again."

Arabella's fingers drifted slowly up my arm, then my neck until she finally found my cheek. I lifted my head just enough to peer down into her face, blinking away the tears that blurred my vision.

"Marry me," she rasped, her dry lips cracking as she spoke the words.

I forced a smile and tried to chuckle, but it died on a stifled sob. Still, I managed to say, "I thought you'd never ask."

Her lips curved ever so slightly, her eyes drifting shut for a moment before she dragged them open again. "I want 'ever after,' Gideon. I always did."

I nodded. "Then you'll have it, lass. I'll hold y'in my arms forever more."

She dragged in a shaky breath. "And we'll live in a cottage."

"And I'll make love to you every night," I reminded her.

Her hand drifted from my cheek to the pendant about my neck, her fingertips caressing the symbols. I drew the necklace over my head and slipped it over hers, letting the pendant come to rest on her chest. Then I drew her up enough that I could whisper my full name in her ear. Instantly the bond took hold, making us both gasp with the intensity of the magic and love infused in the silver.

"I'm yours now," she managed, her voice barely audible. "And you're mine."

I kissed her, fighting back the sobs of dread as her lips grew cold. When I lifted my head, to peer down at her, her eyes were closed, her lips turning blue even as I looked on. I didn't have the king's ability to bind Arabella to me and forbid her to fade away as he had done to his children. But I'd bound her to me in love, that kind of bond the strongest of any I'd ever known. And the king's words drifted to me: *"I believe her love for you was so strong, it kept her in a . . . sort of magical limbo. And, eventually, she made her way back to you."*

I gathered her close, burying my face in her hair as her hand fell away. And I held on to her, held on to her with every ounce of my strength, praying that this time it would be enough.

Epilogue

One year later . . .

"Gideon."

I turned away from the reports on my laptop and swiveled my chair around, a smile growing on my face when I saw the vision of loveliness standing in the doorway of my study, the warm glow from the fire casting a soft light upon her creamy skin. Naked, she strolled toward me, her hair alluringly disheveled from sleep.

I extended my hand to her. "What brings you from our bed, lass?"

"Your absence." Arabella took my hand and let me draw her down onto my lap.

I smoothed my hand down her arm, everything male in me distracted from my work by thoughts of far more pleasurable activities. "I won't be long. I need to finish these reports before the meeting tomorrow."

With mischief twinkling in her eyes, Arabella reached around me to save my document, then shut down the laptop. "I think it can wait, love. The fairy dust distribution business isn't going to come to a screeching halt if you come to bed."

Much had changed in the months since Arabella's *fading*. The king had abdicated his throne to Lavender and had taken the new additions to his brood out to The Refuge to recuperate. And Guinevere had gone with him.

It'd taken a few weeks of dedicated wooing for the king—now returning to the use of the name Lancelot in civilian life—to win his lady love back to his arms, but once there, she'd consented never to leave. They were married soon after and had already seen fit to add a wee one to their already substantial family.

Preferring to dedicate his time to his family, the king also turned over the distribution business to me, insisting that I run it for him. He still serves as CEO, but leaves all the day-to-day operations in my hands. We've not had any additional security breaches since I took over.

Ivy, shaken by her experiences, decided to join her father and his new wife at The Refuge and currently serves as nanny to the younger children. And I've heard rumors that she's taken quite a liking to The Refuge's new school teacher—a rather odd but likable gentleman by the name of Ichabod Crane.

Lily stayed in Chicago, continuing her studies on all brands of magic in her never-ending quest for knowledge, but she's been making frequent trips to Las Vegas. For research—or so she claims. But there's certainly more to that story. And I imagine someday she'll be willing to tell it.

Fabrizio's still missing. I was able to track him to the antique shop to which Reginald had banished the mirror, but there was no record of who'd purchased the relic and so the trail has once more gone cold. But Arabella hasn't given up hope that someday we'll find him and that there will be a way to break his curse.

The Huntsman, too, is still AWOL. There've been reported sightings, but no one has been able to confirm it was really him. He remains a shadow, a threat that the FMA continues to monitor. One day he'll slip up. And someone will bring him down. And if that's me . . . Well, then all the better.

The Seelie mansion was razed after the fire, and I immediately began to rebuild. But it will stand empty when finished except for when the king and his family visit. Arabella prefers the coziness of our stone cottage on the grounds, and so that's where we live, happy in the life we've created. For although much has changed since I held on to Arabella in that icy water, refusing to let her slip away from me, one thing remains the same.

"I love you," I told her, pulling her close for a lingering kiss.

When my hands began to roam over her skin, she pulled back with a grin. "Come to bed, love. You have a promise to keep."

I raised a single brow at her. "Do I now?"

"I believe you promised me that we would make love every night, Mr. Montrose," she purred, smoothing a hand over my bare chest. "And it's already two A.M. Tick-tock."

I chuckled. "Aye, that it is, Mrs. Montrose."

With that, I shot to my feet with her in my arms and charged up the stairs two at a time, making her giggle. But her laughter faded when we entered the bedroom and I set her gently upon our bed. A heartbeat later, I'd shed my clothes and was slipping between the sheets to draw her close.

For a moment, I peered down at her, still marveling at the fact that she was alive and well and content to love me. I smoothed my index finger along the silver chain around her neck and down to the pendant that lay between her breasts, a visible symbol of the strength of the love that bound us, the love that had saved us both.

It seems there'd been something to what Lavender had said about Unseelie magic being stronger than we'd been led to believe after all. But it wasn't just Unseelie magic that was so powerful, it was also the power of our love, the unwavering loyalty that made us so true and noble of heart. And although I couldn't confirm it in any of Merlin's texts, I believe it was the combined strength of my heart and Arabella's that had kept her from her journey to Avalon back in Make Believe and had helped her at last find her way back to me.

When the king had allowed me to create my pendant in the Here and Now, the gift he'd given me was far greater than I could've ever imagined. For in infusing that silver with my magic and my love for Arabella, I'd created the most powerful talisman an Unseelie could possibly forge. And when I'd opened my heart utterly and completely, had accepted her in without hesitation, without reserve as I'd cradled her in that damnable fountain, I'd poured every ounce of my love into that moment—and *that* was enough to overpower Mab's curse.

I couldn't help the grin that curved my lips. I'd never been one for the romantic clichés that seemed to pervade the Tale world—both in Make Believe and in the Here and Now—but in this case I would be forever grateful that love truly *did* conquer all.

"I love you, too," Arabella whispered, drawing my gaze away from the pendant and up to her face. She smiled then, a tender smile that brought dimples to her cheeks and filled my heart with a happiness I sometimes wondered if I was worthy of. But then she drew me down to receive her kiss and all other thoughts vanished. At that moment, she was all that mattered.

The little thief in my arms had stolen my heart, and in doing so had given me a treasure beyond all imagining.

Kate SeRine (pronounced "serene") faithfully watched weekend monster-movie marathons while growing up, each week hoping that maybe *this* time the creature du jour would get the girl. But every week she was disappointed. So when she began writing her own stories, Kate vowed that *her* characters would always have a happily ever after. And, thus, her love for paranormal romance was born.

Kate lives in a smallish, quintessentially Midwestern town with her husband and two sons, who share her love of storytelling. She never tires of creating new worlds to share and is even now working on her next project. Please visit her at www.KateSeRine.com.

Printed in the United States
by Baker & Taylor Publisher Services